ASCENT OF THE NEBULA

ASCENT OF THE NEBULA

THE CHRONOTRACE SEQUENCE VOLUME 3

DJ EDWARDSON

GIRAFFIX

Dedicated to the Yip family. Thank you for your endless encouragement and support.

S.D.G.

The endless cycle of idea and action,
Endless invention, endless experiment,
Brings knowledge of motion, but not of stillness;
Knowledge of speech, but not of silence;
Knowledge of words, and ignorance of the Word.
All our knowledge brings us nearer to our ignorance,
All our ignorance brings us nearer to death,
But nearness to death no nearer to God.
Where is the Life we have lost in living?
Where is the wisdom we have lost in knowledge?
Where is the knowledge we have lost in information?
The cycles of Heaven in twenty centuries
Bring us farther from God and nearer to the Dust.

— T.S. Eliot, *Choruses from the Rock*

NOTE ABOUT TERMINOLOGY

The world of the Chronotrace series is very different from ours. As such, the units of measure, time, and especially the technology used by the characters in these stories may seem unfamiliar to new readers. For this reason a glossary has been provided at the back of this book should a particular term need further explanation.

CONTENTS

ONE
QUID PRO QUO

A<small>N EMACIATED MAN CLAWED HIS WAY UP THE LONG GRAY</small> dune, his tattered coat barely shielding him from the incessant winds. The gusts pounded his paper dry skin, the withering rhythm sounding over and over like hammer strokes striking nails into the lid of his coffin. His death was all but certain, but that was not his chief concern. It was the utter failure of his perfectly crafted plans which gnawed at his soul, eating away what little dignity he had left. Once the master of all he surveyed, he was now made to wander the world alone like some dim-witted beast, and the wind—oh, that cursed wind! It was the reminder of everything that had been his undoing.

Tufts of wispy hair whipped across his face, like the veil inside his mind which kept him from seeing a way out of his torment. How had this happened? How had it come to this? He had lost so much. To him who is given much, much is taken away. He yanked on his hair as hard as he could, attempting to tear the curtain asunder and reveal the answers he sought. The indignant strands, insubstantial as they were, refused to come loose from his skull.

The moment he gave up and let go, the wind blasted him full in the face and sent his hair flying in all directions. His vision returned just as a small chunk of debris smacked him full in the forehead. He felt no pain, but flashes of light dotted his vision. The light jarred something in his memory.

"The shining one," he babbled to himself. "Yes, that is who did this to me...I must be rid of him. But how? His hand is long if he can reach high enough to cast me down from my great throne. What was it they said of him—ah, yes, 'none may look on him and live.' Oh yes, he is terrible indeed. If he wished it, he could snuff out my life with a thought. And yet I must defy him if I am ever to be free of this curse." He raised his eyes to the blazing green expanse above. It roiled threateningly, like water about to boil. He thrust his fist at the skies defiantly. "You followed me here. Yes, you have persecuted me from the beginning. You clothe yourself in light, but your heart is a pit of darkness. Whole worlds you have consumed in that black hole. You promise everything, but all you do is consume. Consume and devour."

Hunger stabbed at his insides again like some rough creature struggling to claw its way out. He fell to his knees and scratched at the sand with his gnarled hands, rooting around for something to eat. When was the last time he'd had anything? He could not remember.

"When will the torment end? How long must I pay for my sins?" he cried out, his voice echoing across the endless waves of sand. There was no answer. Just that infernal wind.

He gnashed his teeth and raked his ragged nails across his skull, dislodging the scabs that had barely begun to heal. For the thousandth time he contemplated ending his life, but no, he could not let that happen, not until he had exacted his vengeance upon those who had wronged him.

"Why does he not just kill me and get it over with?" he

wondered aloud, beating against the ground. Each blow shot sand into his face. He spit and cursed and babbled on until at last his tantrum ran its course and he collapsed into the dust. Dizziness washed over him and the world faded. Where was he, again? Who was he?

At last he heard a voice which came to him upon the wind.

Long you have known of me, and known my will, but you did not listen. You followed the darkness as if it were light. You preferred to go your own way. And now see where your path has taken you. You have lost that upon which all your confidence was placed. And so shall you wander until my will is accomplished. For even when you defy me, you shall find that you serve me all the same.

The madman looked up, trying to find the source of the voice, but there was nothing. He was alone as always. So utterly alone. No, wait. Something shimmered into view before him. A glint caught his eye up ahead. It was something metallic. As he scrambled towards it, he realized that it was nothing more than an old piece of scrap, abandoned and useless like himself. Everywhere he looked he saw more bits and pieces like the first one. He was reminded how careless his enemies were with their creations, casting them aside when they no longer served their purposes.

But it reminded him of something else, too, something also made of metal which he had once possessed. A wave of terror rose up inside of him, a numbing shadow which slipped inside his coat and crawled along his skin. In his memory this...thing, this metallic monstrosity was the proof that what all the voices said were true. He was indeed a murderer and a villain, his heart blacker than any shadow. Worst of all, the apparition shocked loose another memory and he recalled the monster's name—*Nebula*. This was the instrument of his destruction, the weight which hung about his neck, carrying all his guilt, pulling him down to death.

At that moment he might have given up hope of ever escaping the judgment which loomed over him had it not been for another memory.

"But I destroyed it. Yes, after the blood was spilled, I vowed to end my study of war. I became a man of peace. Yes! I repented, changed my ways. The Shining One has no evidence, no proof. He has no means to convict me. The *Nebula* was shattered. I am free. I am free!"

He grabbed handfuls of sand and flung them into the air. The grains rained down around him like confetti in his own private parade. His pain and hunger vanished. He leapt in the air, shouting for joy.

"No more shame. No more guilt. No more sorrow. The *Nebula* is buried in her sandy grave. She went down into the pit and will never rise again. She went down and she shall never be raised, never be raised, never be raised..." he went on chanting that last phrase as he jigged across the desert, a new man.

But in the midst of his celebration, his foot slipped on a piece of metal and he fell, crashing to the ground. As he lay there, the voice came back to him in answer.

Cast your eyes to the horizon. There you shall see the monster rising, rising up from its grave, a silvery resurrection and a monument to your condemnation. For they are building it again, restoring what you thought forever destroyed.

"No," the madman shot back in response, though he knew denial would win him nothing.

You cannot escape your sentence of death. See. Look how it rises again.

And then he saw it, the metal ventricles and alloyed veins

stretched out before him in a vision which brought back with it the pounding inside his head.

"No!" he screamed. "They are rebuilding it once more. And when it is finished they will mount the leviathan and turn it loose upon me, its former master. This cannot be. I will not allow it. My claws and fangs have some sharpness yet. I destroyed it once, I can destroy it again. I am a murderer after all. Best to run headlong into judgment if one cannot escape it. And in so doing I will bring down judgment upon the heads of my enemies, those who are slaves to his will. This time no one shall escape the wrath to come."

Strength infused his wiry frame from some wild, primeval reservoir. The very wind seemed to lift him back to his feet and push him forward. He had to stop them from finishing it or if not, then master the beast himself before they could seize control of it. Rage coursed through him. His feet pummeled the sand with each staggering step. He would find the monster and he would slay it again, for good this time, and all of his old enemies along with it. If oblivion was to come, then it would come by his hand and none other.

The praxis cruiser hovered above the crumbling remains of Oasis, a dark blue star over an even darker city. Mangled ribbons of metal lay trembling amidst three open gashes that cut through the heart of the metropolis, trenches had opened up from the quakes which destroyed Manx Core, the underground military complex of the Collective.

Adan stood in the praxis' Command Center with several of the ship's crew and watched Von's lancer approach through the wide viewing screen. He still found it hard to believe they possessed this massive battleship. The *Maven* wasn't fast, it wasn't streamlined, and it wasn't even a very new design; the logs said the ship was over twenty years old, but what it lacked in spit and sparkle, it made up for by being nigh impossible to destroy.

Though this was the first time Adan had ever been on a praxis cruiser, he had accessed a great deal of information about it from the ship's esolace. Almost everything was connected to this invisible network. The esolace in Oasis had been capable of transporting everything from information to medicine to food. It could also create worlds in the mind which felt more real than ones you could feel and touch. The *Maven's* esolace was not that comprehensive, however. It served only for communication, as a repository of information, and as a means to control the ship. Only someone with a bioseine could connect to it, though.

A bioseine had been grafted inside Adan's body, as well as everyone who had been part of the Collective. This organic augmentation allowed him to communicate with anyone else possessing the same augmentation using only his thoughts, even with no esolace present, though then only at limited range. The one thing all of this amazing technology had been unable to give him, though, was the one thing he most wanted to know: his identity. That had been lost with the destruction of Oasis and Manx Core and the Repository where his memories had been stored.

Raif, the man piloting their ship, didn't need to access the esolace to find out about the *Maven*. He already knew a great deal about these and other ships from his time as a member of the Collective. He had piloted virtually every ship ever produced through the esolace's simulation capabilities. He loved anything that had to do with technology, the more unusual and esoteric the better.

While Raif guided the ship, Adan watched and waited like

everyone else who wasn't out scouring Oasis for survivors or processing the ones they had already rescued from the ruined city. He longed to be free from this place. Every moment they remained he worried the Collective fleet might return and pay them back for destroying their underground installation, though it wasn't actually the Sentients who had done it, but rather this bizarre outburst of seismic activity.

"That's the last of them," Von informed them mentally through their bioseine link. Adan could sense a tenseness in his message, indicating that there may have been more, but it was getting too dangerous to keep searching. Quakes and tremors continued to rock the city, making it almost impossible to land and risky to fly anywhere near the few buildings left standing.

Raif, who was eyeing the massive wall of sand forming up on Virid Ridge in another section of the screen, gave the lancer a passing glance before shifting his focus back towards the dark, churning arm of the oncoming storm.

"Good. I don't want to risk the Maven *getting caught up in that dust storm that's brewing out on the ridge. Not with that hole she's still got in the top of her head,"* Raif replied.

"Is the hole in the fuselage any threat to the overall integrity of the ship?" Adan wondered.

"Well, no, not strictly speaking. I just don't want her getting all clogged up with more dust up top. She'll start thinking I don't care about her." Raif patted the steering column tenderly and gave Adan a wry grin.

Sierra, who had been standing next to Adan while she surveyed the screens, walked over to Raif and swatted him on the shoulder.

"Since when is this your ship?" she asked, speaking aloud. Sierra still preferred to only use the esolace to communicate when she had to. "I'm the one who commandeered her."

Raif frowned. "Aw, come on. You know I couldn't go on without her. Have mercy on a poor miserable tech addict."

She rolled her eyes. "Raif, you're incorrigible."

"So you'll let me keep her? Please, please, please. I'll be good to her, I promise."

Sierra shook her head, but couldn't keep from smiling.

Adan knew it was only playful banter, but somehow their little exchange made him uncomfortable. He still wasn't entirely sure what his relationship with Sierra was, but he felt awkward listening to her joking with Raif. Maybe it was because they'd left him out of it? Or was it something else?

He was relieved when a message from Halerin came across the Collective channel. *"Sierra, they need you in the infirmary. Some of the survivors have injuries that need to be looked at. They are pretty short handed and you have more experience than just about any of us."*

Halerin had been a part of one of the Sentient cells they had rescued from Manx Core. As a former assessor serving with the Collective security forces, he was a natural leader and had volunteered to head up the effort to organize the survivors pouring into the ship.

"I will be right there." Sierra squeezed Adan's shoulder as she brushed past him. His eyes followed her up the ramp, wondering what she was thinking. Normally his memorant abilities allowed him to read her easily, but his emotions were clouding his thinking.

She met Gavin at the door just as he entered. The two exchanged greetings before Sierra disappeared into the hallway.

"Adan, I need to tell you something," Gavin began, using a private channel so that no one else could take part in their exchange.

They met each other at the base of the ramp leading down

from the entrance. Gavin's gaunt face and reddened eyes made it appear as if he had aged since their recent brush with death in the tunnels of the Viscera. He hadn't slept all night, but neither had Adan. It had to be more than that, though. Something was weighing on his friend's spirit and Adan reached out to him mentally to find out what it was.

Inside Gavin's mind loomed the image of the large opening in the docking bay floor, the one that allowed ships in and out of the praxis. It was through that opening that he and Gavin had been rescued and lifted into the ship, but it was also the place where Malthus, one of the leaders of the Collective, had jumped to his death.

Gavin was unable to forget that moment. It lurked behind his every waking thought. But that was not what he had come to Adan about. Layered behind that first thought was another, even more urgent concern.

"It's the tremors," Gavin continued, "I've been recording the land's stress patterns. They're not letting up and I don't think they are going to anytime soon."

"But is that natural? Don't quakes normally go away?"

"Yes. And there have been periods when certain areas have subsided, but only for a time. Then they start up again. And they seem to be spreading. It makes no sense. One thing I do know is that if they don't stop, the Vast will not survive, and neither will any of the people in it."

Adan cast a quick glance around the room. He could see why Gavin had come to him first. They had enough to worry about scanning the city for survivors and monitoring the oncoming storm.

Raif was directing the praxis towards Virid Ridge, on the opposite side from where the storm front was coming in. On the wide view screen he could see the tremors causing the massive ridge to crumble before his eyes. Parts of it had already fallen into Oasis so that only a long slope of shifting rubble remained where once had been a steep rise of silt. Such raw power was more frightening than any threat the Collective possessed. He forced himself to turn his thoughts away from the turbulent scene and back to Gavin.

"*What can we do about the quakes? Anything?*"

"*I think this has something to do with Bryce,*" Gavin suggested. Bringing up the former leader of the Sentients was the last thing Adan had expected. "*Zain told Sierra that he was ramming those tunnelers into a celerium vein.*"

"*But Bryce is dead. What does he have to do with these runaway tremors?*"

"*It's possible that by destabilizing the vein he set off some sort of chain reaction in the planet's crust. I can't say for sure. We know hardly anything about celerium beyond its power amplification properties and we're not even sure how those work. I've got the chronotrace running, trying to get back to what Bryce did after you were separated so that we can get some answers. I'll let you know when it's finished.*"

Gavin had made dozens of improvements to the chronotrace's time mapping capabilities while being held prisoner in Manx Core. Using it to open up windows to the past would certainly give them the answers they needed. But at the moment, that wasn't Adan's chief concern. He was more worried about his friend.

He laid a hand on Gavin's shoulder and surveyed his ragged face. "Are you going to be all right, Gavin?"

Gavin lowered his head. "It never ends, Adan."

"What? What never ends?"

"The evil of this world. The weight of it. One terrible act spills into another until half the world is dragged over the cliff." Gavin stared blankly into the viewing window of the praxis and the broiling storm ravaging the landscape of the Vast.

He blames himself, Adan realized. "But this is just a force of nature, Gavin, this is not evil. It's just the way the world is. And there isn't anything we can do about it."

"I'm not so sure," Gavin replied, "It may be that the fate of this planet and humanity are tied together somehow. I've often wondered if, just like in the physical world, there is not some tangible moral inertia at work in our lives, bringing us to some terrible end. First the storm and now the quakes. I'm beginning to wonder if any of us will survive what comes next."

Gavin turned from the window, his hollow stare passing right through Adan as if he were not even there, his mind caught up in the vision which had seized him.

Adan moved to face his friend directly. "We will fight this. We nearly drowned together and yet we made it out. We walked out of a storm that destroyed an entire city. Alive. Whatever happens, I'll stand with you to the end. And just like always, Numinae will protect us." Adan said these words as much to himself as to Gavin. Numinae, the Creator of the universe, was the one force he could think of that was bigger than these unchecked tremors. But would he put an end to them? One could never be sure just what he would do. Sometimes, most of the time really, he appeared to do nothing at all. Adan thought of all the people he had lost, friends Numinae had chosen not to save. Despite the uncertainties, though, he still had faith. Numinae was at work in all of this somehow, even when he seemed distant and far away. "Don't give up, Gavin. All things, in the end, are passing."

"Thank you, Adan," Gavin replied, a faint light returning to his eyes. As a memorant he surely saw Adan's own struggles and doubts, but the glimmer of hope in his eyes was genuine. "I needed those words. Even if I do not fully believe them."

TWO
THE POWER OF A LIE

B<small>RYCE</small> <small>HAD PROGRAMMED THE BLAST TO TAKE OUT MOST</small> of the mining facility and everyone in it. That was the only way he could eliminate the somatarchs that were after him and the other Sentients. Waking up with his vision blurry and his head spinning was the last thing he had expected.

It was dark, but enough light pierced the cracks above him that he could see where he was. He lay underneath the remains of the hauler. A pile of fused metal crates propped it up and kept the massive vehicle from crushing him.

So that's why I'm still alive. A freak accident.

He crawled out from under the ruined hauler and into the light. Blood dropped onto the rocks beneath him from a gash in his forehead. Cuts and burns crisscrossed his arms. His ankle was twisted so badly it could no longer hold his full weight. But he felt no pain. His bioseine, besides allowing him to interact with esolace technology, regulated his bodily systems and kept him from feeling the effects of his injuries.

As his vision adjusted he surveyed the aftermath of the explosion. All of the carts and tunnelers on his side of the mine were overturned or torn the shreds. The remains of crates sprinkled the wreckage. The bridge spanning the crevice running through the center of the cavern had several chunks missing.

A group of half a dozen white robed somatarchs were assisting a single technician manning an axom crane. The soulless somatarchs looked human, but lacked any true will of their own. They worked silently and tirelessly, helping the man operating the crane clear out the damaged equipment. The crane hauled over large equipment and the somatarchs broke it into smaller pieces with fractal rods. They only had to touch the rods to the vehicles and equipment for a few nanoslices before it separated into smaller components. They then tossed those pieces into a large melter floating nearby, a square container with thick edges and a white glow coming from the opening on top.

Though they were only twenty paces away, they were too focused on their task to notice his appearance, but Bryce ducked back into the shadows beneath the hauler just in case.

He wondered momentarily where all the casualties from the explosion were, but then a body slipped loose out from under some rubble when the crane pulled a tunneler off it. One of the somatarchs, silently and mechanically recovered the body and tossed it into the melter along with the rest of the scrap.

Though the body was unrecognizable Bryce was certain it wasn't one of the Sentients who had come with him to Manx Core. He'd made sure they weren't caught in the blast. Hopefully they had managed to escape and free the imprisoned Sentients, but he had no way of knowing. His bioseine told him that a whole slice had passed since he'd set off the blast. By now their mission would have succeeded or failed. That didn't mean he was out of options, though. The real reason he'd come here wasn't to free prisoners anyway.

But he was getting ahead of himself. First he had to deal with that maintenance crew. He pulled out another contingency trigger. His fingers swiped the glass panels on the compact black disk and ordered up another blast. The crew had helpfully already cleared the ground between Bryce and the crane. He waited for the crane's axom disk to release a large tunneler it had pulled in. The somatarchs moved in with their rods and began fracturing it down into more manageable chunks for the melter. They were all bunched in together, nice and close.

Reaching out from under his hiding place, Bryce tossed the trigger right over to the base of the crane. One of the somatarchs twitched and locked its eyes upon him. But that was the last thing it did. A second blast rocked the cavern, obliterating the crane and the somatarchs in a whirlwind of white light and concussive force.

Bryce crawled out from the shadows and scanned the room one last time. The maintenance crew was just another part of the wreckage now. Satisfied he was alone, his eyes came to rest on three mangled tunnelers near the enormous celerium vein at the back of the cavern. These huge, cylindrical machines had been savaged by his initial blast, but one of them appeared like it might still be operational.

Limping across the wreckage, he made his way towards the vein, drawn as if by a magnet to the smooth dark rock. The finger of stone ran up the cavern wall and disappeared into the bedrock above. The vein both amazed and unsettled him. Its blue flicks glinted, clearly marking it from the surrounding rock. He was mesmerized by the celerium's beauty, but something in the back of his mind told him he should not be looking at this, that he was not meant to be here. The feeling gave him pause. Should he really go through with this? Nolan sent him to destroy the Collective, but he hadn't said anything about the mines or this underground base. They had talked about these strange rocks, though. According to Nolan, they ran all through the crust of this planet. Much of how they functioned was a mystery, but Nolan believed they were alive and that the veins were all interconnected somehow. Destroying one could destabilize all the surrounding veins as well. Before Will had come along with the virus, Nolan had discussed the possibility of using these rocks against the Collective, but the opportunity had never presented itself—until now.

"Everything has to come to an end sometime," Bryce muttered to himself.

Arriving at the tunneler, a quick mental connection with the machine told him the device was still operational. He raised his good foot onto a maintenance ladder on the side, but before he got to the second rung, his other foot caught on something and yanked him to the floor. His head banged against the rocks as he came crashing down. He tried to scramble back to his feet, but a bloody hand reached out from underneath the tunneler and latched onto his foot. The rest of the body remained hidden, as did the face, but Bryce had no doubt it was one of the mindless somatarchs. Nothing else could have survived being crushed like that.

Bryce lunged backwards, but the hand refused to let go. With unbelievable strength it wrenched him in the other direction, pulling him underneath the tunneler. He scrambled to grab onto anything nearby, but only managed to scratch through loose rubble. With a jerk, the hand disappeared along with his foot underneath the machine.

"No!" Bryce screamed.

In the midst of his panic he remembered that he had one last contingency trigger tucked away inside his coat. Running his fingers across it, he programmed the device for a small, localized blast. He knew what it would do to his leg, but he didn't care. He had to get free.

Bryce chucked the black disc into the opening beside his leg. A booming blast rocked the wreckage and the pulling stopped. He would have pulled his foot out then, but there was nothing left to pull. The blast had obliterated it, leaving nothing more than a bloody stump on the end of his leg. No matter, he wouldn't be needing his foot anymore anyway.

Steeling himself, he hobbled up the ladder, relying on his arms and his one good leg. He crested the top of the vehicle and dragged himself over to the banged up hatch. The emergency release lever beside it wouldn't budge. He pulled on it again and again, but nothing happened. Finally, he got out one of the javelins strapped to his back and wedged it into the gap around the edge. Shoving and rocking the shaft back and forth he eventually managed to broaden the gap until the hatch popped open.

He slipped down another set of rungs inside the machine. Once inside, Bryce sat down in one of the operator chairs. With a mental command, he fired up the forward screen and surveyed the celerium vein which flashed into view. He had no assurance that the Developers wouldn't shut him down once he started up the tunneler, but he engaged the drilling cone anyway. The bright blue field of energy shimmered to life in front of the vehicle, but then faded as the viewing screen adjusted to allow Bryce to see where he was going.

The tunneler shuddered and broke free of the fallen rocks around it. It rose off the ground and floated towards the exposed vein of celerium, passing over the remains of the chromium carts and other tunnelers.

Just before the tunneler made contact with the celerium, Bryce hesitated. He realized that if this drilling triggered the sort of reaction he was hoping for there would be no turning back.

Was he really prepared to sacrifice everything to stop the Developers the way he had promised? The blast to free the other Sentients had been one thing, a spur of the moment decision. But this was different. He didn't have to go through with this. Was he really willing to lay down his life?

What life? He reflected back on all of the terrible things he had done. The crimes, the destroyed lives, the violence he had been a part of. It all came flashing past him in one savage rush.

But Nolan had believed in him and Nolan was not like Bryce. He was noble, honorable. This was what Bryce held onto, his path to redemption—death in the service of something greater, an end to the Developer's tyranny, and at the same time an end to his own.

His will resolved, he pushed the tunneler forward into he vein.

Now we'll see if those Waymen legends are true.

The tunneler plunged into the celerium, and immediately jerked to a stop. It drifted uselessly back and forth along the surface, unable to find any purchase in the impenetrable rock. Soon it began slipping off to one side.

Don't do this, a voice inside his head warned, but Bryce ignored it and brought the tunneler back level again.

The blue cross stream cone should have cut through the rock effortlessly, but still the tunneler made no progress. It zigzagged across the vein until it slipped again.

Stop, came the warning voice again, but as before, Bryce pushed it away.

Sweat seeped from his forehead. He forced the tunneler back into direct line with the celerium.

The drilling cone pushed uselessly against the vein before slipping again.

You are making a terrible mistake, the voice warned with a note of finality.

But Bryce would not be denied. This was his choice, the only choice. The Developers had to be stopped.

The funnel of blue energy faced off against the impervious rock once more and this time the tunneler pitched forward: penetration at last. A tiny divot appeared in the rock. Bryce guided the tunneler carefully from side to side, up and down, trying to expand the minuscule opening it had made.

The cone shifted to the side, violently this time. What looked like a shiver ran through the cavern wall in front of him. The sight both terrified and thrilled him all at once. The drilling was finally starting to work.

He brought the tunneler back around to the opening and plunged forward again. The hole opened ever so slightly and again the cavern shook. Dust and a shower of small particles fell into the drilling cone, vaporizing instantaneously. This time the tunneler held onto the small notch it had made.

The opening grew by slivers, but with each minor increase in diameter came a disproportionate amount of convulsing inside the cavern. Large chunks of rock were falling down around him now. Small cracks began to form in the cavern wall around the celerium. If the tunneler had been resting on the ground, it no doubt would have been bucked from its position, but floating in the air, and guided by stabilization algorithms, it latched onto the vein and refused to shake free.

Then Bryce saw something that made him shudder. The black vein *writhed*. For the first time in a long time, real fear gripped him. But then the vein snapped back into a solid formation and he doubled down on his resolve. He would not back down, no matter what.

The cavern disintegrated around him. Rocks banged down on the fuselage in a pulverizing rhythm that threatened to crush it with each beat. He checked other views on the tunneler screens and saw that the bridge was already half buried in rock. The eerie blue light from the river of neophosphorous which ran through the ravine below grew steadily brighter. All around him, the rocks piled up like giant drops of rain, filling up a jar.

The hole grew wider and the vein writhed again. And again. But the tunneler held true, locked in place by Bryce's unshakable will.

Nothing could stop him now. If the Devs had not taken him off system by this point, they never would. The bioseine receiver had probably been trashed in the original blast. The cavern would have to batter him into oblivion before he let up. He would break this world if he had to, so long as justice was satisfied.

This is what I was meant to do, he told himself as the tunneler went under, completely buried by rock. The trembling, quaking walls around him sought to shake their assailant loose. Several times the tunneler did slip, but it always managed to find the hole again.

Finish it, the thought echoed through his mind when the neophosphorous from below rose up into the cavern and started seeping around the tunneler. The neon blue glow soon completely obscured his view of the celerium, but he knew from the tunneler's positioning system that it was still boring into the vein.

The ceiling inside the tunneler began to bend and groan under the enormous weight from above.

"Die," he whispered as a blinding blue light flashed like a warning from within the rubble. The tunneler pressed on.

"Die!" he shouted as the roof of the vehicle punctured and gave way some more, sending showers of debris into the compartment.

"Die! Die! Die!" he screamed as the dust choked his lungs and the rocks pelted his body. The tunneler was shifting and shaking uncontrollably now. The tremors were no longer in response to his drilling. They had taken on a life of their own. But it didn't matter. The world was in its death throes and Bryce would ride the stony spasms into the same fate. Justice demanded it.

Though no one could have seen him, Bryce smiled inside his rocky tomb.

The massive celerium root cracked and splintered. A towering chunk, half the length of the tunneler, crashed down on top of the vehicle, like a death blow from a vanquished foe against his conqueror. The last thing Bryce saw was a wave of scintillating blue light before his body collapsed in on itself.

The drilling stopped, but the underground tempest raged on.

THREE
FILLING IN THE GAPS

Adan and Gavin stood together in the main lab at the center of the *Maven*, but Adan's mind lingered on Bryce's trace. He could not get over that look in Bryce's eyes. It was the most unsettling thing he had ever seen, worse even than looking into the soulless eyes of a somatarch. For Bryce had the light of life in his eyes and yet it burned in a twisted, hopeless way that was worse than if it had never been there in the first place.

"That was so senseless. I didn't think anyone could ever end his life like that."

"Belief is a powerful thing," Gavin answered. *"And Bryce believed in what he was doing. But it doesn't matter how much you believe in something if it's not true. That is why we must be careful about what we choose to believe in."*

Adan let his chin fall to his chest. The sterile smell of the lab felt inexorably linked to the lifeless underground tomb where Bryce now lay and yet it slowly drew his mind out of the trace and back into the here and now.

He stared at the now motionless chronotrace, a black half sphere with a white crystal on top and a silver ring near the bottom. It was not much larger than his hand. Gavin's invention for retracing past events had shown them many things, but it often unlocked more mysteries than it revealed.

"*What do we do now?*" he wondered, trying to take his mind off his morbid thoughts. "*It's obvious that what Bryce did in the mines is the source of the quakes, but if the drilling stopped then why haven't the quakes?*"

"*I don't know,*" Gavin replied. "*So little is known about celerium. Nolan apparently thought the veins were connected in some way. Whether or not he was right, we should get as far away from Oasis as possible until the tremors die down.*"

"*I see why Nolan sent him. Bryce trusted him completely.*"

Nolan was an even bigger mystery than Bryce. A former Developer, he had twice attempted to destroy the Collective, but Adan had no idea why. Nolan had claimed it was out of a sense of justice, but Adan did not believe him. What could they have possibly done to him to justify killing off an entire city? Adan wanted to stop the Collective as much as anyone, but Nolan's methods were nightmarish. And beyond his vendetta against Oasis, his memorant abilities likely surpassed even those of Gavin. Nolan had ransacked Adan's mind while holding him prisoner at Hull. There was no telling what Nolan knew about him, or how he planned to use that knowledge.

"*Did you ever get to meet Nolan when you were a Developer?*" Adan asked.

"*No, I never met him in person. The first time I saw him was in the chronotrace, when he was speaking with Malthus.*" Gavin's face paled at the recollection of Malthus. A former Developer himself, Malthus had taken his own life as well, but unlike Bryce, he had done so out of a sense of hopelessness, not out of some warped sense of justice.

"*If we get the chance, I'd like to do a trace on Nolan some-*

time," Adan suggested, hoping to draw Gavin's mind out of his dark contemplations.

Gavin took a moment to collect himself. *"Yes, that might give us some more answers, but I think our first priority should be to see if we can pick up the trail of the Collective."*

"That makes sense. Sierra saw Nance and several others get picked up by somatarch skiffs. Do you really think we would be able to rescue them though?"

"It would be extremely difficult. If even some of the Collective's ships survived the destruction of the Core we would have little chance of taking them in a fight." Gavin paused, considering. *"Then again, I would not have given you much of a chance of rescuing me from Manx Core, either."*

Cautious optimism welled up within Adan as he recalled the events surrounding their escape from the underground base of the Collective. Despite all the death and destruction, with the cavern literally falling down around them, they had escaped from the Core, and that was something. They also now had the praxis, an incredibly powerful ship. Adan would never have dreamed they would be in this position even a day or two ago.

Then there was the chronotrace. The improvements Gavin had made to the device, combined with the increased efficiency afforded by the celerium core, meant that it was no longer restricted to mapping events at a single location. The fact that they now had a mobile window into the past should allow them to find the missing Sentients, if they were still alive.

Besides the chronotrace they had one last advantage in their battle against the Collective.

"We can always pray," Adan reminded him.

"Yes, you are right, Adan. How quickly I forget," Gavin replied.

Adan and Gavin's thoughts began to mingle in a mixture of

doubt, concern, and wonder. Hopes and fears passed between them simultaneously, like different parts to the same song. But this strain, this outpouring of all that weighed upon them, was intertwined with a deeper, more fundamental melody: a longing to know the will of Numinae, the Creator of the universe himself. They had met his servants, the eidos, but such visits were rare, not something likely to be repeated, and yet Numinae was always listening, even when his servants were not present. And so the two friends sought to find harmony in a song larger than their own, one that would bring all their dissonant notes and far flung scales into a single refrain that would carry them as they went forward.

They prayed for the lost Sentients and they prayed for the ones who had been rescued. They prayed for the native peoples of the Vast, exploited and hunted by the Collective for their experiments, their thoughts going especially to their friend Senya and the captured Welkin in the city of Hull. They also prayed for the savage Waymen who kept them prisoners there, that they might turn from the path of violence and destruction and lay down their weapons. And towards the end of this wordless, shared intercession they prayed for Sierra. Perhaps it was selfish of Adan to direct the prayer in this direction, but their recent conversation had been heavy on his thoughts.

"I want to protect you," he had told her, and yet the only way he would ever be able to do that would be with Numinae's help. As so often happened when his thoughts turned to her, his mind clouded over and he found it hard to know what to pray. His thoughts grew confused and muddled, uncertainty set in. He brought the wordless prayer to an awkward, indefinite end.

"Gavin, there's something else that's been bothering me." Adan began, but then wavered, unsure of how to proceed.

"It's about Sierra, isn't it?"

"Is it that obvious?"

Gavin shrugged apologetically. *"I am a memorant, after all."*

Despite Gavin's gentle ribbing, Adan knew that if anyone could help him sort through his confusion, it would be Gavin. He began to share his memories of Sierra, but more than just the memories, he allowed Gavin to feel what he felt when he interacted with her. The peace, the awkwardness, the excitement, the confusion, it all came through in a flurry of mental confession.

"I can see why you are anxious about this, Adan," Gavin observed. *"There are emotions that we have suppressed in the Collective. Since all of your understanding comes from what Will and the remapping process gave you, you don't have an easy way of processing these feelings. I only have a rudimentary understanding myself, but enough to at least diagnose your situation."*

"So what is going on?"

"I believe the technical term is 'love'." Adan sensed amusement in Gavin's thoughts, which only clouded things all the more. *"Or rather the beginnings of it. Love is something that people share which draws them closer to each other. It is related to friendship and yet it is something more. It takes on a special form when shared between a man and a woman. And judging by the way that Sierra has been reacting to you, I would say that she feels the same way."*

"Love," Adan echoed Gavin's thoughts, only dimly grasping what was meant by the word. *"But if it is more than friendship, then what am I supposed to do next?"*

"To be honest, that's all I know," Gavin answered. *"The Developers were only allowed to understand enough to recognize it when we saw it so we could expunge it during the flat-*

lines. *I can tell you this though, Darius thought it was extremely dangerous.*"

An image of Darius, the wispy-haired former leader of the Developers rose up inside Adan's mind. What did someone with complete control over the Collective have to fear about the fluttery emotions Adan had in his stomach when he was with Sierra? Dangerous? There certainly was an element of anxiousness mixed in with it, but he wondered just how threatening it could really be. The thought occurred to him that perhaps Sierra was somehow at risk. Could these feelings cause her harm in some way? He certainly had no desire to hurt her. He wanted to protect her. So perhaps the danger lay on his end. Perhaps he was opening up himself to be hurt instead. Was that what Gavin meant? He was about to inquire further when the presence of Raif's mind invaded their thoughts.

"*Hey, when you two geniuses get finished with your little history lesson down in the lab, you might want to come topside. Von found something that is pretty interesting.*" Raif's message came to them over the praxis' esolace. Functioning much like the esolace in Oasis, each ship had its own set of bioseine channels to facilitate the exchange of information.

Adan's conversation with Gavin about Sierra looked like it would have to wait. Despite Raif's sarcasm, Adan sensed he had important news to report.

"*Is this another experimental ship design in the praxis' information banks?*" Adan probed, knowing Raif's penchant for all things tech related. Raif had already stumbled upon three such designs in their short stint on the praxis.

"*No, it's something bigger than that. Or actually, it is something smaller. You're going to want to see this one for yourself.*"

Using the lev pads in the access shafts, Gavin and Adan arrived at the topmost level of the ship in little time at all. Raif and Von stood waiting for them in the midst of the central hallway.

Though most of the members of the Collective looked similar to Gavin, Adan had learned to tell them apart by subtle gestures they made or by the clothes they wore. In some cases he could distinguish them by scars or other markings they had received during their struggle for survival after the fall of Oasis. Though they were both wearing gray jumpsuits they had found in the praxis storage compartments, Von had the same serious expression he always did and Raif was sporting his typical goofy grin. But with Raif, Adan immediately noticed a new, distinguishing characteristic.

"What in the world did you do to your hair?" Adan asked.

Raif's hair had been teased into short, bright orange triangular spikes. The color was so vivid it made him look like he was wearing a textured rug dipped in an odd shade of neophosphorous.

"Hey, we're Sentients. We can look how we want, right? Just thought I'd try a little experiment. Gavin's not the only one who can invent stuff," Raif shot back with a playful wink.

Adan chuckled to himself. It was nice to have someone so lighthearted aboard the ship. Von did not share his mood, however. He stood with arms crossed and eyes unblinking, staring at the hole in the fuselage above their heads. It had an irregular, jagged shape, which was odd since the impact from the tunneler should have left something roughly circular. The opening was smaller than what had been previously reported as well, measuring a little over an arm span in length. Above the hole, the olive blur of the sky sped by.

Between Raif and Von floated a mobile chromium workstation loaded down with diagnostic tools, tubes of dense black masa fiber, and a small fabricator. The masa served as raw material for the fabricator, a cube-like device similar to the shifter Adan had used to transform one material into another when he lived in the desert, except fabricators were much more advanced. While shifters only generated raw materials like water, food, and elemental compounds, fabricators could fashion any sort of device or part, no matter how sophisticated. A pair of much larger fabricators down in the maintenance room were currently being used to make parts to create several brand new smaller ships from scratch.

"Looks like you are making progress," Adan said. "But you didn't call us up here just to get a compliment."

"No, but I'll take any compliment I can get. Gavin, how good are you at memory integrity work?" Raif asked as Gavin and Adan came to stand beside them.

"What do you mean, Raif?" Gavin asked.

"You see that hole? It is about two-thirds the size it should be."

"What does that have to do with memory analysis?"

"Because we haven't started working on closing it yet." Raif said.

Gavin's normally placid face wrinkled in confusion. "Are you saying you think this hole wasn't actually caused by the tunneler?"

"We only got here a little while ago and we have only been running tests since then. Does that look like the puncture from a drilling cone to you?"

Gavin ran his hand across his brow as if trying to coax out the answer to Raif's dilemma.

Von picked up where Raif left off. "We were wondering if you could take a look at Sierra's memory of how this happened. She was the only witness."

"To be honest, I don't see how even a tunneler could punch

a hole in the Maven's hull. We haven't found anything that will even scratch it to this point," Raif added.

"You think Sierra's memory of what happened was inaccurate?" Adan interjected.

"Not necessarily," Raif said. "But she was under a lot of stress when it happened. Captured by somatarchs, ship shot down, underground quake throwing rocks down the back of her shirt, watching her friends die—the mind can play diggers on you at times like that."

"That's why we thought maybe Gavin might want to check out her memories to see if there were any deviations," Von explained.

Adan's teeth set on edge with that last remark. Deviations? That was Developer talk. But he checked his impulse to rise to Sierra's defense. Adan had no reason to believe the former assessor meant any harm. Von and Raif were Sierra's friends.

Adan stared back up at the hole. He was not as skilled a memorant as Gavin, but he had experienced Sierra's memories first hand and was convinced she had seen things accurately. He had witnessed false memories in the minds of some of the members of the Collective and he knew what they were like. Manipulated or inaccurate memories were always accompanied by a certain foggy immateriality. That had not been the case with Sierra.

"The tunneler that pierced the hull had one of the cross stream drills," Gavin reminded them. "Have you tried using something like that?"

"Well, no," Raif admitted. "In case you hadn't noticed, the praxis isn't exactly rolling in mining equipment. It's an attack ship. And I didn't think turning the hybrid cannon around and firing on our own ship would be the best course of action."

"Ah, come on now, Raif," Von chided in deadpan fashion. "I'm sure you could build a cross stream drill in your sleep. Or maybe we could try using that spiky head of yours. That hair looks like it would cut through anything."

Raif rolled his eyes. "Okay, so maybe the tunneler could punch a hole in the praxis' skull," he conceded, "but could it make a hole that would close back up again—by itself?"

Gavin's pointed back up to the odd-looking hole. "The shape is certainly not consistent with a drilling cone."

"Yep, that repair job looks like it got run through a random number generator," Raif said, shaking his head.

"We might need to check into the possibility that Sierra's memory might have been affected by stress," Gavin said, his tone even more business-like than before. "My guess is that it was not, but it's best to be thorough. At the same time, I would like for you to search the Maven's systems and find out more about the properties of the ship's hull."

"Got it." Raif nodded, looking surprisingly earnest for a change.

"So we'll hold off on repairing this breach for now, I take it?" Von asked.

"For now," Gavin said. "I'll look into this while the trace on the Collective fleet finishes. We'll meet back down in the control room in the morning to see what we come up with."

"Well, at least you got out of the repair work for a little while," Von put in dryly.

"Hey, if the ship wants to fix itself," Raif fired back with a smirk, "I won't complain."

FOUR

THE MISSING

THE NEXT DAY SIERRA AND ADAN SAT ON A BENCH BY themselves at a table in the commissary. Most of the other Sentients had already eaten, but a handful chatted and ate at other tables nearby. The *Maven* didn't have an invisible viand stream like Oasis to feed its occupants. Instead they used small fabricators in designated eating areas like this one to dispense food. The nutrient fabricators provided fluffy white nutrient cubes the size of the tip of Adan's thumb from a recessed area in one of the walls. It only took around five to fill a person up. Adan had already eaten four, but he wasn't hungry. He sat with his gripper, a short plastic stick with an attractor pad on the end, rolling the last cube around on his plate, tipping it end over end. His eyes remained fixed on Sierra, her beautiful face knotted into a tapestry of worry.

"I only slept two slices last night," she confided to him. "I don't think I will be able to really sleep until we get everybody back. I feel so helpless."

"Gavin has been running trace after trace. We will find Nance and the others soon," Adan said.

Mapping just the right moment when a thought or a conversation took place was the hard part about using the chronotrace. It took a lot of trial and error, but it was only a matter of time before they stumbled upon the right information. Adan didn't feel like telling her that Gavin was analyzing her memories while the traces were running. He didn't think they would find anything and as distressed as she was, he worried how she might take the news. "But I know what you're feeling," he went on, "It's hard knowing your friends are somewhere and there isn't anything you can do about it."

"I know you mean well, but you don't really know what it's like. You barely knew Nance. How could you know what I'm feeling?" Her response had an edge to it caught Adan off guard.

He let the nutrition cube roll to a stop. He twiddled the gripper for a moment in his fingers, unsure of how to respond. Through their bioseine connection, he actually did know exactly what Sierra was feeling and she must have known that. Being a memorant he would have been able to sense something of her thoughts even without his bioseine, but he doubted she wanted to be reminded of that just now. He was on shaky enough ground already.

"The Welkin I met the first time I went into the Viscera are being held in captivity too—in a Wayman city a few days from here," he said, trying to show that he could in fact relate to what she was going through.

Sierra scowled back at him. "What are you talking about?"

Adan reached out to her mind and Sierra uncharacteristically put up no resistance. Images of Senya and her children Halel, Jarem, and Lila passed from Adan's memory to hers. She saw Senya at the Wayman tent serving mosh in the city of Hull. Senya's face wore a look of quiet pain as Adan was carried away from her on the Wayman lev.

Sierra's scowl softened. "I'm sorry, I didn't know about

those people," she said. Her mind drifted away from his. "I guess there's a lot I don't know about you. And a lot you don't know about me," she added. She stood to leave.

Adan rose and touched her arm. "Wait, Sierra. Where are you going?"

"To my quarters," she said. "I think I need to be alone right now."

Adan let out an uncomfortable sigh. This felt like the argument between them when they were trapped inside the tunnels of the Viscera. She had pushed him away like this then too, taking everything on her shoulders.

"I'll let you know as soon as we find out about Nance and the others," he said.

"Thank you." She turned and strode towards the exit, but not before lifting her plate in the air and giving it a shove towards the return cabinet on the back wall. The plate floated across the room, adjusting itself perfectly to avoid the people along its path. The cabinet opened automatically and the plate eased in and filed itself away.

Adan sat back down on the bench after watching her go. It felt considerably stiffer than when he had first sat down. He couldn't help but notice that several of the other Sentients looked their way when Sierra got up and left. Though he and Sierra had kept their voices down during their conversation, it felt like everyone in the commissary could tell she had been less than happy when she left as well. He resisted the urge to scan their thoughts and see what they were thinking.

His eyes zeroed in on the fluffy white nutrient cube in front of him, as if it, too, might get up and abandon him. He popped the tiny square into his mouth and got up and hurried out of the room. His empty plate sat on the table alone for a while until, having not been touched for the required period of time, it rose up and floated back to the cabinet on its own.

Adan couldn't sleep. His thoughts spun perpetually around inside his head, running along the same mental tracks over and over again: the quakes, his relationship with Sierra, the captive Welkin, the prisoners captured by the Collective forces during the escape from Manx Core. He must have tried a hundred times to resolve these dilemmas in his mind, but he kept coming up short.

He knew that he should just use his bioseine to force himself to sleep and trust that everything would work out in the end. After all, Numinae was in control, wasn't he?

Behind all of these concerns, at an even deeper level, the mystery of his past wrapped itself around his thoughts so tightly it felt like it could snap at any moment. He would never truly be at peace until he knew who he was.

When Gavin's mental presence popped into his head as he lay wide awake in bed, he welcomed the distraction.

"Adan, I'm headed to the control room. Can you meet me there as soon as possible? I'm going to contact a few others as well."

Adan wondered who else might be coming at a time like this, but he was too tired to ask. He gave his mental assent, yawned, and rolled out of bed. He did not bother changing out of his tunic, merely putting a silver lab coat over it and slipping on his shoes before shuffling out the door. Leaving his cramped quarters behind, he headed down the hallway towards the nearest access shaft.

His quarters were on level four so it didn't take him long to arrive at the Command Center one level above. He didn't bother with the lev pads in the access shafts, taking the ramps instead. Ever since one of the floating platforms had fallen out from under him in Manx Core, he avoided them whenever possible. Though he knew the failure of the pad had been a deliberate act on the part of the Collective security forces, he couldn't shake the thought that one might fall again.

Adan made his way down the access ramp and the central corridor to a thick metal door, which opened easily, and into the Command Center. All the repairs caused by Nox's explosion looked to have been completed. The image of the Wayman's large frame being inserted inside a black body bag flashed through his mind, as did Nox's horrific grin. Perhaps because he had not been present when he died, Adan still found it hard to believe that he was truly dead. If the volatile Wayman had come swaggering into the room at that moment Adan would not have been surprised.

The bridge was empty when he arrived, but the *Maven* continued flying on auto. In the giant screen which dominated the far wall, the praxis' sensors rendered the terrain over which they traveled as if it were day outside. Pillowy gray dunes stretched out as far as he could see. Like most of the Vast, there was a monotonous sameness to them, but at least the scene showed no evidence of tremors in this part of the desert.

A set of ten black polymeric chairs arranged around a large table occupied the center of the room. On the table rested the chronotrace, powered off and lifeless, a lidless eye staring up at the ceiling.

As Adan approached the table, Von, Raif, Halerin, and two other Sentients whom Adan had not seen before, walked in together. They were discussing the closing of the *Maven's* damaged hull and at first did not take notice of Adan's presence.

Before Adan could ask about the new arrivals, Trey, who had only just been cleared from medical earlier that morning, walked into the room. Adan was surprised to see him present after his near brush with death. He had been put in a coma after getting caught in one of the quakes back in Oasis. Sierra had shared with Adan at length about how advanced the medical facilities on the praxis were and Trey was living proof of her claims. He had a nasty scar that ran down the middle of his forehead, but otherwise he looked well. Many other Sentients had not been so fortunate.

From the little Adan had been told about Trey, he was a quiet person, well-liked even though he usually kept to himself. Before he got hurt, he spent time working with Raif repairing and building equipment, fetching things for Sierra and the handlers, and commiserating with the Waymen, trying to learn more of their ways. It was encouraging to see him up and about.

The two other new Sentients, like all former Collectives, looked very similar, except that one of them wore his hair closely shaved and the other had let his grow out.

Everyone there was wearing the ubiquitous gray jumpsuits, though thankfully none of them had decided to imitate Raif and his ridiculous orange hair.

"Adan, this is Cade." Raif motioned to the man with the longer hair who gave Adan's hand a quick shake. "He was in the same cell as Halerin. Before that, he worked on the atmos array and the energy mesh back in Oasis."

"Greetings," said Cade, nodding. "You're the one who crashed the mesh, aren't you?"

Adan shifted uneasily. He had never meant to bring down the energy mesh which powered Oasis and maintained its protective atmosphere, but when he did, the ensuing storm had taken the lives of nearly everyone in the city. Though he saw no condemnation on Cade's face, he still found himself fumbling for a response. "I—yes...it was an accident."

Cade nodded slowly. "It was terrible what happened, but if you hadn't done it then we wouldn't be free." Cade squeezed

Adan's shoulder warmly. The shift in tone was so unexpected and heartfelt that it rendered him momentarily speechless.

"And this is Jax," Raif went on, breaking up the awkward introduction. He indicated the short-haired man, who gave Adan a curt nod.

"Heard a lot about you," Jax said in a rough voice. "They said you got out before the storm hit, but came back to spring us out of the Core."

Though Adan had not recognized Jax at first, the moment he set eyes on him, he knew who he was: an assessor. And not just any assessor. He was one of the ones who had been hunting for Adan the day Will freed him from the Institute.

The sudden recognition startled Adan. All at once he forgot about the energy mesh and the destruction of Oasis. His mind went back to his last day at the Institute. Though he doubted Jax even remembered that day, Adan's pulse ticked up several beats in his presence.

"I don't remember which cell you were from," Raif inquired of Jax. "Which one was it?"

"B-16," Jax answered stiffly.

"I thought B-16 got wiped out," Halerin said, a questioning look in his eyes.

"That's true," Jax was quick to reply. "I was the only survivor."

"Well, I'm glad you're here," Von said. "We need assessors to help the others realize what they're up against."

"I'll do what I can," was Jax's terse response.

At that point Gavin walked in and down the ramp. He approached the table and motioned for everyone to sit down.

"All right, since you have all had time to introduce your-selves, please, everyone sit down," he instructed them. He was using a private channel, his thoughts limited to the people gathered around the table.

Adan sat next to Raif while Jax took the chair on his other side. Adan tried not to be bothered by this, but found it hard to concentrate with the assessor sitting right next to him. He recalled the word Jax had used to refer to him back at the Institute: *non-viable*. Adan hoped he didn't feel the same way now that he was no longer under the control of the Collective.

"Before you get started," Raif put in, *"I was just wondering why you decided to bring in so many people? No offense, guys, but I thought this was just supposed to be a status update on the hull."*

Gavin, who had remained standing, leaned in on the table and took a moment to gather his thoughts. *"Well, there are a few other things I would like to discuss as well. The Sentients are going to need leaders if they hope to get through what lies ahead. And I think the people at this table are the best qualified to do that."*

Halerin responded first.

"I'm not so sure about that. Half the members of my cell were on Nance's ship when it got shot down. If I couldn't protect them then, what makes you think I'll do any better now?"

"You are exactly who we need," Gavin assured him. *"Because I know you will do whatever it takes to get them back."*

"But they could be half way across the Vast by now—if they are even still alive."

Gavin's eyes sparkled in anticipation. *"We will get to that in a moment. First, Raif needs to brief us on the state of the ship's hull."* Gavin deferred to Raif with a nod.

"Right," Raif began, his head bouncing with enthusiasm. *"Well, in case the rest of you didn't know, even though the Collective was kind enough to loan us this technological marvel, she was damaged goods. She came with a hole two spans in diameter punched in her skull. This hole was how Sierra got on*

the ship, but for some reason we have yet to be able to figure out, the hole has since sealed itself back up. It is completely shut now."

"What do you mean 'sealed itself'?" Cade asked.

"Completely shut? You mean you and your team didn't fix it?" Trey echoed Cade's confusion.

Images of the sealed hole flowed from Raif's mind into theirs, juxtaposed with an image of the breach in its initial state.

"Clear enough?" Raif continued. *"It closed right up like it was a piece of skin and—according to some schematics I dug up in the ship's logs—that's because the hull is, in some strange way I don't understand, alive. It's made of some hybrid form of celerium called velar and it has properties similar to a living organism."*

Varying degrees of disbelief ran through the minds of those present, everyone except Adan. He remembered the way Zain had described celerium to him as somehow alive. Zain might have been the most noble person he had met in his short time in the Vast. Though a member of the savage Waymen who roamed the desert, raiding and looting the cast away machines and parts which littered the dunes, he had never acted like one. He had saved Adan's life more than once and his death in Manx Core had been perhaps Adan's most bitter loss yet. When Zain had told him about the living properties of the rare black rock, Adan had dismissed it as just another Wayman superstition, but after what Raif had shared, Adan wondered whether Zain had really been all that far off the mark.

"That makes no sense. Rocks are inanimate. They're just raw materials," Cade stated, his mind groping to understand the concept. *"The logs have to be mistaken."*

"You are free to look it up for yourself, but that is my story and I'm sticking to it," Raif declared.

A puzzled silence ensued, broken at last by Von's thoughts. *"If that is what you found, Raif, then I have no reason to doubt you. But what about you, Gavin? Did the tunneler actually damage it? Or is it completely invulnerable like we first thought?"*

"Sierra's memories were accurate," Gavin reported. *"It does seem as if cross stream locus energy can harm it. Given what Raif has just told us, that would stand to reason, because that sort of energy can harm both organic and inorganic material. Apparently that's what this velar is, both alive and inanimate at the same time."*

"Okay, so we've got a living—and non-living—ship, whatever that means," Trey put in. *"But I don't see how this gives us much of an advantage over the Collective, especially since we don't even know where they are."*

"But we do," Gavin announced. *"The Collective fleet is currently hunkered down in Breaker's Hollow, a canyon about thirty clicks from here."*

"Are you sure?" Trey followed up. *"Then the trace worked?"*

"I used my memories from my time with Malthus as the seed and worked forward from there. I was able to track the survivors by switching the focus, mid-trace, to another Developer named Cyrith," Gavin confirmed. Nervous excitement, infused with fear about what this all meant, spread across the channel.

"Wait, so since Malthus is dead, is Cyrith in charge of the Collective now?" Jax asked. Adan noted with some discomfort the deep level of respect Jax seemed to have for the man of whom he spoke. Whether it was based out of fear or loyalty, though, Adan couldn't tell.

"Yes," Gavin stated.

"I only ever had contact with about a half dozen of the

Admins," Jax remarked. *"But I remember Cyrith. He was a little different. I can't quite put my finger on it, though."*

"So who is he? Gavin, you knew him, right?" Raif tossed his questions into the mix. As a former Developer, Gavin was the only one that might know anything about what Cyrith was really like. *"What was his role among the Developers? Did he have a military background? Is he mad for power? And, most importantly, what color is his hair?"*

Even Gavin cracked a smile at that last remark.

"Cyrith has brown hair, but that shouldn't surprise you. All the members of the Collective do. We're all based on the same generational map. As for your other questions, he doesn't have any military expertise, though he did help Malthus create the somatarchs. He liked to keep in the background, mostly, and stick to his research, but he had a very important role in Oasis." Gavin gave Adan a telling look. *"He was the head of the Institute."*

An image of the scientist in question flashed through their minds. He looked in most ways just like all the others, but not to Adan.

FIVE

THE PERSEPOLIS

"You are making steady progress, and I have some good news for you," the scientist's words played back through Adan's memory.

Of all the visits Adan had received in the Institute, the one that stood out the most was the first time he had been told about the esolace. He had not known it then, but he realized now that this was when he had met Cyrith.

There was a look in Cyrith's eyes that had made him stand out. The other scientists were distant, as if they were half asleep or perpetually disinterested, but not Cyrith. Intelligence glinted inside his eyes, not cruel and calculating as with Darius, but in its own way just as focused and intense. Cyrith wanted answers. He appeared to be studying things, measuring them all the time. Though many things from Adan's time in the Institute remained hazy in his memory, this was not one of them.

"So he survived the storm and the quakes," Adan commented. *"What are his plans?"*

"Yes, I'd like to know that as well," Von put in. *"Oasis is gone. So is Manx Core. Where else do they have to run?"*

"*Cyrith is not running,*" Gavin declared, eyeing the chrono-trace in the middle of the table. "*He has a fleet of dozens of ships and he plans on using them. Just as soon as the storm dies down enough for an attack.*"

He's trying to ease into this, Adan observed from Gavin's subsurface thoughts. Those didn't come through the bioseine unless a person wanted them to, but Adan's memorant abilities allowed him to see things the others couldn't.

"*Who do they plan on attacking? Us?*" Jax asked, alarmed. "*Do they know our present location?*"

"*No, Cyrith has no idea we survived. Nor would he give it much thought if he did,*" Gavin was quick to assure them.

"*But who else is there to attack?*" Von wondered.

Adan's mind went instantly to the Welkin. Gavin had told him that Malthus had threatened to attack them if he didn't help him with the chronotrace. Maybe Malthus was lying. Maybe they had intended to attack the Welkin all along.

"*He's going after the Wayman city of Hull.*" Gavin declared.

Confusion and bewilderment cascaded through the minds of those gathered at the table, including Adan's. Why would the Collective want to attack Hull? Yes, they had some technology, but it was primitive compared to what the Collective possessed and when Adan had been there the city was still under construction. It would hardly be a suitable base of operations for Cyrith and his fleet.

"*But why—?*" Adan began, before suddenly remembering something—"*Senya.*" The name of his friend burst into the channel like a blast of sand in the face. All thoughts of Cyrith's purpose flew from his mind. "*Senya's there. We can't let Cyrith attack that city.*"

"*I agree, but first we have to—*" Gavin began, but Adan's thoughts kept tumbling out.

"The Collective has no use for Werin. They'll kill her along with everyone else, Waymen and Welkin alike. We have to stop them."

"And risk the lives of everyone on this ship? I don't think so," Jax countered.

"Hold on, let's put a damper on things until we are all on the same page." Raif interjected. *"Who's Senya? And what is this Hull place? I'm getting mixed vibes with all these thoughts flying around. Let's keep everybody in sync here."*

Gavin used his memorant abilities to project a calming presence across the channel, helping the others rein in their emotions. *"Hull is a Wayman city built using a great deal of salvaged equipment from the Vast. The Waymen there have managed to build a considerable amount of new machinery as well, but it is mostly very primitive."*

"Wait," Von responded, *"the Waymen are highly superstitious about technology, aren't they? I thought they generally avoided it."*

"You are correct," Gavin replied. *"But their leader is a former Developer, a memorant named Nolan. And it looks like he has convinced some of the Waymen to embrace it."*

Nolan loomed like a shadow at the back of Adan's thoughts. If anyone could stand up to the Collective it was him, but if Hull did resist the attack, Adan doubted Nolan would stop there. As large as his city was and as many Waymen as he had under his control, the Vast would simply be swapping one tyrant for another.

"But that doesn't explain why the Collective would want to attack them," Jax observed. *"If Cyrith was an Admin, he won't just be doing this out of spite, especially if he doesn't have a military background. He must have something else in mind, another round of experiments, maybe?"*

Gavin sat back in his chair and folded his hands. *He's worried how we'll react once we know the truth,* Adan realized.

Gavin inhaled deeply and drew himself up in his chair. *"Cyrith does have a reason for wanting to attack Hull. And I think the best way for you to understand it is to show you."*

Gazing at the chronotrace, Gavin's eyes glossed over and the ring around the device began to glow with a yellow light. The device spun into motion. A moment later, a new scene flashed into existence all around them. They found themselves in a room nearly identical to the one they were in, but occupied by only two people. They were looking through the chronotrace into the Command Center of the other praxis cruiser in the Collective fleet, the one called the *Persepolis*.

Cyrith stood with his back towards the massive viewing window in the control room of the praxis. There was not much to see there anyway. Breaker's Hollow was a bland, weather beaten bowl of rock devoid of any activity other than the storm that had been raging all day. It covered everything in sheets of sand, blowing back and forth across the canyon walls, scouring them clean.

The thin framed man wore his customary silver lab coat, the mercurial sheen of the fabric shifting subtly in the light. He looked every bit the Institute scientist that he was, but he was no longer at the Institute. He was out of his element and he knew it. Still, he did not trust anyone else to act in his place, including Xander, the other man standing in the room with him. Along with Cyrith they were all that remained of the Developers.

Xander leaned against the railing of the exit ramp. He had traded in his silver lab coat for something more practical. He wore a brown, one-piece jumper. Otherwise, his appearance mirrored that of Cyrith.

The *Persepolis* rested at the back of a large canyon, along with the remains of the fleet from Manx Core. Though they had managed to salvage close to forty percent of the ships from the freak quakes which had destroyed their former base, given what they were up against Cyrith doubted that would be enough.

Besides the losses to the fleet, they had lost the commander of their military forces in the disaster as well. Cyrith had waited over a day for Malthus to arrive, but it was now clear that neither he nor the *Maven* would be making it to the rendezvous point in the canyon.

Could the *Maven* have fallen into the hands of the deviants? Could Malthus have gone rogue? There were too many unknowns and that is what worried him. He liked to know all of the variables before going into an experiment. That way the results were more of a formality, a confirmation of what he already knew. But with war, certainty was never guaranteed.

He was confident that Nolan would not be a problem and felt they could probably handle the deviant threat as well, but the Delegation was another matter. Cyrith had no idea what capabilities they had managed to develop after all these years. The one thing he did know was that they were coming, and he doubted they would be satisfied with simply reclaiming what Darius had stolen from them. Cyrith suspected they would not rest until every last member of the Collective had been annihilated, starting with him.

"*How convenient for Darius to have died,*" Cyrith mused. "*Now we are forced to clean up his mess.*"

"*From everything in the logs we managed to salvage, it sounds like he didn't have a whole lot of choice. The Delegation was killing the planet anyway. Darius just finished what they started."*

Cyrith sighed ever so softly. Of course Xander would say that. As a memorant his thoughts had been more closely scrutinized by Darius than other members of the Collective. Even now, he failed to see that the scalpel which hovered an inch from their necks had been placed there by his former mentor. Cyrith did not yet have a clear idea how Darius had managed to manipulate everyone's thoughts so thoroughly over such a long period of time, but it was clear that his abilities as a memorant far surpassed anything they had previously imagined.

"And yet he clearly did not finish the Delegation off or they could not have sent those scouts," Cyrith replied, checking any judgmental thoughts from creeping into their shared channel. He needed Xander's support more than anything right now and since Xander still held a vestige of respect for the Developer who had created the Collective it would not be wise to disparage Darius too much.

"We still don't have hard evidence that the Delegation sent anything more than those scout ships. And if that's all they have, the remains of the Manx Core fleet will be more than enough to handle them," Xander commented.

Cyrith once again held his emotions in check. Xander was apparently even less skilled in military matters than himself.

"Malthus did not seem to think so," Cyrith reminded him. *"He said the sidereal portals the ships were carrying could mean only one thing: preparation for a zero dimension invasion."*

"But then why send the scouts?" Xander asked. *"Why not just use the same portal we used to get here?"*

"Either they do not know about it, or it was destroyed. Knowing Darius, my guess would be the latter. He would have wanted to burn any bridges between our world and theirs."

"I've always wondered why he destroyed the Nebula,

though. If we still had that ship, we wouldn't have to worry about the Delegation. From what little information we have about it in the logs, it seems like the Nebula was what allowed us to defeat the Delegation the first time. To go to all that work to commandeer it and then just destroy it—it makes little sense."

Cyrith relaxed slightly. Perhaps Xander was waking up to the truth after all.

"Which is why we need to take Hull as quickly as possible," Cyrith remarked. *"If the Delegation ever finds us, we need to be ready. Malthus and I were beginning to make preparations, but now that we've lost half our army, it looks like we'll have to speed things up. Which brings me back to the point of this meeting. Are you certain you can keep the remaining assessors under your control?"*

Xander walked over to stand beside Cyrith, but instead of putting his back to the viewing window as Cyrith had done, he continued to gaze out into the dark gray waves of sand dashing themselves against the *Persepolis.*

"The new Assessor Primary will be easy enough to control," Xander assured him, *"but I'm not Darius. If we had more time and a full-fledged esolace at our disposal I could do a much better job. The lack of memorants also makes things extremely difficult. I am only one man after all."*

Cyrith turned to face the barrage of silt raging inside the viewing window. *"Then I think it is time we recruit some new Developers."*

Xander turned from the screen to regard his fellow scientist. *"But that will take time and the Delegation could arrive any day."*

"I realize that. But if we are going to win this fight, we have to remain unified, working together as one seamless unit. Darius at least knew how to accomplish that. We have little choice but to follow in his footsteps."

"We can begin by seeing what we have in the vault."

"Yes, that makes the most sense," Cyrith answered. *"But we may have to bring in some fresh bodies as well."*

"Agreed," Xander replied. *"If only memorants were not so difficult to come by."*

"I believe the battle at Hull may help us in more ways than one, then," Cyrith concluded, pursing his lips into the barest representation of a smile that the human face was capable of.

The two Developers remained standing there, staring out into the meteorological mayhem. So much sand, yet it looked more like an empty void than an actual mass. Somewhere out there was the Wayman city of Hull, a base cobbled together from scraps and protected by primitive andros, their pathetic brains riddled with superstition and ignorance.

"We will prevail," Cyrith declared. *"We have to. We are all that humanity has left."*

SIX
COUNTER INTUITIVE

THE LIGHT OF THE CHRONOTRACE FADED AND THE *Maven's* command center shimmered back into view. The men around the table kept staring at the device as if they needed the projection to start up again to answer all their questions.

Adan was just as confused as everyone else. The Collective in general, and the Developers in particular, had always seemed invincible to him, their knowledge and power virtually limitless. They had banished disease, hunger, all negative emotions—even death. And yet, based on what he had just witnessed, they apparently had fears and weaknesses of their own. Malthus had told Gavin about a coming conflict, but until now, it hadn't seemed real.

"Are you sure your device was working properly?" Jax remarked after a long silence. *"Those two didn't sound like Admins to me."*

"Exactly what I was thinking," Raif agreed, *"definitely Beta version material there. Maybe even Alpha."*

Adan understood what Raif was getting at, but he wasn't ready to believe Cyrith and Xander were completely incompetent based on a single conversation. They still had the Collective fleet and that gave them the upper hand.

"I'm not sure you understand exactly what is going on here," Gavin cautioned.

"It seemed pretty obvious to me," Jax shot back. *"They're afraid of this Delegation they mentioned and think that attacking Hull will give them an edge. But that is what makes it ring false. The Admins were never afraid of any outside threat because there is no outside threat—there's nothing out here besides the Vast and a whole lot of sand."*

Gavin pointed toward the viewing screen where the dunes rolled by. It certainly appeared as empty and desolate as Jax described. *"It may seem like that to you, but I can assure you that the trace was accurate. I still need to run more to get all the details, but this much I can tell you: the Delegation is real and if war comes to the Vast we don't want to get caught in the crossfire."*

"But you have seen the Collective fleet," Halerin interjected. *"Even though they lost half of it in the Core, what force could possibly stand against that?"*

"Malthus mentioned that they were preparing for war," Gavin continued. *"I didn't believe him back then, but after seeing this, I understand what they were doing in the Viscera. Manx Core was a military installation. They did not build those ships overnight. They knew about this enemy, and they knew there was a possibility that the Delegation might find them."*

"But say the Delegation is real." Raif's mind scrambled to resolve the dilemma. *"What do we care if they've got their sites locked on the Collective? Let them fight it out. They might just do us a favor and do each other in."*

"Can we be certain the Delegation won't do the same to us?" Jax asked.

"I don't know," Gavin confessed.

"I trust your judgment, Gavin," Von replied, even more resolute and grim than usual. *"But either way it seems like the only real option we have is to go somewhere where the Collective —and this Delegation, whoever they are—can never find us."*

"But what about the prisoners?" Halerin reminded them. *"We can't just abandon them."*

"I agree." This brief thought shot through the minds of everyone around the table like a blast from some internal alarm. Were they really going to attempt to go up against the Collective again? The channel rippled with questions and doubts, but Gavin continued on amidst the mental static. *"I have been thinking about this trace ever since I saw it last night. And I have settled on what I believe is the best course of action for us to take. But it won't work unless we're all on board. I warn you, though, this plan involves a great deal of risk."*

"Well, our last plan was pretty cracked, too. Those seem to be our specialty." Raif remarked.

Gavin studied the men around the table. Adan could sense his hesitancy return.

"I think we need to attempt the rescue in the middle of the Collective attack on Hull," Gavin stated.

Jax made a face like he had something in his mouth that he wanted to spit out. *"That would be suicide."*

"Jax is right," Cade put in. *"If we don't get shot down by the Collective, we're likely to get targeted by the forces defending Hull. Our ships look exactly like the ones from the Collective."*

Von's frown deepened. *"A stealth mission—preferably under cover of a storm—would have the best chance of success."*

Adan wrung his hands under the table. Gavin's plan didn't make much sense, but that wasn't what worried him most, it was the thought of Senya and her family. The chronotrace sequence he had just witnessed had convinced him that the

Collective invasion would claim her life as well as those of her sons and everyone else imprisoned in Hull.

"What about the Welkin, Gavin? There are probably hundreds of innocent people inside that city." Adan blurted out frantically.

"Don't tell me you want us to risk our necks for those people, too?" Jax balked.

"Of course we will," Gavin replied. "We're going to save everyone we can, Werin and Sentient both. But one thing at a time. For now, let's figure out how we're going to free the captured Sentients."

"What's your plan? A full-out assault?" Jax scoffed. "They'll see the Maven coming from a dozen clicks away, unless we go under cover of a storm like Von suggested."

Gavin eased back down into his chair. Adan thought he might lose them at that moment, but instead of responding to the assessor's remark directly, Gavin began to unpack his thoughts to the group in a careful, methodical way, forgetting his reservations this time.

"We know that the Persepolis is the only ship with the facilities to hold prisoners. I can use the chronotrace to determine the exact location of the captured Sentients, but even once we find that out, there isn't any way for us to get in by covert means. Not without a great deal more planning than what we have time for. The only reason we got onto the Maven in the first place was because of the tunneler. And since we have no chance in a straight fight, I think we will have to recreate the same set of circumstances that got us inside before."

"So you're saying we just order up a massive quake and drop a tunneler on their head again?" Raif joked.

Jax bristled at the idea. "You cannot be serious."

"It sounds like fun, actually," Raif added. "I will say this, though. I ran a few preliminary tests on the velar hull and cross stream energy does seem to affect it. So Gavin's plan isn't completely crazy."

"We won't need the quake, only the tunneler this time," Gavin clarified. "And we won't have to drop it onto the Persepolis, just land it on top using a citus and then drill in from there."

Each of those gathered wrestled with the idea to varying degrees. Several of them shifted uncomfortably in their chairs. Once again Von took the initiative and responded first.

"I suppose it could work," he offered. This admission relieved the tension in the room somewhat, but Jax remained unconvinced.

"You are all either the bravest men I've ever met or the biggest fools," he commented.

"He is no fool who risks his life for his friend," Gavin cast a glance at Adan.

Von nodded, continuing to warm to the idea.

Jax dug in. "I'm not against risking our lives to bring back the prisoners, but you're asking us to throw them away. They'll never let us get close enough for a stunt like that," he countered, ignoring the growing sentiment of approval within the group for Gavin's plan.

"That is why we will wait until their focus is on Hull," Gavin explained.

"Okay, maybe. But the ships in Hull—are they really sophisticated enough to keep the Collective occupied long enough for the mission to succeed?"

As the only one of them who had ever been to Hull, Adan knew first hand that the Waymen ships would be little trouble for the Collective. The Persepolis alone might have been enough to conquer it since it was doubtful the Waymen had anything which could penetrate its fuselage.

"We will have to add our own ships into the mix," Von surmised.

"I had not gotten to that part yet, but yes, I do think that will give us the best chance of success," Gavin replied.

Jax huffed, but for once kept his thoughts to himself.

"I have to admit, that's a pretty deadly gambit you're calling for there," Raif remarked.

"And yet...it just might work," Halerin put in. "Does anyone else have a better idea?"

The mental exchange ebbed once again as each man mulled over the implications of Gavin's plan. It sounded like it would be nearly impossible to pull off, but Adan trusted that Gavin would not have proposed it if there had been a better one. Adan was still anxious to hear what plan he had for rescuing the prisoners from Hull, though the more he thought about it, the more he realized that freeing hundreds of prisoners who were likely scattered throughout the city might prove even more difficult than boarding the *Persepolis*.

"All right, I'm in," Von declared at length, staring at Jax as if throwing down a challenge for him to join. "The plan is risky, but it is probably the only shot we'll get to free the prisoners."

Von's reply was met with several nods as, one by one, Raif, Cade, Halerin, Trey, and Adan agreed to go through with the plan.

Jax was the last to respond. "None of this makes any sense, but I'll go along with whatever the group decides."

"It's settled, then," Von concluded. "We will bring back the captured Sentients. They would do the same for us."

The tension in Gavin's face finally released, but he retained his solemn air.

"If it's okay with everyone, I'd like Raif to fly on the team infiltrating the Persepolis," he suggested.

"*Sign me up,*" Raif responded enthusiastically. "*I'd love to be the one to punch a hole in the* Persepolis' *skull.*"

"*Actually, I was thinking Cade might take on that role. He knows most of the captured Sentients and I thought the prisoners might prefer to see a familiar face. Cade, would you be willing to man the tunneler team?*"

"*Absolutely,*" Cade replied without hesitation.

"*Raif will fly you in on a citus and pick you up once you get the prisoners,*" Gavin explained.

"*Well, at least you're not leaving me completely out of the party. I'll never turn down a chance to fly one of those streamliners,*" Raif replied.

"*And I'd like to lead the assault,*" Von volunteered. "*If that's all right with you.*"

"*You read my mind,*" Gavin replied.

"*And I'll be his second,*" Jax offered, surprising everyone with his shift in attitude.

Gavin paused. It was clear that he had someone else in mind for that role, but he acquiesced. "*Very well. I'll leave it to the both of you to recruit two additional pilots for the mission.*"

"*I know a couple of men who would be more than suitable for the task,*" Jax stated and neither Von nor Gavin showed any objection.

"*I take it you'll coordinate the operation from the* Maven?" Von inquired of Gavin.

"*Yes, I think that might be the best course to take. I would prefer Halerin to stay with me to help.*"

"*I was hoping to go with Cade,*" Halerin commented.

"*I thought about it, but coordinating the mission from the* Maven *will be just as important, if not more so, than the rescue operation itself. We could use your level-headedness back here on the ship,*" Gavin replied.

Halerin folded his hands and regarded the former Developer with quiet resolve. *"I'll serve wherever I'm most needed. I just hope they don't decide to take the fight to us. Raif's analysis of the praxis defenses revealed that it is vulnerable to disruptor attacks and those have a much longer range than the hybrid cannons. If they manage to disable our shields they could drain our power and drop us like a stone."*

"Our shields are substantial," Gavin reminded him. *"It would take a concerted effort to knock them out. They won't have enough ships to devote to that kind of concentrated attack, not while they're trying to capture Hull,"*

"All the same, I'll keep analyzing the Maven's *systems to see if there is any way around that weakness,"* Raif offered.

"Excellent," Gavin remarked. *"Whatever surprises we can manage to pull off will give us that much more chance for success."*

"And the Werin? What about them?" Adan finally asked, fearing that Gavin might actually have forgotten them after all.

"Well for that part, I do think a more backdoor approach is in order," Gavin answered. He leveled his eyes on Adan who felt his skin tingle in response. *He wants me to do this,* he realized. And though it would likely be just as dangerous as what Raif, Cade, Von, and Jax had just signed up for, he found himself nodding deliberately.

"What do you want me to do?"

SEVEN

GOOD INTENTIONS

News of Gavin's plan spread quickly through the *Maven*. By the following morning, everyone on board had been briefed and most of them assigned a role in the upcoming mission, even if it was just to help process the influx of refugees from Hull.

Since Adan's mission would be physically demanding, Gavin sent him to his quarters to get as much rest as possible. He had been asleep for a slice and a half when his bioseine alerted him to the presence of Sierra coming down the hall towards his room. Though she was still too far away to read her thoughts, he was certain her visit must have something to do with the upcoming mission.

He threw on a soft black robe and dashed over to the dispenser, splashing water on his face to both wake himself up and steady his nerves. He poured himself a cup of water, his hands shaking slightly. As parched as he was, he couldn't bring the cup to his lips; he was too nervous, imagining what Sierra might say and how he would respond.

The door brushed open so silently that Adan would have

missed it had he not been waiting for it. Sierra stood in the doorway with her hands on her hips. She remained like that for several moments, just looking at him, an enigmatic expression on her face. Adan found it impossible to read her thoughts at that moment. Normally, she was the easiest person to read that he knew, but her thoughts were swirling and he could make no sense of them. Ever since she'd found out about Senya and the Welkin, things had not been the same between them.

Since he couldn't read her, Adan found staring at the cup of water an easier proposition. The tiny ripples played across its surface like a mirror of his own agitated spirit.

"Why don't you want me to go on the mission? Does it have something to do with your friend?" She put a peculiar emphasis on that last word.

"No, I told Gavin the reason. Didn't he tell you?" Adan looked up from the cup. He wanted to say more, but his throat clenched. He took a sip of water instead. His parched insides soaked it up in an instant, but his mouth felt as dry as ever.

Sierra stepped inside his room and the door flicked shut behind her.

"Gavin said you were worried about my safety. But after everything we went through in the Viscera, you know I can handle myself. So what's the real reason?"

Adan smacked his bone dry lips. He had thought that she would see his decision as part of his promise to protect her. Sending her on the mission to Hull seemed like the last place Sierra would want to be. She needed to stay on the praxis, where it was safe.

"Sierra, there are hundreds of Waymen in that city, with advanced weapons. Maybe not like what we have, but they're not just using spears there. It's a dangerous place and I don't want you getting hurt. I thought—"

"You thought you'd just keep me out of it—without even asking what I wanted. That's what you thought."

"Sierra—"

"You decided you'd just go off and throw your life away—get yourself killed and then..."

Her eyes glistened with barely contained tears. Suddenly the connection between them flared back to life. Adan understood once again the emotions battling inside her heart.

"Adan," she began, the fire in her voice sputtering, "I've lost Zain and Wik and Yar and Ket, and so many others and I don't want to lose you too. I know it will be dangerous, but if something happened—"

"Sierra, you don't have to do this," Adan said, struggling to swallow the knot rising up in his throat.

"I may be just a handler, but you need one on this mission. Gavin said so himself," she pressed him. "And I'm the only handler who's had experience in hostile situations. It makes sense for me to go."

"But—" he choked on the word, unable to master his emotions.

"I can't—I can't let you go alone. If you didn't make it back, I—" her words faltered as well.

The angry expression on her face disappeared. The old Sierra, that tender person who wore the secrets of her heart so openly reappeared. Gazing into her eyes he realized that, as much as he wanted to keep her safe, she was right. If anyone got hurt, or if any of the Welkin they met were in need of medical attention, her skills as a handler would be critical.

"Okay," he said gently. "I think I see what you mean."

"Not that you seem to need any medical attention to heal," she said lightheartedly, referring to his mysterious ability to rapidly recover from any injury. "But just in case."

Adan breathed out a long sigh, a great weight lifting as the tension between them faded. At the same time he felt a counter weight settling back down onto his shoulders: the weight of knowing that Sierra's life would be in his hands.

The *Maven* passed Breaker's Hollow the following day, but they stayed well beyond the ten click range of the *Persepolis'* scanners. Disturbances in the atmosphere made it impossible to scan beyond that distance, but Gavin wasn't taking any chances. He ran near-constant traces of the Collective's activities to make sure the fleet remained hunkered down inside the canyon.

Meanwhile Adan sat on a bench in the mission prep room, waiting for the rest of his team to arrive. He was nearly half done winding his kaff around his head when Raif sauntered in behind a chromium cart, his shockingly orange hair brightening up the room.

"I come bearing gifts, oh, most fortunate one." Raif gave Adan a mock bow as the cart stopped in the middle of the room. Like the rest of the praxis, the prep area had dark metal walls. They were lined with tall lockers, each large enough for a man to walk into. On the far wall, a reflective screen functioned like an enormous mirror, depicting what was happening in the room, but it could be switched to show other rooms aboard the *Maven* or hook into the view screens in the Command Center.

"You have any solec in that cart?" Adan asked. He wasn't actually serious about needing some of the metabolic enhancing drug, but he certainly needed something to boost his energy. He'd gotten four slices of sleep the night before and even less the night before that. Briefings and planning for the mission had kept him working almost continually.

Raif snapped his fingers. "Fresh out," he lamented. "You've

got to order stuff like that in advance, man. I can only do so much. But I've got a thing or two that will jaunt your juice in a different way." He gestured towards the cart and a drawer slid out from the side, revealing four pairs of black gloves. "Check these out. Fresh from the fabricator."

"What are they?" Adan asked. He already had gloves. He doubted Raif was just bringing him these in case he lost his others.

"Gloves, man, what else? Way cooler than those raggedy looking ones you've got." Raif cracked a grin. "Okay, actually they're cutters. I made a little modification to make them less conspicuous. Here, try one on."

He tossed a glove at Adan who caught it and slipped it on. He inspected it briefly, but saw no indication that they were anything more than well-made, form-fitting gloves.

"Okay, you had me going there—" Adan said, shaking his head.

"No, really. The controls are in the tips of your fingers. That way you don't need a bioseine to use it. Touch your first three fingers to your thumb in sequence to start it up," Raif said.

Adan did as instructed and a yellow blade of light about the size of his palm sprang from the tips of his fingers. Instinctively, he jerked his fingers back, but the beam stayed in the same location, as if it were an extension of his arm and not of his hand.

"Clever," Adan remarked. "How do I control the length?"

"Press and hold your middle finger to your thumb. You've got to give it a little pressure or it won't register. That way it avoids incidental input. Then you press your thumb to your index finger to shrink it back."

Adan followed Raif's instructions, finding that the blade grew or shrank more quickly based on how much pressure he applied. When he pressed hard, the change in length was almost instantaneous.

"Tap your thumb to your fifth finger three times to turn it off," Raif concluded his little tutorial. The blade had barely winked out when he resumed his excited chatter. "Oh, and they're neutralizers too. Great for giving a pesky Wayman a sand nap if he's stressing you out. Just snap your wrist like this." He mimicked the motion for Adan. "But point your arm over that way before you do it, okay? I don't want you messing up my hair."

"I'll try." Adan chuckled at Raif's pretended vanity. Redirecting his hand, he shot a white blast of energy into the floor where it dissipated harmlessly.

"You can also use those to protect yourself from Waymen spears and other thrown weapons if you see them coming," Raif reminded him.

Adan nodded, remembering how the assessors had subdued his entire team with neutralizer blasts when he was in the Viscera—everyone but him. The memory had nagged him ever since, but he hadn't had the chance to ask anyone about it.

"Raif, do neutralizers ever fail to stun their victims? I mean, assuming they hit."

A wounded expression came across Raif's face. "You're questioning my tech and you haven't even tried it out? Man, you really know how to hit a guy where it hurts." He sniffled, but at Adan's confused expression he burst out laughing instead.

Adan couldn't help joining him, glad to have Raif there to take his mind off what lay ahead. But he still wanted an answer.

"No, really, when we were in the tunnels we got attacked by some assessors," he said as their laughter died down. "They stunned everyone with neutralizers, everyone but me. One of them hit me with a neutralizer blast, but it didn't work. I wasn't stunned. That's the reason I was asking."

Raif gave him a dubious look. "For real? That doesn't make any sense. The device must have malfunctioned."

"I checked it after we took them down. It was working perfectly," Adan insisted.

Raif shrugged. "I don't know, then. I've never heard of anything like that. Maybe the Admins did something to you when you went under the articulator. That's the only thing I can think of."

"That's what I was thinking, too," Adan said, taking off the glove and tucking it, along with its match, into a pocket inside his garrick.

"But hey, if you're immune to neutralizers, that's one up for us, right?" Raif slapped him on the shoulder playfully.

The door to the prep room slid open with a whisper and Sierra walked in with Trey right behind her.

"Hey, Raif," Sierra said, her eyes glittering with anticipation. "What do you have for us today?"

Raif motioned to the cart and the open drawer. He repeated his gushing description of the hybrid cutter and neutralizer gloves he'd crafted, adding that Adan had tried to zap him with one of them already and that they better not try the same stunt. Sierra laughed at his antics as she and Trey tested them out.

Adan felt a little odd seeing Sierra come in with Trey. Gavin had told him that Trey was coming with them on the mission, but he had not expected the two of them to walk in together since they were quartered on different floors. It was probably nothing, but uncomfortable thoughts crept in at the back of his mind. And, as happened so often when he was around Sierra, he couldn't quite make sense of exactly what was causing him to react this way.

"You're looking more like flesh and blood again, Trey," Raif remarked. "Sierra fixed you up good, didn't she?"

"Yeah, she's the best." Trey glanced at her with a smile. Adan's face flushed hot when Trey looked at her that way, but he couldn't put a name to the emotion. Whatever it was, he didn't like it.

Trey and Sierra opened the lockers behind them. Each of them pulled out a neatly folded garrick and kaff from inside.

"You know, I've always wanted to try one of these on," Sierra said, unfolding her coat and putting it on. Adan watched her intently, trying to navigate his way out of the maze of his thoughts. Suddenly her expression shifted and became serious and she swallowed hard and brushed away a tear.

She's thinking about Zain and the other Waymen, Adan read in her thoughts.

Suddenly his discomfort with Trey seemed insignificant. Sierra's sadness washed over him, burying his other emotions. The reality of Zain's death brought back the seriousness of their mission. Adan wondered how many of the people in this room would even make it back from Hull. His nerves plucked at his insides and he thought again about asking Sierra to remain behind.

Adan forced himself to take a deep breath and close his eyes. He felt like he should pray. It had been a while since he had. Slipping back into that sacred place within himself, the tension drained from him. He let his mind drift towards the infinitely distant and infinitely near Creator of the universe. Adan still knew so very little about him, but he knew enough to know that they needed his protection now more than ever. Everything, Adan's mission as well as Gavin's, ultimately depended on him.

A swishing sound interrupted his prayer as the door opened once again. Adan looked up to see a man wearing a weathered brown garrick walk into the room. It was Tarn, the fourth member of their team. His darkly complected face and sharp-looking eyes were typical for a Wayman as was the tattered kaff that hung loosely about his neck. The concept of youth was still new to Adan, but he had learned to see some of the signs: an absence of care about the face, a freshness to the skin, an expectant gleam in the eyes. Tarn had all these and a sure footed step as well. He greeted each of them in turn with curt, respectful bows.

Adan had only met Tarn a few days before, but Sierra and Trey had known him before that. He was a companion of Zain's and having him there was a little like being in the presence of his friend. Gavin believed a Wayman guide would be helpful on the mission and Adan didn't think he could have picked a better one.

Tarn was even more confused by Raif's new gloves than Adan had been, but he caught on surprisingly fast to Raif's instructions. Unlike most Waymen Adan had met, he showed a keen interest in technology.

"Right," Raif said, clearing his throat after he got Tarn up to speed. "Now just one last piece of equipment and you're ready for launch. Tarn won't have one of these since he doesn't have a bioseine, but three should be enough."

He caused the chromium cart to swivel around. A drawer on the side slid open revealing three silvery oscillathes and four polymeric pouches inside. Adan recognized the oscillathes by the thin tapered bodies set on rounded stocks, eerily similar to the hand held pistols so often carried by the somatarchs.

Raif passed out one to Trey, Sierra, and Adan. The deathly cold metal stung Adan's hand. Memories of the deadly whispers from these weapons echoed through his mind as he shoved it into a belt loop at his side. Gavin had insisted that they take them, but Adan would gladly have left them behind.

"You should know that these have been modified," Raif explained. "They're only able to stun someone. But that means the range is longer."

This bit of information eased Adan's fears. He wasn't interested in killing anyone. Hopefully there wouldn't be any fights at all if everything went according to plan.

"What's in the pouches?" Trey asked. "Are those for us too?"

"Yep," Raif answered. "Just some food, the tracking band you can use to find your way back to the ship, and a few other surprises. You can check that stuff out later. Gavin's waiting for you in the bay. You better hop and skip."

Adan looked over the three other people who would be going on the mission with him. Why in the world had he taken on this responsibility? He was no leader. He wanted to save Senya, yes, but he hadn't thought through what it would mean to lead a group into a place like Hull. The Waymen who ruled the city were as tempestuous and unpredictable as the desert winds. His temples throbbed with the memory of the riot that broke out among them when the Waymen assembled to attack Oasis. Adan had almost been trampled to death that day and he couldn't shake the thought that he was leading these people straight back into the midst of a frenzied mob.

EIGHT

A CRACK IN THE HULL

Gavin stood before Adan, Sierra, Tarn, and Trey amidst the massive cargo bay. Next to them rested the attack skiff the team would use to travel to Hull. The oscillathe cannon on the front had been unmounted from the cramped, triangular platform to make more room for more passengers. The skiff had no cockpit, only a seat for the gunner and a column for the pilot to stand behind and steer the ship. Two polymeric chairs had been grafted onto the rear section to bring the ship's riding capacity up to four.

Silence fell over the massive chamber. The maintenance crews around the perimeter of the bay paused in their work to observe the sendoff.

Gavin placed his left hand on Tarn's shoulder. "Wind at your back," he said. The words, as well as the gesture were part of the traditional Wayman parting.

Eyes glowing with anticipation, Tarn echoed the address back to him.

Gavin repeated the farewell to Sierra and Trey. Trey fumbled his reply, his nerves getting the better of him, but

Sierra's response was as clear and bright as her unblinking eyes.

Finally Gavin came to Adan. After going through the same formalities, he looked his friend in the eye. "So it is time for us to part again."

Adan kept his hand on his friend's shoulder.

"At least we are parting on our own terms this time."

"You saved my life—twice," Gavin reminded him. His face flushed with a rosy sheen, but his eyes shone clear. "If anything happens to you, know this. I will come for you."

Adan nodded wordlessly. His tongue felt thick and cumbersome and words failed him. If he had not known it before, he knew now that he was looking into the eyes of the greatest friend he had in all the world. Adan squeezed his shoulder and released him.

Gavin turned to address the team as a whole.

"It won't take long before you will be out of communication range. If anything goes wrong, do not hesitate to abort the mission or send someone back. After you make contact with the captives you will stay in the city until the time for the extraction arrives. Stealth is your best weapon. Do not engage the Waymen unless absolutely necessary."

Adan adjusted the oscillathe on his belt. Strictly speaking, it wasn't uncomfortable to wear, but he noticed it every time it chafed against his jacket, even slightly.

Gavin motioned towards the skiff. "I think it's time."

Adan took in a deep breath. *So this was really happening.*

The team boarded the ship, Sierra settling into the gunner's seat while Tarn and Trey took their places at the back. Adan stepped onto the skiff last. He gave Gavin what he hoped was a confident nod and then pulled back the steering column. The skiff lifted gently into the air. The circular opening in the middle of the bay floor grew steadily wider. Howling winds swirled up from below and a musky, sandy smell rushed into the chamber.

The wedge-like ship glided gracefully towards the hole. Not for the first time, Adan wondered how they were going to pull this mission off.

The ship passed over the middle of the empty aperture. It was only about halfway opened, but gave them ample room to maneuver safely down and out of the cargo bay. Adan paused long enough to catch the gaze of Gavin one last time. He waved and then, gripping the steering column with sweaty hands, he plunged the ship into the sandy swirl of the open Vast.

Six slices after they left the *Maven*, Adan landed the skiff in the midst of an outcropping of rocks. The natural barrier surrounded a shallow depression, the perfect place to stash their ship. The only way to find it would be if someone walked in through the surrounding rocks or flew overhead. Working swiftly, the team battened down a faded gray tarp over the ship to shield it from the wind and prying eyes.

The grotto was a little over three clicks from Hull. They would have to walk through open terrain, but in the pitch black night of the Vast they would be almost impossible to spot unless the Waymen had some form of zoetic sensors. Based on what Adan had seen the last time he had been here, he doubted they possessed such advanced technology.

Adan's foot slipped on one of the smooth rocks as he stepped off the skiff. Catching himself on the steering column, he narrowly avoided falling face first onto the rocky terrain.

Not a great way to start the mission.

The texture of the surrounding rocks had been entirely blasted away by the wind. They were covered with just enough sand to make them treacherous to walk on. The others followed behind Adan, everyone stepping lightly.

Once out of the grotto, they took a moment to survey the rolling dunes which lay before them. A massive dust storm shrouded the horizon. The city would have been invisible to them had it not been for their lentes. These green lenses allowed them to see through the debris as if it were nothing more than semi-transparent smoke. The massive outer walls looked like pieces of scrap, strung together in a line across the surface of the Vast, stitched into the ground by little knobs which represented the towers.

The team set off towards the city. Barely half a slice into their journey it became clear that the storm was not content merely battering Hull. It swept towards them at an ever-increasing rate. Hurriedly the team tied themselves off with polymeric cords which they pulled from a small tube Raif had included in their gear as one of his "surprises." Each tube had enough cord for a hundred micro clicks, but they only needed about fifteen each. Adan took the lead with Sierra, then Trey, and then Tarn tied off at the rear.

The storm broke over them a few microslices later. The winds sent waves of dust slamming against them. Though the garricks held up against the constant blasts, the winds knocked them about, making the dunes twice as hard to traverse. The gusts seemed intent on pummeling them into submission. Sierra stumbled on nearly every dune and would certainly have fallen behind had it not been for the polymeric cords.

The only entrance to Hull which Adan knew of was in the northeast section of the wall, but he had no intention of going anywhere near that. It was too closely watched. Instead, he angled the team towards the southwest as far away from the towers as possible. Once they reached the outer wall they would use their cutters to slice their way through. The feeding tent where Adan had met Senya was in the western part of the city and the plan was to look there first. Once they found Senya, she would hopefully be able to help them get in contact with the other refugees and start organizing the escape.

As they pressed on through the storm the winds rose and fell, but overall grew in strength. The howling drowned out all speech and scrambled their bioseine signals, making even mind to mind communication impossible.

Tarn yelled something at Adan, but all he could make out was the word, 'shelter' and he wasn't even sure about that. Adan wondered if the Wayman wanted them to unfurl their garricks and use them as emergency protection against the storm. But if they had to wait it out, there was no telling how long they'd be trapped on the dunes. If the Waymen spotted them out in the open when daylight hit they might never make it inside. Adan decided it would be better to press on and reach the protection of the city's walls. It was not far, less than a quarter of a click away now.

The relentless winds fought them every step until the fused scrap walls rose before them. Two hundred paces more and they would be within their shelter. Watchtowers stood resolutely against the tempest on either side, looming in silent vigil over the metal encrusted city. No lights or figures peeked through the narrow slits in the tower walls, but no doubt they held Waymen inside.

While Adan paused to study the turrets, the cord behind him snapped taut. A moment later it jerked him off his feet and sent him tumbling down the side of the dune he had just climbed. The tower, the dunes, and the horizon spun together before he rolled to a stop at the base of the slope.

He whipped his head around to see Sierra flailing in the wind, a full body length off the ground. The only sign of Tarn and Trey was the abrupt end of the polymeric cord jittering behind her.

"Sierra!" he cried out, not knowing if she could hear him.

He grabbed the cord with both hands and tried to wrestle her back to the ground, but the wind refused to surrender her. He dug his heels into the rocks. Sand showered his face, stinging his eyes, but he kept hold of the cord, wrangling it from side to side. The winds shifted again and a downdraft plunged Sierra into the sand. Adan scrambled over to where she had fallen.

As he knelt down beside her, her eyes fluttered open and met his. She looked shaken, but not in any serious pain.

"Are you okay?" he yelled.

She nodded feebly.

"Come on," he said, not bothering to yell this time, speaking more out of habit. He gathered her up in his arms and helped her to her feet.

The untethered end of Sierra's cord followed limply behind her, only coming to life at the occasionally stronger gusts. It must have snapped from the force of the wind. Adan scanned the ever shifting dunes they had crossed, hoping to spot some sign of Tarn and Trey, but all he saw was a sandy void. As time wore on and the winds continued to surge Adan realized that if they didn't make it into the city soon, he and Sierra would be lost as well. Waves of numbness seized his insides as he realized that Tarn and Trey had been swallowed up by the storm.

Adan and Sierra were alone.

Adan slumped against the outer wall of Hull.

If only I hadn't kept pushing, he thought. *We should have waited out the storm like Tarn wanted.*

Why hadn't he recognized the danger in time? He pounded his fists against the gravelly sand. The mission had barely started and he had already lost half his team.

Sierra said nothing, but he read in her eyes that she wanted to go back and search for the others. Surveying the swirling dunes, Adan saw nothing but his own helplessness in the face of the beating winds. The sand storm had already cost them valuable time, forcing them to arrive at Hull almost a full slice later than they had planned. They only had half a day to find all the prisoners and organize the evacuation. But even setting all that aside, he knew it would be almost impossible to find Tarn and Trey out in that mess. And if he did go back he risked losing Sierra as well.

Adan returned her gaze, shaking his head slowly. By the crushed look on her face he knew she understood his decision. He wished he could say something to console her, to let her know how difficult it was for him to go on, but the storm raged on, claiming his voice just as it had his friends. He swallowed the bitter taste in the back of his mouth and powered on the cutter in his glove. A yellow diamond shape flickered into existence at the ends of his fingers. Shielding the light with his body, he carved out a small hole in the wall, just large enough for them to crawl through on their bellies.

They had little trouble passing through to the other side, emerging beneath some dilapidated scaffolding at the end of a debris-filled street. They gathered what scrap they could and piled it in front of the hole to hide the breach.

Inside the walls, the storm lost some of its force, but the buffeting blasts still raged overhead and sand eddied along the ground. Bioseine communication was still scrambled, but at least it was quiet enough to speak. Sierra opened her mouth to say something, but Adan quickly placed a finger over her lips. There was no telling how their voices might carry along the street. He gestured up ahead and, taking her by the hand, led her out from under the scaffolding into a narrow alley between the half-finished framework of two buildings. Both structures rose three stories high, the panels clinging to their skeletal walls, weathered and beaten and barely adequate to resist the unceasing winds.

Memories from his time in Hull came rushing back to him, his brief encounter with Senya, his time in the pit, and his interrogation by Nolan. Of all the danger the streets of this city held, he feared the Reeve more than anything. Waymen at least could be fought, but fighting someone who could break into your mind was another matter. Hopefully he would be in and out of the city before the leader of Hull ever knew he was there.

But the mission had hardly gone according to plan so far. Casting a glance back into the street, Adan fought back a fresh wave of grief. Thoughts of Tarn and Trey lying dead in the desert overwhelmed him. He found himself breathing hard, trying to keep from giving in to despair. He realized that he could not go on like this. He sunk to the ground in the alleyway, tears rushing into his eyes and forcing him to pull the lentes from his face.

Inside the cramped lane the howls of the wind dulled to the point that they could no longer mask the sounds of Adan's sobbing.

Sierra wrapped her arms around him tightly.

"It wasn't your fault," she said, so near that he could feel the warmth of her breath on his cheeks.

Though he did not believe her words, her arms around him gave him strength in the midst of his own internal storm. He was about to thank her when he caught the sound of footsteps at the end of the alley. Adan hurriedly wiped his eyes so he could put his lentes back on, but only managed to gouge them with bits of sand which clung to his fingers.

Sierra turned to see what had startled him and let out a cry.

"Adan, it's—" she started to say but then took off without finishing.

Adan blinked away enough of the sand to be able to reattach his lentes. When his vision returned he could make out a figure approaching at the end of the alley.

Sierra cried out again as he rose to his feet. Then she threw her arms around a man whose tearstained face glowed with joy. It was Tarn. He had pulled down his kaff and removed his lentes because he too found it impossible to cry with the lenses in place.

Adan ran to join in their embrace. The three of them holding each other in the confined space meant that their bodies were squeezed uncomfortably against the walls on either side, but it did not matter. Tarn was alive. Everything else melted away.

"Tarn! What happened?" Adan babbled, barely able to get the words out from all the excitement coursing through him.

"The storm," Tarn said, wiping away the last of his tears. "I went flying into the air and I must have taken Trey with me. The wind snapped Trey's cord on both sides. When I came down I blacked out for a time and when I came to I...I couldn't find him, I couldn't find any of you."

Tarn's words blindsided Adan. He had been so overjoyed to see him he hadn't noticed that he had come alone.

So Trey was gone after all.

"I'm sorry," Tarn said. "I did my best, but the storm...a curse on this desert and all its fury."

Sierra placed a hand on Tarn's shoulder. "There was nothing you could have done. If you had kept looking for him the storm would have taken you too."

"Sierra's right," Adan said. "You did the right thing. And as much as it hurts, we have to move on and pray that Trey finds his way to us. If you found us, then there's hope for him, too."

Tarn straightened himself up tall in the darkness. Pulling a clean rag from his garrick, he rubbed away the dampness around his eyes.

With heavy steps, Adan led his friends back out into the dim, dusty streets of Hull.

NINE

SCRAP IN THE SCRAPYARD

ADAN PEERED OUT FROM BEHIND ONE OF THE DILAPIDATED carts which littered the street. Tiny stalls made of poorly soldered sheet metal huddled together up and down the thoroughfare, trembling in the wind. If a single one of these shaky constructions were to fall, it would probably bring down the rest of them with it.

He had not come this way the last time, but from his bioseine he knew they were headed in the right direction. They needed to find the food tent where Adan had met Senya the last time he was in Hull. Her living quarters would hopefully be nearby. That was the idea anyway. It was never the strongest part of their plan, but at least they could search for her under cover of night.

They padded through the deserted streets, hitting dead ends once or twice and doubling back, but they met no one out on the stormy pathways. At last they arrived in the part of the city where he expected to see Senya's tent, but there was no sign of it. Instead, a jumbled barrier of fused wire loomed a span and a half high at the end of the street. Beyond the makeshift fence were piles and piles of scrap. A gate consisting of a single, battered piece of corrugated metal provided access into the scrapyard, but it was guarded by two Waymen. One of them had his head bowed and appeared to be asleep. The other looked less concerned with watching the street than he was about shielding his eyes from the debris-filled winds gusting around him.

"We need to get through that gate," Adan told Sierra, grateful the storm had dwindled enough for them to be able to communicate via bioseine.

"Couldn't we just go around?" Sierra suggested.

The two of them were hunkered down beside each other behind a sizable cart that must have blown over in the wind. Tarn crouched just inside an alleyway on the opposite side of the street, waiting to act on a sign from Adan.

"No, we need to get into the scrapyard. If we cut through the fence, someone might spot the opening, and it's likely that whatever other gate we find will also be guarded. This is our best shot, especially with only one guard awake. If we knock them out whenever they wake up they will just think they dozed off."

"Okay, but are you sure the tents you are looking for are in there?" Sierra asked.

Adan eyed the massive piles of debris beyond the fence. It certainly didn't look like there were any tents in there, but they might be hidden on the other side of all the scrap. Several of the heaps towered well above the fence.

"I don't know. Maybe we'll find it after we get past all those piles. We at least have to look."

Sierra gave her mental assent and Adan motioned for Tarn to follow.

"I'll hit the one who is still awake," he told her. *"You hit the other to make sure he doesn't come to."*

Adan and Sierra pulled out their oscillathes and crept

forward. They advanced down the street, edging closer to the guards. Sheets of sand cascaded around them and swirling winds masked the sound of their approach. Adan's hands coated the grip of his pistol in sweat.

You're only going to stun them, he told himself, but his mind still recoiled at the thought of actually firing one of these weapons. He had seen so many people die from one of their evanescence blasts.

They pulled up behind an empty stall in front of one of the buildings. Mentally syncing their shots, Adan and Sierra ducked out from behind their cover and fired at the same time. Two invisible, crackling blasts blanketed the two figures beside the gate, sending both to the ground.

The team rushed the gate. Adan knelt beside the man he had downed and rifled through his garrick. Within a few moments he found a short stick of metal with several prongs on one end. He hoped it was the key to the dingy-looking lock securing the gate, but when he inserted it into the keyhole it wouldn't budge. After several anxious moments, and worried that someone might come by, he asked Tarn to give it a try. Though smaller in stature than Adan, he applied considerably more force in his attempts and, after a couple of failures, the lock snapped open and the door swung free.

The three of them darted through the gate, Tarn clicked the lock in place behind them. The mountainous heaps formed a maze of discarded oddities around them, but a single clear path meandered through the mess ahead. The wind rattled through the mounds of junk, threatening to topple them over, but they held together despite the constant battering. Like the rest of the cast off material which littered the Vast, Adan recognized none of what he saw. The only thing he could tell for sure was that a tremendous amount of work must have gone into collecting and hauling so much scrap into one place.

After passing a dozen piles of debris, they arrived within sight of a clearing at the base of a hill. According to his bioseine, this was where Senya's tent should have been, but, as with the other tents, not only was it gone, there wasn't even room for anything like it. The whole space had been converted into one giant scrapyard.

Morning light threatened to peek over the city walls soon and they were no closer to finding Senya than before. Once people began stirring it would be much harder to move about the city. Adan was about to suggest they head off to search the streets before the populace awoke when Tarn nudged him, pointing to a shack on the edge of a cleared out area up ahead.

The structure's walls braved the wind at different angles, none of which were plumb. A weak light flickered between the cracks around its flimsy metal door. Though the shack had no windows, Adan and the others ducked around a pile of scrap on the outside of the clearing on the chance that someone might come out the door.

A terrible scream split the night. It came from inside the shack.

Adan peeked through a gap between two pieces of scrap to see what was going on. The door burst open, nearly flying off its hinges. A figure came hurtling through the opening. The crumpled stranger landed in the dusty clearing like a pile of trash that had just been tossed out. It was a man dressed in tattered robes. His unfurled kaff lay beside him. He did not stir or even moan in pain. Another figure stormed out of the shack, but this one came on his own power, kicking up clouds of dust wherever his feet stomped the ground.

The second figure's appearance startled the fallen man into action. He scurried to his feet, looking like he meant to defend himself, but his wiry frame and lack of height meant he was no match for the thick-bodied brute advancing on him. The second man wore a newly-stitched garrick and kaff. Two men dressed in similar fashion strode from the shack behind him, their pitiless eyes intent on the hunched figure in the middle of the clearing.

"No, please," the frail man pleaded. "I was half-asleep. I didn't recognize you Sunder Rak! I'll go rouse the others. We'll start back to work at once—"

Whatever else the poor, cringing figure meant to say was cut short by a backhand to his face from Rak. The blow spun him halfway around, and he landed heavily on his knees. Blood glistened in the weak half-light in splotches on the ground. The fallen man breathed in great, stuttering gasps, his eyes darting between his attacker and the men to either side of him as if wondering from where the next blow would come.

"The storm take you for all I care, Barlo!" Rak bellowed. "I give you an extra wink of sleep and this is how you repay me?"

The sunder grabbed a wad of Barlo's tattered collar and yanked his head upright.

"B-but the storm is still..." Barlo gestured feebly at the swirling dust around them.

"I don't care if all the sand in the Vast dropped on your head. Orders are orders." Rak slapped him again. "But you won't have to worry about disobeying me again. I'm promoting Othan to foreman. You work for him now." He dropped Barlo unceremoniously into a heap.

"But—what about...?" Barlo begged, pawing at the hem of the man's coat.

Rak kicked at Barlo's groping hands. "Clean up this mess, shivs," he commanded, gesturing to the other two Waymen. "This swedge isn't worth the time and effort it would take to gut him. I've got shipments coming in at dawn. I'll see you back at the docks."

The words only set off another, more desperate round of

entreaties from Barlo. He begged Rak for his life, promising to work himself ragged, but the burly Wayman paid him no heed. The other two figures moved swiftly to descend upon him.

Adan could read in their eyes even from this distance what they meant to do. Though he had watched the scene in shock and outrage up to that point, he now realized that he had to act. All thoughts of the mission fled his mind as did any sense of what the consequences might be. He dashed out from behind the pile of scrap and charged headlong into the clearing.

"Wait, what are you doing?" came Sierra's incredulous question as he charged out from his companions and the safety of their hiding place.

"I've got to save him," Adan replied.

He sensed Sierra's confusion, but he didn't give her any further details because, at that moment, he wasn't even sure he knew what he was doing himself.

One of the Waymen bore down on Barlo, lashing out gleefully at the trembling figure. Barlo raised a wiry arm to ward off the attack, but at that moment Adan barreled into his assailants, knocking both of them off their feet.

A cry of confusion turned into one of rage and then somehow Adan was on his back, staring up at the furious Rak. "Who in the Vast are you?" he shouted.

Landing on his back shook Adan to his senses. He was in over his head.

Rak reached down to grab him, but Adan shoved the man as hard as he could and scrambled backwards, putting some distance between himself and the vengeful sunder. One of the Waymen Adan had knocked down leapt up and punched him in the small of his back. Adan doubled over in pain, clutching his sides. He tensed up, bracing for another blow, but instead several crackling blasts went off nearby.

All three Waymen dropped to the ground, instantly unconscious. Tarn and Sierra rushed towards him, Sierra's silvery oscillathe in her hand.

"Adan, why did you let these men see you? If we leave them here, they'll come looking for you the moment they wake up," Sierra reprimanded him as she rushed to his side. Frustration, mixed with fear, fought for control of her face.

"I'm sorry," Adan replied. *"I thought they were going to kill him."*

"We saw it too, but what about the refugees? How are we going to find them now?"

"Please don't hurt me," came Barlo's shaking voice as he wobbled to his feet, wincing in obvious pain. "I don't know who you are, but if the Reeve sent you—"

"We're not from the Reeve," Sierra said, holstering her oscillathe.

"Wait—you're a...you're a woman?" Barlo gasped.

"We're here to help," Adan said, gritting his own pain to regain his feet.

"But—but...What thral are you from? You're not from Hull." A panicked look gripped Barlo's face. He looked more terrified of his rescuers than he had been of Rak.

Tarn stepped up and gave Barlo a curt nod. "We're not from here and neither are you. You're Welkin, aren't you?"

"Yes," Barlo admitted, his fear softening somewhat at Tarn's words. "There are many Welkin here. Everyone knows that. But who are you and why did you knock down the sunder and his men? They'll light me on fire when they come to. Probably throw me off the outer wall and watch me burn to death in the sand."

Adan stared at the incapacitated Waymen. The beginnings of a hurried and desperate plan began forming in his mind. "Barlo, we don't have much time. We need your help."

"Help? From me?" Barlo stared back at him in confusion.

Adan wavered. He was tempted to tell this man about their intentions to free the Welkin. He was clearly no friend of the Waymen, and yet Adan decided he should hold off until he found out more about him.

"We're looking for someone. The last time I saw her they were here. There was a big tent around this area then."

"The feeding grounds?" Barlo cocked an eyebrow.

"Yes, do you know what happened to it? Or, more importantly, where the women are who served the food?"

Barlo's jaw worked back and forth like he was chewing on a mouthful of ideas. "And why should I tell you?" he spit out the question suspiciously.

"Because one of them is a friend of mine. And I really need to find her. She may be in danger."

"Humph, we're all in danger," Barlo scoffed, but then he tugged at his chin in a thoughtful way. His eyes sparkled suddenly. "So what if I do know her? What's in it for me?"

Adan suppressed a sigh. Apparently saving this man had done little to influence his opinion of them. He was either highly distrustful of strangers or exceptionally opportunistic. Either way, it meant that dealing with him would be less than ideal, but given the swiftly encroaching daylight and unfortunate circumstances Adan's rash decision had put them in, he didn't think they had much choice.

"We can protect you," Adan declared. "If you take us to my friend, I promise to take you to a place where the Waymen won't ever be able to hurt you again."

Barlo eyed the fallen Waymen, a conspiratorial look on his face. "Hmm...what's your friend's name?" he asked in a low voice, as if he didn't want the unconscious men to hear.

"Her name is Senya. Do you know her?"

Barlo's face brightened at the mention of Senya's name and, for the first time since they'd met him, all traces of fear faded from his countenance. With a surprising amount of tenderness in his voice, he answered, "Know her? She's the only spark in all this sprawling pit of darkness."

"Could you take us to her?" Adan asked, his hopes reviving.

Barlo's lips twitched excitedly. "It would be my singular and sincerest pleasure. Any compa of Senya's is a compa of Barlo. Come, follow me." He turned to leave, but Tarn grabbed him by the shoulder.

"Wait, we need to tie up these shivs, don't we?" he said, indicating Rak and his men.

"They should be out for a while, but perhaps you're right," Adan said.

"No good." Barlo shook his head. "Othan, the new fore-man, will be here shortly after dawn anyway. You'd only be wasting your time. Hurry now, we're wasting time." He hobbled off through the scrapyard at a surprisingly rapid pace for someone who had just endured such a severe beating.

"I don't like this," Sierra's thought came into Adan's mind. He agreed, but there was nothing to do about it now except hurry after Barlo.

They fled the shack, leaving Rak and his unconscious henchmen lying in the middle of the heaps of debris. Hopefully it had been dark enough that when they woke up they wouldn't be able to identify who had jumped them outside of Barlo's shack, but somehow Adan doubted that would be the case.

TEN
TWISTS AND TURNS

Their newfound ally Barlo led them off the main path and through the maze of refuse. They wound their way through the morass until they arrived at the fence surrounding the scrapyard. Their guide leaned forward and latched on to the wire barrier with both hands.

"He's not going to climb it, is he?" Tarn mumbled under his breath.

Barlo motioned for them to keep quiet and began twisting part of the fence with his fingers. At first Adan thought he was trying to pull apart a section of wire. He soon saw that what he had taken for a deformity in the metal was in fact a small tumbler lock attached to one of the chain links. Barlo flicked the tiny dials with practiced ease and a rectangular shaped opening in the fence popped free and swung open.

Though Barlo walked with a pronounced limp, they struggled to keep up with him as he ambled through the streets of Hull. They traveled always on the narrowest, most twisted pathways imaginable, never staying on a single one for very long, though generally heading towards the northwest section of the city.

The pathetic dawn of the Vast had mounted over the walls of Hull by the time they arrived at their destination: a massive, one-story structure made from patchwork metal paneling that looked like a much larger version of Barlo's shack. It showed the signs of a hasty, temporary construction. Most of the metal panels were flimsier than those in the piles in the scrapyard. In fact, if someone had told Adan that this scrap had blown itself together into this corner of the city and formed itself into this structure he would have almost believed them.

Two weary-looking Waymen sat near the door, but they quickly jumped to their feet when Barlo and the others appeared. They were armed with shivs and pinions and physically imposing despite their unenthusiastic expressions.

Barlo walked straight up to them. At a word from the Welkin, they grumblingly pulled open the sliding panel behind them which served as an entrance to the catastrophe behind them disguised as a building. The whole thing shook a little when the panel stopped moving. Adan flinched, expecting the structure to fall on top of them, but it settled back into the same sorry state it had been in before. With great misgivings, Adan followed Barlo inside.

They entered a long metal hallway with unsightly gaps in the floor every few paces. Stepping carefully across the jigsaw floor, they emerged into a wide, oblong room with more than a dozen chairs and a few small tables. The furniture was worn, but appeared to be slightly better made than the building surrounding it. A few lumins dangled from cords in the ceiling, giving the room just enough light to avoid seeing the full extent of the negligence on the part of its builders. Another pair of Waymen, outfitted as if they were meant to be on guard as well, were passed out in opposite corners in two of the chairs, their heads lolling back against the wall.

"This way," Barlo whispered, taking one of the two passages which led out of the room.

They went down several more topsy-turvy hallways, every one of them a mess of angles and an assault on the laws of geometry. They passed several doors along the way, but Barlo showed no interest in them. They paused at one of the open rooms where a woman sat by herself at a table. Her eyes were closed and her head was bowed, but she was clearly not asleep. Her arms were lifted above her head, her palms facing upwards.

She is praying, Adan realized. He had seen Senya in that posture when he visited her home. He hadn't understood what it meant then, but now he recognized it for what it was.

Barlo hurried through the room without giving the woman so much as a glance and led them down several more night-marish passages. At last he stopped at one of the gray metal doors in the middle of what passed for one of the walls of a hallway.

"I think this is the one," he muttered to himself before giving the door a few soft raps with his knuckles. He waited for a response, his legs jittering impatiently. Then he knocked on the door again, louder this time. He repeated this process of knocking and waiting three more times, the volume of his knocks increasing each time until at last the door shuddered and swung open.

A woman with disheveled hair and tired eyes squinted at him from within a cave-like darkness.

"What is it?" she asked in a groggy voice.

"We need to talk to Senya," Barlo said, stepping towards her.

"She's not here," the woman answered hastily, now very

much awake. She eyed Barlo with visible fear now that she recognized him.

"Bah!" Barlo dismissed her with a wave of his hands and attempted to push his way past. "Don't play games with me. This is important."

Barlo had no room to get by so he simply bowled her over, shoving her into the room along with him.

"Wait—" Adan said, attempting to stop Barlo by placing a hand on his shoulder. But Barlo either didn't notice or didn't care and kept going.

"Barlo, you can't do this—" the woman protested, but to no avail.

"Senya," he said in a boisterous whisper. "Senya, it's Barlo. I've got some friends of yours here to see you." The room was dark, but enough light trickled in from the hall to see two sets of cots strung from poles on either side of the room. Mounds of hair, blankets, and clothing showed that two of them were occupied, but Adan could see little more.

"Barlo, I told you, she's not here," the woman insisted, tagging helplessly along behind him.

Sierra gave Adan a worried look. He wasn't sure whether to try and rein Barlo in or stay out in the hall so as to not further invade this woman and her companions' privacy. The cramped space favored the latter option so he called out to Barlo as loudly as he dared.

"Barlo, please come back out—I think you might have the wrong room."

"Nah, this is hers, all right," he shot back, leaning over one of the beds. After scrutinizing the face of whoever was beneath the hair and sheets, he let out a grunt and went to the other bed, all the while fending off the protests and pleas of the poor woman whose quarters he had invaded. "Shh! You're liable to wake the guards," he snapped, raising his hand as if he would strike her if she didn't keep quiet.

She backed off and lowered her voice, allowing Barlo to examine the second bunk in relative peace.

"Not here, either," he growled at the woman in the second bunk. She stirred and woke, letting out a frightened gasp and ducking back under her covers. "Where is she?" Barlo demanded of the poor woman who had first opened the door.

Adan had seen enough. He started to move into the room when Sierra stepped in front of him.

"Barlo, stop. You can't do this," she insisted.

"What?" Barlo exclaimed, making a surprised noise that was something between a wheeze and a growl.

"I apologize for disturbing you," Sierra said, addressing the woman. "We're looking for someone named Senya. Do you know where she is?"

"My guess would be the infirmary," the woman said. "She usually goes there in the mornings early."

"Well, why didn't you tell me that in the first place?" Barlo huffed.

"I tried telling you she wasn't here, but you wouldn't listen," the woman said meekly.

Barlo tromped sourly past both women and out of the room. Sierra followed, apologizing once again for the disturbance.

"Thanks for nothing, Maira. See if your rations aren't a little tighter for a ten span," Barlo threatened over his shoulder. Then he motioned for Adan and the others to follow him. "Sorry about that," he muttered, resuming his former, less belligerent demeanor and flashing a look of regret. Then he limped off down the hall without waiting for a response.

Adan, Sierra, and Tarn had little choice but to follow him

down the pock-marked passage, but Adan was wishing he had chosen to rescue someone of less questionable character.

The passage twisted capriciously as their journey through the haphazard building resumed. They traveled along three more passages like it before coming to another empty room with tables and chairs. As they made their way through yet another hallway, the immensity of the building impressed itself upon Adan. The sheer amount of scrap required was staggering. It may have been horribly put together, but a tremendous amount of work had gone into gathering the materials for its construction.

At last they reached a set of double doors. These were actually well made and they slid away when Barlo stood on a pressure plate in front of them. On the other side, two men sat behind a massive metal slab of a desk. The room was well lit and, though not the cleanest of places, had more or less straight walls and floors with no large holes or gaps in them. The ceiling was even partly tiled. It was a poor job, but at least an attempt had been made.

Two doors, separated by about three paces, stood facing them on the opposite wall. The men at the desks wore brown cloaks and were unarmed, but from the way they eyed Adan and his group, especially Barlo, it appeared that they functioned as guards of some sort, controlling access to the doors behind them.

"What do you want, Barlo?" asked the older looking of the two.

"Aren't you supposed to be at the scrapyards?" added the other.

"There was a storm, in case you hadn't heard," Barlo quipped. "My shift got canceled."

The first man regarded him with suspicion. "Okay, fine. Who are you here to see?"

"I need to speak with Senya. I was told she was working in the infirmary," Barlo stated.

The man coughed. "She's busy. Besides, we're only allowed to let people visit the sick, not the healers."

"But these people here need to see her. It's urgent," Barlo said, gesturing towards Adan. "Surely it's not a serious infraction to bend the rules a bit. She could step out for a moment or two," he suggested. Though his words came across smoothly, his anxious expression told a different story. Judging by the reactions on the faces of the men he was speaking to, they did not have a very high opinion of him.

"She's treating Malloc's leg injury," the second man reported, glowering at Barlo.

Barlo's expression darkened. "I know what you're thinking. But you can't blame his injury on me. It was an accident."

Adan gave a start. "Malloc is here?"

The last time he had seen the Welkin leader he was lying unconscious in the Viscera after a fierce battle with several somatarchs.

"That's not the first accident on your watch, Barlo," said the first man, ignoring Adan's interruption.

"If people would just follow orders, there would be a lot fewer accidents," Barlo said defensively. "Malloc has been trouble from day one."

Adan pressed up against the desk. "Please, I need to see him. It's very important."

The second man looked Adan up and down. He seemed skeptical, but the other man answered before he could reply.

"We can let this man and his friends in, can't we Var?"

Var stifled a groan. "Fine, but Barlo has to stay here. Putting him and Malloc together would only cause trouble."

Barlo threw up his hands in protest. "But he's a patient. What could he do?"

"We'll tell Senya you're out here as well, okay?" Var responded curtly. "If she wants to come back out with these people to talk to you that will be her decision, but we're not letting you in there."

"This is an insult!" Barlo protested, shaking his fist at the man. "You'll suffer for this, Var. Mark it in stone."

"Like Malloc?" Var replied. "I guess that's a chance I'll have to take."

"Don't worry," Adan said, laying a reassuring hand on Barlo's shoulder and stepping between him and the attendants. "We'll come back as soon as we can."

Barlo's face twisted into a vicious sneer, but he stifled whatever outburst he was tempted to make. "Just make sure and tell her that it was Barlo who brought you here. You can do that much at least, right?" His ingratiating expression made it very hard to sympathize with him.

"Yes," Adan promised and then stepped towards the door.

Var manipulated something under the desk and a loud beep sounded. The left door slid open with a light scraping sound.

"You may pass through," Var said, waving them in.

"Thank you," Adan said as he, Sierra, and Tarn passed into the short hallway beyond. Like the entrance room, some care had been taken in its construction. Dingy white tiles covered the floors and there were no holes to speak of. The hallway soon turned to the left and opened up into another small alcove. A woman sat behind a desk here as well.

"Who are you here to see?" she asked.

"Malloc," Adan answered, remembering that it was the custom to visit sick people here and not those who were attending them.

"Eighth door on the left," the woman said, pointing.

Adan walked down the hallway, his heart beating fast with

the knowledge that Senya was near. Though he had only met her once, he had never forgotten her. He remembered the look of quiet resolve on her face when she had spoken to him of the pain of losing her husband, *"All things in the end are passing, even death,"* she'd told him, and that phrase had given him strength at his darkest moments.

Adan paused just before he reached the door and took a deep breath.

Then he touched a glass panel in front of the door. It slid open and he walked inside.

ELEVEN
OLD GRUDGES

A SINGLE LUMIN EMBEDDED IN THE CEILING DRAPED TWO figures in warm light. Below it, on a plain metal bed, lay a sleeping man with his right leg covered in yeso, a hard white material the Waymen used to set broken bones. The injured leg was propped up on the lip at the end of it and the other lay bent beneath a thick white sheet. This was supposed to be Malloc's room, but at first Adan hardly recognized the Welkin leader. His hair had been cut short and his sunken face made him appear wasted and frail, a shadow of the imposing figure Adan had met in the Viscera.

Standing between the bed and a waist-high cabinet was Senya. Her hair was disheveled and her faded robe was more patches than actual garment. She had her sleeves rolled up and was in the middle of washing a rag in a basin of water on top of the cabinet. She too looked worse than Adan remembered, but she still had that same familiar blend of weariness and hope in her face. She stared at him for a moment, no recognition showing in her eyes.

"Did they finally send the medicine I asked for?" she asked.

Adan remembered then that his face was still covered by his kaff. He quickly pulled down his desert scarf and stepped into the light.

"Senya, it's me," he said.

A spark of life leapt onto her face. She dropped the rag onto the floor and rushed across the room, throwing her arms around him and bursting into tears.

"Oh, praises to the Holy One, you're safe," she said, her tears soaking into his filthy garrick.

"He has protected you as well," Adan whispered. "He has protected us all."

For several moments she said nothing, overcome by her tears. Adan, conscious of those behind him, pulled away.

"We've come to get you out of here, Senya, to free all the Welkin and any Waymen who want to escape this place." Adan turned to introduce his companions. "This is Sierra and Tarn. They're here to help, too."

Senya, wiping her tears, quickly brightened, regarding them with the same warmth and hospitality as if she were receiving visitors in her home.

"Thank you for coming," she said. "We were all praying, just this morning—and now this. I can hardly believe it. And yet, why shouldn't I? We prayed—" Her voice broke with emotion.

"It's good to meet you," Sierra said, forcing a smile.

"We are glad we found you," Tarn added, his tone formal, but genuine.

"And Malloc?" Adan gestured towards the big man. "What happened to him?"

"I don't know," Senya said. "He got hurt in the scrapyards. A large slab of metal fell on his leg. It should have killed him, but he's stronger than most men. They said it was an accident, but Malloc...he doesn't think so. He's been feverish all night, going on about it. I ordered some more medicine for him to help break the fever, but the supplies are extremely low."

Adan studied the Welkin leader, his thick chest rising and falling too quickly, as if it were a struggle to breathe.

"Some almamenth would help," Sierra said, stepping beside him. "I brought some with me." She patted one of the pouches around her waist.

"Oh, yes," Senya said. "That would be wonderful."

Sierra pulled out a small tube of the dark green paste. "Would you like to apply it, or shall I?" she asked.

"Why don't you rub it in while I get a fresh rag to moisten his forehead," Senya suggested.

At a nod from Sierra, Senya bent down and picked up the rag she had dropped. Then she opened up the cabinet and pulled out a fresh cloth. Sierra began spreading the greenish paste from her tube onto Malloc's arm while Senya set the old rag down beside the basin and proceeded to dampen the new one.

Gently wiping Malloc's forehead with the rag, Senya said, "How did you manage to escape from the Waymen? I asked where they had taken you and they said to the pits. I was so terrified that you were going to die. No one ever comes back from there."

"It's a long story," Adan said. "I was rescued the next day. I wanted to come looking for you, but I couldn't. I'll tell you the rest later. Right now, we need to get the word out to everyone about how and when we're going to escape. We've got a large ship ready to carry you and your people out of here."

Senya gave him a blank look. "A ship..." she mumbled the words. "How big is it? There must be close to a thousand prisoners here."

"It won't be easy," Adan said. "And we have to be especially careful not to alert anyone who might give away our plan." He paused, unsure of how Senya would react to his next statement. "That means we may have to leave some people behind. You can only entrust this information to people you are sure will keep it secret."

Sierra finished with the almamenth and returned her tube back to her pouch. She proceeded to retrieve her activator, a short silver rod used for diagnosing someone's condition, from her coat. It emitted strange patterns of light across Malloc's body.

"We can inform the leaders," Senya stated, her eyes captivated by the colorful yellow lights dancing across Malloc's skin. "They will know who is safe and who isn't."

"Right," Adan agreed. "How many are there? And how do we get in touch with them?"

"There are six Welkin leaders amongst the prisoners, but I don't know if they would believe me if I told them. Most Welkin are just as suspicious about technology as the Waymen, at least the Waymen outside of Hull. I don't think they would understand what a 'ship' was. Honestly I don't understand it myself."

"It's a large...vehicle...that you get inside of." Adan stumbled to find the right words to explain it to her.

Tarn jumped in to assist him. "It's like one of the water-vessels—the ones from the legends, except it floats—in the air."

A dim light of recognition flickered in Senya's eyes. "And it will be big enough for all of us?" she asked.

"Yes. It's large enough to hold more than a thousand people," Adan assured her.

At that moment Malloc gave a low groan and began to stir. Sierra put away her activator. "The medicine he received was laced with tiferum, a poisonous drug. Most men would have died from the amount he received, but his constitution is remarkably strong. The almamenth will cleanse it out of his system."

"Tiferum?" Senya asked. "How did that get into the medicine?"

"I don't know," Sierra said. "But it does not occur naturally, so either someone made a mistake when they stocked your medical supplies or someone put it in there on purpose."

Senya's hand went to her mouth. "You're saying someone tried to kill him? But that makes no sense. Malloc is head strong and has often been punished for not obeying orders, but if the Waymen wanted him dead, they would have just run him through with a pinion."

"Hopefully it was just a mistake," Adan said. "But we'll probably never know. Either way, you'll soon be free of this place and we can get Malloc out of whatever danger he is in here."

Malloc coughed loudly and opened his eyes. His initial look of confusion quickly gave way to one of anger.

"How did this traitor's friend get in here?" came the hoarse, yet powerful voice of the Welkin leader.

Adan's mind flashed back to the last time he had seen Malloc. Will had been with him then, and Malloc despised Will, blaming him for the death of his son. Weak as Malloc was, that same fiery hatred for Will which Adan had seen back then still burned in the Welkin's eyes.

"Hush, Malloc," Senya scolded. This took the edge off his anger for the moment. "Adan, where is Will? The last time we met I wanted to ask you, but there wasn't time."

Adan's eyes fell to the floor. His heart still ached at the memory of his friend's death and he was reluctant to inflict the same pain into Senya's heart, but he had to be honest. "He died in Oasis," he said softly. "He was killed by the Waymen."

Senya covered her eyes and shuddered. Adan stepped

towards her, wanting to say something to comfort her, but no words came. Wisdom told him that the wound was too fresh to apply a salve.

"A fitting end," Malloc muttered.

Senya's eyes darted at Malloc in astonishment.

"I'm sorry, Senya, but some men are beyond forgiveness." Malloc coughed again and turned back to Adan. "Why are you here, Wayman?"

Adan straightened and returned the man's gaze, refusing to allow the Welkin's caustic nature to affect him. He needed this man's help to save these people. Though his heart ached for Senya and her grief, the more quickly he could get beyond old grudges and earn his trust, the better.

"Because I long to see your people free of this place," Adan said. "I am here to help."

Malloc snorted derisively. "I don't need the help of a coward who fled in the midst of battle to free my people." He coughed several times before continuing. "Once I get my strength back, I'll find a way to untangle my knit from their bindings."

Senya gently touched Malloc's shoulder, taking a moment to collect herself. "Do not let your pride get in the way of helping your people," she said soothingly. "These are friends. They are here to help us. This woman just brought you some almamenth. She may have saved your life."

Malloc grunted and nodded begrudgingly in Sierra's direction.

"Is he always this stubborn?" Sierra asked, earning her a stern look from the large man, but he said nothing this time, clenching his jaw shut in a rare show of restraint.

"We need you to help organize the other leaders for the escape," Adan said, trying to mimic Senya's tone. "You are the only one who can rally them in time."

"I told you we don't need—" Malloc began, but checked himself mid-sentence. "Wait, you're speaking our cant. You can't possibly have learned it since the last time we met."

"It's from the technology which Gavin's—I mean Mendigo's—people gave me," Adan said.

Malloc's expression softened a bit. He took a moment to study Adan and his friends. "I still don't like you," he stated flatly.

A long silence fell over the room.

"I am not impressed by your wizardry," Malloc grumbled, shaking his head.

"Forgive me, elder," Tarn said, "but now is the time to act. We have taken a great risk in coming to this city to help your people escape. If these strange drugs they gave you have not affected your mind, then you need to help us get the word to your people."

A look of shock came over Malloc's face at the bluntness of Tarn's words. "And who are you? I don't remember seeing you before," the Welkin leader shot back.

"My name is Tarn. Sierra and her friends rescued me from the ruins of a city destroyed by storms and quakes. I owe them my life. Now I want to help your people the same way they helped me."

Though Tarn's words came across as sincere, Malloc's expression remained callous. "I refuse to be lectured by a Wayman. Senya, why did you let these people in?"

"Tarn is here to help," Senya said, unfazed by his continued ill-temper. "These people have a way for us to get out of here. You have to listen to them, Malloc. Now is not the time for pride and anger."

Malloc's dark complexion flushed burgundy at Senya's rebuke. "What has gotten into you? The Wayman have attacked our knit dozens of times. Tell me why I should trust any Wayman—ever!"

Adan was beginning to think they were wasting their time with this man. "Malloc, if you care more about old grudges than you do the fate of your people, then we will have to find a way to rescue them without your help."

Malloc snapped upright in his bed and lunged at Adan without warning. Instinctively, Adan jerked backwards, causing Malloc to swing at the open air. The Welkin leader collapsed back onto his bed, wincing in pain.

"Malloc!" Senya reprimanded, her voice at last losing its respectful tones. "I think perhaps Tarn is right. That medicine must have affected your mind as well as your body. You are not being reasonable."

Malloc stifled a groan and rolled his head from side to side in response.

"Senya, we don't want to cause any problems," Adan said. "Just let me explain how you can find the ship and then you can—"

"No, wait," Malloc said, raising a trembling hand. "I will listen. It's just…You don't understand. We have been betrayed so many times that it is difficult to trust. Even here in Hull, there are Welkin who would sell us out if they thought it would improve their standing with our Waymen taskmasters. It was one of them who put me in this bed."

"You still think Barlo did this to you?" Senya asked. "He may be working for the Waymen, but he's not a murderer. Besides, it was a tremor that caused that beam to slip. I don't see how Barlo could have caused that."

"I know it was him, Senya," Malloc said, grunting again either from the pain or his disdain of the man of whom they spoke.

Adan wondered if he should mention their connection to

Barlo, but suspected it would only cause further trouble with the temperamental Welkin.

"Have you had tremors here at Hull too?" Adan asked.

"The one yesterday was the strongest, but there have been a few smaller ones since then," said Senya.

"The place we came from has been experiencing quakes for several days now. If they are spreading this far out, that is all the more reason to get you out of here and onto the ship where it's safe."

"The Viscera is all connected," Malloc said. "When one part of the body is in pain, it is felt elsewhere."

"You experienced tremors before? Back in Aldea?" Adan asked.

"No," Malloc answered, "but the legends speak of them, in the time before the Severing."

"The Severing? What was that?"

"That was when the Waymen and the Welkin went their separate ways," Tarn answered. "According to legend."

Malloc fixed his fierce eyes on Adan, but they no longer flared with anger. Instead they shone with intense interest. "You have convinced me, friend of Nacio. He may have killed my son, but if you can truly help us, I would be a fool not to listen to you...Tell us about this 'ship' of yours and about your plan to help free my people."

Relief washed over Adan. Malloc may have been difficult to win over, but now that he was on their side, they might actually have a chance to pull off this rescue.

TWELVE
CAUGHT IN THE SPOKE

Malloc's scowl deepened as Adan finished explaining his plan to liberate the captives. "So you're certain the attack by this mechanized army will come on the day you have predicted."

"If I was not, I would not have risked my life to come here," Adan said.

Malloc stroked his mountain of a chin, pondering all that Adan had said. He was still deep in thought when a man's voice burst into the room, startling everyone.

"Senya, there are Waymen heading down the hall towards you," the voice said, breathlessly. It sounded like the voice of Var, the attendant at the door, but more artificial, like something coming through a tube or pipe. "I tried to keep them out, but they have the master switch," the voice added.

Senya's face went pale.

"Wait, what is he talking about?" Sierra asked.

"What was that voice?" Tarn asked, his eyes darting about the room.

"That was one of the guards at the entrance to the infirmary," Senya said. "They have a way of projecting their voices into the rooms here, though I don't really understand how it works." She gripped Malloc's arm in a panic. "What are we going to do?"

"Hurry, Senya,there are lots of them," warned the voice in the air.

"Leave," Malloc commanded, his powerful baritone filling the room. "I will stall them as long as I can."

Despite the clarity of Malloc's order, Senya hesitated at the side of his bed.

"Go, Senya. Show them the way out," Malloc said.

"We'll find you before the ship leaves," Adan told Malloc, taking hold of Senya with one hand and urging Tarn and Sierra out the door with the other. "Tell the other leaders what I told you. We won't leave without you. I promise."

Malloc's solemn nod was his only reply.

They ducked out the door and Senya led them down the hallway in the opposite direction from which they'd come, further into the infirmary. Glancing over his shoulder as he ran, Adan saw that they were too late. A line of Waymen, at least seven or eight, rushed up from behind them, the tips of their spears glinting in the dim light.

"Ho there!" one of the men cried out. "The Reeve of Hull commands you to halt!"

Adan's heart sank, but only for a moment. They were outnumbered, but the men coming after them were in perfect position to fire his oscillathe. This time he did not hesitate. There wasn't time. He pulled the weapon off his belt in one smooth motion and fired.

A static-filled boom bellowed down the narrow hallway, sweeping up every last Wayman in its wake. The entire contingent dropped to the floor. The combined thud of so many men hitting the ground was like an echo from the blast of the weapon.

They sped down the corridor, doors whisking past on either side. But their freedom from pursuit lasted only a moment. The echoing sounds of running feet filled the hallway up ahead.

"They must have sent every guard in the Spoke," Senya said.

Their headlong sprint down the passage came to an abrupt halt in the middle of an intersection.

"Which way?" Adan asked, his heart pounding.

"I don't know," Senya replied, shaking her head. "They must be coming through the back entrance as well."

With no time to deliberate, Adan took off to the right. They had not gone twenty paces when a set of double doors in front of them swished open and another half dozen Waymen surged through.

Adan fired at the Waymen on the left and Sierra shot up ahead. Though his aim had been true, six more came through the doorway after the shot, leaping over their fallen comrades. Two of them let their spears fly.

Adan flinched and Senya let out a terrified cry.

But instead of running them through, a white light enveloped the spears and cast them to the ground. The blast from Tarn's neutralizer has come just in time.

By now, Adan's oscillathe had recharged, but Sierra fired on the six newcomers first, dropping them where they stood.

As brief as the exchange had been, running footsteps from behind indicated that more men were just behind them.

Adan took off running, hoping to get past the double doors before more Waymen came through, but before he could reach them, four more attackers rushed in.

Two shivs flashed in front of Adan and though he jumped back a stinging pain sliced through his arm. Almost reflexively, he flicked his wrist and a white burst from his neutralizer dropped his attacker. His attacker's weapons clattered to the floor, one brushed along the edge with fresh blood.

It only took two neutralizer blasts from Sierra and Tarn to disable the remaining three since the Waymen were bunched so close together.

Adan's arm flushed white hot like it had been dipped in fire. Without hesitation, he let his bioseine suppress the pain, but that was no long term solution. Blood flowed freely through the rip in his garrick sleeve.

All thoughts of his injury vanished when another group of Waymen rounded the corner. They let their spears fly, half a dozen filling the air. Senya screamed again, but Adan, Sierra, and Tarn, dismissed the attack with blasts of white energy.

Adan and Sierra followed up the defensive maneuver with blasts from their oscillathes. A moment later, a carpet of unconscious Waymen filled the hallway.

"Too many," Senya muttered, visibly shaken. She rushed to his side, her eyes fixed on his arm. "Adan—you're hurt. We've got to wrap it before you pass out."

Adan surveyed his arm. From the elbow to the wrist, dark wet streaks coated his sleeve. Because he felt no pain, for a moment it failed to register that it was really his arm that had been hurt.

Sierra ripped open the sleeve with the yellow beam from her cutter glove to get a better look at the wound. It was not deep, but it ran nearly the length of Adan's lower arm. "Senya is right. We need to bind that wound."

"Senya, do they have any special way of tracking us in here? If we stop won't they find us?" Adan asked. He didn't question Sierra's judgment, but he also didn't want to put everyone at risk just to save himself.

"I'm not sure. What do you mean?" Senya replied.

Adan shook his head, "Never mind. Let's head into one of these rooms and get this taken care of." Even if the Waymen could somehow track them, hopefully their oscillathes and neutralizers would get them out of trouble.

"This way," Sierra said, swiping the panel to the closest door with her hand. Thankfully the room was unoccupied. Everyone filed in and the door swung shut behind them. It was identical to Malloc's chamber with only a bed, a mobile cabinet, and a single lumin for light.

"Tell me about this building. How can we get out of here?" Adan asked, sitting on the edge of the bed while Senya handed Sierra a roll of thin fabric from the cabinet.

"The Waymen call it the Spoke," Senya said. "It's the largest building in Hull, I think. Parts of it are still being finished, but they moved most of the prisoners in here a few days ago so they could expand the scrapyard."

"Is there any place in this building we could—" Adan started to ask when a tin-sounding voice coming over the sound system interrupted him. It wasn't Var this time.

"Attention infirmary patients and attendants, we are locking the doors. Everyone is ordered to stay in their rooms." Red lights running along the base of the walls began to pulse in time with a loud siren. "Remain where you are until the alarms have stopped. Anyone caught in the passageways is subject to the wrath of the Reeve."

Tarn rushed to the door and tried swiping the panel several times with his palm, but it would not open.

"I didn't know they could control the doors like that," Senya said. "They will catch us now for sure."

"They can't hold us in here," said Sierra, working the bandage rapidly around Adan's forearm. "Tarn, cut us a way out of here."

A bright yellow ray sprung from the end of Tarn's hand.

His quickness with the blade was impressive. Wielding it like it was one of the Waymen shivs, Tarn quickly converted the door into a metal slab which fell clanging onto the floor just as Sierra tore off the end of the bandage.

Adan, upset at the delay his wound had caused them, leapt to his feet. The four of them hurried out into the hallway, glancing up and down its length. It was empty, but Adan doubted it would remain that way for long.

"Where do we go now?" Sierra asked.

"I know a place where we might be able to hide you for a little while—the kitchen," Senya said, but Adan shook his head in response. While Sierra had been binding up his arm, he had been thinking about their situation and had come to a difficult decision.

"They would probably find us there too. We can't stay here. We need to get out of this city. The longer we stay, the more danger you and the other Welkin are in."

"But what about the escape? I thought you came to free us," Senya said, giving Adan a questioning look.

Adan reached into his pack and pulled out the tracking band Raif had given him. The black elastic loop was singularly unremarkable. "Put this on your wrist," he said, handing it to her. "Tomorrow, at exactly one slice before midday this band will give off a slight pulse that you will be able to feel when you are wearing it. It will pulse again whenever you head towards our ship and it will pulse more frequently the closer you get to it. Before then, you need to gather everyone you can and head northwest, beyond the city walls. After you feel the pulse, it shouldn't be long until you see the ship. If a storm comes up, or if you get lost, don't give up. Just use this tracking band and it will lead you straight to us."

Though her confused expression did not vanish entirely, Senya nodded and slipped the band around her wrist. More questions clouded her face, but instead of voicing them, she leaned forward and embraced him warmly.

"I had hoped to take you back to the boys, but that will have to wait. I'll get Malloc to rally the other elders. We'll see you soon enough—tomorrow—after midday."

"Everything will be all right," Adan said. "You should go back to Malloc. I'm sure the Waymen will question you. Just tell them you don't know where we went."

Senya's eyes, moist with tears, settled on Sierra. "Take care of them," she said.

"I will," Sierra said. She paused, embracing her awkwardly.

Senya then turned to Tarn. "You look like you have a good heart," she told him. "You remind me of my sons."

"Thank you," Tarn replied timidly.

"May the favor of Numinae be ever upon you," Senya said.

"And you." Tarn lowered his eyes respectfully and gave her an abbreviated bow.

"We'll meet again soon," Adan promised, trying not to think about what the Waymen would do if they caught her. He hoped they would go after his team instead. They were the intruders after all.

"I know," was all that Senya said, but Adan could read the same doubts he himself had in her eyes.

THIRTEEN

THE PATH OF THE DESERT

THE THREE COMPANIONS SPRINTED AWAY FROM SENYA. The red lights pulsed maddeningly and the beeps blared down the passage, but there were no sounds of pursuit. It was not long, however, before the passage came to an abrupt end.

"Now what?" Tarn asked.

"Great—a dead end," Sierra growled, bouncing her shoulder against the wall. There were doors on either side, but they likely led only to patients' rooms.

But Sierra's frustrated comment gave Adan an idea. "This is perfect, actually," Adan said. "They won't be expecting us to come out from this end of the infirmary."

Exchanging glances with Tarn, he saw that the Wayman understood his idea without him having to explain.

"Which side, right or left?" Tarn asked, the tips of his cutter gloves flashing a yellow beam that reflected off the metallic walls.

Adan pointed towards the closest door on the left.

"If we punch through the far wall in that room it should lead us back towards the way we came in. That's the best route to take since we don't know how big this place is. We would get lost if we headed off in a new direction."

Tarn sliced the door off at the hinges. They rushed into an empty room, propping up the dismantled metal slab to cover the opening as best they could. Tarn dropped down behind the bed and began slicing through the back wall. He was careful to make the opening as small as possible and not let the section he cut off fall into the hallway on the other side. Once he completed the incision, he removed the elliptical cutout and laid it against the wall.

Tarn peeked his head through to make sure everything was clear before slithering into the hallway beyond. Sierra followed and last came Adan. He squirmed his way out of the infirmary, pulling the cut out section back across the hole.

The hallway they found themselves in looked more like the ones they had walked through on their way in, dilapidated and made from scraps. Though Adan didn't know exactly where they were, he knew their position relative to where they had entered the infirmary. If they headed back in the general direction they had come hopefully they would be able to retrace their steps out of the Spoke.

No flashing lights or alarms were going off in this hallway. There were barely any lights at all, just a few lumins dangling from cords. They walked briskly, trying to look as normal as possible.

They passed through an intersection without meeting anyone, but a moment later, Adan's heart skipped a beat when a door they were just about to walk past swung open.

A man in a dingy robe pushed a cart right out in front of them, blocking their path. He gave them an angry look, but appeared unarmed. Adan suffered a moment of panic, thinking the man might attack with his fists or shout out a warning, but then he realized that the look of anger was actually one of annoyance.

"Excuse me," the man said petulantly. "I'm trying to work here." He waved in front of his cart, indicating his desire for them to let him pass.

Adan and the others obliged and the man shuffled down the hallway, muttering under his breath. They left him behind, soon drawing close to the entrance to the infirmary. They were just about to make the final turn into the hallway where Adan expected to see the outer doorway when they heard sounds of commotion.

They halted and listened. It sounded like a large group of men were heading into the infirmary. Harsh laughter mingled with various voices. In the midst of it came the sounds of someone being struck several times, followed by the loud cries of a familiar voice: Barlo.

Adan risked a glance around the corner and saw the last of a group of Waymen entering the infirmary, leaving behind a writhing and moaning Barlo on the floor.

Adan's first impulse was to run and see how badly he was hurt, but he checked himself to make certain it was safe. When no one appeared for several moments, he turned to the others.

"Barlo is hurt, but the hallway looks clear. I'll go see if he's okay. You keep watch in case anyone comes out of the infirmary."

Tarn nodded. "Be careful."

"Hurry," Sierra urged. "Those Waymen might come back at any moment."

Adan padded down the hallway until he came to Barlo's side. The man had blood splattered around one ear and matted in his hair. The dark red liquid also trickled from his mouth. He was so wrapped up in his own misery he failed to notice Adan's presence.

"Barlo, what happened to you? Why did they beat you again?" Adan whispered. He pulled out a tube of almamenth and yanked up the man's tattered sleeve. He was about to rub it into his skin when Barlo recoiled in horror.

"What? Who? Please, no more," he begged, clearly dazed. He brushed a handful of wet, stringy hair from his eyes. "Oh, it's you!"

Adan put a finger to his lips. "Shh. They'll hear us," he warned.

"Ah...yes," Barlo said, lifting up a limp hand. "Here, help me up."

Adan pulled him up to where he could lean against the wall. "Are you well enough to move on your own?" he asked.

Barlo coughed, a terrible sound like sand and rocks being stirred in a barrel. "I suppose I'll manage somehow. Only don't let them beat me again. I don't think I can take another round of that."

"Don't worry, Barlo. We'll protect you," Adan promised. He motioned for Sierra and Tarn to come down the hall.

"Where are we going then?" Barlo asked, looking up at Adan with droopy, blood-shot eyes.

"Somewhere safe," Adan said. "Remember that place I promised you? Well, we're heading back there a little sooner than expected. We can take you now if you think you're in good enough condition to keep up. Just let me rub this into your arm first. It will help."

"Yes, of course," Barlo replied, nodding. Adan promptly began working the greenish paste into his skin. The familiar, pleasant aroma filled the hallway as Sierra and Tarn appeared at Adan's side.

"Adan, even with that almamenth, I don't think we should take him back to the praxis," Sierra told him privately. *"At least*

not now. He'll slow us down. I think we should leave him behind to escape with the others."

"But you've seen the beatings he has taken. If they go after him again he might not live long enough to be rescued."

"We've got to go," Tarn said, his eyes trained on the door. "It's not safe here."

"Fine," Sierra acquiesced. *"I just hope we don't regret this."*

"Let's get going, then," Barlo said, stutter-stepping forward like rusty gears cranking into motion. "This way."

He shuffled ahead, holding his ear the whole time, heading back towards the entrance to the compound.

They passed two women in the hallway wearing plain robes who gave the injured Welkin anxious looks, but he did not even acknowledge them, trudging right past.

Several times Barlo looked back over his shoulder as he navigated the hallways, but there were no signs that anyone was following.

They were about halfway to the exit according to Adan's bioseine when Barlo made a left turn and began taking them in a new direction. Adan rushed up beside him and asked where they were headed.

"Oh, what?" Barlo blurted out, jumping at Adan's sudden appearance. He immediately shifted his gaze, focusing on the hallway up ahead. "Other way's too dangerous," he muttered. "Bound to be guarded now. This way's better. A secret way. Much safer."

Barlo surged forward down the new hallway without waiting for Adan's reply. Adan caught up to him just as Barlo stopped in front of a thick door. The door was surprisingly sturdy for the Spoke, and did not at all fit with any of the others they had seen, except perhaps those in the infirmary.

"Wait here while I go inside," Barlo said.

"Barlo, we have to keep going," Adan said. "The Waymen are looking for us."

"I'll only be a moment, I promise," Barlo insisted, his face simultaneously pained and imploring.

"Adan, no," Sierra interjected.

"But I—I need to make certain it's safe," Barlo pleaded, clinging to Adan's arm.

Adan shook his head. He wished that the decision did not rest with him, but he knew that whatever decision he made, it had to be quick.

"All right," he said, nodding at Barlo. "But if you're not back in a hundred count, we'll have to leave you behind," he warned.

Barlo nodded profusely. "I'll be back in half that," he said. He pressed his hand to the panel on the door, but he had to do so several times before it opened. When the door finally slid away, all Adan could see was another doorway just beyond it. It looked as stout as the first one, but the first door closed before it opened, leaving Adan, Sierra, and Tarn to wait for Barlo out in the hall.

"I don't like this," Sierra said.

"Me either," Tarn added.

"He said he'd only be a moment," Adan tried to reassure them, but inside a quivering sensation rolled through his stomach.

"We're risking an awful lot for someone we barely know," Sierra said, her voice on edge.

"Hopefully, he's just making sure everything is clear," Adan said.

"I don't like this place," Sierra said quietly. "I don't like anything about this city. There's something not right about it, but I can't put my finger on it."

Adan checked the fragmented map of the Spoke which his

bioseine had formed in his mind. It looked like all the hallways they had traveled spread out from a central hub, somewhat like the layout of Oasis, though with corridors instead of streets.

The most important detail of the building's layout at the moment was their proximity to the only exit he knew about. If they continued along the current passage, they would be moving further away from it. Adan was so focused on studying the map that he completely missed when the door whispered open.

Tarn grabbed him by the shoulder, shouting "Look out!"

A contingent of Waymen stood on the other side. Before Adan or his friends could react, they hurled several small, dark balls at them. Two struck Adan square in the chest and several others impacted against Tarn and Sierra. The Waymen who threw them were too close to miss. From the green dust and pungent smoke which exploded in the air around them, Adan knew at once that they had been hit by sopor pods, a Wayman concoction for knocking people out.

Adan felt his eyes grow drowsy and his legs begin to buckle underneath him, but then he caught himself and shook off the haziness. Sierra and Tarn were not so fortunate. They keeled over, knocked out cold. Had his bioseine counteracted the drugs? But if so, then why hadn't it saved Sierra?

There was no time to resolve the mystery. Adan yanked his oscillathe from his belt and blasted the Waymen in the doorway with a crackling burst of invisible energy.

They were jammed so tightly together, all six of them hit the ground with one shot. Seeing that no one was left standing, Adan knelt beside his friends, placing his hand on Sierra's shoulder. The neutralizer in his gloves could revive people just as easily as it could render them unconscious. After a short jolt from his gloves, Sierra responded with a sharp breath and her eyes opened wide.

"What happened?" she asked, looking startled.

Adan opened his mouth to reply, but before he could answer he caught a flicker of movement out of the corner of his eye. He turned just in time to see the doorway swish open and a figure fling something at him from the other side. The pinion sunk deep into Adan's side. Though he felt no pain because of his bioseine, the force of the blow pushed him backwards and he toppled to the ground. A stream of blood began pouring from him onto the floor. It seemed impossible that a single person could have that much blood inside of them.

Though he remained on the ground, in his mind Adan continued falling. The memory of that first death he had seen in the Basin came rushing back. Like some terrible nightmare, he was living inside that memory again, only this time he was one of the victims, not some distant observer.

"Adan!" Sierra shouted, rushing over to him. "Adan, no..." The look on her face was impossible to miss, even in his confused and shaken state: the wound was fatal. "Hold on," Sierra cried. "I'll get some almamenth."

Adan checked his bioseine to see if even almamenth would help. The system told him that it would only delay his death. It would take something much stronger to save him.

But she was not given the chance to apply the treatment. At that moment a dark figure shot through the opening, closing the gap between them and kicking Sierra in the ribs. She collapsed back to the floor.

She rolled over slowly and struggled to rise, but failed to get up.

"Don't touch him," she threatened, gritting out the words.

The dark figure sneered at her. "We'll do whatever we like," he spat back, dashing over and giving her another kick. But she saw the blow coming this time and managed to avoid the full force of it. Even so, the impact sent her colliding with the wall.

At last Adan got a good look at the man's face. It was Rak, the man they had saved Barlo from.

Sierra pulled out her oscillathe, but she was still too dazed from the blow to react in time. Rak kicked it from her hand, cackling boisterously.

A red blade flickered into existence at the end of Sierra's hand. Adan could see in her eyes that she was prepared to fight to the death. For once Rak pulled away from her, keeping his distance from the weapon.

"Sierra, you don't have to..." Adan tried to tell her, but she just grimaced and pushed herself back to her feet.

Adan hoped she would make it out of this, even if he himself did not, but she looked so weak he wondered how long she would even be able to keep standing. Something whizzed through the air from behind Rak and struck her in the shoulder. A puff of green dust filled the air around her and she toppled back to the ground.

Another figure emerged from the opening, coming up alongside Rak.

"Nice shot, Barlo," Rak said, regarding the weathered face of the treacherous Welkin beside him. "It looks like you'll keep your position as foreman after all."

Barlo responded with a mocking smile, leering down upon the people who had been trying to save him.

Adan felt strangely weightless, like he might at any moment start floating towards the ceiling. His mind told him this couldn't be happening, that this must be a dream, but his blood soaked garrick and the awful presence of Barlo standing over him said otherwise.

"Why?" Adan asked. "We rescued you."

Barlo avoided Adan's gaze. He fingered his blood encrusted ear as if the pain from that wound had flared up again.

But the shock of Barlo's betrayal lasted only a moment. Adan had his friends to think about. If he did not do something fast they would be captured or killed.

He reached for the oscillathe at his waist, but it wasn't there. His eyes darted around the room searching for it. He wondered if he had dropped it when he ran to help Sierra, but he couldn't spot it from his prone position.

Rak stepped forward, eyeing Adan warily. "Barlo is a Wayman, gearhead. He knows the only way of life is the path of the desert: put others beneath your feet before they put you under theirs."

Feet pounded the metallic floor down the hallway, moving towards him.

"You never told me you were friends of Malloc," Barlo muttered in murderous undertones.

Though Adan's senses were dulled by the bioseine controlling his system and keeping him alive, his mind was still clear enough. In that moment he knew that Malloc's injury hadn't been an accident after all.

Rak snapped at Barlo, "Silence, shim. Who gave you permission to speak?"

Barlo withered beneath the large man's threatening glare.

Adan clutched the spear in his side. Pulling it out would only hasten his death. Given the circumstances, he didn't see what choice he had. There were only two of them. If he could get close enough with his neutralizer, maybe he could take them down before more Waymen arrived.

He sat up and grasped the pinion with both hands.

"Empty shaft! Are you mad?" Rak cried out, starting forward.

Adan was just about to yank out the spear when a dozen

armed Waymen burst into the hallway. He froze. There were too many for him to hope to escape.

The Waymen swarmed in and surround him. Adan read in their faces that they were actually afraid of him, perhaps because he was a man with a pinion sunk deep in his side who refused to die.

Adan stared at his gloved hands, trying to think of some way out. But even if he took them all down, his bioseine couldn't sustain him indefinitely. It was already going through and shutting off everything not critical to keeping him alive.

"I'm sorry," he said under his breath to Sierra and Tarn.

"Take him, you miserable swedges," ordered Sunder Rak.

The next moment Adan's bioseine shut down his consciousness and he knew no more.

FOURTEEN
THE POWER OF PRAYER

Adan's eyes opened to a bright light glaring above him. His head felt thick, like it was wrapped in invisible gauze, but the cold metal table underneath him and the dark, blurry figures in the corner shocked him fully awake. His first thought was that he was somehow back at the Institute.

He started to sit up, but a voice sounded from behind him.

"No sudden movements. The surgery is still fresh."

As disoriented as Adan was, there was no mistaking that voice.

"Nolan."

The knowledge that he was in the presence of the leader of Hull drained him of what little energy he had. If he was here it was almost certain that Sierra and Tarn had been captured. He studied the fuzzy figures standing near the edge of his bed, trying to make out which was him.

Adan sat up slowly and the room gradually came into focus. A table of silvery instruments and tools sat up against the wall. A metal door was the only exit. The tall bearded figure of Nolan stood before him, dressed in elegant robes. His imposing gaze caused Adan to shrink inside himself. A Wayman stood on either side of him, both armed with pinions and shivs.

Adan's bioseine told him that the wound he had received from the spear had closed. It was not entirely healed, but based on past experience it soon would be. Adan's accelerated healing ability was as much a mystery to him as the fact that he was still alive, but he had no time to contemplate such matters now.

"Where are my friends?" he asked, trying not to let his imagination fill in the details.

"I save your life and all you can think about are your friends?" Nolan commented.

"Tell me where they are. Are they alive?" Whether or not Nolan had saved his life was inconsequential. All he cared about was the fate of Sierra and Tarn.

Nolan drew closer. "You really shouldn't worry so much. It's a sign of weakness. You would be much better off if you simply concentrated on the things within your control."

"Tell me what you did to them." Adan studied Nolan's eyes to see if he could catch a glimpse of his thoughts, but he sensed nothing behind his vacant stare. His expression made him look even more detached than the Collective scientists, more mechanical than human.

Nolan had to be masking his thoughts, ensuring that Adan did not use his memorant abilities to discover what he was thinking. In the meantime, Nolan was no doubt attempting to penetrate into Adan's mind as well. But Adan was not the same memorant he had been the last time Nolan captured him. This time he knew about the miasma channel, making it possible to invade the thoughts of anyone with or without a bioseine, willing or unwilling. As desperate as, he hesitated. Was he ready to force himself inside someone's thoughts? It felt too much like what the Developers would do.

Nolan's eyes flashed with sudden insight.

"So you've discovered the miasma channel. You continue to surprise me, Adan." The corners of his lips rose in smug satisfaction. "You would have made a marvelous memorant with the proper training."

He knows about the miasma channel. The thought shivered through his mind like a crack in a pane of glass. That explained how he had been able to get inside Adan's thoughts the last time. Adan shifted his awareness to that part of his mind which knew about the channel and felt Nolan's presence there. He was probing for an opening. It was only a matter of time before he got in. Adan could still try to use the miasma channel on Nolan in a counter attack, but Nolan had a head start and was far more skilled than he was.

He didn't have many options left. He decided to take a risk.

"If you can promise me that my friends are still alive I'll tell you whatever you want to know."

"Everything?"

"Yes."

Nolan shook his head. "Adan, I know you better than that. Even as honest as you are, there are certain things you would keep back from me. Perhaps it would not even be intentional, given your promise, but something would go missing. My way will be much more sure."

Adan's mind went momentarily blank. Nolan meant to extract everything he knew and there was no way Adan could stop him. In the face of such helplessness, the only thing he could think to do was pray.

He closed his eyes and tried to forget about Nolan and all of the danger he was in. His mind filled instead with the awareness of his creator.

Numinae, protect me. Please don't let him inside my mind again. Help me find out what happened to my friends. Keep them safe. Please, oh, please, hear my prayer.

The petition lasted only a moment, but when he opened his eyes, Nolan was staring at him, his brow furrowed. It was the first time Adan had ever seen that expression. If Adan didn't know better, he would have said he looked worried.

Please help me get out of this room, he continued. *My friends need me. Just let me find them. I don't know what Nolan has planned, but please keep him out of my mind.*

When he had finished praying the second time, he looked up again. Nolan's expression was even more upset than before.

Had his prayer been answered? Nolan definitely had not entered his mind like the last time. Adan had a strong intuition that his prayer had something to do with it. Whether it was because Numinae had answered him or that the mere act of praying itself had somehow protected his thoughts, he wasn't sure. Who could say what really transpired in the realm of the mind during prayer? Perhaps some part of him was no longer present during real, honest prayer, but wandered elsewhere, suspended between the Vast and the Eversky, the realm where Numinae was said to dwell? Adan had no way of knowing the truth, but he kept praying all the same.

Why have I not sought you more often, or more earnestly? Surely you have been with me every step of the way and yet I have never been more aware of your presence than at this moment.

"Stop!" Nolan commanded, his voice reverberating throughout the room.

Adan opened his eyes. Nolan's forehead was pulled taut. The Wayman guards shifted behind him, regarding Nolan with concerned expressions.

Adan stared straight into Nolan's eyes. "I won't let you know anything until you tell me what happened to my friends."

Nolan glowered back at him. The Reeve could order his guards to tear him to pieces if he wanted to, but Adan was not about to give him anything until he found out what had happened to Sierra and Tarn.

After a long silence, Nolan finally let out a long, exasperated sigh.

"Fine," he said, biting out the word between the infinitesimal gaps of his clenched teeth. "You want to know what happened to your friends? They're alive. Being held in a cell not far from here."

"Take me to them," Adan demanded, not willing to take the Reeve at his word.

"Only if you let me into your thoughts."

"I have to know that they're alive."

"You have my word."

"Which is next to useless."

Nolan started forward, his eyes narrowing as he pressed his face up next to Adan's. "Drop your resistance to my probing or you'll never see them alive again."

Adan refused to flinch, though inwardly he began to doubt just how much of an advantage his new discovery gave him.

"My patience for these delays of yours will not last much longer, I can assure you," Nolan threatened.

Adan wavered. *Please Numinae, tell me what to do.*

"Guards," Nolan raised his voice.

"Yes, oh great Reeve?" one of them responded.

Adan braced himself. Would Nolan order his men to kill him? Drag the dead bodies of his friends before him? He prepared himself for the worst, but trusted that Numinae would give him strength, no matter what happened.

Nolan shook his head, giving Adan a look of begrudging respect. He smoothed his robes as if his clothes, and not his inability to get what he wanted, had been the source of his irritation.

"Bring his companions," he said.

The guards returned his order with looks of bewilderment.

"Ah...yes, of course. We could use the relay system and send for them—" one of them offered.

"No, you are to bring them personally. In the meantime I want to speak with this prisoner—*alone*."

Then Adan did flinch, half from fear and half from shock. It appeared that Nolan was finally giving in. And yet there was something sinister about the way he said that last word.

The guards opened the door awkwardly and disappeared into the hallway beyond.

After the door shut, a change came over Nolan. His regality, his air of superiority diminished, though it did not disappear altogether. He looked less like the Reeve of Hull and more like an ordinary, common man. And this terrified Adan more than anything. The thought that the same man who had convinced Will and Bryce to risk their lives attempting to destroy Oasis, who had harnessed the murderous instincts of the Waymen for his purposes, and who had twice sent Adan to his death, could be anything other than a twisted genius was unthinkable. Of all the men in the Vast he was the least to be trusted and the most to be feared, especially since Darius, the leader of the Collective, had been killed. The possibility that Nolan was a mere man sent tingling waves of fear across Adan's skin. It was one thing to fear a monster, it was quite another to entertain the possibility that the monster was no different than you.

"You think of me as a killer, a tyrant, no doubt," Nolan said. Again, his tone made Adan even more suspicious than ever. Nolan was not the sort of person to talk in an apologetic manner. "But I am no different than you. I am merely an instrument in Numinae's hands. Some of his servants he uses as implements of destruction, others he has consigned to be destroyed."

Adan's mind began to spin. The metal slab beneath him felt several degrees colder. *Numinae? Had he really just mentioned the name of the being Adan had been praying to? Had he been reading Adan's thoughts after all?*

"What are you talking about? What's Numinae got to do with this?" Adan shot back.

"What's Numinae got to do with this? Everything. You of all people should know that."

"What do you know about Numinae?"

"A great deal more than you. It is his path I follow."

Adan shook his head vigorously. The more Nolan talked, the less sense he made.

"So you're saying that the destruction of Oasis, the amassing of this army of Waymen, your enslavement of the Welkin, that's part of following the path of your Creator?"

Nolan's face was calm, almost grave. "You were there when Oasis fell. I may have sent Will and the Waymen, but tell me, in the end was it I who destroyed Oasis or was it Numinae himself?"

"Yes, but..." Adan's response sputtered and died on his lips. Nolan had to be twisting things by bringing Numinae into this, but why? Was he simply trying to shake off responsibility for his actions? Or was he trying to gain Adan's sympathy to manipulate him into revealing what he knew?

"Did Gavin ever tell you about a man named Illiud?" Nolan asked.

Again Adan was rendered speechless. Gavin? Illiud? What connection did they have to Nolan? Gavin and Nolan had both been Developers, but Illiud? He was a Welkin holy man, a maneusis, who had been killed in Oasis. What could he possibly have to do with Nolan?

"Well, did he tell you about Illiud or not?" Nolan repeated the question.

"Yes, he told me about him," Adan admitted, anxious to see where this was going.

"And did he tell you about the prophecy?" Nolan continued.

Adan nodded in reply. *He knows about that too?* Adan tried to remain outwardly calm, but each revelation from Nolan shook him like a blow to the temple, staggering his concept of what he thought was true.

"'The blood of the dead who have been trampled underfoot cries out for justice,'" Nolan recited, slowly and deliberately. "'The skies shall fall upon that city of iniquity and destruction shall walk its streets.' Those were the words of the prophecy which the eidos spoke to him."

"Yes, but that wasn't all," Adan corrected. "He also said, 'if the people of that place should repent from their wickedness, Numinae will stay his hand. For long is his arm, but just as great is his mercy." Adan had learned the words from Gavin— no, that wasn't actually true. He had learned them from Gavin's memories, the ones in the extractor. And now Adan realized how Nolan must have learned about Illiud and the prophecy, from the same place Adan had—the extractor. Bryce had brought it to Nolan after the fall of Oasis.

"You are correct," Nolan went on. "And it is clear that they did not repent. The sky fell upon them and the streets were torn asunder."

"And how did you learn of the prophecy?" Adan asked, testing to see if Nolan would confirm his theory.

"Illiud told me," Nolan announced.

"Really? When was that?" Adan asked. Nolan had to be lying, but there was no point in calling him on it. Better to see where he was going with this first.

"When he freed me from the Institute."

Adan stared at the Reeve in disbelief, trying to imagine

what Nolan hoped to gain by concocting such an outrageous story.

"Illiud was a Welkin. He knew nothing about technology. How could he have freed you from the Institute?"

"Is anything too hard for Numinae?" Nolan lanced a predatory glare at him. For the first time since the guards had left, the proud ruler of Hull returned. "He caused Illiud to wake up while he was in the Institute. Darius was planning on wiping my mind because the remapping of Malthus' son's memories into my consciousness failed. I knew I wasn't his son almost from the beginning. He may have erased my memories, but he could not erase the person behind the memories."

This part did have some truth to it. Nolan had been implanted with the memories of Malthus' son, Dane. Gavin had seen it in the chronotrace. But the part about Illiud had to be a fabrication. There was no way a primitive Welkin could have rescued Nolan from the Institute.

"Please forgive me if I find this hard to believe," Adan said.

"Your doubts are perfectly understandable. Numinae's ways are indeed mysterious, but I assure you that I am telling the truth."

"But why reveal this now? And what does any of this have to do with Numinae. You still haven't explained that."

Nolan approached the edge of Adan's bed and looked down upon him with the closest thing to desperation Adan had ever seen on his face.

"You may not approve of my methods, but when you are fighting a war the rules get re-written. You think I wanted to slaughter everyone in Oasis? You think I took pleasure in Will's death? But the Collective had to be stopped. And Numinae sent Illiud to free me because he knew that I was the only one who could do it. Illiud said that Numinae had chosen me to enact his vengeance upon the Collective. He personally anointed me as the savior of the Werin, the instrument who would 'restore his people back from their dispersion.' Those were the exact words he used."

"You're lying," Adan countered. He had had enough of Nolan's games. It was time to call his bluff. "You found out about Illiud in the extractor. If you knew about the virus you could have found out about the prophecy as well. And then you made up this story just to, just to..." Adan fumbled for a reason, but nothing came.

Nolan latched onto his arm, all hints of the Reeve of Hull fleeing from his face. "Adan, you have to believe me. I had to do things the way I did because it was the only way. I am the only hope these people have against what the Collective is doing. It is them or us. They will slaughter every last one of the Werin and us as well. You've seen what they're capable of. Maybe you resent me for manipulating you into fighting them, but ask yourself, would you have sacrificed yourself to destroy Oasis if I had asked you? No, you had to remain ignorant. You never would have sent the virus if you had. But none of that matters now, because the storm didn't destroy all of them. And sending you again, along with Bryce and Nox didn't stop them either. My scouts have spotted the Collective ships out in the Vast. I need to know what you know about their army and their plans. If you allow me access to your thoughts I promise that you and your friends can go."

Adan sat in stunned silence at Nolan's plea. He realized now that he knew next to nothing about the man before him. He half wondered if the real Nolan had been remapped and replaced with this newer version. It was highly unlikely, but at present, anything seemed possible.

So he knows an attack is coming. Should I help him defend this city? Should I tell him what I know? Would it even make any difference if I did?

Adan never got to answer those questions. Sirens roared from out in the hallway, shattering the silence inside the room. With the blast of noise, his thoughts scattered.

Nolan spun and faced the exit.

"They're coming," was all he said.

The awareness of what he meant hit Adan in the gut like another Wayman pinion.

"It's the Collective, isn't it? The attack has begun."

Nolan glared back at him. The imposing, prideful Reeve stood before him once again.

"You should have told me," he said. "Now all is lost. None of us will survive."

FIFTEEN
FROM THE STARS

Two Waymen guards burst into the room. Neither Sierra nor Tarn were with them. In fact, they weren't the same guards from before.

"Reeve, the city is—"

"Yes, I know about the attack," Nolan said. "Take this prisoner to the new cells. I don't care which one. I never want to see him again."

With that Nolan stormed from the room, leaving the guards to stare suspiciously at Adan, as if the attack on Hull were somehow his fault. In the back of his mind, irrationally, Adan wondered if somehow it actually was.

The guards escorted him out of the room and down the hallway. It was well made, rivaling the construction of the passages at the Institute. At the end of the hall they waited for a wide door to open. When it did, Adan saw the reason for the wait. It was an elevator. It took an inordinate amount of time for the doors to open again. As the elevator descended Adan worried about what would happen to Sierra and Tarn. Would the Collective level the city? Would they all die together in their prison cells? As long as those sirens kept blaring, he had little hope they would make it out of this alive.

At last the doors opened again and the Waymen herded him along a new corridor and through two more thick doors. On the other side was a hallway unlike any Adan had ever seen. It was lined with transparent walls allowing views into a series of identical rooms. Two more guards sat behind a transparent wall at the head of the passage, their dark eyes looking Adan up and down.

"Prisoners? Now?" asked one of them.

"Reeve's orders," replied one of Adan's guards. The answer got a shake of the head, but the other Waymen waved him through.

Adan's escorts moved him quickly along the new corridor. Inside each room they passed, he saw pairs of men sleeping on metal framed cots on opposite sides of the room, dressed in the same drab gray clothing Adan was wearing.

They stopped in front of a room occupied by a single man. One of the guards touched the clear wall facing them with the palm of his hand and the entire panel retracted into the ceiling. Then they shoved Adan inside and the panel whisked back into place.

The Waymen departed hurriedly without a word, leaving Adan to take in his cell. The chamber had no internal lighting, the only light coming from a lumin outside in the hallway. It was enough to make out a few details about the figure sleeping on one of the cots. He had gray, slightly thinning hair that went down to his shoulders, but he lay with his back towards Adan so that the particulars of his face remained hidden.

Adan sat down on the opposite bed. His strange encounter with Nolan still lingered in his mind. He wondered how much of what he had said was true or if he had been manipulating Adan in some way he had failed to see. But more than Nolan, his heart was heavy with thoughts of Sierra and Tarn. The most likely outcome was that they would be killed by the Collective forces. Or maybe they had been killed already. Adan had no reason to trust Nolan's word.

He touched the transparent wall facing the hallway. It felt like some kind of plastic. It looked too thick to break, but he tapped on it a few times for good measure. It sounded just as solid as it looked.

"If you're looking for a meal, they only serve it twice a day," came a husky voice from behind him. The man on the bed rolled over and stared at him through bleary eyes. Rubbing his face, he tossed his legs over the side and sat up. His stubble-ridden face was reminiscent of char, flecked with black, white, and all shades in between.

Adan paused to consider the man's comment. He couldn't remember the last time he ate, but his hunger was of little concern to him at the moment.

"I was just testing it to see how strong it was," he said.

"Where are you from?" the man asked, scratching the bristly whiskers which covered his face and neck. "You don't look like you're indigenous."

Adan scratched his forehead. The man must have been referring to the Werin, but the term indigenous was not typically used. He didn't look like he was part of the Werin either, now that Adan stopped to think about it.

"I don't know," Adan stated. "I have no memory. I don't remember anything past a few days ago."

"That freak Nolan get inside your head too?" the gray-haired man asked, scraping the sleep from his eyes and sizing Adan up. Despite his grogginess, there was a cunningness to his look.

"No, it was a group of scientists. Have you heard of a city called Oasis?" Adan asked. He didn't know whether or not this man could be trusted, but at that moment he really didn't have much choice. The man had been here longer than Adan and that meant he knew far more about Hull and this prison.

The man shook his head. "No. Is it one of the native camps?"

"It's a city. Actually it *was* a city. It was destroyed by a storm. The scientists who erased my memory built it. It was even larger than Hull. It had hundreds of buildings, some of them fifty stories high."

"Why would anyone build a city up on the surface? It's not safe." The man stood up and stretched, letting out a low groan.

"I'm not sure, actually. They did have atmos generators to protect them, but when those went down, the storm leveled almost everything. Have you been through a storm out in the open desert?"

The man grew agitated at Adan's question. "Yes. I know what they're like," he snapped.

The sudden change in the stranger's mood perplexed Adan.

"How long have you been here?" he asked, still trying to gauge how much the stranger knew about the prison.

"Don't know," the man muttered through a yawn and scratched the back of his head. "Nolan's got me drugged up, playing with my mind. Everything's all jumbled up. Dates, times, they're hard for me to pin down. It all runs together."

"Drugged? Do you remember anything at all?" Adan asked, staring at him with a newfound sense of pity. His story sounded eerily similar to Adan's, only this man had been captured by Nolan instead of the Developers.

A distant look came into the stranger's eyes. He no longer appeared fully present. Adan caught a glimpse of his thoughts. Dark tunnels flash through his mind, reminiscent of the ones in Manx Core. He walked through them carrying a rifle of some sort in his hands. He wore a helmet and a metal suit, but Adan somehow still knew it was him. Machinery and vehicles revved and hummed nearby, but Adan couldn't see them.

The scene blurred. When it came back into focus, a million motes of bright white light sparkled overhead. Their beauty pierced Adan's heart. It reminded him of the neophosphorous cavern in the Basin only this was much, much larger.

But the longer Adan contemplated the vision, the more he realized that something wasn't right. The ceiling was different than what he had first thought, in fact, it wasn't a ceiling at all. It was just black, empty space interspersed with points of light. But then, what held the lights up there? And how far away were they?

The ground stretched out perfectly smooth before them in every direction, lit by the faint lights above, giving it an eerie, wan cast. There were no walls to speak of. Adan realized that the man was no longer underground. No cavern could possibly be that large. He had to be outside, but where? There was no place like this anywhere in the Vast as far as he knew. There was no sand, no hills, no mountains. The terrain was featureless. And the sky had never looked that clear. The utter absence of clouds made Adan feel exposed despite the undeniable beauty of the expanse above.

"The stars..." the man mumbled. "I came from the stars. Kelm Brennan, escalon, sidereal scout class. Yes, that was my name. But what am I here for? Why did they send me?"

Kelm slumped back onto his bed as if he had been struck by a dizzy spell.

"Are you all right?" Adan asked. Something was definitely wrong with this stranger. With the sirens still whirring off in the distance, Adan was beginning to think he might be wasting his time trying to find out what this man knew.

Kelm brushed off the question. "I don't know how I got

here. But I know it took a long time. Maybe I've been sleeping the whole time. Maybe I'm just now waking up."

"Where are you from, Kelm?" Adan asked. That was the biggest piece missing from Kelm's puzzle, if only he could remember it.

The man rolled over to face the wall in response. Suddenly his whole body shook like he'd just woken up from a dream. He turned back to face Adan, blinking and looking around as if seeing the cell for the first time.

"You said something about stars. I've heard about those before. They're up in the sky—beyond the clouds, right?"

The man's head bobbed up and down, an excited look of recognition bursting onto his face.

"Yes, yes, that's right. You've been there, too?"

"I'm afraid not—" Adan began, but the man rambled on.

"Are you sure? I could have sworn you were an escalon too, maybe even someone from my division."

"No, I think you must have me confused with—wait, what are you talking about? Are you some sort of soldier?" The gun and metal suit in the man's vision made it seem like he must have been at one point, but Adan didn't know how far back that had been or whether it was just part of his imagination.

The man's eyes opened wider and wider as the words spilled from his mouth.

"Yes, and you remember it too! I knew I'd seen you before. You were one of the first ones they sent."

"What?" Now it was Adan's turn to feel disoriented.

"Yes, they sent us out one by one," Kelm said. "I remember now. Not many of us had the skill and training for such a long mission. They sent us out a few at a time and waited to hear back, waited for the signal, but it never came. We had to find them, we had to hurry....but why? And who? Who were they?

Do you remember? What was the prime directive? What were we looking for?"

As a memorant, Adan sensed that Kelm's mind was poised somewhere between ignorance and insanity. And yet the eagerness with which he spoke must have had some basis in reality, even if the details were all mixed up and out of place.

"Listen, I don't know who sent you, or if anyone sent you at all. I told you, they erased my memory—" Adan said.

"But not mine." Kelm rushed at Adan and grabbed him by the shoulders. "Nolan only confused it. And I do remember you. That mind jammer may have jumbled everything up, but I still have the pieces. And your face—I swear I've seen it before."

SIXTEEN

THE LOST MAN

Adan pulled away from Kelm. Excitement washed over him, but a layer of doubt bubbled just beneath it. That this man claimed to know him seemed too incredible to be true. It was just as likely his claims were the product of a drugged and muddled mind. And yet Adan so wanted to believe that Kelm was speaking the truth.

"Kelm, are you sure about this?" Adan asked. "Perhaps you only imagined it."

The insight brimming in Kelm's eyes vanished as quickly as it came, replaced by desperation. "No, I...I remember...you were..." his voice trailed off as he wandered back over to his side of the room.

Adan felt a deep sense of pity for this man. He wondered if this is what Nolan did to all of his prisoners and whether he planned on using the same drugs on him if Hull survived the attack.

"Your face," Kelm rambled on like a man fumbling for something he had lost in the dark. "I saw it once. I just...oh, you're right, how can I be sure of anything? It's all swirled together inside my head, like I've lived the lives of a hundred people instead of just one. I can't tell which memories are my own." Kelm slouched onto his bed and began to fiddle with his long hair, twisting it around his fingers.

Answers about Adan's past, like his chances of getting out of this cell, seemed more distant than ever.

The light out in the hallway flickered and Adan stood and returned to the transparent wall. This time he felt it tremble slightly.

Raised voices erupted at the end of the hall. He missed the first part of what they were saying, but pressing his ear to the wall he caught some of it.

"...a breach on the top floor. Report to the weapon vault immediately." The voice sounded hollow, like it was coming from the sound system inside the building.

"But what about the prisoners?" asked one of the guards.

"One of you stay there. If it gets worse and we have to send for you, just release the gas and abandon the block," came the answer from the sound system.

"Right," was the guard's response.

The prison's main door whisked open, followed by the drumming of footsteps retreating in the distance. The prison walls shook again, visibly this time. A low rumble echoed through the building.

Kelm's head jerked up. "What was that?"

"The building's been damaged," Adan said. He wasn't sure whether or not he should tell Kelm about the attack.

"It's happening again, isn't it?" Kelm said, his expression wilder than ever.

"What? What's happening?"

"Another purge."

"What do you mean?" Adan asked as he got down on the

floor to examine whether he could wedge his fingers under the wall. It was sealed tight.

"The Delegation. They poisoned the air, killed my...who did they kill? My family? Did I even have a family? I can't remember. Oh, why did I survive and they didn't? It's because the commander he...did something to me. He...changed me. He changed all of us," Kelm thrust his hands into his hair, tearing at his scalp as if he meant to pull out his memories by force.

"The Delegation? Kelm, you know about the Delegation?" Adan stared at him in shock, momentarily forgetting the danger they were in. Surely this had to be more than just the ravings of a broken mind.

The building shook again. Another ominous rumbling rippled through the cell.

"No, it wasn't the Delegation who caused the Purge. It was Deliverance. The Delegation wanted to, but...the Doctor, he stole their fire. He stole it for Deliverance and he...he destroyed the world before the Delegation got the chance." Kelm babbled on, his voice joining the chatter from the nearby prisoners as they voiced their fears about what was happening.

Deliverance? Kelm made less and less sense the more he talked.

"Kelm, whatever happened to you, it doesn't matter now. We've got to get out of here. The building is under attack." Adan rose and grabbed hold of his cellmate by the arm and looked him in the eye. "Listen to me, Kelm. I overheard the guards saying that they are going to use gas on us. We need to—"

The building shook again, halting Adan mid-sentence. The other prisoners started pounding on the walls of their cells, demanding to know what was going on. The men across from him pressed up against the transparent walls, straining to get a glimpse of what was going on.

"Kelm, do you know any way out of here?" Adan asked.

"If I knew a way out of this place do you think I'd still be here?" Kelm replied, giving Adan a helpless look. "But it doesn't matter. Even if we escape, the purge will kill us all in the end. We're too close to the surface."

"The surface? What's that got to do with it?" Adan shook the man, trying to snap him out of whatever vision was over-shadowing his perception of the here and now. "We've got to get out of this place, Kelm, before it falls down around us or the guards kill us."

Kelm's shoulders went limp. "It's no use." He wagged his head, his eyes misting. "They'll kill us all this time. They won't make the same mistake twice."

"Kelm, if you know anything that can get us out of here, you have to tell me now."

The building shook twice in rapid succession. The pris-oners shouted and banged their plates, beds, anything they could find, demanding to be let out. Adan wished they would stop. The cacophony made it hard to concentrate.

"We're going to die," Kelm cried out, his voice joining with the others. "We're all going to die."

Adan abandoned Kelm to his ravings and returned to the transparent wall. He pressed his fingers frantically around the edges, searching for some crack or vulnerability. It was a slim possi-bility, but he hoped the shaking might have damaged it somehow. But even as more tremors wracked the building, increasing both in frequency and intensity, the wall remained frustratingly intact.

A muffled voice came over the sound system, echoing down the hallway, but Adan couldn't make out anything over the uproar from the prisoners.

"They'll clean the world once and for all this time," Kelm moaned, sitting on the edge of the bed and rocking back and forth to some tuneless rhythm. "And all the works of men shall vanish in the light. That awful, terrible light..."

Adan noticed a fine, white mist drifting up from the floor. It was the gas. He pounded on the clear wall, joining the rest of the riotous inmate population, demanding to be freed.

A thunderous blast erupted down the hallway. It shook the walls of the cell in all directions and the roar of it drowned out the voices of the clamoring prisoners.

The prison grew quiet in the aftermath of the shot. Even Kelm stopped moaning. He stared at the clear wall, a terrible look of resignation on his face. Adan could no longer look at him. Instead he prayed silently for courage as the white mist caressed his feet and legs.

Rapidly approaching footsteps broke the silence. A flickering yellow light came along with them.

"Adan!" a voice shouted down the hall. "Adan? Are you in here?"

Adan recognized the voice. It belonged to Trey. Before he could respond, his friend stood in front of his cell, the prominent scar on his forehead glistening from sweat. The yellow light of a cutter shone from one hand. In his other he wielded a massive thick-barreled gun.

"Trey—you're alive," said Adan. "But how? And how did you find me?"

"I'll tell you later," Trey said, eagerness and relief mingling together in his expression. "Hold on. I'll have you out of there in no time."

Trey's cutter slashed through the transparent wall in a web of light, carving an opening in a matter of moments.

Adan tried to connect to Trey's mind, hoping he would be able to quickly fill him in on everything that had gone on since they'd gotten separated, but it came up blank.

"Trey, something's wrong. I can't sense your thoughts," Adan reported.

"I know," Trey said. "That's what made it so hard to find you. This prison must have some sort of inhibitor broadcasting into it. But it doesn't matter any more. Come on, let's get you out of here before this whole place falls down on top of us."

Adan started to step through the opening when he noticed that Kelm still sat trembling on the edge of the bed, staring at Trey's cutter in abject fear.

"Kelm," Adan said, returning and grabbing him by the arm. "Come on, this is my friend. He came to get us out. This is our chance. Let's go."

Kelm's shaking subsided somewhat.

"He's...he's not part of the enemy forces?"

"No, no. I told you. He's here to help us." Adan took Kelm by the hand and coaxed him to his feet. The white mist was growing thick around the floor and he wanted Kelm breathing as little of it as possible.

Kelm began to calm down, but he still showed little interest in following Adan. "Why leave if the whole world is going to be destroyed anyway? We'll never get down far enough to avoid the purge."

"Adan, we've got to hurry. This building won't hold together much longer," Trey warned.

Adan dragged Kelm towards the opening.

"Even if you're right and we're all about to die, we're not going to die here in this cell. We'll face whatever dangers are out there together."

Kelm allowed himself to be led out into the hallway, all the while shaking his head and mumbling unintelligibly.

The passage shook again. Prisoner's faces pressed frantically up against the transparent panels along the corridor, terrified by the gas billowing around their feet.

"Get us out of here!" they screamed. "Save us!"

"Trey—" Adan began.

But Trey had already taken off down the hall.

"We can't just leave them," Adan protested, running after him. Kelm stumbled along behind, half dazed.

Trey disappeared out of the prison before Adan could catch up. He either hadn't heard Adan, or he wasn't interested in saving the other prisoners. Either way, Adan had no choice but to run after him.

The thick metal door to the prison block lay twisted and broken on the ground just in front of the opening. The body of a guard lay behind the transparent wall in a bloody mess of shrapnel and charred metal. Adan quickly averted his eyes.

As he burst into the corridor outside the prison he caught sight of Trey sprinting up ahead. Adan flew after him, exceeding his breakneck pace so he could close the gap between them.

They sped by doors and intersections as the rumbling of the building droned on like a sort of primitive alarm system.

"Trey," Adan shouted when he was almost caught up. "What about Sierra and Tarn? We have to save them, too."

"Listen, Adan, the Collective is up there," Trey said between heaving breaths. "We're three floors below the surface and they've been hitting this building hard. We're going to get buried if we don't get out of here as fast as we can."

As if to confirm his point, the building shuddered again. A long metallic groan seeped through the ceiling, terminating in an ear-splitting crash somewhere behind them.

"I won't leave them behind," Adan said, slowing down. "If you want to get out yourself, that's fine, but I'm going to find them."

Trey hesitated, breaking stride.

"She saved your life," Adan reminded him.

"All right," Trey relented, shaking his head. "The guard I interrogated told me how to get to both prison blocks on this level so they must be in the other one. But if they're not there I can't help you."

The two of them shot off to the right, down a new corridor. The passage lighting cut in and out, the world tilting helter-skelter as they ran. The building shook again. A light mist of dust sprinkled down from the ceiling in front of them.

Trey pointed to a door like the one to Adan's cell block. "There. Just up ahead," he said.

Seeing the cell door, Adan suddenly remembered Kelm. In his race to catch up to Trey, he had forgotten all about his mentally unstable cellmate. Adan turned back to see if he was following them, but there was no sign of him. He wondered whether or not he had even left the prison.

"Kelm!" he shouted. "Kelm, where are you?"

Trey jerked Adan by his collar. "Forget about him. We're barely going to have enough time to save the others as it is."

Adan winced in frustration, wishing he had paid closer attention to Kelm. Given his mental state, there was no telling where he might have run off to. But as awful as Adan felt, he could not turn back now.

A ball of fire flashed from Trey's massive weapon, obliterating the prison door in front of them. The little that remained of it lay about the entrance in heaps of smoldering ashes.

A terrified shout came through the gaping hole and Trey pulled out an oscillathe from inside his coat. The crackling blast which burst from the gun, instantly silenced the cries. As Adan stepped through the mangled ruins of the entrance he saw the body of the Wayman guard under the wreckage of the front walls. He was still burning from the after effects of the explosion.

"Trey...you didn't have to..." Adan stared at his friend in disbelief.

"You wanted to get into this prison block, didn't you?" Trey snapped back. "Casualties are part of war, Adan. There was nothing I could do."

Perhaps Trey was right. But his words did nothing to dispel the sickening emptiness Adan felt inside.

"Come on!" Trey pointed at the row of cells. Clouds of white mist fogged up the clear walled chambers.

Fear for Sierra and Tarn washed away his other emotions. They bounded down the hallway, scanning the cells for any sign of their friends. The prisoners lay sprawled out on the cell floors or slumped up against the transparent walls. They failed to stir even amidst the rumbling and shaking.

The building trembled again. The ceiling buckled. Snapping sounds crackled through the structure above. The building had to be on the brink of collapse. Fear sapped Adan's strength, but he forced himself to keep moving.

As they reached the second to last pair of cells, Trey tapped him on the back and pointed to the one on their left. Tarn and Sierra lay huddled together against the transparent wall. Their eyes were closed and they were not moving.

"No!" Adan screamed, pounding his fists against the transparent wall.

"We're too late," Trey said. "They didn't make it."

SEVENTEEN
PRISON TRANSFER

"Sierra...no," Adan whispered. He sank down in front of the transparent wall. Not since he first awoke in the Institute, not since those long lonely days as a subject in the Collective's lab, had he felt this empty and alone.

"We should go," Trey said. "It's not safe here."

"No," Adan said, barely able to speak from emotion. "I won't leave them."

Trey grunted in frustration. "Do you want to throw your life away, too?"

Adan wondered how someone who had been so close to death could be so callous to it when it came to others. Adan stood resolutely and held out his hand.

"Give me one of your gloves," Adan ordered him.

"What? You'll release the gas out into the hallway if you cut through that wall. They're dead. Can't you see that?"

Adan grabbed at his hand, but Trey jerked it away.

"You're losing it."

"Give it to me or I will take it from you," Adan said bluntly, his nostrils flaring, every hair on his skin standing on end.

Trey flinched and Adan saw fear in his eyes. "Fine," he relented, exhaling deeply. "But let me do it. It will be faster that way."

Adan nodded and stepped away from the wall. The numbness consuming his feet crept up his legs.

Trey cut a hole in the wall, smaller than the one he'd made for Adan's cell. Gas poured into the hallway, eagerly lapping around Adan's feet, but he didn't care. He ducked through the opening while Trey backed away.

"Think about what you're doing, Adan," Trey pleaded. "We can still make it out if we leave now."

Adan ignored him and dragged Sierra's body out into the hall. The gas seeped into his lungs, covering them in its drowsy webs. His limbs, like enormous magnets, threatened to pull him to the floor. It took tremendous effort to keep them moving. As he pulled Tarn out into the hallway he nearly passed out, but the sound of Trey's voice yanked him back to his senses.

"Please, Adan," he begged. "This is pointless. You can't save them."

Up to that point Adan had been acting on pure emotion. Looking down at his friends, Trey's words finally sank in. What was he really hoping to accomplish? Did he intend to drag the corpses of both Tarn and Sierra through the maze of this crumbling building just so that their bodies would not have to be buried beneath this cruel Wayman city? What difference could that possibly make?

Numinae, please tell me what to do. I don't want to lose my friends—and Sierra, you know that she was much more than that...

As Adan opened his eyes from the prayer, he saw something that made him pause. He blinked, rubbed his eyes, and then he saw it again. Sierra's chest rose and fell ever so slightly. Joy surged through him. Sierra was alive. He was sure of it.

"Quick, Trey, give me some almamenth," Adan said.

Trey pulled a tube of the healing paste from his pouch and tossed it to Adan, but remained back where he was, away from the gas. Adan was amazed he had not passed out yet himself, but then again he had resisted the Waymen sopor pods as well.

He smeared the almamenth wildly, using far more than necessary. He quickly finished with Sierra and then jumped over to Tarn and did the same.

It only took a few moments for the healing agent to counteract the poisonous gas. Sierra and Tarn's eyes both opened and they sat up. They moved slowly, but appeared otherwise unharmed.

"What—?" Sierra began but then caught sight of Adan.

In that moment all was forgotten: the shaking building, the gas, the Collective attack, the fallen Waymen; Sierra was alive and all he could think about was the radiance streaming from her eyes. They had never looked more beautiful or so full of life.

I think I understand what love is now, he thought.

"Oh, Adan, you're alive," Sierra exclaimed, falling into his outstretched arms. As they embraced, the warmth inside his heart flooded his entire body. A wave of weakness rushed over him, nearly as strong as the effect from the gas.

"We should go," Trey's voice jarred him back to reality once again.

"Right."

"Trey?" Sierra stared at him, eyes blinking in disbelief. "Is that you? How did you find him, Adan?"

Trey shifted uncomfortably. Adan decided not to say anything about Trey wanting to abandon them. Trey had only been acting as any rational person would have in that situation. He thought their friends were dead and was trying to save Adan from a similar fate. If anything, Trey had been the one who acted wisely. Adan had been so swept up in his emotions he had been willing to risk both their lives. But sometimes Numinae honored the rash course of action, apparently.

"Trey found me, actually," Adan said. "But there's no time to explain. We need to get out of here. The Collective is attacking the city and this building isn't safe."

Tarn rose beside them, his face beaming at Trey. "So we are together again. I knew the wind would not carry you far. Lead the way."

Adan grabbed hold of Sierra's arm and Tarn hobbled along behind them. With the ceiling and walls still cracking and shaking, they hurried down the corridor and away from the smoking cell.

"Where will we go?" Sierra asked as they fled the prison. "Aren't there still Waymen here? And if we do manage to get outside, won't we get captured or killed by the Collective forces?"

"We're going to the praxis," Trey declared. "It's waiting for us just outside this complex."

"I thought the praxis was was going to stay outside of scanning range of the city," Adan said.

"When you didn't show up, they decided to come looking for you," Trey explained and then set off down the passageway before Adan could get anything more.

Adan didn't like the thought of the praxis flying into the middle of the fray just to save him, but he had to assume that Gavin would not risk the ship unnecessarily.

They raced through the hallways, the building rumbling and shifting all around them, until at last they came to a small door and slowed to a stop. Trey reached for the handle, but before he could open it, six Waymen appeared from around a corner right next to the door. Both groups hesitated, barely two steps between them. Trey pulled out his oscillathe, but Adan grabbed hold of his arm and yanked it down.

"Wait."

Trey bristled at the command, but the delay afforded the Waymen the opportunity to shout, "Get out of the way!" and plow past Trey through the small doorway.

"They're trying to escape, just like us," Adan said.

The appearance of these men reminded Adan of the reason he came to Hull in the first place. He wondered what had happened to the Welkin. Had the praxis come and saved them already? Had the escape attempt been foiled by Rak and the other Waymen? He thought about asking Trey, but now wasn't the time.

"Come on," Trey grabbed Adan by the arm, pulling him through the doorway.

The four of them plunged through the doorway. Inside they found a dimly lit ramp. The sounds of fleeing Waymen echoed down from higher up. Everyone sprinted after them, running circles around a central metal column. They fled upwards, the structure shuddering with each successive tremor. Locus pulser fire whistled through the air, growing louder the higher up they went.

As they reached the end of the ramp, Adan nearly collided into the Waymen in front of him who had come to an abrupt stop. Trey shouted at them, ordering them to get out of the way. Adan felt a twinge of fear, thinking that perhaps these men had decided to stand and fight after all. But his confusion passed, as did Trey's anger, as soon as it became apparent what was hindering them. The ramp had ended. There was nowhere else to go.

They stood on top of what was essentially an isolated platform in the midst of a swath of desolation. The building they were in, whatever it might have once been besides a prison, was a flattened mess. Gnarled metal beams and shattered rooms lay open to the sky. Tendrils of dust rose up from the wreckage, writhing as if in pain. The ramp stood above the remains of the building, a full floor higher than its surroundings. The ceiling had been ripped away and the walls, except on one section, were little more than stubs. The place where they were standing was small, maybe twenty paces across, but it gave Adan a perfect window from which to survey the devastation which had been inflicted on Hull.

In between pockets of dust clouds blanketing the city, dozens of ships flashed in and out of view. Most of the towers along the walls lay in ruins, though most of the buildings remained untouched. Only the prison building beneath them and the docking area for the Waymen ships had suffered any major damage. Not far away, like a giant metallic eye, the praxis hovered in the air just as Trey had promised.

Adan was about to ask Trey how he planned to get them onto the ship when someone tackled him from behind. At the same moment, the ramp shook with such force that Adan and whoever was on top of him went hurtling towards the edge.

The drop-off zoomed towards him, but Adan was helpless to halt his slide. He braced himself to fly over the edge, but when his feet hit the end of the ramp someone grabbed his collar and jerked him back. He looked back and saw Trey holding onto some sort of cable with one hand and with his other gripping Adan's collar.

As Adan scrambled back up the tilting platform, he saw that the one wall that was still intact had been cut in two. The Waymen were nowhere to be seen, gone along with the other half of the floor. Tarn and Sierra clung to the central column, unable to move. If they did, they would be joining Adan and

Trey at the edge of the platform and probably send everyone over the edge.

Two attack skiffs piloted by somatarchs circled back around and a pair of lancers converged on the shattered ramp from a different direction. But as the ships sped towards them, a small pocket of ballast cruisers and sand dusters broke through the dust clouds and opened fire. Though their yellow rays dissolved harmlessly into the shields of the Collective ships, the attack drew their attention away from the ramp. The Collective forces veered to meet the incoming threat. Two dusters were instantly shredded by yellow beams from the skiffs, the various sections scuttling into the wreckage below.

"We've got to get to ground," Trey cried out over the thunderous impacts of the ships.

The yawning gulf dangled beneath Adan's feet. They were four stories off the ground at least, and even had they been closer, there was nothing but jagged wreckage to land in.

"It's too far of a drop," he shot back, vertigo sloshing around inside his head like wet char in a bucket.

"Trust me. I'm going to let go," Trey said. The platform listed further in their direction. Metal groans from below told him the ramp was in its final moments. The structure swayed dizzily in the gusting wind.

"Wait, don't—we'll die if—" Adan began, but Sierra's scream swallowed up the rest of his words. She lost her grip and careened towards him.

"Adan, help! I can't stop!" she shouted. Tarn came sliding after her. They were heading straight for Trey and Adan and there was nothing they could do about it.

Trey didn't wait for the impact. He let go, sending himself and Adan plunging into the open air. The ramp gave a shuddering boom and tumbled after them, girders and beams reaching out for them like twisted metal fingers. If they didn't die from the fall they would certainly be killed from the building falling on top of them. But instead of falling along with the building, Adan's headlong plunge stalled out in midair. It felt like the air compressed around him, cradling him in its invisible grip. The building cascaded into the scrap heap below, burying itself in a burst of dust and flying shrapnel.

Though the wind was rushing around him, that alone could not have saved him. In fact, the winds did not seem to be affecting him at all. His body floated forward like the time he had been rescued out of the storm in Oasis. He was drifting straight towards the praxis.

His head darted in every direction, searching for what was keeping him aloft. Suddenly he recalled when he and Gavin had been rescued out of the neophosphorous flows in Manx Core. They had been lifted up into the praxis by the ship's axiom field. That must be what was happening now.

Trey glided beside him. Just behind them, Tarn and Sierra floated towards the ship as well, buoyed by the same invisible forces. Unlike the last time, they were not headed towards the underside of the ship and the cargo bay. Instead, they were being pulled toward a small opening about a quarter of the way up the side of the ship.

Adan spotted two lancers flying past the praxis. They must have been part of the Sentient forces because the cruiser wasn't firing on it. They headed off in the direction of the skiffs and lancers which had been circling the prison ramp. Those ships were now engaging a ballast cruiser. Flashing bursts of yellow and white lit up the rolling mass of dust clouds around them as the cruiser shot down a sand duster.

Moments later, the landscape of war and rushing winds disappeared as they were sucked up into the praxis. The opening closed behind them and they found themselves within the safety of the *Maven* once again.

They stood on a black disc at one end of a long room covered in metal paneling. Adan had hoped that someone might be there to greet them when they arrived, but he never expected the sight which met his eyes.

A dozen somatarchs stood in a semi-circle before them. Each held a silver oscillathe in its hand, the weapons trained on Adan's group. Adan's first thought was that the praxis must have been overrun. He started to connect his mind to the black disc beneath his feet, to force it to take them back outside the ship, but Trey's voice interrupted him.

"Don't bother trying to escape," Trey said, stepping off the platform. "You won't be leaving this ship anytime soon."

Unbelievably, he began walking towards the soulless somatarchs, who made no effort to attack or impede him in any way.

"Trey, no..." Sierra gasped.

Trey regarded her coldly, "Stay on the platform, Sierra. You'll be safe there."

A chill washed over Adan. "Trey, what's going on?" he demanded.

"I should have thought it was obvious," Trey replied. "You've been captured by the Collective. They have need of you."

Adan took a step forward. "But I don't understand. You're not one of them—"

Trey lifted a hand in warning. "Don't try anything, Adan. I know you're a memorant, but these somatarchs are outside of your control. Come quietly and no one will get hurt."

EIGHTEEN

ANOTHER EXPERIMENT

"Two faced swedge!" Tarn lurched forward, his fists clenched, but Adan grabbed him by the shoulder and pulled him back.

"Why, Trey?" Adan asked. "The Sentients saved your life. You've been with them from the beginning."

"No, not from the beginning," Sierra said. "He joined our cell a few days after the storm hit. He never did explain how he survived all that time on his own, but we were too busy fighting to give it much thought. We needed every person we could get."

"You'll see in time that it was for the best," Trey said. "The Admins only want to help."

"What happened to Raif and the rest of the ship?" Tarn demanded, straining against Adan's grip.

"This is the enemy's ship, Tarn," Adan said quietly. "They have one just like ours."

Trey eyed the Wayman cautiously, but there was no way they could take down that many somatarchs. Trey was right about them. These weren't the kind Adan could control. But maybe he didn't have to. With the miasma channel, he could connect to Trey's mind and control them through him.

Adan closed his eyes and reached out to Trey's mind, but the moment he did so crackling energy filled the air. He collapsed, along with Sierra and Tarn onto the black disc.

The room went blurry. Adan felt sure he was going under, but then he snapped back, fully awake. His limbs still tingled, but he didn't need to move. His mind was a more powerful weapon than his body.

He sought out Trey's mind again. Since no one in the Collective knew about the miasma channel he expected to seize control of him instantly, but instead he found nothing. Trey was blank, just like back in the prison. His bioseine had either been removed or shut down or...

Trey pulled up his sleeve, revealing the inhibitor he wore on his wrist, a black band with a small yellow chip in it.

"The Developer's aren't taking any chances with you this time," he said.

Adan wasn't close enough to use the miasma channel without bioseine augmentation. If he could get close enough though, he could access Trey's mind directly.

Warmth flooded into this limbs as the feeling returned. He started forward, but ran smack into a shimmering barrier of white light which burst into existence around the black disc, imprisoning Adan and his unconscious friends in a translucent bubble of locus energy.

"Like I said, not taking any chances," Trey said.

Still surrounded by the field of energy, the lev rose just up off the floor and whisked them down the corridor to the end of the hall.

He pounded against the wall of energy with his fists, but it was no use. He might as well have been banging against solid metal.

The platform soon left Trey and the somatarchs behind. The look of cold satisfaction on Trey's face was the last sight Adan had of him. Adan might have felt the sting of his betrayal more if this had been the first time a friend had turned on him. As it was, he could muster nothing beyond sadness and pity for him. He doubted Trey had much say in what he had done in any case. He was a part of the Collective. His thoughts and motivations were not truly his own.

Adan, Sierra, and Tarn passed through a doorway and into one of the access shafts. The platform shot upwards, ascending through the heart of the ship.

Adan took a deep breath and tried to collect himself. If only he still had his cutter gloves, he could cut through this barrier or at least revive his friends. All he could do now was watch while the mobile prison surrounding them careened upwards.

Moments later, the ascent stopped. The lev moved forward through another doorway and out into a hall. It spun to the left and then shot off down another passage. At the end of this, the disc finally stopped in front of a much wider doorway. After a brief wait the new doors slid silently open.

The lev floated into a large room with a rounded ceiling and walls that mirrored the shape of his lev prison. The disc transporting Adan glided to a stop in the center of the room, still encased in its glowing bubble of light.

"Greetings, Adan," came a voice from behind him.

Adan spun around to see Cyrith in a silver lab coat standing between himself and the doorway.

"Cyrith..." Just saying the name felt like an admission of defeat.

"You remember me," said the scientist in crisp, efficient tones. "Do your remember our conversation as well? I was thinking we could pick up where we left off."

Those words drained any hope Adan had of escape. The

last time Cyrith talked to him he had explained what would happen when they initialized Adan's bioseine for the first time.

He's going to erase my memory. No. I can't let that happen.

Adan's thoughts returned to the miasma channel. It hadn't worked on Trey, so it was even less likely to work on Cyrith, but he had to try. He focused in on the man before him. It only took a moment to confirm what he had already knew would be the case, there was nothing there.

"Your memorant abilities must be considerable," Cyrith remarked casually, as if he were commenting on the color of Adan's clothing or some other incidental detail. "We have learned that you are not to be underestimated. That is why I am speaking to you here as a projection. There is something unusual about you. And we intend to find out what that is."

"What are you going to do to me?" Adan asked, guessing the answer to the question before Cyrith replied.

"We will incorporate you back into the Collective, of course." Cyrith's expression was as dispassionate as his voice.

Adan tried to maintain his composure, but it was one thing to see something horrible coming, and quite another have the horror arrive. His stomach turned in knots.

The door to the chamber slid away and half a dozen somatarchs marched into the room, their white robes swaying mechanically in rhythm like a single, giant, multi-legged organism.

Adan swallowed hard and attempted to keep his voice from wavering. "Why did you send Trey after me? I thought Hull was what you wanted."

"Because you are a dangerous person, Adan," Cyrith said.

The somatarchs marched towards him.

"Why? What's so special about me?" Adan asked, his eyes strayed to the white robed figures coming his way.

Help me, Numinae, he pleaded.

"You are a memorant who has twice broken through our security and caused inconceivable damage to the Collective. There's something you know that we don't. A secret, Xander suspects. And we are not very tolerant of secrets in the Collective," Cyrith said, continuing with his clinical tone.

Adan tried not to think about what was about to happen to him, and about what would happen to Sierra and Tarn. It would be better not to know. He didn't think he could take it, even if Cyrith told him the truth.

The somatarchs fanned out around the sphere. Three of them pulled zoeliths from their belts, the silvery discs on the end of the stocky black instruments reflecting the multitude of lighted panels in the walls.

The energy barrier surrounding him faded, but the somatarchs made no move towards him, as if waiting for him to act first.

Whatever happens to me, please protect my friends, he prayed. *Especially Sierra. Don't let her forget.*

Cyrith's voice interrupted his prayer. "You will be fine once we restore you back to the baseline generational map. You will learn to thrive in our society. If you knew what was best for you, you would embrace the path before you."

"You can't just make people into what you want them to be. Forced salvation is no different than slavery," Adan said defiantly.

"You would choose freedom over life itself?" The slight lift in Cyrith's voice suggested that Adan's response had evoked some measure of actual curiosity.

"You can't treat people like this. I'm not just another experiment." Adan's lips began to quiver. He couldn't tell if he was about to scream or burst into tears.

Cyrith responded with an impassive stare.

Though Adan knew it was only a projection, he rushed

forward, charging the Developer as if he could wring an answer from the man's anemic throat.

"Tell me who I am!" he shouted.

The somatarchs rushed in around him and smothered him, ramming him into the floor and knocking the wind out of him.

As soon as he caught his breath, Adan screamed out, "Tell me!"

All possibility of discovering the answer vanished with the cold metal of the zoelith connecting to his forehead.

NINETEEN
ASSAULT ON HULL

The long, sleek citus dropped out of the underside of the *Maven* and into the swirling torrents of sand. Raif piloted the ship above while Cade and three other Sentients rode in the tunneler, held fast beneath the citus by its powerful axom field. Von, Jax, Conner, and Lan followed after them inside their lancers. Together the five ships which comprised Dreamer flight soon distanced themselves from the floating fortress from which they had emerged.

"Okay, dreamers, are we ready to crack this giant floating skull?" Raif asked over the ship's audio relay system. The ships flew in tight formation, close enough for mental communication, but they needed to use the audio to stay in contact with the *Maven*.

"We'll follow your lead for now," Von answered back.

"Just be sure not to get in range of the *Persepolis'* weapons until we give you the go," Jax said.

The warning was extremely premature. The *Persepolis* was nowhere in sight. But that was the way Jax liked to roll, everything squared and prepared. He was about as tight as a sonic screw, but Raif didn't let it bother him.

"I'll be glad when the *Maven* is the biggest cog in the machine," Raif said. "Then we'll put her through her paces and take her on a tour of the whole Vast. There's got to be more than just dunes and dust on this giant rock."

"Let's not get ahead of ourselves," Von cautioned. "This plan is hardly foolproof."

Raif shook his head inside the cockpit. Von was little better than Jax when it came to keeping up people's spirits, but Raif wasn't going to let those two get sand in his eye. All Dreamer flight had to do was keep the Collective ships and the *Persepolis* distracted long enough for Cade to get in, free the prisoners, and get out. And since they knew the prisoners' exact location from the chronotrace, that shouldn't take long. Add to that the fact that the Collective would be focused on attacking Hull and they had the element of surprise as well. All in all Raif felt fairly confident about their chances. And if the mission went sour, he had a few tricks up his sleeve.

Part of his confidence also came from the nimble little ship he was flying. Even weighed down with the tunneler, the citus was the fastest thing in the Sentient fleet. Though it could respond directly to his thoughts, he kept his hands on the manual controls because he liked the supple feel. He rode in one of the two pilot spots face down with his legs hugging the seat and kept his eyes focused on the view screen in front of him. The ship streaked across the desert, keeping low to the ground and kicking up scattershot dust clouds in its wake.

They flew in and out of sand storms, but the viewer gave Raif perfect visibility regardless of the conditions. It took them nearly a slice and a half before the outer walls of Hull came into view. There was no sign of battle in or around the

Wayman city, but they decided to circle around the edge just in case.

"All clear," Von said.

The ships finished the circuit and glided to a stop, hovering just above the dunes.

"Now we just sit back and wait for the fireworks to start," Raif said.

"I'm a little nervous," Cade confessed from down in the tunneler. He had access to his own view screen there.

"Just remember why we're here," Von told him.

The faces of Nance and the other captive Sentients flashed through Raif's thoughts.

"I'm a little nervous myself. But that's not such a bad thing. The bravest ones are those who admit their fears. You'll be fine." Raif said.

"*Maven*, we are in position," Von reported.

"I've got you on the screen, Dreamer flight. We're in position as well, three clicks behind you," Gavin answered from the Command Center on the praxis.

"I sure hope this works. We're only going to get one shot at this," Jax put in.

"We have the element of surprise," Gavin reminded them. "And that is not a small thing."

"We'll give those hardwires enough juice to jump their circuits," Raif said.

"Circuits?" asked Cade. "What's that, Raif?"

"Aw, it's just an expression. They used to use circuits on some of the vintage ships."

"You sure do use strange words."

"Picked them up from the esolace," Raif said. "I used to spend days off-loading old ship designs. I lost a lot of my memories, but for some reason those stuck."

"All right, enough chatter," Von said. "We need to stay alert. The Collective could show up at any moment."

Raif stifled a groan. Von could be such a zero sometimes. But there was no point in arguing. Keeping his eyes trained on the citus' view screen, he shifted in his seat and tried to get comfortable. Waiting was not one of his strong suits.

Twenty lancers appeared at the edge of the citus' sensors. Raif zoomed the view screen in on them to get a better look. They were flying in a ragged formation and at various altitudes, roughly three columns of ships in rows of six or seven, and they were coming in fast.

The *Maven* was too far back to detect them, so Von informed Gavin of their arrival.

"All right, then," Gavin's voice came in over the audio. "Fall back, until you get a visual of the *Persepolis*."

Based on the lancers' present rate of speed, they would reach Dreamer flight's position in less than two microslices. Since Raif had boosted the scanning range of their ships at the expense of some of their weapons systems, the Collective should not have spotted them yet. Dreamer flight moved off as far south as they could while still keeping the enemy ships in range.

Two microslices later the *Persepolis* appeared on Raif's sensors, coming in behind the lancers. Two hovland cruisers flanked the giant flagship. The wingspans of the hovlands were nearly a quarter the diameter of the praxis. A mix of lancers and attack skiffs, piloted by somatarchs, flew in front of them. Above those soared a formation of eight vapors.

"Flying oscillathes" was the nickname for this last set of ships, because that was the primary weapon they employed.

They had one purpose and one purpose only, to take human life. As deadly as they were, Raif could not suppress a wave of admiration at seeing this last group of ships. They were flat, silvery discs with a small, rounded compartment in the center for the crew. Wide, blade-like crescents extended from a central sphere along four separate arms, one in each direction. The vapors boasted omnidirectional flight capabilities and were second only to the citus' when it came to maneuverability and speed. What truly set the them apart, though, was their blinking capabilities. These let them perform particle shifts over short distances, usually not more than a few hundred spans, but the erratic nature of these jumps made them almost impossible to target, even with automated weapon tracking.

Hopefully they would be able to get Cade down onto the *Persepolis* without having to tangle with this new group of ships.

Raif whistled inside his cockpit, "Vapes. Not good. I was hoping those things got crushed in the quake."

"Wait for the Waymen forces to engage the *Persepolis*," Gavin reminded them. "We'll rendezvous on the far side of the city at the rally point for the Welkin after you've freed the Sentients."

"Hull doesn't stand a chance against that force," Jax said.

They watched in silence as the Collective forces closed in on the unsuspecting city. Not a single ship had lifted off from Hull. It looked like they had taken the Waymen completely by surprise. Raif hoped Dreamer flight would be able to give the Collective the same treatment. *But if Hull doesn't put up some kind of a fight, all the surprise in the world isn't going to help.*

Raif had almost died a dozen times since escaping the Collective's rigid technocracy. Despite that, the possibility of death wasn't something he thought all that much about. The thing he feared most was the kind of life he had lived in Oasis,

that numbness to anything beyond what the Admins wanted
him to think or feel, having every decision made for him to the
point that he didn't even know who he was anymore.
Compared to the possibility of going back to that, not much else
scared him, though the sight of the Collective fleet flying
unchecked over the dunes did start his foot tapping in nervous
anticipation.

The Collective forces descended on Hull hard and fast.
Though the hovland cruisers hung back with the *Persepolis*
about two clicks away, the rest of the ships drove relentlessly
onwards. Raif thought it strange that the hovlands didn't open
fire in advance of the attack. They certainly had the range, but
their weapons were designed to take out large targets like buildings and generators. Perhaps the Collective wanted to keep the
infrastructure of the city intact for some reason, though it
wasn't much to look at. Hull was the most cobbled together
excuse for a city Raif could imagine. The outer wall rose and
fell for no apparent reason. Half the buildings were unfinished.
And the ones that were looked more like failed art projects than
functional structures.

Just pitiful all the way around.

The lancer's disruptor beams knocked out the canons
mounted on the walls, striking unerringly against the stationary
targets, while the skiffs carved up the guard towers, toppling
them with their glowing locus beams. Around the edges of the
city, the vapors hung back, blanketing the buildings with
evanescence pulses. Though the attacks were invisible to the
naked eye, the *Maven's* targeting systems tracked them and
projected shimmering facsimiles onto the view screens and
targeting maps within Dreamer flight's ships. The pulses
passed straight through the walls, detonating inside and causing
no damage to the structures, but disintegrating anyone within

the radius of the burst, like dozens of oscillathes being fired at once.

Raif bit his lip. *Char-buckets. Firing on defenseless people.* He wanted so badly to see the Collective melting in a hot pot at that moment. But five ships and a tunneler wasn't going to cut it. *Come on, fight back,* he silently urged the Waymen.

Collective ships were racing through every part of the city by the time Hull mustered any kind of response. The yellow locus canons from the eastern wall opened up and returned fire on the lancers and skiffs. Most of the shots missed their mark, landing well wide of the fast moving vanguard, but even the ones that hit dissipated harmlessly into shards of fragmented light, absorbed by the Collective shields.

On the northern side of the city, the one furthest from where Raif and Von were positioned, three ballast cruisers and a dozen sovos ships took to the air in defense of Hull. They had barely risen above the walls when several lancers peeled off to engage them.

The triangular lancers focused their fire on the smaller ships, disabling two of the sand dusters before they could get in position to return fire. Meanwhile the skiffs targeted one of the thick ballast cruisers, slicing off the end of it and carving up several of its guns. The weapons that remained intact managed to return feeble fire, but again to no avail. The ships they were up against had shields and they did not, and they were outnumbered three to one; it was a losing fight from the start. More dusters came in support, but the skiffs shredded the new arrivals into shrapnel pinwheels, sending them spinning apart in all directions.

Raif's mind churned helplessly. *This is worse than I thought.*

He kept waiting for the *Persepolis* to enter the fray, but it sat back at a comfortable distance, flanked by the motionless hovlands. Raif now realized the fatal weakness in Gavin's plan. If Hull didn't mount some sort of meaningful resistance, enough so that the praxis would be forced to get involved, they would never be able to pull off the rescue.

"We've got to do something," Von said. "The Waymen are getting carved to pieces."

Von's words were met by an uncomfortable silence. Raif fingered his two control sticks anxiously, deciding if it was time to flip the script on their plan. He loved improvising and prided himself on his ability to think on his feet, but for once, he hesitated. Would the little surprise he had whipped up even work?

"All right, men. This is your time," came Gavin's unexpected, but heartening voice over the audio system. "Target the hovlands. The *Persepolis* is invulnerable to your ships' weapons, but that might draw their attention away from Raif. The mission is a go."

"Now you're talking," Raif said, grateful that no one questioned the order. "Let's get this fire started." He didn't think they had any real chance of success, but he was getting sick to his stomach watching the Collective lay into this helpless city. He squeezed the control sticks tight and adrenaline rushed through him as their ships surged forward.

Von took the lead, the four lancers flying in a tight line. Raif's citus brought up the rear. Von sent out an attack plan mentally, each ship passing it to the next in turn.

Attack from above. The hovlands have no countermeasures against overhead attacks. All they will have is their shields. The praxis will have fewer weapons to target us as well if we keep on its topside. It will take longer to bring them down, but this fight is not about winning. It's about getting Raif and Cade the time they need to locate the prisoners and get them out.

The plan had barely been communicated when Raif spotted several ships issuing forth from the cargo bay beneath the *Persepolis*. Though he was flying in the back of the formation, because of the way his viewer worked, the rest of the Dreamer flight ships were nothing more than faint outlines on the screen.

Eight new ships appeared, each one a sleek, silver vapor. They did not set out to join the other ships attacking the city. Instead, they headed straight for Dreamer flight.

"They've spotted us," Von said.

"Or they knew we were coming all along," Jax said hotly. "There are too many of them. This is a trap. We need to call this off."

"We can't. If we flee, they'll chase us back to the *Maven* and then we'll put everyone at risk." Von said.

"And we can't outrun them," Raif said. "At least you can't."

Jax growled derisively. "Then let's scatter. Let them chase us half way across the Vast if they want to, but this is suicide."

"Did you hear what Raif said?" Von replied. "We can't outrun—"

"I want to save them as much as anybody, but I know when I'm outmatched," Jax shouted back.

Raif listened in stunned silence. For a while no one said anything. But the vapors kept coming. Then Gavin's voice came in over the audio.

"Abort the mission, Dreamer flight. I repeat, abort," he said breathlessly. "Return to the *Maven*. The mission is off. "

TWENTY

THE MENDAX GENERATOR

The ships from Dreamer flight scattered, swiveling in place and jetting off in the opposite direction. In the time it took for Gavin to relay his order and for Raif's group to work their way back up to maximum velocity, the vapors had already closed a quarter of the distance between them.

"Gavin, are you sure about this? If we head back, they'll follow us right to you." Von said.

"That is a risk I'm willing to take," Gavin responded from the Command Center. "I am not going to lose another five Sentients today if I don't have to."

"But there might not be another day," Raif was not on board with Gavin's decision. It seemed rash for someone who was usually so level headed. Then again, military decisions weren't exactly his thing.

"It doesn't matter either way," Jax said. "There's no way we can outrun them."

"We stick to the plan, even when the plan changes," Von said. "We all heard Gavin's order. End of discussion."

In the ensuing silence, the vapors continued gaining on

them. Despite Von's fine words, Gavin's order still didn't sit right with Raif. They were going to get caught by these ships. Gavin had to know that. And though the *Maven* could probably handle the vapors, once its location was discovered that would put everyone at risk.

Raif swerved his ship back around, nearly swiping Von's lancer as he zoomed by. He respected Gavin, but following orders wasn't really his forte. It hadn't worked out all that well when he was part of the Collective and he didn't see it turning out much better this time around.

"Raif—what in the Vast are you doing?" Von exclaimed. "Is your ship malfunctioning?"

"Just the opposite," Raif said as the citus streaked towards the oncoming vapors. "She's humming right along."

"Well then, do you mind telling me what's going on?"

Raif checked the vapor's position on the view screen, getting ready to time his jump. "Jax is right. We can't outrun these ships. So I'm heading for the *Persepolis* on my own. There's still a chance to salvage this mission."

"Raif, your ship doesn't even have any weapons," Von fired back.

"Who needs weapons when you can fly like I do?" Raif chuckled with false bravado.

"Hey, Raif, care to fill us in down here?" Cade piped up from below.

"I'm heading back, Cade. I can take the tunneler in myself if you don't want to do this. I'll drop you off in the desert and you can hunker down in the dunes until everything blows over."

"Like that would work," Cade's comment was followed by low chatter from the rest of the team in the tunneler.

Cade was right. The idea had sounded a lot better in Raif's head.

"We discussed it and we're all in down here," Cade came back. "We knew what we were signing up for when we got on board. We're with you."

"Raif," Gavin called in from the *Maven*, "Turn the citus back around and scatter. You cannot take on the *Persepolis* alone."

"Gavin, in case you've forgotten, if Sierra hadn't pulled off something like this, you'd still be gurgling blue soup. Trust me. I know what I'm doing. The *Persepolis* is as blind as a beta-tester when it's got ships up close."

"The *Persepolis* may lack close range weapons, but it's surrounded by ships that don't. And this time there won't be any collapsing cave to keep them off you," Gavin warned.

"You may be right and I may be crazy, but I've got to do this," Raif said. He checked the view screen again. The vapors were almost within firing range. There was no more time for debate. "Raif out," he said, killing the in-ship audio. He didn't need the distraction.

"I trust you," Cade's thoughts came into Raif's mind from the tunneler. *"But I'd trust you even more if I knew what you had in mind."*

"Hold on. First I've got a little jape for these vapes."

Raif reached inside a pouch at his waist. Once he had what he was hunting for, he opened the window on his left with a mental command.

I sure hope this works, he thought as he flicked one of several small metal spheres out the window. The tiny bead buried itself in the desert sand below. The little device was a mendax generator. He had come up with the idea for them back when he was in Oasis, but he'd never thought it would work until he got hold of the chronotrace. Studying the way Gavin's invention could project events had opened up all sorts of new possibilities, but this was the only one he'd had time to implement. He threw it in with his gear on a whim and it looked like now was as good a time as any for that field test he'd been planning.

He engaged the citus' after-burst and shot above the vapor formation almost as fast as blinking. The *Persepolis* came up on the view screen like a giant rock hurtling straight at him. He checked the citus' energy well as the ship slowed back down to normal flight speed. After what happened in Manx Core, he wanted to make sure that the ship would have enough fuel for two after-bursts. Looking at the levels, it still had plenty left.

Raif timed the burst so that he came out hovering just above the *Persepolis*, but he the little present he'd left for the vapors in the form of an exact duplicate of his ship was still flying back behind him, on a course straight for Hull. He held his breath, waiting for it to flicker out or give itself away, but the projection held together, gliding above the dunes as if it were a real ship with a real pilot. It even left sand sprays in its wake.

Raif engaged the audio again, trying to contain his giddiness. There was still plenty of time for the generator to fail. "Von, that's not my ship back there, just so you know. I'm flying over the *Persepolis*. Hopefully those vapes will follow the decoy and give you time to vanish."

"Raif—what are you talking about?" came Von's sharp reply.

The first of the evanescence pulses launched from the vapors at the false citus. The copy, also hauling the tunneler and looking every bit a perfect copy of Raif's ship, banked hard to the right, managing to dodge them. Traveling along its new course, it offered the vapors a tantalizing shot at its flank.

"It's just a projection. I modified our sensors so that we can tell the difference," Raif explained. "The citus that just dodged the vapors is a fake." He didn't have time for anything more. Von was a smart guy. He'd figure it out. Raif cut off the audio again before Gavin could jump in and tempt him back to sanity.

"*I think I'm starting to get the picture,*" came Cade's thoughts. "*Do you really think you'll be able to last long enough for me to get in and out with the prisoners? Dodging those vapors was a clever trick, but those aren't the only ships in the fleet.*"

The citus descended towards the top of the massive enemy flagship. With perfect precision, Raif eased the tunneler down onto its surface and released it.

"*Don't you worry, I can bob and weave around this giant ball bearing for an eternity and then some. I'll be here when you get out.*"

Raif could tell Cade didn't have the greatest confidence in the plan, but an understanding passed between them. There was no turning back now.

"*Cade, if something does happen to me,*" Raif added, "*use the altitude capsules and try to escape on foot, okay?*"

"*Right.*"

Raif knew that if it came to that, they wouldn't make it, but it didn't matter. For now they had the tunneler and the citus. Mathematically, they still had a chance.

Cade engaged the cross stream cone as the citus pulled away. The blue energy flared brightly, reflecting off the multi-faceted hull in a hundred places. The tunneler dipped forward, boring into the velar sheathed outer shell.

At the same time the praxis, as if irritated by a tiny creature attempting to scratch its way into its skin, began to move.

"Why is the praxis advancing on the city?" Von asked over the audio. "Is Hull finally starting to put up some kind of resistance?"

Gavin scanned the section of the view screen trained on Hull. Half a dozen ballast cruisers lumbered through the air accompanied by about twice as many of the smaller sovos, but they had yet to down a single Collective ship. Worse, without shields the Collective was ripping them to shreds almost as soon as they lifted off. Half their fleet was gone already.

The *Maven* was nearing the pickup location for the Werin. They may have lost their chance at rescuing the Sentients, but he hoped the forces of Hull would hold out at least long enough to let the prisoners get free.

"From where we are the Collective doesn't look like it's having any trouble," Gavin reported.

He shifted his attention back to the tactical map inside his mind. The praxis continued closing in on the city, leaving the hovland cruisers behind. He could only assume the reason for the *Persepolis'* advance would eventually become clear. In the meantime, Von's group was fleeing and Raif's ship had suddenly duplicated itself. Everything was falling apart. Gavin knew that the plan had been risky, but he never expected things to go this wrong this fast.

The vapors were close to being within firing range of Dreamer flight. Two of them had peeled off to engage Raif's projection, but the other six were still bearing down on the main group. Gavin had hoped they would abandon their pursuit and return to the main battle at Hull, but Raif was right. They were going to overtake Von and the others. It was only a matter of time.

"I'm sorry I sent all of you into of this," Gavin said. The weight of his decision fell heavy upon him. He tried desperately to think of a way out, but all of his abilities as a memorant and a scientist were useless in this situation. He couldn't bend reality to his will or go back and change the past.

"With all due respect, Gavin," Von said, "We're not dead yet. We may still get out of this."

I should have waited, thought this through, Gavin told himself.

"The vapors are pulling back," Jax broke in. "And six—no eight lancers just came out of nowhere. They're advancing on the *Persepolis* along with Raif's extra...whatever that ship is."

"Yes!" Von let out a cheer that echoed across the channel from the other pilots.

Gavin could hardly believe how quickly things had turned.

The vapors banked and turned to set course for the *Persepolis*. Were they heading off this new threat to the praxis? But where did the lancers come from? The Waymen had no ships like that as far as he knew. Then it hit him. Raif had said his citus was an illusion, some sort of projection which appeared, both to the naked eye and to scanning technology, to be an actual ship. The lancers must be projections as well.

"Those are Raif's aren't they?" Von arrived at the same conclusion.

"He's full of surprises today," Gavin said.

"Typical Raif. But I doubt those illusions will fool them for long. Permission to resume the mission."

Gavin hesitated, knowing he would be risking these men's lives all over again. But Von was right. Once the Collective saw through the projections, those vapors would be breathing down Raif's neck. And the *Persepolis* was finally heading to Hull. They just might have a chance.

"Permission granted. Engage the enemy, Dreamer flight. Give Raif and Cade the time they need."

Gavin watched Von's ships on a tactical map on one of the view screens as they doubled back and reformed. The vapors, besides being faster ships, already had a significant head start on them and quickly closed the distance to the *Persepolis*. The phantom lancers swarming the praxis reacted with amazing skill, pivoting and darting behind the *Persepolis* to get out of the vapors' line of fire.

Pursuing their targets, the vapors flew straight at the Collective flagship as if they meant to ram it. But just before crashing into the praxis' velar carapace, the dots on the map disappeared and reappeared again on the other side, sending the unsuspecting lancers scattering in response. Pulses from the vapors bloomed on the tactical map in the aftermath, peppering the lancers with a deadly bouquet of evanescence. The bursts swallowed four of the phantoms and partially hit two more. Since shields were useless against oscillathes, the four lancers inside the blast waves plummeted to the sand, maintaining the ruse that they were piloted by actual men who had been killed in the blasts. The rest of the phantom ships continued to zip around the *Persepolis* like particles in orbit, dispersing in every direction to avoid getting caught in a cluster again. The vapors, still taking the bait, flared out in pursuit.

Though only four of the phantom ships had "survived" the vapors' attack, the distraction bought Dreamer flight enough time to get within firing range. And unlike the fake ships, their lancers had actual weapons to fight back.

"All right, Dreamers," came Von's voice over the audio. "Let's see if we can't clear the skies a little."

The Dreamers targeted the two vapors that were closest. Gavin saw the disruptor fire of the lancers across the tactical map. Two of the four shots connected. Though they failed to bring down either of the vapors, an orange-yellow circle appeared around the outside of the vapor's dots on the tactical map indicating that their shields were damaged. One or two more hits and their shields would be gone. That was the one weakness of the vapors. So much of their energy was devoted to their oscillathe cannons and their blinking capabilities that their shields were almost nonexistent.

In the midst of the tense engagement, Cade's voice blasted across the audio, "The prisoners are not at the specified location, *Maven*. We've been ambushed by somatarchs. Attempting to flee—" Then the audio went silent.

A stillness settled over the Command Center.

"I'm going in after him, Gavin," Raif said, breaking the silence.

"No, Raif, you have no chance by yourself," Gavin shot back.

"You're not controlling my ship or my mind, Gav," Raif said testily. "Just fire up the chronotrace and find out where they moved the prisoners to or this is going to be another one way trip. I'll hit you up again when I'm inside."

"Raif, you can't—" Gavin began, but Raif had already disconnected from the channel.

Gavin sighed, wondering how Raif could be so intelligent and foolhardy at the same time. Then he remembered that his own plans didn't always turn out as expected either.

Raif might be a loose canon, but Gavin couldn't let him run around blind inside the *Persepolis*. Using the *Maven's* esolace, he connected his mind to the chronotrace inside the lab and interrupted the current sequence it was running. He restarted it on a new trace, using an archived sequence from a little over a day ago as the starting point. He set Cyrith as the focus. He had been experimenting with thought and speech filters on the device and set the machine to alert him of any reference to the captured Sentients in the Developer's thoughts or conversation.

"Lan, you've got three vapors bearing down on you, pull up," Von warned over the audio channel, jerking Gavin's thoughts back to the battle.

The tactical map flipped into Gavin's mind just in time to

see Lan's ship caught in a trio of evanescence bursts. The next moment, his lancer stalled and went crashing to the ground. The green dot representing his ship disappeared from the map.

"Blanks," Jax cursed under his breath.

"Keep it together," Gavin said, but his words came out as if by rote. He had known that men would likely die on this mission, but the suddenness of Lan's death still struck him like a blow to the face.

"Stay on the offensive," Von urged, his voice steady. "Jax, Conner, follow my lead. Attack my target on my signal. Let's make Lan's death count for something."

"Got it," Jax said, his voice even stonier than Von's.

Conner muttered a hurried, "Okay."

Von's ship shot up above the nearest vapor and Jax and Conner flared out to either side of it.

"Now!" Von ordered.

Only two of their shots connected, but that was all it took to erase the ship's shields. A red circle started flashing around the vapor's dot on the tactical map. One more hit might have finished it, but the ship blinked away before they could get off another shot.

"He jumped. Argh!" Jax howled in anger.

"He came out under the *Persepolis*," Conner reported. "I've got a visual."

"Quick, before his phase engine has a chance to recharge. He's only vulnerable for a short time," Von spurred them on.

Von's ship pivoted to follow the dot representing the vapor. It zipped beneath the praxis and popped out the other side, catching one of the phantom lancers by surprise. The elusive vapor brought the projection down with a single pinpoint shot.

Jax and Conner dodged the blasts of several more vapors as they sped around the sides in pursuit of one of the enemy ships. Von nearly collided with one of them when he came tearing around the edge. The near collision forced him to veer off course and ruined any chance at getting off a shot. Jax got the drop on it, though, emerging around the side just in time to peg it dead center with a disruptor beam. The vapor went spiraling off course and crashed into the sand.

"Finally!" Conner cheered, but his celebration was short lived.

Four vapors blinked into existence near his ship. He had no way of avoiding the combined fire which smothered the airspace around his lancer.

No one said anything as Conner's empty ship plummeted to the ground. Gavin's stomach turned. He wanted to look away from the view screen, but knew the others needed him to stay focused on the battle.

It was not supposed to be like this. Where was the counterattack from Hull?

Heavy breathing filled the audio channel for the next few moments. The remaining two lancers dodged and swerved through the crowded airspace, avoiding the evanescence clusters, the vapors, and the praxis. All but one of the phantoms went down in quick succession, leaving the lone projection and what was left of Dreamer flight to harry the seven remaining vapors.

Gavin was tempted to order another retreat. Cade's group was lost and probably Raif gone along with him. He couldn't see any way to salvage this mission.

At that moment an alert from the chronotrace came through via the esolace.

Location of the prisoners discovered. Level 3, Cell block C.

"Raif, I found the prisoners," Gavin reported over the audio, but there was no response. "Raif, connect your audio, you fool," he muttered, striking the railing he was standing next to. The other crew in the Command Center, whom he had all but forgotten, stared at him momentarily before returning to monitor the view screen and flight controls.

"Raif, this is the *Maven*—" Gavin tried again. This time Raif cut in.

"Okay, Gavin, you better have what I need, because this ship is hotter than a glide engine after a test run. I've got hollow men crawling all over me."

"Raif!" Gavin shouted breathlessly. "I've got the location. They're on Level 3, Cell block C."

"No way," Raif fired back in astonishment. "I'm on Level 4 right now. I'll be there in a microslice."

"Excellent. Be careful, Raif," Gavin told him, his tortured stomach spinning like a vortex.

"We'll buy him the time he needs," Von promised.

"I know you will," said Gavin.

There was still little chance of success, but Gavin took courage from Von's resolve in the face of such overwhelming odds.

Even as hope began welling up inside him, Gavin felt like they were still missing something. He knew he should pay attention to the tactical map and give whatever support he could to Jax and Von, but something was nagging him at the back of his mind. His plan had been risky, but almost every thing which could have gone wrong had. He may not have been the greatest military mind in the Vast, but he wondered if something else was going on.

On a hunch, he connected his mind to the chronotrace and pulled up the sequence depicting the information about the transfer of the prisoners which the device had just uncovered. He closed his eyes, the scene flashing through his mind. As the sequence played out inside his head, his stomach kept on churning.

TWENTY-ONE

THE TRAITOR'S SEQUENCE

CYRITH STOOD WITH XANDER IN ONE OF THE *PERSEPOLIS'* sick bay units. The walls were lined with the same metal paneling as the rest of the ship, but with a raised ceiling to accommodate the equipment stored above the operating tables. Motionless bodies occupied two of the tables, thick polymeric straps holding them in place. Their brown hair and pale complexions were identical to that of the two Developers present except for the bluish tint to their skin. They were fresh from the vault.

An articulator, a monstrously large, bulbous device hung from the ceiling over each of the patients. One of them had been lowered over the table where Xander and Cyrith stood. They were busy manipulating the articulator's multiple, serpentine appendages with their minds, making countless incisions into the body prostrate before them. It was another remapping procedure, one they had performed countless times before.

The body jerked, betraying the fact that the motionless figure was still alive. Perhaps the subject was dimly aware at some level of the fact that the two Developers were recreating his identity with every puncture, slice, and slit.

The cables and instruments the scientists were using to restructure the patient's memories stopped abruptly in the middle of their writhing. One of the machine's impossibly slender blades hovered next to the patient's neck, reminiscent of a proboscis belonging to some giant metallic insect.

Ship incoming, came a message from the Command Center to the two men present. *It's an attack skiff.*

Cyrith took in a shallow breath, what passed for exasperation in the subdued scientist.

This is why we had a team of Developers, to deal with trivialities like this. He was about to answer with a suitable remark, something to the effect that he had full confidence the personnel running the Command Center could handle the situation, when he remembered something of vital importance: the infiltrators. Perhaps one of them had survived the quakes. Or it could have even been Malthus.

When the ship is in range give me a visual of the pilot, Cyrith instructed.

Certainly, came the response from Com.

The operation resumed silently, but lasted only about a microslice longer before the instruments paused again in the midst of their coordinated frenzy.

A mental image of the incoming skiff appeared in Cyrith's mind. It was piloted by a single man dressed in desert gear like one of the andros.

Get me an iris scan, Cyrith ordered.

Half a moment later, the information from Com came streaming into his mind. *Collective member 24602.*

Excellent, Cyrith replied. *One of the infiltrators made it after all.*

He opened his eyes and directed his thoughts towards

Xander. "*I know it will take you more time without me, but you'll have to finish this one alone. I have an urgent matter to attend to.*"

"*I understand,*" Xander responded.

The articulator gracefully resumed its sinuous ministrations under Xander's direction. Cyrith walked through the sliding door and made his way towards the cargo bay. Strictly speaking, he did not need to go meet the new arrival in person, but he preferred to communicate one on one over a private channel. With the security breaches of late, they could not take too many precautions. As he walked, Cyrith contemplated how it was that they had let the rogue memorant escape not once, but twice from the Collective's facilities. Either Malthus, the former chief of security, had been slipping or this memorant was more dangerous than anyone realized. Having worked with Malthus for many years, Cyrith was inclined to believe the latter. Hopefully this visit would shed some light on that problem.

Cyrith arrived at the precise moment in which the cargo bay doors in the floor opened up to allow the attack skiff to rise and enter into the heart of the praxis. Navigating its way to an open spot amongst the other skiffs, vapors, lancers, and levs, the small ship set down gently. The pilot stepped off and proceeded to march briskly in Cyrith's direction.

"*What do you have to report, Trey?*" Cyrith began as soon as he got in range to communicate over a private channel. Malthus would have reprimanded him for his long absence in making contact, but Cyrith did not stand on protocol. All he cared about was whether Trey's time with the deviants had yielded any sort of useful information.

"*One hundred and fifteen Sentients are alive and in command of the praxis* Maven," Trey responded. His clothes were covered in sand and ripped in several places, but his bioseine indicated that he was uninjured.

"Am I to take it then that Malthus is dead? Or has he joined their side?" came Cyrith's pedestrian reply, as if the possession of a massive warship by their enemy were a relatively inconsequential matter.

"Malthus committed suicide," Trey answered, his thoughts likewise betraying little emotion.

"And the attack on Manx Core—do you have any information as to how they were able to free the prisoners? We lost a lot of subjects who were slated for remapping in that attack."

Trey allowed Cyrith to access all of the information he had been able to glean about the attack from Gavin, Adan, and the other Sentients in the aftermath of what had happened in the Core. In this way Cyrith quickly learned about their plan to board the *Persepolis* and rescue the other prisoners. Most interesting of all, he discovered the means by which Gavin had been spying on them all this time.

"The Chronotrace. So it actually works. And why were you not able to warn us of the deviants' plans to free the prisoners from Manx Core, seeing as it was your cell which initiated the incursion?" Cyrith asked, still contemplating the implications of what he had just learned.

"I was injured in one of the quakes. I was in a coma when they infiltrated the Core," Trey answered apologetically.

Cyrith stared out across the array of assembled ships in the bay. He was not overly alarmed at Malthus' death, or even by the destruction of Manx Core. He was a realist. He could move on and so would the Collective. What truly concerned him was this memorant called Adan. Letting him escape so that they could track down Gavin had turned out to be one of the Developers' more costly mistakes.

"You did well to find a way to escape without them realizing it. Now that we know their plans, they will be easy enough to counter. But your work with the deviants is not entirely complete. I want you to go back to them. Find Adan and bring him back to me. Since they're sending him on a mission into the Wayman city, we'll bring the Persepolis *into Hull during the attack and you will persuade him to come on board."*

"That shouldn't be a problem. I will leave at once."

Without so much as a good-bye or nod of the head, Trey returned to the skiff and it floated back through the opening by which it came.

Cyrith connected his mind back to the *Persepolis'* esolace and sought out the new Assessor Primary. *"Prestin, we need to move the prisoners. Put them on Level 3, Cell C. We may be having some visitors on board soon and we wouldn't want to make it too easy for our guests to find them."*

Gavin looked around the Command Center in disbelief.

So Trey had been an agent for the Collective. How had he missed this? Was he slipping as a memorant? No, he had simply been too busy to notice.

He stared out over the other Sentients piloting and monitoring the *Maven* inside the Command Center and he had to wonder. How many of them plants from the Developers as well?

He did not have time to delve into their thoughts to find out. The trace he had witnessed was nearly a day old. If the *Persepolis* reached Hull, Adan was as good as dead.

"Raif, do you have the prisoners yet?" Gavin asked, pacing aimlessly up and down the ramp near the exit to the Command Center.

"Almost," Raif informed him in hushed tones. "I took out the guards with a contingency trigger and now I'm cutting my way into the cell block. I'll let you know as soon as I've got Nance and the others in hand."

"Excellent..." Gavin wasn't sure he wanted to tell Raif about what he had just discovered. Raif had already made enough rash decisions for one day. Gavin didn't want him running off to look for Adan as well.

He focused in on the tactical map. The *Persepolis* was not a fast ship, but it was already within half a click of Hull's western wall.

"Gavin," Halerin's mental presence slipped into his thoughts. He stood on the opposite side of the Command Center, deeply absorbed in a scene from one of the view screens. *"We've got a visual of some of the first Werin prisoners fleeing the city."*

Gavin's gaze flitted to the screen. There, a few tiny figures were emerging on the outskirts of Hull.

"Good. Put our last two ships on standby in case they need to run interference in that area if any of the forces from Hull decide to stop them," he answered. Normally he would have been elated to see the bedraggled Werin staggering across the sand, but he was too worried about Adan at that moment.

"Gavin, I've got Nance and the prisoners," Raif said, his voice bubbling with excitement. "Cade's group wasn't there, though. You don't think the somatarch's killed them, do you?"

"I doubt it. The Devs don't usually kill Collectives unless they have to," Gavin said. "Now listen to me, Raif. Go ahead and get those prisoners on board the tunneler. Von will provide you cover so you can after-burst out of there."

"I'm not leaving without Cade," Raif told him.

Gavin sighed. Nothing was ever easy with this man.

"Fine. But at least wait to go back for Cade until after you get the others to safety. We'll look for them in the chronotrace while you are helping the prisoners."

"Right," Raif agreed.

Gavin turned his attention to the visual of the cargo bay on one of the screens. The pilots Halerin had ordered to oversee the rescue operation were mounting up to head out.

"*Wait,*" Gavin told one of the pilots through the esolace. "*Seth, I'm going to need you to take me into the city.*"

"*But what about the refugees?*" Seth replied.

"*Arn will have to fly this mission on his own. There are other people in the city who need our help.*"

Seth offered no further resistance, mounting his skiff and waiting for Gavin to arrive.

"*What's going on?*" Halerin asked, his thoughts disoriented by the sudden change in plans.

"*I'm going to help a friend,*" Gavin declared.

Halerin strode over to stand in front of him.

"*You can't go out there, Gavin. We need you here on the* Maven."

Gavin cast the image of the *Persepolis* closing in on the city into Halerin's mind. "*Adan failed to contact us at the agreed upon time. I have reason to believe that he might be on that ship. He saved me twice before. I have to find him.*"

"*How do you know this?*" Halerin asked.

"*The chronotrace. Check the logs if you want to see what I saw,*" Gavin replied. "*I have to go. Use the chronotrace to find Cade and relay the information to Raif.*"

"*But Raif's already on the ship—why don't you send him to look for Adan?*"

"*There's not enough time for him to do two more rescue missions. As it is he will be lucky to get off that ship alive,*" Gavin answered, already heading up the ramp. "*If I'm not back by the time you've rescued the Werin, take off without me.*"

"I still don't think this is a good idea," Halerin replied.

"Well, Raif isn't the only one capable of making rash decisions."

TWENTY-TWO
MAVEN OUT

Though Gavin no longer had access to the tactical map, the *Persepolis* was too large to miss as it closed in on the beleaguered city of Hull. Seth piloted their tiny skiff across the desert straight for it.

The wind blustering across the skiff drowned out all other noises, but the silver extractor Gavin wore around his neck projected the chatter from the Sentient's audio channel straight into his mind.

"Dreamer flight, you've got a large ship heading your way," Halerin warned, pulling Gavin's attention away from the *Persepolis* to a new ship rising up on the western side of the city. "It looks like it's from Hull. We certainly never saw anything like this in Manx Core."

"I've got a visual," Jax replied. "Looks like a...what in the— is that a gendarm?"

"That's what it's coming up as on the *Maven's* sensors," Halerin reported.

If the ship was part of the Wayman fleet it was certainly the largest vessel they had. It was about a third of the length of the praxis, though much narrower. It had a flattened, pill-shaped body encased in bronze colored metal plating. More importantly, if it really was a gendarm, it would have two layers of invisible shielding surrounding its chassis. A ship of this class was designed for running blockades, surviving by diverting half the ship's energy to shields, and most of the rest to the thrusters. These ships typically had only a smattering of weapons, but they were strong enough to make it past more heavily armed ships. As soon as it cleared the buildings, it pivoted and headed off in the direction of the *Persepolis*.

"The vapors are pulling off us, now," Von observed. "I think that new ship has their attention."

The vapors swarmed in front of the *Persepolis*, reforming for an attack vector on the gendarm. At the same time, the praxis opened fire on the new ship.

The skyline of Hull lit up with the yellow locus pulses and white disruptor fire that pelted the newly launched ship. The gendarm managed to dodge a few of the strikes while the rest dissipated into its shields, causing no visible damage, but this was only the opening salvo. The *Persepolis* was just getting warmed up.

"Stay close to the praxis if you can," Halerin ordered. "Raif should be coming topside any moment. You need to make sure the prisoners get off without any trouble."

"I'm one step ahead of you," Raif chimed in. "We're coming up now."

"I see you," Von said. The two remaining Sentient lancers circled the *Persepolis*, steering clear of the path of fire between the praxis and the gendarm.

"Do you have all the prisoners?" Halerin asked.

"Yes. Nance and the whole crew. Had to plow through a

bunch of somatarchs camped out around the opening, but nothing a few contingency triggers couldn't handle. Nance will bring them home in the citus. I'm going back for Cade."

"Great work, Raif, and great timing, too. I've got the location where Cade is being held. Level 5, Cell block D," Halerin informed him. "Be careful. It's heavily guarded."

"I'll be fine, Hal. Most the assessors are out flying the ships. I can out dance a few more hollow heads," Raif said.

"We'll be here to pick you up when you get back," Von promised.

"We're in the citus," Nance reported a few moments later. "The tunneler's loaded up. Taking off now."

"All right," came Jax's rumbling reply. "We just might pull this off after all."

The ship lifted off, after-bursting away from Hull so fast it sailed out beyond the *Persepolis'* firing range in a burst of light.

They did it, Gavin thought. *They actually did it.* He closed his eyes and said a silent prayer of thanks. Now if Raif could just find the prisoners and get off the ship.

The vapors were well within range to fire on the gendarm by now. The ship was large enough to weather substantial amounts of conventional fire, but the people inside would have no defense against the vapors' oscillathe canons.

The gendarm returned fire with an anemic barrage from a handful of locus cannons on either side of the ship. The squat barrels spat out yellow beams at the vapors, but the shots seemed to be random at best. It looked like they weren't even using targeting systems, just firing with the naked eye. A couple of shots connected, but none of the vapors went down.

More Collective ships moved in from other parts of Hull. Three lancers and a dozen attack skiffs were now heading for the gendarm, fresh from their disposal of some of the lesser

Waymen ships. The *Persepolis* let off a second volley with similar results, causing no visible damage, but no doubt further weakening the shields.

"That ship is taking a pounding," Jax muttered. "The shields won't hold up much longer. And if the praxis doesn't finish them off, those vapors are wreaking havoc inside her."

"It's a defensive ship," Halerin said. "If the leaders of Hull had any sense, they'd be flying it the other way, trying to save as many of their people as possible."

"Good thing for us, they don't," Jax said.

"I just hope it can hold out until Raif gets back," Von said.

Dreamer flight spiraled around the praxis, unmolested for now, but the gendarm wouldn't last long.

The Wayman ship hurtled towards the *Persepolis* like a giant metal fist, blunt and angry. From the speed and trajectory of its flight, the gendarme's intentions were clear: it was going to ram the Collective flagship. Under normal circumstances, that might have been a viable tactic, trade one ship for another. But the velar hull of the *Persepolis* was no ordinary hull. As large as the Wayman ship was, the gendarm wouldn't even scratch it.

Gavin's skiff crested the walls of the city in time to witness with his own eyes as the lancers and attack skiffs opened fire on the gendarme.

The Wayman ship took massive amounts of fire, but would not be denied. Its shields held and the gendarm met the *Persepolis* just outside of the city. Dreamer flight scattered to the winds as the two hulking ships connected in midair.

The collision sent a hurricane of light and shrapnel exploding through the air, forcing Gavin to shield his eyes. When it was safe enough to look, he saw the last bits of the gendarm plummeting beyond the city walls. Massive chunks of mangled metal sank into the desert, joining the menagerie of endless artifacts which littered the Vast.

The *Persepolis* burst through the cloud of debris, as pristine as the day it was built and crossed the outer wall of the city. Though pockets of Wayman resistance remained, Gavin's heart sank. With the fall of the gendarm, the battle for Hull was all but over.

The newly arrived lancers and skiffs, as well as the six vapors, reformed and swooped back around towards the Sentient ships orbiting the praxis.

"Looks like trouble," Jax said.

"Stay separated and keep them busy," Von instructed.

"I'll do what I can," Jax said grimly.

As the two lancers shot out from beneath the *Persepolis* to the other side, Gavin lost sight of them momentarily.

The Collective ships fanned out to head off the two rogue vessels darting around their flagship.

"Halerin, we can't take on this many ships," Von pleaded. Gavin thought for the first time he heard real fear in his voice.

"At least we'll die free," came Jax's hollow reply.

Hurry, Raif, Gavin pleaded silently.

Jax looped his ship back around the praxis and emerged on top of it. The maneuver put him in perfect position to unload on one of the newly arrived lancers, but it also made him an easy target for the two vapors next to it.

The Collective lancer swerved to escape the bulk of Jax's disruptor fire, clipping one of the vapors in the process. The vapors must have gotten off a shot anyway though, because Jax's ship sailed aimlessly off course, dropping rapidly and crashing into the sandy abyss below.

No, not Jax too...

Jax's death had barely registered with Gavin when Von's ship slingshotted around the *Persepolis* into a swarm of enemy ships. Von opened fire on them and many of his shots hit, but only a single vapor went down.

"I'm sorry, Halerin," Von apologized, his voice cracking. "And I'm sorry, Raif. I did what I—"

The transmission cut short. Gavin's skiff had just descended into the city so he couldn't see whether Von's ship had been shot down or not, but Halerin's words confirmed his fears.

"You did what you could, Von. That's all we could have asked." Halerin's voice was barely above a whisper. "Dreamer flight is gone, Gavin. Whatever you and Raif do from here on out. You're on your own."

Gavin wanted to close his eyes and shut out the world around him, but he feared that if he did, he might never open them again. This was madness. Why was he even here? The faces of Von, Jax, and the others flooded his mind. Their blood was on his hands.

No. They had agreed on the plan together. Their deaths were not in vain. They did what they set out to do. They rescued the prisoners. Gavin had to focus on that and put their deaths aside. He didn't have the luxury of giving into grief. He had his own mission to accomplish.

Seth maneuvered the skiff through the frenetic streets of Hull. He flew high enough to avoid the streets below, but low enough not to be easily picked off by the Collective ships above. Pandemonium reigned over the city. Everywhere men, women, and children fled to safety, abandoning their homes like streams of blood pouring from open wounds. Everything whipped by so fast that he could barely take it in, but the images would forever be burned in his memory.

The skiff zipped through the jigsaw maze of buildings until it came to the ruins of what must have once been one of the larger buildings of the city. Gavin's skiff just missed being spotted by a pair of lancers as they ducked in between two large piles of rubble. On the edge of the ruins, their skiff was exposed to any ships coming in from the east, but Gavin gave that little thought because of the sight before him. He had reached the *Persepolis* at last.

He jumped off the skiff and gave his final instructions to Seth. *"Stay here as long as you can. If you get spotted or if the* Persepolis *takes off, I want you to flee back to the* Maven. *Do you understand?"*

"Yes, of course," Seth replied.

Gavin took off through the rubble. While he ran he opened up a connection to Halerin through his extractor.

"Halerin, I need you to have the chronotrace follow Cyrith to see if you can find out if Adan has been captured. Be sure to monitor his thoughts as well."

"We're taxing the *Maven's* energy supply pretty heavily with all of this processing," Halerin warned. "But I'll do what I can."

"Just tell me if you find anything." Gavin cleared the end of the street he was on and the massive praxis came into full view above the ruins of a flattened building.

He had to enter the ten-story cruiser through Cade's hole up top. He could have had Seth drop him off there, but Gavin didn't want to put him in any more danger than he already had. Fortunately, Gavin had grabbed one of Raif's utility pouches before he'd left.

As Gavin sprinted towards the massive ship, he pulled an altitude capsule from the pouch on his belt. Without slowing his step, he twisted the black cylinder and felt it start to hum beneath his fingers. He took a few more strides, shoved his hands into the straps on either side, and then leapt into the air. At the same moment, he swiped the device with his thumb in an upward direction.

With Gavin clinging to the capsule, it gradually floated off the ground. As Gavin rose, his reflection in the mirrored hull of the praxis rose steadily along with him. In less than a microslice his soft-souled feet made contact with the outer surface of the praxis half way up the side. Still gripping the capsule above his head, he began running along the velar plating.

Padding his way up the smooth circumference, he passed an endless array of cannon barrels, triangular beam intensifiers, disruptor batteries, and other assorted anti-ship and antipersonnel weaponry. Once he reached the crest, he slid the altitude canister's level down to nothing. He tucked the capsule back into his pouch and rushed over to the hole on the cruiser's topside. Cade's tunneler was parked beside it, held fast to the surface of the *Persepolis* by its own axom field.

Though the pallium generator he had tucked away inside his belt would mask his presence from anyone with a bioseine, the administrators of the *Persepolis'* esolace could detect him if they went off system. Normally Collective security forces didn't do that because it required too much power, but Cyrith had been one step ahead of him all along, so Gavin had to be on his guard.

"All right, Halerin, do you have anything for me?" Gavin asked, before jumping into the hole.

"He's definitely on the ship, but he's been on the move ever since he boarded. I'm waiting for the chronotrace to catch up to give you the closest location. Adan's team entered on level five. That's as far as it's gotten. Start heading that way and I'll give you an update as soon as I can pin it down more precisely."

Gavin ground his teeth together. Five levels down and five levels back up meant it would be that much harder to get them out. But at least he had something to go on.

Unfazed by the two span drop to the floor, Gavin launched himself into the perforation made by the tunneler. His bioseine enhanced reflexes kicked in, causing him to tumble gracefully when he hit the floor and then spring to his feet. No one was present in the hallway below, but piles of white clothing, all that remained of several somatarchs, lay in quiet heaps on the floor, evidencing Raif's handiwork. Gavin touched the oscillathe he had on his belt, hoping he would not have to use it as well.

"Hey, Raif, Where are you?" Gavin spoke into the emptiness, his extractor sending his voice out across the Sentient audio channel.

"I'm on level five, still trying to clear a path to Cade. They must be scanning for pallium generators because I've had to fight somatarchs on every level just to get here." Raif sounded winded.

"Sit tight if you can. I'm headed your way. I might be able to help." Gavin set off down the passage.

"Okay, I suppose two guns are better than one. I'll keep your seat warm," Raif said. "Unless they send more hollow heads out to get me. Then I may have to jam."

The layout of the *Persepolis* was the same as the *Maven*. The safest way to get to level five undetected would be to travel through the maintenance conduits running between the various levels and on the outside of the ship.

Stopping at the white plastic door at the end of the hall, Gavin flicked on his cutter glove and made himself an opening.

Beyond the doorway he grabbed onto the maintenance rungs running along the curved space between the outer hull and the rest of the ship. He started his descent at once, passing several of the excess vents to the outside on his way down. He was just passing the shaft leading back into the ductwork between levels four and five when Halerin's voice came into his mind through the extractor.

"Gavin, it's too late. I'm not sure what they plan on doing to

Sierra or Tarn, but they're going to wipe Adan's mind with an articulator," Halerin said, anxiously.

Gavin nearly slipped from the rung at the unexpectedness of the message.

"Wait, what room? What level?"

"Gavin, you have to get off that ship. They're tracking you. They know where you are. They know where Raif is. Both of you have to get out of there now."

"But we can't leave Cade and Adan. We can handle these —" Raif interjected.

"They're sending a team of assessors after the both of you and Xander is leading it. This is your last chance to get out before they reach your position."

Gavin hung suspended between two rungs of the ladder. If Halerin was right, then there wasn't any way to save Adan, Cade, or any of the others. But if the Devs really did know where they were, there wasn't much chance of him or Raif escaping either.

"Halerin, thank you for that information," he said, resuming his descent. "But I think our best chance out of this is to stand and fight."

"I'm with you," Raif said. "Kick the door down or choke on the lock. Either way, we won't go quietly."

"Gavin, Raif, I completely disagree with your decisions," Halerin said desperately. "Don't throw your lives away like this. You could still—"

"Maybe if there was a way out, we'd try it, but even if we get off the ship, they'll just track us down. This is the way it has to be." Gavin said.

Halerin was quiet for several moments. "Very well," he said at last. "I may not agree with it, but I respect your decision. I should inform you, then, that we've already started receiving refugees. We've taken in over fifty so far. The *Maven* will soon have to take off, so if you do survive, it's unlikely there will be a ship for you to return to. Whatever happens, I want both of you to know that I admire you tremendously. It has been an honor knowing and working with you. *Maven*, out."

With that the audio channel went silent.

TWENTY-THREE
JETTISONED

RAIF'S JAGGED GRIN FLASHED IN THE CORRIDOR OUTSIDE the prison block. Though Gavin was panting, still recovering from his headlong run, Raif sauntered towards him as if they had casually bumped into each other on board the *Maven*.

"Glad you could drop by." Raif squeezed Gavin's shoulder with his free hand. In his other he held a shiny oscillathe pistol.

"You're a hard man to track down," Gavin said, and then got serious. *"So we probably have less than a microslice before they arrive."*

"Relax, I've got this one. You just watch my back and get any I miss."

Gavin pulled out his own oscillathe. *"You have a plan?"*

Raif reached into a pouch on his belt and pulled out a black disc and a small metal bead. *"Don't you know it. Round things. A somatarch's greatest weakness. They like everything straight and squared at the corners. They can't handle my curves."*

The black disc was a contingency trigger and Gavin had a hunch about the ball. *"Is that what you used to fool the Collective ships?"*

Raif's grin widened. *"It's called a mendax generator. This little combo has served me pretty well so far. Let's just hope it gets us through one more time. Wait here."*

He ran down the hallway into the middle of a T-intersection and flicked the ball up to where the ceiling met the wall and it stuck fast. Setting the black trigger on the floor just around the corner, he hurried back to join Gavin.

"Ready?"

"I'm not sure that Xander and the assessors will be so easy to fool," Gavin commented.

"I guess we'll find out."

Within a few moments the sound of distant footsteps rumbled down the hallway. Gavin and Raif could not take cover in the passage they were in, but that wouldn't matter if the Collective forces were using oscillathes. The two men stood in the middle of the hallway about equal distance between the intersection and the closed metal portal leading into the prison block.

Gavin focused his thoughts on the door behind them. *"What's stopping them from sending another force from inside the prison?"*

"Oh, don't worry. I took the door off system for a bit. Should hold long enough for us to wipe the floor with these hollows and be on our merry way."

The thud of booted footsteps grew louder. Soon Gavin could feel the vibrations in the floor. Two projections appeared in the middle of the intersection. They looked exactly like Gavin and Raif, down to the drops of sweat on Gavin's brow.

"Not bad, eh?" Raif beamed.

"I'm far more handsome in real life," Gavin remarked.

Raif shook his head. *"Next time you get your brain reworked, have them put in a sense of humor."*

The duplicate images took off running down the hallway in

opposite directions. Though the images lacked any definitive substance, the sound of their feet pounding the metal floor rang through the hallway in believable fashion, the auditory information projecting into the bioseines of anyone within range.

"*Where did you find the time to invent all these things?*" Gavin asked.

"*Coming from you that's pretty funny. I actually copied the projection technique from the chronotrace. I just tweaked it a bit to make it show something false instead of something real. I'm surprised that it actually worked. I have a million more ideas where this came from. Kind of like someone else I know.*"

"*We need to talk when we get back to the* Maven," Gavin replied.

A group of ten somatarchs rounded the corner of the intersection. The first five or so took off running after the false images and Gavin indulged himself with a silent cheer.

Then the other five appeared, but instead of following the projections, they rounded the corner and headed towards the real Gavin and Raif. Their momentum carried them right into the path of the contingency trigger. The passage lit up with a brilliant burst of white light and a muffled whisper drifted through the hallway. When the light faded, the only things that remained were clattering guns and suits of white clothing, spiraling towards the ground.

"*That takes care of another patrol of hollow heads,*" Raif declared.

"*But what about the assessors and Xander?*"

The sound of footsteps still resonated down the connected hallway, though the number was fewer and the pace had slackened.

A black ball the size of Gavin's fist rolled into the middle of the intersection from the direction of the incoming forces. It hit the wall and exploded into another, smaller burst of white light.

The sounds of the fleeing mendax phantoms went away, replaced by the synchronized marching of the returning somatarchs.

"*They disabled the generator.*" Raif's thoughts turned this way and that, trying to think of what to do next. "*We have to do something before the somatarchs get back. Let's take out whoever tossed that disruptor.*"

Gavin grabbed Raif by the shoulder and pulled him back. "*Halerin said they're tracking us. They'll know when we're in range.*"

"*So we fire first,*" was Raif's succinct reply.

"*But they could be assessors.*"

"*I don't want to kill anybody either, but do we really have a choice?*"

Gavin squeezed his oscillathe. Raif was right. They weren't getting out of this without a fight. "*I suppose they won't be expecting a counterattack.*"

"*Look,*" Raif went on. "*If they do fire on us, there's no reason both of us should go down.*"

"*They won't kill a memorant.*"

"*They tried to kill Adan once,*" Raif reminded him. "*Look, either way, I don't see why both of us need to risk our necks. If anyone's going to flame out it should be me. You've got a better shot of getting out of this than I do.*"

"*No, I've got this,*" Gavin pulled up his sleeve, revealing a nondescript, segmented black band. "*Malthus gave it to me. It projects some sort of dispersion shield, but it's better than any shielding technology I've come across. It's able to modulate and protect from almost any weapon.*"

"*Even oscillathes?*"

"*Yes, though I never had time to actually test it. I would have made one for everyone, but I haven't had time to reverse engineer it and figure out how it works.*"

"You're just full of sur—" Raif's thought was cut short by the appearance of a floating black sphere in the intersection. It whipped around the corner and headed straight for them.

It came so fast, they didn't even have time to run.

"A contingency probe!" Gavin barely got the thought out before a dozen white neutralizer beams arced towards them. Several hit each of them, dropping Raif instantly, but fizzling harmlessly in the sudden shimmer which enveloped Gavin.

Gavin's cutter glove blaze yellow and he charged the shiny black probe, slicing it neatly in two.

The sounds of the returning somatarchs reverberated down the hall. Their white forms came into view, but they were still at least a hundred paces away.

Gavin ran back towards Raif, but a voice from behind stopped him in his tracks.

"You've got some intriguing technology if you can withstand a neutralizer blast from a probe," Xander said, standing in the intersection with three gray robed assessors. He himself wore a plain brown jumper. The three assessors had oscillathe rifles trained on him. Their range was much greater even than Gavin's modified pistol. Xander appeared to be unarmed.

The oscillathe blasts would not hurt Gavin. At least he was *fairly certain* they wouldn't. But they would kill Raif.

"We've tried bringing you in peacefully," Xander went on. "Don't force me to destroy a perfectly good memorant."

Xander was bluffing. He would never kill another memorant. He was just waiting for reinforcements.

Gavin backpedalled until he was standing just over Raif. He could jolt him awake with his gloves, but then what? The somatarchs would reach the intersection any moment.

It only took a moment for Gavin to make his decision. "Sorry, my friend," he said, looking down at Raif. Gavin turned on his heel and sprinted down the hallway.

"After him!" Xander shouted. At that moment the somatarchs arrived. They quickly passed the assessors and began gaining on Gavin.

He reached the first connecting hallway just in time to beat a second force of somatarchs to the intersection, but they caught him a few steps past it. They bowled him over, but he activated the dispersion band and his hand glowed red. He sliced backwards, cleaving through two somatarchs with one motion. They fell instantly dead to the floor. The other four jumped him, heedless of his glowing hand and all of them fell, dismembered and mutilated to the floor.

But the fight, brief as it was, had allowed another group of three contingency probes to appear in the intersection. They lit into him this time not with neutralizer blasts, but with locus pulser fire. They were actually trying to kill him!

His multi-colored screen shielded him from the attacks, but the dispersion band pulsed on his wrist afterwards and sent a warning to his bioseine.

"Shields reduced thirty percent. Approximately five microslices before full recharge."

What? This thing had a limit? Maybe it wasn't as different from conventional shields as he thought. But if they knew about the dispersion band, maybe they weren't trying to kill him after all. Maybe they were just trying to reduce his shields. Either way, he had to get out of there.

He charged the mindless probes and sliced them into scrap with his cutter. The other group of somatarchs was by now only fifty paces away.

As Gavin turned and ran again, he fumbled around in his pouches and jacket for anything that might help him. His fingers brushed against a few viand nutrient patches, a tube of almamenth, a spare bismine crystal, a pair of lentes, and the altitude capsule, but nothing useful. If only he had another trigger like Raif's, or even a disruptor pellet.

A hissing sound signaled the opening of a door up ahead. How had he missed it? Two assessors stepped out. These were not armed with oscillathes, but long sleek locus rifles. They lit into Gavin with repeater fire, sucking his shields down.

But Gavin refused to use his oscillathe on the assessors. He kept charging, his prismatic screen absorbing hit after hit.

The dispersion shield was down eighty percent by the time he got in range to put them down with two neutralizer blasts from his gloves.

"Fifteen microslices to full charge," the bands told him.

He could not take another round of that.

The somatarchs were within twenty paces now.

As he passed the door, it hissed shut and the sound jostled loose an idea. *The altitude canister.* Such devices had been known to malfunction when punctured, releasing all of their fuel in a short amount of time and sending whoever was using it plummeting to their death. But as the fuel ejected, it caused the device to generate tremendous lateral force from where it was punctured. At the end of the hallway was one of the maintenance shafts Gavin had used to crawl through the ship unnoticed. If he hit it at high enough speed, he would burst through the flimsy plastic door at the end of the hallway and fall down the shaft and out through the trash vents and then...well, the praxis had been floating about fifteen spans off the ground so it might end up very badly for him, but he had his bioseine to repress the pain.

I'm sorry I couldn't save you, Adan. I'll come back for you, though, I promise.

A yellow streak of locus energy to appeared once again at the tips of Gavin's fingers.

The somatarchs were within ten paces. Behind them ran Xander with the assessors and also a new pair of probes.

Gavin clamped one hand onto the capsule, fastening it to the tube using the safety lock. With his free hand he sliced the end closest to him clean off and ducked. Air spit forth from the capsule, starting off at a low fizzle, but ratcheting up quickly to a furious whistle. An inky green light shot forth from the tube and Gavin was launched down the corridor like the tip of a spear formed of green lightning. He remembered to suppress the pain just before he hit the white plastic door. He splintered the door and impacted the wall of the shaft. His body jerked to a near stop for half a moment before the canister shifted course and angled his trajectory downward.

The momentary drop in speed allowed him to see the light at the end of the chute. A moment later he burst out through the trash vent. Immediately a single thought seized his mind.

Oh no, the Persepolis *took off.*

Gavin could not see the ground for all the swirling clouds below. He plummeted like a rock, the spent altitude capsule in his hands powerless to stop his fall.

TWENTY-FOUR
LAID OUT ON A TABLE

ADAN AWOKE IN A HIGH-CEILINGED METAL ROOM. HE assumed he was still aboard the *Persepolis*. Above him hung a tangled ball of cables fused together and embedded in the ceiling, capped by a large metallic bulb. The bulb glared down at him, a giant, mutilated eye, merciless and unforgiving. A second, identical ball hung to its left.

He tried to rise, to get up and move out from under the eye's unsettling gaze, but his arms, legs, chest, and waist were held fast by thick straps. He had a metal band around his head as well, but it did not hold him down.

Adan's mind flashed back to the alembic chamber in the Institute. The scientists had tied him to a machine there to help him recover his strength. The treatments had been excruciatingly painful. Was something similar in store for him?

His last conversation with Cyrith came back to him, causing him to shudder. *They're going to erase my memory,* he realized. *And they're going to use that ball of cables to do it.*

No sooner had that thought entered his mind when

another, even more devastating thought, exploded inside his head. *I'll forget Sierra. She'll forget me.*

A door on the opposite wall swished open and a chromium cart floated through. It had a body strapped on top of it the same way Adan was. Two somatarchs stood at the door, watching the cart drift through, but they remained outside when the door closed. The cart came to rest a few paces away from him.

Adan didn't recognize the man on top of the cart. He was clean shaven with closely cropped hair, after the style of the scientists, but his nose and jaw were far too angular and well defined for him to be one of them.

When he turned and locked eyes with Adan, Adan gave a start.

"Nolan? What are you doing here?"

Nolan regarded him with amused pity. "So, they captured you as well."

"Hull was taken, wasn't it?"

"Yes," Nolan said, eyeing the looming bouquet of cables overhead. "And soon they'll take our memories as well. If the Collective has one treasure, it's their memorants. We're too rare and valuable to let them pass us by."

Adan tried not to think about what was going to happen. Nolan was here, and whatever else he was, he was resourceful. Twice he had plotted to bring down the Collective and had nearly succeeded both times. If anyone could find a way out of this situation it would be him.

"It doesn't have to end like this. We could escape," Adan said, but Nolan's response was swift.

"Out of the question," he said, shaking his head. "This is the end for both of us. We've had too many second chances already."

"What do you mean?"

"I know when I'm beaten. You may look for help if you wish, but no help will come." Nolan closed his eyes as if he intended to just lay and wait for the scientists to come and erase his memory.

"I thought maybe Hull would be able to fend them off," Adan said. "You had all those ships."

"If I had thought my army was a match for them, I would have attacked the Collective a long time ago and you would not have been needed." His eyes opened and a spiteful grin crossed his face. It was so odd for Adan to see him without his beard and long hair. He looked less enigmatic now, his expressions more exposed. He seemed smaller, too, laying there beside Adan. They had divested him of his elegant, gold trimmed robe and finely-crafted staff. He now wore the same simple gray robe as Adan. "A cog in the wheel, that's all I was in the end," he continued. "However many other cogs moved because of me, I was just a part of a larger machine. I have failed in my mission."

"What mission? Are you working for someone else? And don't tell me it was Numinae again. I won't believe you."

"Why ask the question if you plan on eliminating one of the possibilities beforehand? That's the first sign of a defective mind—a predisposition to a certain set of answers. You will not get very far with that sort of thinking," Nolan lifted his chin and for a moment appeared to recover some of his former pride.

What was Nolan getting at? Did he mean to continue the ruse about Numinae even now, when they were both caught, both facing the same fate? Adan couldn't see what he had to gain by doing so.

"So you're sticking by your story then? It was Numinae who sent you?"

"What does it matter now? Everything that comes to pass is his will. Don't you see that? We're just puppets in a theater."

Adan stared back at Nolan, trying to resolve the riddle before him in the form of a man. Was he just speaking out of bitterness and hopelessness? Adan wondered what he really believed about Numinae, though he was at a loss to say exactly why it mattered so much to him. Maybe it was because of the implications to his own beliefs. What if Numinae did use cutthroats and schemers to carry out his ends? It was a troubling thought. Wasn't he the source of goodness itself? Why did he allow evil to exist at all?

"You're still saying that he told you to attack Oasis?" Adan pressed him.

Nolan glared back, weary of the constant questions. "Through Illiud, yes. 'The skies shall fall upon that city of iniquity and destruction shall walk its streets,' remember?" Nolan rattled off the prophecy in a droning, monotonous voice, as if by rote.

"But Gavin was given that prophecy. Not you," Adan maintained.

"Can you be certain of that?" That old cleverness flashed in Nolan's eyes.

Adan faltered. He had categorically rejected Nolan's story about Illiud, along with Nolan's claim to have been sent from Numinae, but staring at Nolan now, on the edge of losing his memory, Adan's confidence in that rejection wavered.

"But how could Illiud have found you? It took a Developer to free Will. Illiud was just a Welkin."

"Honestly, I don't know how he did it," Nolan said. "I assume Numinae must have shown him. Nothing is impossible with him, after all. But it doesn't really matter. I failed and now I will be cast into the fire along with the rest of Numinae's useless vessels."

"What are you talking about? You think he's abandoned us? You think you're outside his help if you ask?" As Adan spoke, he wrestled with whether he believed the same thing as Nolan at that moment. Perhaps Numinae didn't care what was going to happen to them. Perhaps this was what he had wanted all along.

"Numinae does not stoop to listen to our requests. That is Welkin talk. The best one can hope for is to stay clear of the swath of destruction which he leaves in his wake." Nolan's expression grew bitter once again.

Adan was tempted to give into hopelessness like Nolan, but he reminded himself that Numinae wasn't like that. He couldn't be.

"You're wrong about Numinae," Adan said. "He has answered my prayers before. And he has saved me from worse than this. Besides, even if he didn't answer my prayers in a way that I could see, that's not the point. We pray to find out his will, like...like little children do with their parents." A heaviness washed over him as he remembered his friend Zain, the one who had shared the analogy with him.

"You are right about that. Conformity. That is what the ruler of the universe desires. And none shall stand in his way. In the end, he's really no different from the Collective."

"That's not what I meant. You make him sound cruel. He's not like that."

"And what do you know of Numinae? You're nothing more than an organically enhanced pawn of the Collective, the Delegation, *and* the so-called maker of the universe. Getting used is the only thing you know how to do. But not all of us are content with our slavery." Nolan's lip twitched in a sneer.

Adan felt blood rush to his face in anger. This, from the man who had twice sent him to his death to do what he dared not do himself.

"Maybe I'm not as powerful as you," Adan said quietly, working to stay in control of his emotions. "But I know

Numinae will protect me. And if you asked, I know he would do the same for you."

Nolan strained against his bonds again, his expression tightening and his eyes smoldering with an inner fire.

"Who do you think sends the storms which ravage this world? It is Numinae. Who do you think allowed me to send you to Oasis the first time? The self same lord. Who do you think spurred the army of Waymen to their deaths? Your precious Creator each once again. And who do you think sent us to this cursed planet to begin with? It was the ever-loving, all-kind, all-good, supernatural being whom you pray to with such faith and sincerity. Now tell me again who it is that answers your prayers."

Adan stared at Nolan in shock, the words he had just heard whirling through his mind. He wanted to counter them, to defend Numinae as he had before, but they shouted down his arguments, drowning out any possible response. One phrase rose above the rest.

Who do you think sent us to this cursed planet to begin with?

The words settled in Adan's mind like a hazy reflection clearing in the water.

"What did you say—this planet? Someone sent us here? What are you talking about?"

"This world is not our home," Nolan said cooly. "I would have thought Kelm had enough of his mind left to at least tell you that."

Adan's response sounded hollow in his own ears, as if in a dream. "Kelm did try to...tell me something...I think." The prisoner's ravings danced back through Adan's mind. "He said he had seen me before...but that you did something to his mind. He wasn't altogether there, so I didn't believe him."

"I suppose that makes sense," Nolan said.

"He said you drugged him."

"That's what I made him think. It sometimes helps the mind accept memory manipulation more easily to believe it has been drugged."

"But why? Why did you do that to him?"

"He was far too dangerous to set free. I could have just killed him, but he knew too much about the Delegation to just simply dispose of."

"Wait, slow down. Kelm was trying to call the Delegation? Why? Who is the Delegation?"

"The Delegation came before the Collective. Their leaders were more conventional, ruling by their military power and shrewd political acts where that failed. But their civilization was shattered and their cities leveled. The few survivors took refuge below ground since their planet was no longer inhabitable.

"It was the Collective who destroyed their world, though they did not call themselves by that name back then. They were merely a resistance movement. Deliverance was their name in the beginning. They struck before the Delegation even realized the threat by capturing the prize of the Delegation armada, an interstellar ship called the *Nebula* through an act of betrayal.

"Malthus was in command of the ship, and Darius promised to restore his son Dane to life if he would yield control of it to Deliverance. I was Darius' mentor back then, and foolish enough to trust him with the secrets of the memorant path. But in an act of double betrayal, my life was forfeited and my mind and body used to host Dane's thoughts, personality, and memories.

"And thus the *Nebula* came into Darius' hands. It was an enormous structure, capable of housing thousands of people. More importantly, it possessed a weapon called the omniclast, the World Breaker. With it, the leaders of the Collective brought an end to the war and turned their home world into a burnt out husk. Kelm was an advance scout in the Delegation's army, sent out across the stars to find out where the Collective had fled to and signal back their location."

Adan stared off into nothing, lost in thought, trying to take it all in. Other planets? An army capable of crossing the stars? He wasn't sure what it all meant. "And you learned all of this from Kelm?"

"Most, but not all. Illiud told me some things as well. He said that I was not from this world and that if I would raise an army and fight against the 'wicked ones' as he called them, that Numinae would deliver me from this place and give me a new home."

Adan hung on Nolan's every word. He could not believe that he was finally getting answers now that he was on the edge of losing everything.

"What do you mean when you speak of another planet? You make it sound like there is something else beyond the Vast. But what is it? A star? Another land? Or perhaps just another word for the Eversky?"

"You and I come from another world," Nolan spoke slowly and letting his words sink in. "You have to pass beyond the clouds to get to it, and even then it is impossibly far away, but it is not the Eversky. The Eversky is a myth made up by the Welkin to get their people to follow Numinae. He dwells beyond all time and space. There is no way to get to him. He is wholly other. But our planet, and the planet where the Delegation comes from, is the planet of Kess, and it can be traveled to via space ship. An interstellar ship like the *Nebula*."

"What happened to the ship after the Collective used it to destroy the Delegation's world?"

"The leaders of the Collective crashed it onto the surface of this planet. I don't know why. Maybe they thought that since the Delegation was gone they didn't need it anymore. Whatever the reason, they were fools to destroy it. But now they've realized their error and want it back."

"How do you know that?"

Nolan's face grew grim once more. He replied in low, bitter tones.

"Because I was in the process of rebuilding it. Do you think the attack on Hull was an accident? I wasn't any threat to them. They attacked this city because they wanted their ship back. The city of Hull *is* the *Nebula*."

The door to Adan's room whisked open before the full weight of Nolan's words could sink in.

Trey and Xander, wearing silver lab coats, passed into the room. Trey's reddish scar glistened in the light like a warning beacon, heralding the terrible fate that awaited Adan.

Xander took the lead, his movements and mannerisms more rushed than was typical for a Collective scientist.

"We do not usually do warm-bodied remapping," Xander said, not taking his eyes off them as he approached. "But in your case we have decided to make an exception. You are both extremely important to us."

Trey's eyes shifted nervously.

The two men took positions beside either cart, Xander standing next to Adan and Trey beside Nolan.

"You know, no matter how many people you absorb into the Collective, you'll never be able to survive the Delegation attack when it comes," Nolan said, his tone as deep as it was threatening. "And it will come, you do know that, don't you?"

"We have ways of dealing with them," Xander said, though Adan heard little confidence in his reply.

Xander's eyes glazed over a moment later and the tentacled ball of machinery above Adan descended. Trey did the same and the second ball lowered over Nolan.

Adan had to do something before it was too late, but his mind seized up. He was a memorant. There was some way for him to tell what Xander and Trey were thinking, but he couldn't remember how to do it. He strained to recall the knowledge, but it eluded him, vanishing on the edge of his thoughts whenever he reached out for it.

They already took that away. They erased it when I was unconscious.

"Xander, please don't do this," he begged.

But the expression on Xander's face, or rather the lack of any at all, told Adan that it was pointless. To Xander, Adan was an object, a thing, nothing more.

Numinae, please stop this, Adan prayed, knowing that this was truly his last resort. *I don't want to lose myself again.*

"You're not going to die," Trey assured him, his eyes briefly regaining focus. "In fact, this is the only way you're guaranteed to survive."

The words were met by Xander's cold stare and Trey went silent.

"You cannot escape the punishment for your crimes. Judgment will be meted out on all who disobey." Nolan said, his words reminiscent of the eidos from Gavin's memories.

Neither Xander nor Trey seemed to hear him. The mechanical bulb hovered so close to Adan he could have touched it if his arms had been free.

As he stared out at the loss of all he held dear, he tried to remember the people who were important to him, to hold on to his memories for one last moment. Gavin, Senya, Raif, Von, and Lila, Senya's precious little daughter. And Sierra, above all Sierra. How would he ever hold on to her?

He remembered the way Senya had talked to him about the death of her husband. The pain of her loss was a tangible thing in her eyes, and yet there had been a spark of light behind that pain, her connection to him unbroken even beyond death. He wished he had been able to share that kind of bond with Sierra. But instead his hopes and memories would be consumed by that pitiless mass of tessellated coils hovering over him. The slinking cables sent shivers of fear through his body.

Nolan shouted defiantly and that was when Adan realized there was no hope. He would never remember who he was again.

He gripped the edge of the table, his whole body one large, tense ball of muscle and fright.

"Numinae, you are my only hope," he cried out loud. "Save me, please!"

They were the last words Adan spoke.

TWENTY-FIVE
FOUND IS LOST

GAVIN'S MIND GROPED FOR THE LIGHT. A DISTANT sensation beckoned him. It felt like something was chipping away at his skin, but his skin was somehow made of stone. The blows came fast and furious, each one more jarring than the last. Finally, one hit him near his neck that was so fierce that it shook him from his stupor. One of his eyes flew open, casting its gaze along the porous stretch of rock upon which he lay. His other eye, along with half his face, was buried beneath it. He attempted to jerk his head behind him to where the noises were coming from, but the stone held him fast. He realized that he wasn't laying on the rock, but in it. The right half of his body was encased in this ash colored prison.

The chipping sensation stopped. Everything was quiet for several moments. Gavin began to think that perhaps it had been all in his mind. The only things moving were the currents of sand, sidling across the barren plateau. The stony ground gave way to sand some fifty paces from where he lay.

"Oh! You're awake," said a scratchy voice from where the smashing sound had come from. "Didn't hit you did I?"

"Uh...okay," was all Gavin could manage to voice through the half of his mouth not locked in stone.

"What's that?" came the voice.

Gavin mumbled and grunted in reply. "I con heek."

There was an answering grunt and then footsteps coming around to the front of his vision. At first all he saw was a pair of cracked canvas shoes like the Waymen wore and the hem of a dusty gray robe. Their owner got down on his knees and pressed his face near the ground so Gavin could see him. It was a man with stringy gray hair and the scraggly beginnings of a beard. His eyes were wild with fatigue, or pain, or sadness, or perhaps a mixture of all three.

"I con heek," Gavin repeated.

"You can't speak, is that it?" the stranger asked. Gavin blinked twice in response. Somehow the man picked up on the gesture and nodded in reply. "Yes, yes, I see. Well, that's under-standable. But at least you're awake now. And that's a good sign, isn't it? Yes, I'd say so. It's not every day you get stuck in the middle of a giant rock, is it? How did it happen?" The man stared at him, as if by doing so he could somehow unravel the mystery of Gavin's predicament.

Gavin traced back through his own thoughts, trying to solve the puzzle himself. He remembered falling from the *Persepolis*. His hand was locked tight around the punctured altitude canister. His garrick shuddered in the wind. Below him swirled clouds of sand. His bioseine told him that he had seven nanoslices before impact. He tried to stay calm, to think of a way out. He thought about using his garrick's storm sash to break the speed of his fall, but knew it would not be enough. All he could do was pray he would hit an exceptionally soft dune, but even then death was all but certain.

He caught sight of the ground right before impact. A large dark gray mass came rushing at him. He braced. And then...he could recall nothing between that moment and now. But if the rock he was on now was the gray mass he had slammed into, the impact should have killed him instantly. Surely he had landed in one of the dunes nearby. Perhaps he had been blown onto this rock afterwards. But then how had he become encased in it?

Then he remembered the dispersion band on his wrist. Its shields absorbed not only attacks from energy weapons, but any sort of kinetic force. Could it have protected him from his impact with the ground? Perhaps. But that didn't explain how his body survived the sudden stop.

"I'll tell you what. Just sit tight," the man said. "It might take a while, but I'll get you out of here eventually. I think I've almost got one of your legs free at any rate."

Gavin blinked twice again and the man gave him an encouraging nod and stepped over him and out of sight. The chipping sounds started up again. The pounding droned on for ten more microslices before Gavin's right leg finally came free. After that came his other leg, then the upper parts of his body, each one more quickly than the last, but his head was another matter. The man took great care not to accidentally strike him there. The force of his blows grew so weak that sometimes it took several strokes before any noticeable progress occurred.

While he worked, the man spoke to Gavin, apparently eager to have company, even company as uncommunicative as Gavin. At first Gavin could only make out the odd word or phrase here and there in between all of the banging. But towards the end, as the man worked more carefully around Gavin's head, he was able to make out more and more.

"But I'd rather be facing a storm, I suppose, than be back in that dark cell again," the stranger said.

As he kept speaking, Gavin learned several things about this man who was working so tirelessly to free him from the rock. He had very little knowledge about the Vast, for one thing. He knew a few things about the Waymen and it sounded like he had spent time in Hull, but he seemed surprised that the storms were so frequent.

"And the clouds," the stranger added. "There's something wrong with them. They never break, never clear, never give way to let you see the stars."

The more he went on, the more obvious it became that something was not right inside the man's mind. He referred often to a conversation between two people called the Lord of Death and Sentinel Orin. From the bits and pieces Gavin overheard, The Lord of Death went back and forth between being either the friend or the enemy of Sentinel Orin. Orin blamed him for the destruction of some other world, while at the same time, entreating him to help him conquer new ones. It was very disjointed and Gavin could piece together little beyond the fact that Sentinel Orin was flying on a ship through space on his way to wherever the Lord of Death wanted him to go.

"I've never seen the Death Lord myself, but I've *felt* his presence," the man said in hushed tones. "Awful cold in space, it is. The Death Lord is what fills up all that emptiness between worlds. Jiggles the brain just to think about it. But Sentinel Orin, he's a crafty one. He'll find a warm pocket in the middle of all that cold. If anyone can do it, it's him. And then he'll burn it all up and it'll go cold again. Make more room for the Lord of Death."

He paused in his efforts, breathing heavily.

"Not too warm here, though," he continued. "But not too cold either. It's like they say in that story, 'just right'...Though I do wish the wind would stop. Sounds too much like voices at night. Might be the Lord of Death at work. Or it might just be wind. You never know."

With these words, the last of the rocks entrapping Gavin

broke away and he was free. He lifted his head and rubbed his chin, massaging the squashed side of his face back to life. His muscles felt limp, but amazingly he was otherwise unharmed from his fall.

"Thank you for setting me free," Gavin said, grateful for the ability to speak once again. "I am in your debt."

The man shrugged and tossed aside the rock and metal wedge he had been using to chisel Gavin out from the stone.

"I couldn't just leave you out here. Not with those savages running around. I got captured myself by them once. Wouldn't wish that on anybody."

"You mean the Waymen? You got captured by them?" Gavin asked, taking in the stranger's full appearance for the first time. He was underfed, his clothes hanging off his slight frame. His robe was ripped in multiple places, and covered in sand. He looked like he had been living out in the open desert for several days.

"Is that what they're called? They spoke a strange dialect, but they could make themselves understood well enough. Cruelty is a universal language."

Gavin tried to rise to his feet, but he was too weak to do so on his own. The stranger was quick to lend a hand, his grip much stronger than expected.

Gavin brushed off the layer of dust which coated his garrick. "My name is Gavin," he said. The man stood blinking at him, as if he hadn't heard what Gavin said. So Gavin repeated his name, and added. "And your name is...?"

The man snapped back to attention. "Kelm. Kelm Brennan, escalon, sidereal scout class," he answered mechanically.

"Escalon? Scout? What do you mean? Are you part of some sort of army?" Gavin began to study the man even more closely. He was relieved that he didn't see any weapons on him. Gavin did not think it would be safe for someone in Kelm's mental state to possess any form of weapon.

"The army, yes. We are all part of the army now. What unit do you serve under?" Kelm asked.

"I'm not part of any army, Kelm. What army do you belong to?"

"The—the...it's a secret, actually," he said, clamping his mouth shut and giving Gavin a suspicious look.

"A secret? I see...Are you all right, Kelm? Are you in some sort of danger?"

"I suppose so. We both are," he whispered confidentially. "This storm could turn for the worse at any time. And I've been searching all day and still haven't found any water."

Kelm grew more anxious by the moment, but Gavin didn't think his pained expression came just from the scarcity of water or potential storms.

He certainly did not look to be in the best of health. Perhaps dehydration was actually the cause of his delirium. Gavin checked to see if he could connect to Kelm's bioseine to find out the exact state of his health, but if Kelm had one, it had been disabled; he was as blank as any Werin. Even with his memorant abilities, Gavin could get no sense of what was going on inside Kelm's mind. The thoughts were too disjointed and incoherent to make sense of, as opaque and impenetrable as the swirling clouds above.

Gavin studied the sheet of rock upon which they stood. It was the only such rock in the surrounding terrain. There were a few small rocks scattered about, but those were smooth and worn and this one was rough and porous. It was then that he realized that it was an etram stone, or what the Waymen called a 'vadi.' For reasons no one in the Collective fully understood, these rocks transformed into a sort of spongy, fibrous substance from time to time. It took several days for the transition, but once complete, the etram provided a source of water for days before drying up again. When dry they held their present consistency and hardness.

He must have fallen into the etram when it was in its spongy state. That, combined with the dispersion shields might have been enough to protect him from the full effects of his fall. But the rock was hard now. How long had he been out? He checked his bioseine to see how long he had been unconscious and discovered that it had been three and a half days since he had fallen from the *Persepolis*. He had, in fact, suffered some internal bleeding as a result of the fall and his bioseine had taken that long to contain the damage. He was still in need of medical attention, but he was not in any immediate danger.

"We should probably get back," Kelm muttered, licking his cracked lips. "When I look at those clouds on the horizon it makes my skin itch. I always get that feeling before a storm."

"Get back where?" Gavin asked.

"I found a little cave. That's where I've been living ever since the attack," Kelm said, eyeing the craggy plateau off to the south.

Gavin turned his attention from the plateau to a line of dingy-looking dust clouds about half a click off to the west. They didn't look like they were moving all that fast, but that could change in an instant.

"I agree. We should head for shelter," Gavin replied. "Do you have any supplies there?"

"A little water that I've been storing in a shallow depression. I kept some extra from the first one of those water stones I found."

Gavin felt inside his utility pouch for the four viand strips nestled inside. He handed one of them to Kelm.

"What's this for?" Kelm asked.

"It's a food replacement patch. Stick it on your arm and it will inject nutrients into your system."

"Oh no, I shouldn't take it. You need it a whole lot more than me."

"I've got three more," Gavin said, slapping one of them on his arm through a rip in his sleeve.

"Well, I'm twice as glad I found you, then," Kelm said, smiling for the first time, though in a rather strained sort of way. He pulled up his sleeve, but then stopped. His eyes flitted back and forth between the patch and his arm. Gavin had to assure him several times that it was safe before Kelm would put it on and even then, he stared anxiously at it for some time, as if expecting some awful side effect to occur.

Gavin touched the extractor around his neck. Connecting his mind to it, he discovered that the *Maven* was no longer in range.

"Hopefully we can wait out the storm in your cave. Once it clears, I should be able to contact my friends."

"You—you have friends?" Kelm asked.

"Yes, lots of them, actually. And they've got a large ship—assuming they survived the battle of Hull."

Kelm's face brightened at the news. "Will you take me with you—onto the ship I mean?"

"Of course."

"I had some friends once...but I don't remember much about them. I would really like to meet yours," he said wistfully.

"What were you doing before you got captured?" Gavin asked.

Kelm's matted strands of hair swayed back and forth. "I—I was with the army. I already told you that."

"Where are the rest of your fellow soldiers, then?" Gavin asked, not really sure Kelm was correct about this detail, though

Kelm certainly seemed to believe it. "It might help me to get you back in touch with them if you can tell me where they are."

"No, I can't, it's a...what am I saying? I don't even know anymore. Lost is found and found is lost. It's all the same. They were doomed to die just like me." Kelm pressed his hand to his forehead as if it hurt.

"But you didn't die, Kelm. You survived and maybe your friends did too. Once we find my ship, I'll see to it that you're protected and we'll find out what happened to your friends." Gavin placed his hand on Kelm's bony shoulder. The muscles were as tense as the rock beneath their feet.

"Wait," Kelm said, his eyes glinting. "I do remember something now. There was another man—a prisoner in my cell that I left behind. I have to go back for him." He swiveled away from Gavin and started heading off to the north, perpendicular to the oncoming storm.

"Kelm, no," Gavin said. "You can't go looking for him now. It's not safe. We've got to get back to the cave, remember?"

"But I left him. You never leave a man behind. It was the building that made me forget him—it was shaking, and things were coming down, and I, I couldn't tell where I was going. I've got to go back and find him."

Gavin was almost certain that Kelm must have been in Hull when it was attacked.

Kelm set off at a quick trot, but Gavin was too weak to keep up with him. "Kelm, come back. The battle for Hull was over three days ago. Your friend is probably long gone or..." Gavin thought it wise not to mention the other possibility.

"I can't believe I let him down," Kelm rambled, trudging on ahead of Gavin.

"We can search for him later, after the storm blows over," Gavin said. At that moment he reached the edge of the etram and stepped onto the sand. It was much more loosely packed than he had expected and he slipped and fell.

Kelm cried out in alarm and ran back towards him. "Are you all right? Are you all right?" he shouted.

Gavin gladly took hold of his hand and Kelm helped him to his feet. "I'm fine. I just slipped, that's all."

Kelm shook his head and stared reproachfully at his feet. "I'm sorry," he said. "Here I was babbling on about not leaving a man behind and look what I did to you. Left you behind. It's like they whipped all my training right out of me, but that's no excuse."

"Don't be so hard on yourself," Gavin told him. "You freed me from the rock. If you hadn't done that I probably would have died out here in the desert."

The wind hit them both with a sudden blast of sand. The wall of rolling dust clouds was still some distance off, but the gust reminded Gavin of the need for shelter.

"We can look for your friend once we're safe. Either way, we'd better get moving."

Kelm's eyes searched the clouds again. It looked like they were getting even darker.

"Okay, let's go," he said. "I just hope Adan is all right."

Gavin cleared his throat, feeling a sharp sting of anticipation run through his chest. "Did you say, 'Adan'?"

The light of intelligence light sparked from beneath the matted hair covering the man's face. "Ah, I see that you know him as well," he said.

TWENTY-SIX

STORMS OF THE MIND

As they trekked across the desert, Kelm shared the details of his encounter with Adan. The words spilled out of him, one on top of the other, and Gavin did not bother to interrupt with questions. He didn't have to. For the first time since they had met, Kelm's mind was focused enough so that Gavin could actually see Kelm's memories unfolding as he spoke.

By the time they reached the cave, almost a click away, Kelm had finished his story and the memories began to fade, and with it his clarity of mind.

From the outside, the cave was little more than a large, flat rock. Though it stretched on for another fifty paces, the rock rose no higher than Gavin's shoulder with an opening near the ground. The mouth was so low the two men had to crawl to get in. The entrance sloped down and, the further in they went, the taller the cave became. By the time they reached the end of it, about forty paces in, they could stand at their full height. In the middle of the cave a small pool of water half filled a shallow depression, maybe enough for the two of them to down nine or ten gulps each. The rest of the chamber lay hidden in shadow.

Kelm and Gavin sat down beside the basin across from each other. The whistle of the wind outside rose as the storm picked up. Gavin checked the extractor again to see if he could connect to the *Maven*, but as before there was nothing. The storm was probably too close anyway, even if the ship had been in range.

Gavin moved his gloved hand so that the smallest sliver of yellow flickered to life, pushing back the darkness. Kelm failed to notice the tiny light. His slumped shoulders and the look of resignation on his face mirrored the same hopelessness Gavin was fighting against.

"Kelm, what if I told you that I could help you recover some of your memories?" Gavin asked, sensing that this was at the heart of his despair.

Kelm's eyes flashed feebly in the light from the cutter. "What do you mean?"

Gavin paused, suddenly unsure of whether or not he should go on. Kelm had saved him, but he was still a stranger and Gavin had no indication of what his motives or intentions might be. But curiosity about Kelm's identity overcame his reservations. He decided to take the risk.

"I have a device which allows me to see into the past," he explained. "It's called the chronotrace."

"The chronotrace..." Kelm repeated the word reverently, as if the mere utterance of it had the power to bring back his past. He pressed close to the edge of the puddle and leaned further into the light. "I would do anything to get my memory back." Though his words were respectful, there was something desperate in his tone that caused Gavin to wonder once again just how safe this man really was.

"I won't be able to show you everything. But we can look for important things, and maybe those might jar other memories loose."

Kelm's face sprang to life. "You would do that? For me?"

"You saved my life, Kelm. I think I owe you at least that much."

"Yes, yes, that's true. I hadn't thought of that—so when do we start? I'm not really that tired, you know. And your machine will be safe inside this cave, protected from the storm."

"Oh, I don't have it with me, Kelm," Gavin said. "It's back on the ship. We won't be able to use it until we get back there."

Kelm's hand darted across the puddle, grabbing Gavin's leg. "I don't want to wait for the ship. I want my mind back now." He had a gleam in his eye, like a man dying from hunger who had just been told there was no food left.

"I'll call the ship after the storm. They can't be far. Don't worry, we'll get your memories back, I promise."

Kelm did not let go.

"What if you can't reach them? What if the storm doesn't end? What if it blasts this cave into oblivion, or fills it with sand?" Kelm's eyes throbbed with urgency.

Gavin now regretted saying anything to Kelm. "There's nothing I can do about it right now, Kelm, I—"

"But you said you owed me." Kelm looked more and more delirious by the moment. His grip was fantastically strong. His fingers, whether consciously or unconsciously, started to dig into Gavin's leg. Kelm's entire aspect transformed into that of someone trapped in a corner, ready to fight for his life.

"Calm down, Kelm," Gavin said in as even a voice as he could manage. "I told you I would help you. Don't you trust me?"

"Trust? Why should I trust anyone? You might drug me too for all I know, lock me up in another cell and take away all my secrets. Maybe I shouldn't have saved you. To be honest I thought you were dead at first and I thought—well, I thought that I would—and then a voice told me no, I'd better not. And then I thought maybe you would help me. And then you even promised to, and now—now I find out that you lied to me. Just like everyone else. They're all liars. Schemers. Never telling the truth!"

Kelm had worked himself up into just short of a frenzy. His lips were covered in spittle and his skin stretched tight across his face. Gavin knew that Kelm's anger had nothing to do with him; he doubted Kelm's mind was even fully present. He was lashing out and Gavin just happened to be there, but that didn't change the fact that Gavin was still in danger. He rubbed his fingers together, ready to activate his neutralizer gloves the moment Kelm sprung on him.

"Kelm, I'm not trying to mislead you. I promise—"

"Words! Words! Empty air is all it is!" Kelm screamed. Gavin pulled back in fear and yanked Kelm forward. The maneuver forced Kelm to release his leg or risk falling into the puddle.

Kelm's eyes fell upon the murky water and he caught his maniacal reflection staring back at him. He looked shocked and afraid of what he saw. The vision seemed to blunt his rage. After a moment, his aspect began to change.

Kelm shrunk back across the puddle, returning to his usual vulnerable, confused state.

"I will help you get your memories back," Gavin said, massaging his leg where Kelm had been gripping it.

Kelm nodded tentatively and kept staring at the water. "Ah, why bother?" He appeared to be on the verge of tears. "The device probably won't work anyway. It probably isn't even real."

Gavin held his tongue, hoping that Kelm would drop his obsession with the chronotrace of his own accord.

Kelm withdrew from the edge of the pool. He seemed to wither and shrink as he did so. He curled up in a ball on the other side of the puddle. "I should have known better. I knew it wasn't safe to trust anyone..." he mumbled sleepily.

Gavin eased away from the water and stretched out on the floor a comfortable distance from the unpredictable man.

"Never trust anyone," Kelm said to himself. "Not even yourself..." The listless look in his eyes told Gavin he had given up on finding his memories. "No hope," he whispered under his breath. "No hope."

Kelm closed his eyes, nuzzling his head into his elbow. He let out a weak sigh. Within moments his breathing grew heavy and took on a steady rhythm. Gavin continued to eye him for some time, trying to get a glimpse of his thoughts, but Kelm's mind remained as turbulent as the storm raging outside the cave. Gavin could make no sense of the dizzying, dancing patterns he saw flitting by. Eventually he gave up trying and drifted off as well, falling into a guarded and fitful sleep.

Kelm was relatively docile during the following day. After their second day together, Gavin convinced him that they needed to abandon the cave if they were to have any hope of making contact with the *Maven*.

They wandered in and out of storms, across cracked plains, rocky hills, and endless dunes until Gavin did not think they could go one day more. Unlike Gavin, Kelm had no bioseine to compensate for the lack of food and harsh conditions, yet he endured every hardship, stubbornly clinging to life despite his obvious hopelessness and shattered mind. Perhaps it was that very brokenness which allowed him to keep going when a sane man might have given up.

It was near dark when Gavin finally felt a tingling at the base of his neck which told him his extractor had an alert for him.

The Maven *is within range,* the device informed him. *Would you like me to connect to its audio relay?*

"*Yes, yes, a thousand times, yes,*" Gavin rapidly assented. Exhausted as he was, his mind became instantly alert.

"Kelm," Gavin whispered hoarsely, barely able to make his voice heard over the pestering winds. "Kelm, I found my friends. We're going to make it."

Kelm received the news with no visible display of emotion.

Gavin collapsed on the ground and waited for the *Maven's* reply.

Halerin was the first person Gavin saw when he and Kelm floated up into the cargo bay, carried inside by the *Maven's* axom field generators. Halerin wore a look of joy even if Gavin was too far gone to respond in kind. Beyond him, the bay bustled with activity as a dozen mechanics worked to repair a handful of ships. In addition to the repairs, several ships looked to be of brand new construction. They were vapors, which had previously not been a part of the Sentient fleet. Gavin nodded in satisfaction. Halerin and the Sentients had not been idle while he was gone.

Halerin placed his hand upon Gavin's shoulder in the customary Wayman greeting. Gavin returned the gesture with as much enthusiasm as his broken body could manage. Kelm stared blankly around at the open bay, oblivious to Halerin's presence.

"You made it back," Halerin said.

"Yes, thanks to you. You kept looking. You didn't give up. I won't forget that," Gavin said, his voice cracking.

"It wasn't easy. We couldn't scan the area around Hull for fear of getting into another fight with the *Persepolis*."

"Another fight? What do you mean?" Gavin asked.

"They came after the *Maven*. They hit us as we were

boarding the last of the prisoners. It was horrible, Gavin. We had to leave some of them behind. In all that terrible battle, that was the hardest thing I had to do."

Gavin saw the tortured memory play out behind Halerin's eyes, the dozens of people left reaching towards the sky as the ship took off, some of them holding children in their arms. The distance soon erased their horrified expressions from view, but they were forever stamped in Halerin's mind.

"They came after us with lancers outfitted with cross stream weapons," Halerin went on, "We barely escaped alive."

"How did you make it?" Gavin resumed his grip on Halerin's shoulder, both to keep himself upright and because this news hit him hard as well. His sense of relief at seeing Halerin quickly evaporated.

"The chronotrace saved us. One of the energy mesh technicians used it to unlock the code for the Collective's ship to ship channels. We were able to jam their communications. After we did that, they were forced to abandon the attack."

"Brilliant," Gavin said, forcing a smile.

"I guess that's one of the reasons we call ourselves Sentients," Halerin said.

As they spoke, Kelm wandered in the direction of the wide bay doors. The ship's mechanics gave him puzzled looks. When Gavin realized what was happening, he followed after him, trying to reach him before he touched something he shouldn't or interrupted the repairs.

"Halerin, this is Kelm, the man who rescued me," Gavin said, spinning a confused Kelm around to face Halerin.

Kelm stared in Halerin's direction for a moment before turning away and mumbling something about looking for his quarters.

"We'll find you a place, Kelm. We're glad to have you on board," Halerin said.

Kelm ignored him, fixing his attention on Gavin instead.

"When can we use your machine, that chrono device you told me about?" he asked, his beady eyes unblinking.

"Soon, Kelm, soon," Gavin promised.

Kelm regarded him with rapt attention, smacking his lips together as if anticipating a hearty meal. "Wonderful. Just lead the way."

Despite Gavin's promise, he was unable to help Kelm recover his memories right away. There was too much to be done aboard the *Maven*.

In the engagement with the *Persepolis*, the Collective forces had damaged the celerium power core. The *Persepolis* had targeted the *Maven's* energy systems specifically. Just like Raif had said, the praxis cruisers were not invulnerable. Halerin had attempted to disable the *Persepolis* in the same manner, but the Collective fleet was much larger. They whittled down the *Maven's* shields before the Sentient forces could do any significant damage.

The crippling of the core had forced them to operate on bismine reserves. The crew of the *Maven* had been working day and night to repair the damage, but the energy mesh which powered the ship was still extremely weak. Before the battle they had been using celerium to power the chronotrace, but that was no longer possible. Worse, with the reserves dangerously low, they had sent out groups to mine the desert for fresh bismine, but that had proven problematic as well. Quakes continued to wreak havoc across the desert, interrupting several of the mining expeditions. One of the tremors had been so strong two Sentients had actually been killed. And the quakes were only getting worse, increasing both in intensity and frequency.

"*It's too dangerous to travel on the surface now,*" Halerin told Gavin as they sat in a small, circular meeting room just off the Command Center.

As Halerin described the quakes, memories of Gavin's escape from Manx Core came rushing back. The ceiling and walls of that place had started coming apart, followed by the glowing blue streams of neophosphorous, which poured down like blood gushing from a massive wound. He could almost taste the metallic floes again as he recalled the sludge pouring over him and pulling him under. He had never imagined something like that ran through the Viscera. Nor did it seem possible that such a cataclysm could still be raging beneath the surface of the Vast.

"*The quakes from Manx Core started days ago,*" Gavin remarked. "*How can they possibly still be going on?*"

"*I don't know. It doesn't make any sense. And they're spreading. We're more than a hundred clicks out from Oasis and they've already made it this far. We're safe because we're in the air, but the power requirements to keep us aloft are enormous. We're running through bismine faster than we can recharge it.*"

"*How long before the celerium is fully functional again?*"

"*That's hard to say,*" Halerin replied. "*The technicians are baffled by what is going on with the core. Conventional diagnostic tools are useless. The only thing they've been able to determine is that it's somehow repairing itself, similar to the way the velar hull did, but we have no idea how long that will take.*"

"*But if it's repairing itself, shouldn't we be able to transfer some of the power needs back onto the core?*"

"*That's another odd thing. Every time we've tried to connect it back into the energy mesh it ceases working altogether. It looks* like the only thing we can do is wait until the core is fully repaired before reconnecting it."

"This ship won't stay airborne forever," Gavin reminded him. "Not to mention the fact that without the core, we're limited in the kinds of sequences we can run with the chrono-trace. We need to find out what Cyrith is thinking and planning. And we need to find out where they're holding Adan and the others."

Halerin's mind buckled under the weight of so many unknowns. The responsibilities of leading the Sentients had taken their toll on him.

"There's something else that's troubling you besides getting back the core and finding Adan, isn't there?" Gavin probed.

"I was just thinking about all the Werin we rescued. They've been asking ever since they got here when we would take them to their families. I was so busy trying to find you and so focused on repairing the ship that I put it off. But I've been having nightmares about them ever since we lost the two Sentients to the quake. What about all the people living in the Viscera? We can't just leave them down there."

"You're right. They're not safe," Gavin agreed. "Finding them and getting them on board needs to be our top priority, even if it means ignoring the Collective for a little while. We can't wait until the core is functional."

"This is all my fault. I should have gone after them earlier," Halerin remarked, his eyes staring hollowly into space. "It's just...I thought if we could find you first, you would know what to do."

"I left you in command and you did what you thought was best. I blame myself more than anything."

A somber air descended upon the room. The weight of regret worked on Gavin, draining his will. His efforts to save Oasis had failed, and now the same thing had happened with his attempt to rescue Adan. Both had failed miserably, each time ending up worse than if he had done nothing at all.

As helpless as he felt, Halerin felt worse. He had been forced to abandon Gavin and then abandon the Werin as well. Gavin did not blame him for anything. Halerin had done a tremendous job under the circumstances, but Gavin sensed his friend was weary of bearing all these responsibilities on his own. It was time for his burdens to be lifted. It was time for Gavin to take back command of the ship.

"We may be down, but we are not helpless," Gavin declared. *"Halerin, head to the Command Center and get ready to set a new course."*

"Where to?" Halerin answered, roused temporarily from his doldrums.

"I'll tell you after you get there." Gavin arose and left the meeting room. *"First, I have to visit an old friend."*

TWENTY-SEVEN
A FORGOTTEN FRIENDSHIP

Senya sat across from Gavin as motionless as the bare metal table jutting out from the wall between them.

He gave her a smile. He hoped it did not seem too forced. She returned it with one of her own, an expansive expression which lit up her caring eyes. For all his supposed perceptivity as a memorant, her actual thoughts eluded him. Even so, common sense told him that the little quivers at the corners of her mouth meant that she, too, felt the awkwardness of the moment.

Though her skin showed lines of worry and her straight brown hair hung simply at her shoulders, there was an understated beauty about her.

He hurriedly shifted his gaze to her folded hands upon the table and took a deep breath, still wondering how to begin.

Though Gavin had known Senya for more than a year, even living with her family during a portion of that time, those memories had been erased by the Developers when he went back to Oasis. Nothing from his time with the Welkin remained except for a few second-hand accounts he had received from Adan. He knew that she had three children, two boys and a little girl. Her husband had died several years before Gavin arrived. Everything else was lost.

He opened his mouth to speak, but the words hung in his throat. What to say to a stranger who is supposed to be a friend? Gavin did not feel equal to the task, especially with the news he was about to give her. He lifted his eyes to meet hers. From what Adan had told him, Senya was courageous, strong, and resilient, and the clarity in her gaze confirmed that, but still the words did not come.

"It's good to see you again," Senya said finally, the kindness in her voice matching the expression on her face. "When you left...you had a look in your eyes like you might not be coming back."

Gavin cleared his throat, acknowledging her words with a nod. With their utterance he felt the anxiousness chains within loosen, at last freeing him to speak.

"I'm glad our paths have crossed again, but as Halerin has told you..."

"I know. You don't remember us anymore. You're like Will was at first. They...did something to you, didn't they, in that city the elders told us not to speak of?"

As the tension in the room eased, Gavin's memorant abilities began to quicken and return. He could finally read the emotions running through her. She felt sorry for him, and yet there was a kind of reserved respect there as well. She remembered how kind he had been to her family, but wasn't sure what to expect from him now.

"Yes, but my memories are not what's important at the moment," Gavin said. "What is important is that you're here and you're safe. Even though I may have failed in what I set out to do, that much, at least, came to pass."

A cold ball of nerves rolled down his back as he spoke, but

Senya reached out and placed her hand over his. "Thank you for saving us," she said, squeezing it softly. "If it were not for you, Adan, and your friends, we would have all been killed."

A pleasant warmth washed over Gavin as he returned her gaze. He struggled to find a fitting response, but words eluded him. It was not from awkwardness this time, but simply because he realized that words were inadequate for what he felt at that moment. He couldn't remember ever being in the presence of someone so obviously honest and good. Hope radiated from her, promising that, despite all that had happened, everything would turn out all right in the end. As much as he wanted to give in to that hope, his analytical mind would not surrender so easily. The loss of Adan and the other Sentients, as well as the fact that the Collective was reestablishing itself in the city of Hull, weighed heavily upon him.

"Senya, one of the things Adan gave back to me was my memory of the eidos and the revelations of Numinae. He said that most of the Welkin believe in him too, especially you."

"Yes, that is true. He is the source of my hope." Senya's eyes searched his, as if she sensed the doubts lurking in the back of his mind and sought to banish them through the light of her gaze.

"Do you think he will help us? As safe as you may feel here, everyone else on this ship in terrible danger. And I really don't know if I can fix things this time. There are so many things out of my control."

"Gavin, it's not your fault we were captured by Waymen," Senya said.

"If I had stayed I could have protected you."

"But you told us that leaving was the best way to protect us. And, as you said, that part came to pass."

Gavin withdrew his hands to he edge of the table, rubbing the corners nervously. The material was so unyielding, the flawless surface immune to scratches and blemishes. Why was it not the same with the human will? Why did it have to waver and collapse in upon itself so easily? Why could men not impose their will upon the events of life in the same way they produced this perfect rectangle of purpose and design?

"Senya, there's something I have to tell you. Halerin would have told you earlier, but he was too busy looking for me."

"Is it about Adan?"

"No, it's about your daughter and the rest of your knit. Halerin said that they fled east of the Basin after I left."

Senya's hand went to her lips. It trembled as she spoke. "Is she all right? Did something happen to the knit?"

"No, not that we know of. But they may be in danger and I thought you should know about it."

"Oh, Gavin, what is it? The Waymen? More of those flying ships?" For the first time the light in her eyes wavered.

"No, it's the land itself. It's not stable. Something's not right. The tunnels of the Viscera are collapsing in on themselves and we don't know why. It may be that the part of the Viscera where your knit fled to remains untouched, but we just wanted to let you know that we're doing everything in our power to—"

Senya reached over and clutched his hand once again. "Take me to them. Please, Gavin, you can do that, right?" Tears tumbled down her cheeks. "Oh, Lila, my little girl..."

Gavin covered both her trembling hands in his. "Senya, that's one of the reasons I came to see you today, to find out where your people fled to so that we can go and find them."

Senya made no effort to wipe her tears, but the hopeful light in her eyes blazed anew.

"Of course I will tell you where they are. Anything to find my Lila and help our people. But before I do, you asked me about Numinae. You asked if he ever intervenes. I believe he does. I've seen terrible things happen to our people, but I've seen help come at unexpected times and in unexpected ways as well, ways that could only be from him. He will help us if that is his will."

Gavin sighed, his hopes buoyed as much by the light in her eyes that shone through the sadness as by her words.

"I used to know him, didn't I?" Gavin asked plaintively.

Senya brushed her tears away at last and quickly grabbed his hand. Her touch was no longer desperate, but gentle.

"Your faith was very strong, Mendigo. That's what we used to call you. It means 'beggar.' You told us that you came seeking the truth and so the Maneusis chose that name for you."

"Beggar...an odd word. We had no need to beg in Oasis. We had everything we needed."

"Not everything. Otherwise you would not have left."

"You are right," Gavin said. "And it seems that Numinae had a hand in helping me see the emptiness at the heart of that city. Even abundance can be lack if he is not a part of it. I just wish I knew what he was planning now, so that I could go and do it. I feel so helpless."

"We will seek him, then, as we did in our hogar when you were with us. And he will hear us now as he did then," she assured him. "And it may be that, in time, he will also reveal to us what his plan may be."

Then, at a nod from Gavin, she bowed her head and lifted her hands in prayer.

It turned out that the part of the Viscera where Senya's people had fled to was two and a half days away from their present location. It was a place the Welkin referred to as The Cata-combs. These tunnels served as a burial grounds for their dead, though many caves within the Catacombs had yet to be given over to this purpose. Normally it was uninhabited, but in times of emergency, the Welkin sometimes fled there since the Waymen feared to come near it. The *Maven*, with Halerin at the helm, set a course for this place based on the information Senya provided.

Gavin spent the rest of the day and most of the night in the lab, tweaking the chronotrace, trying to improve its capabilities without the use of the celerium core. Though it still had a small celerium wafer inside it, this proved inadequate to re-enable the thought mapping or accelerated temporal projection algorithms he needed. Early in the morning, he gave up and retired to his quarters. He was still recovering from his ordeal in the desert, so he applied some almamenth to his skin before going to sleep.

Barely two slices later, Halerin invaded his consciousness with a mental message which roused him from sleep.

"Gavin, I'm sorry to disturb you, but I have some important news. It's the celerium, it seems to have made a complete recovery during the night. We've already connected it back to the energy mesh and everything seems to be working perfectly."

Gavin sat up and groped for the lab coat which he'd cast at the end of the bed. *"Wonderful. I'll meet you in the Command Center and we can plan where to go from here."*

"I'll see you in a bit, then," Halerin replied.

Gavin rubbed the sleep from his eyes. Donning his robe, he stepped out the door. He turned to head down the hall, but hesitated when he spotted Kelm emerging from his room at the same time. Though the two shared quarters next to each other, this was the first time Gavin had run into him since their arrival.

Halerin had informed him that Kelm had been asking several of the Sentients about the chronotrace, specifically when he would be able to recover the information about his past. The other Sentients had done their best to explain the situation to him, that the chronotrace was not functioning properly, but Kelm did not take the news well, accusing Gavin and the other Sentients of treachery and false promises. On one occasion he had even attacked one of the Sentients and had to be pulled off him by two Waymen who happened to be nearby. Kelm had backed off rather quickly after being confronted, going so far as to apologize for losing control.

Gavin had planned on addressing these matters at some point, but had wanted to wait until they got the chronotrace working. Now, as Kelm hurried his way, it looked like Gavin would be forced to address the situation sooner than he had hoped.

"Oh, Gavin, you're up," Kelm exclaimed. "I couldn't sleep either. Were you up all night working on the chronotrace? Is it fixed?"

Gavin took a quick breath. "I'm going to talk to Halerin about it now. I'll let you know as soon as everything's ready." He made to take his leave at that point, hoping that would be enough to resolve the issue, but Kelm stepped in front of him, blocking his way.

"So there's hope that you'll be able to find out about my past soon? Do you think it will be today?" Kelm asked.

Gavin sensed Kelm fighting to control his emotions, to not let his desperation master him.

"Not today, Kelm," Gavin said, regretfully. "But don't give up hope. It should be very soon. As I said, I'll let you know as soon as I start the trace of your past. Right now, though, I've got to go. I'm on my way to a meeting with Halerin."

"I—could I go with you? Maybe I could help?" Kelm offered, his voice sounding feeble and pathetic, as if he hoped to move Gavin into a display of compassion.

"I'm sorry, Kelm," Gavin said firmly. "I'm afraid I need to meet with him privately. I hope you understand. How about if I stop by your quarters tonight and fill you in on what we find out? Would that be all right?"

Kelm started grinding his teeth. Gavin sensed an outburst might be imminent so he took advantage of Kelm's momentary hesitation to dart past him. "I'll talk to you tonight," he blurted out over his shoulder as he strode briskly down the corridor. He didn't bother looking back and thankfully Kelm said nothing in reply. Gavin hoped he would not take this further delay too hard and do something rash.

TWENTY-EIGHT
INCIDENT IN THE LAB

With the energy mesh finally back at full strength, Gavin and Halerin focused their efforts on coordinating the rescue of the families of the refugees they had taken in from Hull. The two Sentients met with representatives from the various Welkin knits and Waymen thrals on the ship to discuss their plans. Since Senya's knit was the closest, it was decided that they would be the first to be rescued.

But even though this decision made sense, it generated some resentment among the Waymen. This in turn set off Malloc, the leader of Senya's people, who glowered at the Waymen gathered and shouted that none of them deserved to be rescued at all. Both sides fell to bickering, the Waymen claiming that they had been on the ship first and the Welkin recounting the atrocities they had endured from the Waymen raids. The two groups nearly came to blows. Only by hastily adjourning the meeting was an out and out brawl avoided.

As the agitated gathering dispersed Gavin hurried towards the Command Center and tried to put the meeting behind him by turning his thoughts to the chronotrace. He was anxious to find out what the Collective planned on doing with Hull, but more than that, what they had planned for Adan and the other captives. He had some ideas and none of them were good.

The thoughts of Dillon, the chief energy systems technician in Raif's absence, came to Gavin through the esolace. *"The majority of the bismine reserves should be fully charged before the end of the day. We will be near one hundred percent by tomorrow."*

"I would like to renew my work with the chronotrace as soon as possible," Gavin replied. *"Do you think we could transfer the core to my lab before the reserves are fully charged?"*

"If necessary. Even with the reserves at half charge, we can power basic flight capabilities and normal operational systems for up to seven days."

"I should only need it for a day or two to complete the traces I need. Whenever the reserves get to fifty percent, have the core sent over," Gavin replied.

He sensed Dillon's mind interacting with the system monitoring the bismine reserves. It was a little like watching someone assemble a puzzle, only at a very fast pace. *"We should hit that in just over four slices from now,"* Dillon informed him. *"We'll have it in the lab half a slice after that."*

"Excellent. I appreciate all your work, Dillon."

Finally, some good news at the end of a long day.

Once again, the intrusion of someone else's thoughts shook Gavin awake. It was Dillon.

"I'm sorry for waking you, Gavin, but I thought you should be alerted. There appears to have been a malfunction with the chronotrace. Its energy signature is no longer appearing on the system."

Gavin rolled over and threw one leg off the edge of his bed, still half-asleep. *"That's odd. When did it go off system?"*

"Almost half a slice back. I'm sorry. I was doing some optimization on the energy mesh and didn't notice it had gone down."

"Perfectly understandable. I'll head down to investigate the issue." Gavin had learned his lesson from last time and had slept in his lab coat.

"I have a team on the way," Dillon told him. *"You don't have to go yourself. I just wanted to let you know what was going on."*

"No, I would prefer to see it first hand. The chronotrace is my invention and I would like to find out what went wrong and resolve the issue as soon as possible. Every moment we lose delays us finding the Sentient captives."

"Very well, should I recall the two men I sent?"

Gavin was about to answer yes, but then thought better of it. If the problem was with the celerium core someone might need to transfer it back into the energy well for testing.

"No, I will meet them there," he replied.

He slipped on his shoes and headed out the door. Quick steps soon brought him to the lev shaft at the end of the hall. With a brief mental command, he called for a disc to carry him down to the lab level, but the esolace informed him that the lev in that particular shaft was out of commission. He tromped away from the access door and headed to the ramp. He picked up his pace to make up for having to take the long way. When he came out on level five, he finally stopped to catch his breath, looking down the corridor towards the lab. Immediately he realized that something was wrong. The door was open. Doors never stayed open on the ship; they always closed automatically. Looking closer, he noticed someone's hand laying across the threshold, unmoving.

Gavin rushed forward to see who it was. The lab entrance was about fifty paces away, but when he got within thirty, a powerful, acrid odor crawled up his nose. He became light-headed and staggered, catching himself against the wall. His thoughts became fuzzy, but he had enough clarity of thought to send a message across the *Maven's* esolace before his mind went all the way under.

"Halerin? Halerin, are you there?" His mind groped through the mental darkness. There was no answer. Halerin must have been asleep, Gavin reasoned, but then he couldn't remember whether or not that would have made any differ-ence. He forced his thoughts in a different direction. *"Dillon, something's wrong. I can't find Halerin. Do you know where he is?"* He slid down something smooth and hard. Or maybe he was being pulled up instead. He couldn't tell. He was so dizzy.

"Gavin, what's wrong? Your mental signature is fading. I can barely make it out." After that Dillon's thoughts collapsed in a mangled heap of unintelligibility.

Gavin's mind dimmed to almost black and then, unexpect-edly, his head began to clear.

"Gavin? Gavin, can you make out what I'm thinking?" Dillon pressed him.

"Yes, it's getting better. I can think again."

"Good. You started to fade on me so I ran a diagnostic and found a high concentration of namarin in the air at your loca-tion. I recycled the vents in that sector hoping to neutralize it before I lost you."

"Good thinking. You need to let Halerin know what's happening."

Dillon paused briefly before answering. *"I can't reach him. It looks like he disconnected from the system about two slices before midnight. No trace of him after that."*

"Strange."

"What about the namarin? Do you know where that came from?"

"We had some in the lab for surgical purposes, but it was stored in gel form, not as a gas. Something must have gone wrong in there, an accident of some sort," Gavin conjectured.

"Did Anders and Quinn make it? They're the technicians I sent," Dillon asked.

"I don't know."

Gavin worked his way to his feet, his legs still lethargic from the effects of the gas. *"I think at least one of them passed out from the gas. I see a hand in the doorway, that's all."*

Dillon's thoughts clouded over. Tension often made a person's thoughts opaque. Like the rest of the Sentients, Dillon had only been awakened from the Collective a few days ago. He had no idea how to handle a situation like this.

"Dillon, I need you to focus," Gavin attempted to draw him out, but it was no use. Once again, their connection began to fade. Gavin started thinking of random things. Unconnected words and concepts popped into his brain. Neon, spastic ribbons, floundering cloth jars, crusty fuchsia clouds. Whatever odd thing he could think of. It was a memorant technique to shock someone's mind into letting him in. After a few more moments of technicolor speculation it worked. Dillon's mind came back.

"They are both off system as well," he finally reported. *"You were right, they probably got hit by the gas. By the time you got there it must have dissipated enough so that you didn't go down right away."*

"At least they're not hurt. I'm going in to investigate," Gavin informed him.

"Wait until I get there. I don't want you going in alone. It could be dangerous," Dillon warned.

"Fine, but hurry."

Gavin stamped his tingling feet, trying to get them to wake up while he waited for Dillon to arrive. How had this happened? He ran through possible explanations in his head. A massive fluctuation in the energy levels would have done it, something similar to what happened when Adan used it in Oasis the first time. But Gavin had put in failsafes since then. Maybe the algorithm generator had gone bad, or maybe the celerium was acting up again. It could have been one of a hundred other things as well.

Eventually, he grew so frustrated churning over hypothetical scenarios that he decided to check the logs. He started searching for any clues as to why Halerin had gone off system. The only detail that stood out as unusual was the fact that he had gone to the cargo bay to check on some problems the technicians were having assembling one of the new vapors. He could have done that from the Command Center, but Halerin liked to interact with people face to face as much as possible. He said it made him feel more like a Sentient, more human.

Unlike the esolace in Oasis, the *Maven's* logs were not exhaustive. They did not record Halerin's thoughts, but they did record his words and what he saw. The last thing he laid eyes on was the hallway between the cargo bay and the Command Center. Gavin checked to see if any other Sentients had been present, anyone who might have seen what happened to him, but the passage had been empty; he had been alone.

Three microslices passed before Dillon arrived. Two new technicians trailed behind him as he exited the ramp. Both of them wore cutter gloves and held oscillathes. Gavin thought it a bit unnecessary, but it was probably best to err on the side of caution.

When they arrived at the door, Gavin saw the other technicians lying stretched out on the floor. The room looked the same as he remembered it except for several empty tubes on top of a table. Those must have been the ones filled with namarin. He was about to check the labels when he noticed the celerium core in the corner of the room. The chronotrace that was supposed to be on top of it was gone.

He rushed over to see if it had fallen behind the column. Splotches of dark red blood glistened on the floor at the base of the core.

"No..." the word escaped Gavin's lips as he went around the back of the column. The lifeless body of Halerin lay slumped against it.

TWENTY-NINE
A HARD DECISION

G<small>AVIN LEANED OVER THE TABLE</small>. A <small>DIZZY SPELL CAME</small> over him, but it wasn't the namarin gas this time. It was the sight of his dead friend.

He didn't bother looking up when Dillon and the others rushed over. There were gasps, confused questions, but Gavin barely heard them. He wandered inside his own mind, spinning in a gyre of despair. What had happened? What had gone wrong?

By the time he came out of his mental and emotional spiral, the cart carrying the body of Halerin was floating into the hallway, accompanied by the technicians. Anders and Quinn, who had first arrived on the scene, were revived and sent on their way after some brief questioning. Gavin and Dillon were left alone in the lab.

Though Dillon had purified the air in the room, nothing could expunge the intangible dread which hung over it. It was tasteless, odorless, and invisible, but it made Gavin's skin pale and his heart beat slowly and painfully. It was the emptiness and enduring chill which comes from death, like wind rushing through a hole in his stomach.

Dillon's stare bored into the empty tubes, an angry light smoldering in his eyes.

"*How could this happen?*" he asked. "*We're all Sentients here. Anyone on this ship would give his life for anyone else. It doesn't make any sense. Could it have been one of the Waymen?*"

Only some of the Sentients knew about the Waymen before they came on board and Dillon wasn't one of them. Even so, he didn't pose the question in an accusatory manner. Like Gavin, he was just grasping for answers. But why would the Waymen attack Halerin? What did they possibly have to gain by doing so?

While Dillon struggled through his own mental fog, Gavin began to come out of his.

He used the esolace to bring up the lab records. It only took a moment to find what he was looking for.

"*I just checked the portal access history, Dillon,*" he reported. "*There is no record of Halerin entering the lab all day.*"

"*Do you think he was killed before he came in?*" Dillon wondered.

"*No, there's no sign of blood in the hallway or anywhere else in the lab for that matter. I think he was killed in this lab.*"

"*He must have disconnected his bioseine from the esolace. That's the only reason I can think of why the system doesn't record him entering. But why would he do that?*"

"*Maybe he was forced.*" As thoughts flew between them, Gavin's intuition latched onto something. "*And there is only one person who would have done something like that, and he's not a Sentient or a Wayman.*"

It took Dillon a moment to catch on. *"Wait, Kelm? But why? Do you think he got in another fight?"*

"No, I'm guessing he brought Halerin in here on purpose. Kelm was desperate to find out about his past. Maybe he decided to take things into his own hands. He could have forced Halerin to use the chronotrace and then killed him after he got what he wanted. He might have taken the chronotrace so that no one would find out what he discovered."

Dillon ran another mental check through the esolace.

"Are you sure? Halerin's mental signature doesn't show up on the Maven's system as accessing the chronotrace either."

"You see these tubes left out on the table? Whoever opened them didn't even bother tampering with the labels or removing them. Only two of them were filled with namarin. The other three, when mixed together, form vexam, a hypnotic, hallucinatory drug. It can be used to implant suggestions in the mind of someone affected by it. Kelm said he was some sort of scout in an army. If so, he might have known how to create vexam. If he drugged Halerin, he could have convinced him to connect directly to the chronotrace without using the esolace and we would never know about it."

"Do you really think Kelm was capable of something that meticulous? He didn't seem like his mind was all that together."

"Sometimes madness conceals extreme cunning. And who knows just how much of his instability was feigned and how much of it was real," Gavin conjectured.

"But he saved your life, didn't he? Why would he turn around and kill Halerin?" Dillon gripped the edge of one of the tables so hard his knuckles turned white. Halerin and Dillon had been in the same Sentient cell together after the fall of Oasis. The memories of their time together flashed through Dillon's mind. Halerin had saved Dillon's life on more than one occasion and now his friend was dead.

Gavin couldn't help but feel that he was to blame. He had promised to help Kelm, but have gotten wrapped up in rescuing the Werin and finding Adan. If he had never mentioned the chronotrace to Kelm in the first place, maybe this never would have happened.

Now Halerin was dead because of his mistake. It should have been Gavin lying with his head split open against the core, not Halerin.

"Security, there's been an incident in the cargo bay," came a message from one of the technicians, shattering the morbid stillness of Gavin's thoughts.

Dillon and Gavin shot out the doorway, starting to run before even answering back. The cargo bay was not far, at the opposite end of the hallway from the lab.

"What is it?" Dillon asked.

"I just came in with another technician to take over for one of the night shift teams and we found all four mechanics passed out. They seem okay, but they won't wake up."

Dillon and Gavin picked up their speed. A quick mental check of the system showed traces of namarin in the air supply in the bay.

"We're on our way, but you should get out of there for now. There may be an enemy in that area," Dillon advised. *"We'll meet you outside the main entrance."*

The gas had probably dissipated by now, but Dillon accessed the vent system in the cargo bay and set it to recycle just to be sure. He also called for a security team of six Sentients to head to the bay, but he and Gavin got there first.

They met the men who had sent the initial alert as they left through the main entrance. A zoetic scan of the area through the esolace, as well as a more rudimentary physical search, failed to detect the presence of anyone else inside the bay beyond the four unconscious technicians.

They called in some medical personnel to revive the mechanics. While they waited for them to arrive, Gavin went out and questioned the two men who reported the incident. He learned nothing more during the brief interrogation other than that one of the citus' was missing from the cargo bay.

He called up to the Command Center and had them scan to see if there were any ships in the area. They reported the departure of a citus a full slice earlier speeding northwards, but it was out of scanning range now.

"Did you try to make contact with the ship as it left?" Dillon asked Nance, who, since his return from captivity on the *Persepolis*, had been assisting Halerin in the Command Center.

"Yes," Nance replied. *"But he wouldn't respond. We did get a visual though. It was Kelm. We didn't think it was worth risking one of our ships to go out after him, though, especially since he was on a citus. We'd never catch him."*

"I see," Gavin answered. *"Thank you for the information."*

Dillon shook his head. *"He's gone for good, isn't he?"*

"There is a way we can find him," Gavin came back.

"How?" Dillon looked over at Gavin, his eyes blinking rapidly.

"The chronotrace."

"But Kelm took it."

Gavin smiled, renewed hope taking the edge off his numbness. *"Yes, but the chronotrace is still inside my head. I can build another."*

Halerin's death cast a shroud of darkness over the *Maven*, but the rescue of the Welkin lessened it somewhat. The operation into the Catacombs went better than expected. That part of the Viscera had suffered only minor quakes and the Welkin living there had all been brought on board, eighty-five more people joining the ship's population. Though frightened and confused at first at the sight of the enormous praxis cruiser, being reunited with their friends and family helped make it easier to adjust to life in the floating fortress.

Now Gavin sat in the commissary, surrounded by friends at the end of a savory dinner of mosh, atol, and a tangy, stringy dish the Welkin called asada. This was the first time he had been able to share a meal with Senya and her children and he took great delight in the lighthearted interactions between them. Despite all that had happened to Senya's boys, Jarem and Halel, and her daughter Lila, the children still held on to a settled innocence which Gavin found both remarkable and comforting.

Little Lila, who barely came up past her mother's waist, had not seen her family for many days, living with family friends in the Catacombs. Yet she remained a bright-eyed, bubbly little girl who winked and made faces and snorted atol out her nose when overcome by fits of giggling.

The boys were a little more dour, but, in spite of having been pressed into hard labor, processing scrap for the Waymen in Hull, their eyes glowed with the embers of an unbroken spirit. Being reunited with their family was all they cared about. And their confidence in themselves and in their leaders to overcome any future threats to that union seemed unshakable.

"Numinae has protected us this far," Jarem said at one point during the meal. "He will see us through to the end of days."

"We can carve out a new home quickly in the Viscera with these machines, right mother?" Halel added.

"Oh, if we do, can I have my own room this time?" Lila piped up, her whistle-like voice rising above the noisy room.

Even Malloc was affected by the general mood pervading the celebratory dinner. In honor of Gavin's role in rescuing his knit, the big man had deigned to share a table with him. He had yet to grumble or say a harsh word, though his face often clouded in a scowl whenever the children got too carried away. At any other time the Welkin leader would have reprimanded them for their lack of dignity, but today he let it pass.

Perhaps the presence of the Maneusis, the diminutive, wrinkled Welkin who shared the table with them, was another factor in Malloc's docility on this occasion. This bent old holy man was short on stature, but long on the respect he commanded among his people. The twinkle in his eye hinted that he perceived far more than he let on and that eye seemed to be upon Gavin every time he glanced his way.

The few times the Maneusis did speak, his words were full of wisdom. Gavin thought he heard echoes of Senya in his speech, or perhaps it was the other way around. Gavin drank in the words, finding them more fulfilling than anything that had been served at the meal. More than anything else that night he was looking for guidance, looking for some indication as to whether he should go through with what he had planned. And yet he could not confide in anyone about what those plans were. He knew what they would say if he did. He was a memorant, after all. Still, he wished he could tell someone.

Three days had passed since Kelm escaped and it had been a day and a half since Gavin had rebuilt the chronotrace. The trace of Kelm's past was complete and now Gavin had the answers he's been looking for, though they weren't anything like what he had been expecting.

"Gavin, I think it's time we retire to our rooms," Senya's voice spoke into his musings. He realized that he had been quiet for some time and that the celebration was winding down around him.

Senya rose, along with her three children, and made her way towards Gavin on the opposite side of the table. He stood to see them off.

"All right, then," Gavin muttered, recovering his senses enough to go through the motions of returning their embraces.

Malloc had actually left a little earlier, after having eaten three times more than anyone else at the table and claiming the need to 'walk it off.' Only the Maneusis remained seated, gazing at Gavin and Senya as they exchanged their goodbyes.

"Do you have any games we can play in this big metal ball?" Lila asked. "It gets kinda boring around here, you know."

"Lila, shh," her mother chided. "If you need something to do, I'm sure Gavin could find some work for you."

Gavin gave a distracted smile in their general direction. "I'll see all of you again soon," he said, his eyes glazing over.

Lila's eyebrows squiggled across her forehead. "What's the matter with you, Mendigo? You look sleepy. Or maybe just woozy. You got too much mosh sloshing around in your belly or something?"

"No, no. My mind is just on other things," Gavin said hastily, acutely aware of the odd looks the others were giving him. All, that is, except the Maneusis, whose expression rarely changed.

"He's worried about Adan, Lila," Senya said, touching his shoulder. "Do not worry, Gavin. Take your concerns to the Everlord. He will take care of Adan better than any of us ever could."

"I hope so," Gavin said, trying to sound optimistic. "It was a wonderful meal, Senya. Go enjoy your family."

"I have you to thank for that." She embraced him tightly one last time, then she and her children bowed respectfully to the Maneusis and made their way towards the exit. Lila gave

Gavin one last mischievous wink before her brothers dragged her out the door.

The moment the door shut, the Maneusis rose and stood in front of Gavin.

"You have dark thoughts swirling around in that head of yours, my son," said the elder, speaking in the Welkin tongue. "I have seen that look before."

"Are you saying you can read my mind?" Gavin asked, trying to make light of the man's comments.

"I cannot read minds, but the well of the eyes rises up from the heart. It is not difficult to see the truth if one keeps his eyes open," the Maneusis answered in his raspy voice which, if it were skin, would have been as wrinkled as his face.

Gavin hung his head. If anyone could give him advice about what he should do, he sensed that it would be this man. And yet, he dared not mention his plans.

"So when did you see this look?" Gavin asked.

"Before you left us the last time," the man said softly.

Gavin could not bear to meet his eyes for fear he might give too much away. Though the Maneusis was certainly no memorant, he was in many ways just as perceptive.

"Well, times change," he said, hedging his words, trying not to reveal too much.

"But the heart of a man does not. Not when it is set on a given path. And I believe you have been on this path ever since you left the city of your people."

There was a long silence in which Gavin wished he could think of something to say, but all he wanted to do was leave. The Maneusis was right. The decision had already been made and every moment he stood there only delayed the inevitable.

"Go and do what it is that you must do," said the Maneusis, his voice losing its rasp and becoming strangely resonant. "And may Numinae ever be your guide."

The words of this shriveled little man somehow set Gavin free to make his decision. Even more than that, the fierce compassion in his eyes told Gavin that at least one of his worries, about who would take care of Senya and her family, could be laid to rest.

"Thank you," Gavin whispered.

The Maneusis nodded slowly.

Gavin bowed and took his leave. He left the commissary and returned briefly to his quarters, just long enough to record a mental message, leaving instructions for Dillon and Nance in his absence. Then he walked in calm, measured steps towards the lev shaft, reflecting again on what he had seen in the chronotrace. By the time the lev stopped on the central floor, he was sufficiently clear on his decision to wonder how he ever doubted it. He made one last stop at the lab to gather the things he needed and then headed towards the cargo bay.

He did not remember what he had felt when he left the Welkin for Oasis last time, but he wondered if it was similar to what he felt now. Inadequacy. Misgivings. Despair. He was almost certain that his plan would fail, but that did not bother him. Success is not measured in the outcome, but in being faithful to do what was right, no matter the cost. All men die sooner or later and he had lived longer than most. Better to live bravely and truly to the end than to wait for death in the cold dark corner of cowardice.

Despite what he told himself, and the overwhelming sense of inevitability which coursed through him, he hoped this was not the end.

He was not quite ready to leave this world just yet.

THIRTY

A NEW ASSIGNMENT

Two researchers in silver lab coats walked stride for stride through the *Nebula's* corridors. They had just come from a debriefing in the Orientation Room and were on their way towards the Repository on the other side of the ship. The *Nebula* was nearly half a click across, but the lev waiting for them at the end of the hallway would make the trip little more than a brief inconvenience. They mounted the black disc floating just above the floor and rode off along one of the lev lanes.

The only Collectives they passed on their way were supervising somatarch crews busy repairing the ship. The researchers sped through several unfinished corridors, some of which were little more than bare frameworks revealing open sky churning above them.

"It seems hard to believe they will be able to finish the reconstruction on time," Aaron remarked.

"The plan seems sound enough. The somatarchs are quite efficient at these sorts of repetitive tasks," answered Donovan, the other researcher. He had more of an engineering mindset,

having worked on the construction of others ships before coming onboard the *Nebula*, so Aaron trusted his opinion.

"At least there's something left to repair," Aaron commented. Most ships would not have survived crashing into the surface of a planet, much less left any survivors, but the *Nebula* was no ordinary ship. Most of the crew being in cryo-sleep had certainly helped. The interstellar cryo-chambers were located in the most well-protected parts of the ship.

"The hard part will be finding another suitable planet to start over on again," Donovan observed. Aaron could not tell whether the comment was meant to express concern or merely a statement of fact. Donovan was a hard man to read. He rarely shared as much through his bioseine as he could have.

Aaron hoped that this might be one of the rare instances where Donovan was incorrect. He was more than ready to resume their interstellar journey. As an environmental investigator, his skills would be put to good use in finding the Collective a new world to colonize. He would perform a more in-depth analysis of the possible candidates this time. The decision to enter Nai's atmosphere without sending in recon ships had been a mistake. Then again, they didn't have much choice. Getting inside the atmosphere was the only way to avoid the Delegation's interstellar scans.

Of course, there was no guarantee of finding any habitable worlds within scanning range. Even if they did stumble across one there were always risk factors on unexplored worlds—interstellar scans didn't pick up everything. Nai was a perfect example. It scanned out as having suitable metrics, but now that they were here he could hardly imagine a more inhospitable place. Resources were scarce, long range communication impossible, and the weather completely unpredictable, defying all known modeling algorithms.

"There are several planets within a reasonable distance,"

Aaron stated. *"But we won't really know anything definite until we send out some scout teams. Either way, I'm just glad we won't be going back into cryo-sleep."*

"Let's hope not. We're still under evaluation, though," Donovan reminded him.

"Maybe one of us will test out as a memorant. That would help. I wonder why they didn't test us before the journey began, though? Why wait until after they've promoted us to the Development team?"

Donovan's thoughts became guarded. There he went, close to the vest again. Was that a sign that he had been wondering the same thing, too?

"I'm not questioning their methods," Aaron followed up, trying to reassure him. *"I'm just curious, that's all."*

"I'm not so sure that's the way they'd see it. I'd keep those kinds of thoughts to myself if I were you if you want to stay on this side of the cryo-vault," Donovan warned.

The curt response caught Aaron off guard.

"You're right. Sorry for bringing it up." Aaron felt awkward apologizing. They had not even been Developers for a single day and already he was out of step. Not for the first time he wondered why they had even promoted him to this level. *They must be getting desperate,* he thought, but squelched the notion as soon as it popped into his mind. He had to be more careful, toe the line like Donovan.

Aaron glanced through one of the windows along the corridor as they passed by. He could see other sections of the ship and crews with portable fabricators braving the sand storms to finish them. The fabricators had long, low frames with floating material ejectors constantly maneuvering themselves to create panels, struts, and other components needed to rebuild the infrastructure of the *Nebula.* The ship was close to eighty-five percent complete. If everything went according to schedule, it was projected to be completed in less than a ten span.

The black disc Aaron and Donovan floated on scuttled beyond the windows and into a passage with a checkpoint. The platform slowed briefly when it passed through several bands of yellow lights and then picked up speed again. Security had become tighter than ever of late. There were too many exposed areas where outsiders could get in. The checkpoints were designed to keep them from getting very far.

A few moments later, the disc dropped the two researchers off outside the door to the Repository. It swished aside and they stepped into the chamber. Black metallic memory blocks and large neon canisters of remin fluid were stacked floor to ceiling along the walls. The glowing green solution reflected off the metallic surfaces, giving an overexposed appearance to the room. The spacious warehouse of memories was larger even than the *Nebula's* bridge. So many thoughts, so many lives, all within the confines of a single room.

Xander stood in between two rows of memory blocks. The black cubes came up to his shoulder so that from the doorway all that could be seen was his head. His eyes were glassy, his gaze fixed on some spot on the wall to their right. He was using the esolace. Since neither Aaron or Donovan had access to the channels he was using they walked over and waited for him to finish.

"Your orientation went well, I take it?" Xander acknowledged their presence through the Development channel, though his eyes remained unfocused.

"Excellent," Donovan replied. *"It was a lot to take in, even with a bioseine, but I feel much more up to speed with the situation now."*

"Good. We will continue to monitor you to ensure there are no side effects from your extended time in cryo-sleep. Once

everything checks out, we will submit you for memorant testing."

A sense of mild alarm arose in Aaron's mind. In the back of his mind he had already been wondering about the side effects of coming out of cryo-sleep. He had heard strange things could happen to a person in that state. He hadn't felt quite himself since coming out and even Donovan at times seemed to act in odd ways, more like a stranger than the long-time friend Aaron knew him to be.

"Understood," Donovan replied, taking the news in stride. *"How are repairs to the ship progressing?"*

"Well, but it may not be enough. We have reason to believe that the Delegation may have discovered our presence on this planet. We found a radial jaunter abandoned in the desert this morning. It was damaged and inoperative, no doubt a victim of the same sorts of storms which grounded the Nebula, *but there was no indication that the pilot died in the crash. We assume he will construct a new ship and open a sidereal portal as soon as possible if he has not already done so. Then he will call in what's left of the Delegation fleet to finish what they began on Kess."*

Xander relayed the news quickly and efficiently, as would be expected from such a veteran Developer, but Aaron struggled to suppress the rising panic inside of him. The Delegation was coming to this planet? Wasn't it enough that they destroyed the Collective's home world of Kess? Did they mean to eradicate all life on Nai too? Whatever their intentions, the Collective was in no shape to position them, not with the *Nebula* in the state it was in.

"That's terrible news. Is there anything we can do to help accelerate the repair of the ship. I know that's not our area of expertise..." Aaron allowed the dangling thought to shrivel away. Once again he had reacted without thinking, making

suggestions to his superior on a subject which he knew nothing about.

Mild concern registered on Donovan's face, which only deepened Aaron's regret at having let the thoughts slip through.

"We actually have something else for you to work on, though it is of no less importance," Xander replied.

"What would that be?" Donovan asked.

"The survivor of the crash has not contacted the Delegation yet as far as we know. If we can find him before he calls in our enemy's forces we can stop this war before it ever starts."

"We'll do whatever it takes to protect the Collective," Donovan promised.

Xander nodded distractedly. *"I need you to resume a project that has been abandoned for some time. You were briefed about past deviants during your orientation. The project in question belonged to one of our most prominent defectors."*

Aaron and Donovan exchanged worried glances. Working on deviant technology was inherently dangerous. They didn't want to get sucked in to aberrant ways of thinking.

"Do not be concerned," Xander assured them. *"The decision to resume this work has been approved and gone through the proper channels."*

"Which deviant are you referring to?" Donovan asked.

"Gavin, one of our archivists."

"And what was he working on?" Donovan followed up in his typical, businesslike fashion.

"It's a device designed to retrace time and playback events from the past. According to the logs he never finished it while he was a Developer, but now we are not so sure. We have had several inexplicable security breaches of late and are wondering if this device might have played a part. We have decided to investigate the possibility of crafting one for ourselves or at least finding a way to render any others ineffective."

"Difficult times demand unorthodox approaches," Donovan remarked.

"Sounds interesting," Aaron commented, intrigued in the project despite the device's clandestine origins. *"So what is this device called?"*

"The chronotrace," Xander replied.

Light from the chronotrace filled the lab, glinting off the instruments and the blue-tinted visors worn by Aaron and Donovan. The device had been running for almost half a slice, its longest period of continuous operation yet. Without warning a blossom of white light consumed it and it spun to a stop. The malfunction coincided with a brief shaking of the walls, but they often shuddered like that from the quakes. The tremors had been happening ever since they crashed, but they rarely lasted for very long and had only damaged the ship significantly on one occasion, collapsing a newly framed-up wall. Yet another of Nai's many instabilities.

"We're tracing an area one tenth the size of what the chronotrace should be capable of and it still can't handle the presence of zoetic entities," Aaron remarked, lifting his visor. *"You would think the celerium coil would mitigate the power fluctuations."*

"The way things are going, I doubt we'll have it ready before the launch," Donovan replied. The exact time of launch was not known, but both thought it would be no more than a few days.

"It took Gavin years to perfect this device," Aaron commented. *"I don't see how they expect us to finish it in less than a ten span."*

"But we have access to all of his research." Donovan also removed his mask and the two of them walked over to their

prototype sitting on top of a column of celerium. The ebony stone was a bit wider than Aaron's body and came up to his shoulder. The chronotrace attached to it was burnt out so they could no longer sense it with their minds. They'd have to replace the bioseine interface again which meant it would be close to a full slice before they could perform another test.

Donovan picked up the disabled device and brought it to a nearby table. He pulled out a tool connected to a sectioned cable which stretched down from the ceiling and set to work dismantling it.

While Aaron watched his colleague work, he ran back through the logs, going over all of the successful test runs Gavin had recorded. In reviewing the notes about these experiments, Aaron noticed a detail that he had missed.

"Donovan, did you see these references to the sub-rational algorithms in Gavin's notes?" Aaron asked.

"Briefly, why?" Donovan replied, not bothering to look up from his work.

"All of the successful tests included them," Aaron replied.

"Not exactly. You're forgetting the field test he did during the storm. The Developers ruled that out as a malfunction," Donovan reminded him.

Aaron studied the section on the failed peer review and found that what Donovan reported was true. Though Gavin had initially claimed that test as a success, the Developers had rejected it. But Aaron decided he needed to see it for himself. Through the esolace, he jumped to the test in question, accessing the trace recorded in the logs. Speeding up the sequence, he went straight to the end where the malfunction occurred. A tall silvery being appeared at that point, near the edge of the projection. It looked vaguely human, but its mercurial skin and otherworldly appearance marked it as a strict anomaly. It made sense that allowing for the possibility of nonstandard events might cause the chronotrace to malfunction like that, but following Gavin's thought process might help them break through the wall they kept running into.

"What if we included the sub-rational algorithms on a few runs—just to see what would happen?" Aaron asked.

"And waste more time? I don't see the point," Donovan countered.

Aaron knew he was right, but he didn't see the harm in trying. Ordinarily, he would have simply gone with what he knew to be true, but he had reached the end of his ideas.

"What are the proofs against the sub-rational?" Aaron let the thought out without realizing it. He had meant to keep it to himself, but his vigilance slipped for the briefest of moments.

Donovan's face wore the closest thing to shock Aaron could ever remember seeing. The expression jarred Aaron to his senses.

"I don't know what I was thinking," he added hastily, *"I'm sure the proofs are so elementary that they didn't bother including them in the knowledge base..."* Aaron decided to simply withdraw his thoughts instead of continuing on. He was only making things worse by trying to explain himself.

Donovan's stoic expression returned and no more thoughts were exchanged on the subject. Aaron did not know whether this meant that the matter would be forgotten or if Donovan would report it when it was more convenient. Knowing Donovan, he suspected the latter, and yet Aaron had the sudden impression that he didn't really know Donovan as well as he thought. After all these years, his friend was sometimes as big a mystery to him as this device they were trying to create.

At that moment the door to the lab slid open and Cyrith entered into the room exhibiting the same plastic expression as always. He usually checked in on their progress once per day, but this time he was earlier than usual.

"*What is the status of the project?*" he asked, the unspoken tenor of his thoughts as brusque as his expression.

"*We had a run of nearly six microslices today,*" Donovan reported.

"*What about zoetic entities? Have you made any progress in that area?*"

"*None, but we're working on it.*"

Cyrith's stare remained unwavering, though Aaron detected a notable shift in the nature of his thoughts. There was an uncharacteristic urgency to them.

"*Every moment the device remains unfinished our enemies may be moving against us. Until we have a way to discover their plans everything here on the* Nebula, *everything the Collective is working towards, is at risk.*"

"*We will have it working soon,*" Donovan assured him. "*Our goal is still to finish before launch.*"

"*Then you will have to get it working by tomorrow,*" Cyrith came back.

"*Tomorrow?*" Aaron chimed in, knowing it would be impossible to fix everything by then.

"*We've decided to move up the launch. We cannot afford to remain chained to this wasteland prison any longer. The quakes show no signs of letting up and we cannot afford risking further damage to the* Nebula. *We will mount skyward in the morning.*"

"*But the ship—will all the repairs be finished?*" Aaron asked.

Cyrith stared blankly ahead, his mind consumed in endless calculations. "*No. But if we don't clear the planet's atmosphere in time we will have no chance against the Delegation.*"

These details left Aaron reeling. Things were worse than he thought.

"*What sort of weapons does this ship even have? We've been* working on this project ever since we got out of cryo-sleep so neither of us have been briefed on the ship's capabilities," Aaron probed.

"It has only a single weapon. The omniclast. And that is the only weapon we shall need."

THIRTY-ONE

THE OMNICLAST

AARON AND DONOVAN WERE NO MORE MILITARILY MINDED than Cyrith, but the longer they worked on the chronotrace, the more it was starting to look like a long shot at best. The *Nebula's* weapon systems were probably their only means of salvation from the coming Delegation onslaught.

"In what part of the ship is the omniclast located?" Aaron asked, expecting Cyrith to mention one of the sections which was still under construction. He had been in most of the other ones.

"You have the wrong concept," Cyrith answered. *"It is not that the omniclast is part of the ship, it is that the omniclast is the ship."*

"The entire structure serves as a weapon?" Donovan asked, his mind immediately going to work to conceive of what he was being told. Neither of them had heard of a weapon that large. The *Nebula* could have accommodated close to five thousand people if it had been completely built out. Even in its present condition it could hold close to three thousand.

"Essentially," Cyrith replied. *"The ship's exterior panels*

harness galactic sub matter and focus it into a paroxysm. The ship's enormous size allows it to gather enough matter for a planetary class attack."

"A planetary class attack?" Aaron asked. No wonder the Delegation was after them. An organization like theirs would seek to possess such power, whatever the cost.

"If it utilizes sub matter, I see why we need to clear the atmosphere. Even then it will take some time to charge," Donovan observed. *"But aren't paroxysms inherently unstable outside of a controlled environment?"*

"That's the point," Cyrith replied. *"If enough sub matter is focused on a single point, it quickly converts into locus energy and from there into an entropic feedback rift, literally tearing a hole in the fabric of the universe. It spreads out in all directions, consuming all it touches. Hence the reason for the weapon's other name, 'the world breaker.'"*

"I believe the process of consumption is called excoriation. But how do you stop it once it starts? That is the problem with paroxysms, isn't it—stopping them?" Donovan asked.

"The reaction will eventually collapse in on itself," Cyrith stated.

"Yes, but the magnitude of such an attack might take out the Nebula *itself if it's too close to the blast,"* Donovan conjectured.

"True. It's not really designed for ship to ship combat. Which is why we must engage them at long range. And that brings me back to the reason for my visit. What are the barriers keeping you from completing a working prototype?"

"All the algorithms from Gavin's archives have failed," Donovan reported.

Cyrith's shoulders dropped slightly. *"I suspected as much. You must forge ahead on your own then. We need a break-through. Other than preparing for launch, this project is our highest priority. As powerful as the omniclast is, If we can stop the scout from creating the sidereal portal, we can avoid this conflict altogether."*

The pressure of time, multiplied by ignorance built up inside Aaron to the point of bursting. There was no way they would be able to finish the chronotrace in time.

"Thank you for informing us of the situation," Donovan replied.

Cyrith exhaled quietly as if to mark the completion of his task there in the lab. *"I have every confidence that you will get the job done. Inform me the moment you have a working device."*

Then, with a barely perceptible nod, he left the room, leaving the two recently-appointed Developers to wonder how they were ever going to complete the project on time.

The madman scratched at the door with his long, ragged nails, but the metal surface refused to give way. He gave the door one last punch for good measure and abandoned it in search of another. He would try them all if he had to. Surely one of them had been left unlocked. Surely his enemy had made one mistake.

The winds whipping past him obscured everything except the outer walls of the ship. He was forced to feel his way around. He pawed along the paneling, mumbling to himself as he went. "The beast can't fly. No, no, no, its wings are broken. But, but...what if they fix it, what then? They'll use it against me, yes, yes, they'll purge me from this world. No. I must purge them first. Then I'll have peace. Peace at last."

He fought the wind and his fears, babbling to himself all the while, slipping in and out of the awareness of his surroundings. At times he thought he was in this world, at times back on his home world, a respected leader, a man coming into his own, longing to right the wrongs he saw in a corrupt and dying civilization. And still at other moments he wandered in the dark fearing he had passed from this world into the next.

In the midst of his wandering between worlds, the wall along which he was groping ended. Empty space greeted his probing fingers. His body shook, half from anger half from fear. Was he back out in the open desert again? Perhaps. But no, he remembered that the *Nebula* was a round thing and that circles did not end. He ventured forward determined to find something solid. He shuffled ahead, step by cautious step, suspecting a trap, or thinking that his mind was playing tricks on him again. A few moments later, however, his perseverance paid off when his fingers brushed up against another metal wall.

His hands quivered in anticipation as he pressed his way along the new surface. He noticed a gradual change as he went. The winds were dying down. The sand chafed his exposed skin less and less. And then something even more strange happened; a light shone up ahead. He went more quickly now, scurrying towards the light, though he had no idea why it seemed so promising. But his faith was rewarded when he reached it at last. A glowing orb hung from the ceiling, a miniature star pulling him into orbit. But no, it wasn't a natural light. It was artificial. That was a good sign. He must be in some sort of corridor, but it was either unfinished or badly in need of repair. Half the paneling was missing from the walls and several struts extended out into nothing.

The madman pressed on, soon seeing another light, and then another. He was in a nearly finished section of corridor now. Because of that, the storm all but died away. A few steps later and he came upon an abandoned maintenance lev with a fabricator on top of it. His heart warmed at the sight. He now knew two important things: he was inside the ship, and they had not finished building it.

His ever wandering gaze fell upon a maintenance hatch above him. He licked his lips in rapt anticipation. The black lines around the edge of the hatch told him he was in one of the northern corridors of the *Nebula*. He hopped deftly onto the lev and vaulted towards the ceiling, catching onto the indented lip around the metal hatch. Dangling from the ceiling with one hand, he pounded the hatch with his other and it flipped upward.

His hands quivered in anticipation so that he nearly lost his grip, but he was too close now to be denied. Driven by desperation, he yanked himself up until his head was almost level with his hands. Then, with one last maniacal surge, he slipped an arm over the edge and dragged his emaciated body up and into the maintenance shaft which ran above the corridor.

He had made it at last. He was inside the *Nebula*. He was inside the belly of the whale. Now all he had to do was find a way to destroy it.

———

Despite everything Aaron and Donovan tried, they could not get the chronotrace to work. They were fairly certain they had perfected the time-mapping algorithm as it pertained to inorganic matter, but organic substances blew up the trace every single time. Such entities were simply too complicated for the device to handle all of the possible permutations. The mapping algorithm demanded an ordered universe and life was the chaos which tore all of their calculations asunder.

Aaron's mind turned from the useless prototype to the impending launch as he and Donovan stood beside each other, carried along by the circular lev on their way towards the bridge. All of the Developers were to report there to witness the launch.

About half way there the surrounding corridor quivered, telltale signs of another quake. The corridor walls rippled threateningly, as if some terrible worms were burrowing beneath the surface, but the lev floated safely above the turbulence and they quickly passed into a safer area. Hopefully it was only an aftershock.

The night before a much stronger quake had nearly taken out the main fuel well, endangering the launch. They only saved it by pulling the celerium core out before the fuel chamber collapsed. The technicians couldn't salvage much of the primary bismine cores, but they still had enough left in the reserves for launch and they could recharge the energy supply fairly quickly once they reached space.

"I know you're worried," Donovan observed. *"But you didn't come to the Developer meeting last night. We have a plan in place if the Delegation gets the jump on us."*

"What is that?" Aaron asked.

"They have set up a secondary bridge. If the Delegation boards us and manages to seize the Command Center, we can retreat there and still maintain control of the ship for some time, hopefully long enough to charge up the omniclast and wipe out the enemy fleet."

Aaron had missed the meeting because he stayed working through the night on the chronotrace. Not that it had done any good.

The disc zipped down one final corridor, up a ramp, and through a wide metal doorway onto the bridge. Seven men in silver lab coats were already there, five other new Developers plus Cyrith and Xander. Cyrith had been informed about the failure of the chronotrace project earlier that morning, but had shown no reaction one way or the other. The ship's launch was all that mattered now.

The circular bridge rose slightly above the rest of the ship. Metal panels covered the walls, most of them overlaid with screens displaying information about the ship's operation: fuel levels, navigational charts, and equipment status. The *Nebula's* esolace was not powerful enough to stream all of the information simultaneously, making it necessary to utilize visual representations. Some of the panels had transflex windows. These afforded a view of the ship and the endless desert from which they sought to escape.

The *Nebula* spread out in every direction, a giant, spoked wheel with multiple connections between the spokes. Many of the spokes were still broken and unfinished. Except where the ship was damaged beyond repair, the sub matter intensifiers dotted the top of the *Nebula* like insects pollenating a giant flower. These devices had circular bases with giant funnels on top and rods radiating out around the edges. Sixteen of the twenty intensifiers were still intact and operational, lit by subtle guide lights on the ends of the rods. This meant that the omniclast would take slightly longer to power up, but once it did, it would be capable of wiping out whatever the Delegation threw at them.

"Everyone is present. It is time to engage the launch sequence," Cyrith informed the group.

From all across the ship, the humming of the enormous thrusters beneath the *Nebula* ramped up.

The Developers showed no reaction, except perhaps to stare even more vacantly at the dozens of view screens. A massive dust storm raged on all fronts, but the *Nebula's* sensors allowed them to see through the deluge of sand and debris.

"In space we can begin again, free of the shackles of this

hollow world," Cyrith declared, his eyes glinting with uncharacteristic anticipation.

Mixed emotions coursed through Aaron at the thought of leaving Nai. Though every stretch of this planet was a miserable, inhospitable wasteland, he regretted that he had not been able to see it first hand. He had traveled halfway across the galaxy to be a part of the colonization effort on this planet and now he was leaving without ever having set foot on its surface.

And what awaited them above the planet's turbulent atmosphere? For all they knew the Delegation was waiting to shoot them down the moment they cleared the clouds. No one in the Collective was safe, not even inside the *Nebula,* not until the omniclast was charged or they found the Delegation scout. Aaron wondered if he might not be able to take one last stab at getting the chronotrace to work before they broke atmosphere. He vowed to run a few last tests if he got the opportunity.

The humming of the engines died down gradually and then, just as gradually, the patchwork scaffolding surrounding the ship fell away and the *Nebula* began to rise. They escaped the billowing dust below and rose towards the swirling clouds above, and beyond that, the endless expanse of space. Aaron felt that mysterious pull which the stars exert on every human being who leaves his terrestrial confines and mounts the unconquerable sky. Though he had been in space before, he could not shake a sense of nervous expectation. His heart stirred at the prospect of floating in the midst of that impossibly open expanse. He had not felt such powerful emotions since before going into cryo-sleep, and their intensity rose along with the *Nebula* as it slowly slipped its planetary bonds.

THIRTY-TWO
ASCENT OF THE NEBULA

THE ASCENT OF THE NEBULA WAS LITERALLY LIKE LIFTING
a small city off the ground. It took time to build up speed. The
dark green clouds above remained impossibly far away and
since the ground below was nothing more than swirling sand it
hardly felt like they were moving at all, but the altimeter read-
ings on the screen tracked their progress. Every moment
brought them closer to their rendezvous with the stars.

A vague sea of impressions floated through the group, but
the general mood was optimistic. Though the ship still needed
repairs, it was for the most part fully functional. Achieving this
status in such a short period of time had been a testimony to the
technological prowess of the Collective. Their small team of
Developers, coordinating with a few dozen assessors, several
hundred Collectives, and the less capable, but far more numerous, force of somatarchs had achieved their goal of launching
before the arrival of the Delegation.

Amidst the personal musings shared by the Devs, a thought
from Trey, the chief navigator, surged to the forefront.

"Tracking three large objects descending out of the clouds," he reported.

Aaron's gaze went to several red dots which flashed onto the navigational screen. They were not far from the *Nebula's* current position and were closing rapidly.

Another view screen flipped on, showing a visual of the ships. They were very large, about five times larger than a praxis cruiser, though less than a tenth of the size of the *Nebula.* Their hulls were covered in black and gray paneling arranged in chevron patterns which made them look more sleek than they actually were. The bodies of the ships flared out in the back, narrowing to a fine tip as if they were enormous, metallic droplets floating through the air, their tapered ends pointing straight at the *Nebula.* Two thin wings jutting out from either side were the only break in the otherwise smooth exteriors.

Cyrith stared, unflinching, at the screen, waiting for the diagnostic routines to identify the ships.

"They are derringer attack ships with interstellar capabilities," the *Nebula's* system conveyed the information directly into their minds.

Cyrith studied the tactical readouts. *"We stand no chance against ships of that size."*

"Should we send out the fleet?" Xander suggested.

"It is the only choice we have. We must at least attempt to delay them, to buy us enough time to break the atmosphere," Cyrith replied. Despite the dour admittance, he remained as calm as ever.

The moment Cyrith's thought entered their minds half the team exited from the room. They needed no further instructions. This scenario had been prepared for. Even so, Aaron didn't see that it would make any difference. The *Nebula* was barely half way to the lower reaches of the atmosphere. They would never break through in time.

"Trey, transfer all excess power to the shields," Cyrith instructed. *"When they cannot take any more, use what's left to boost our ascent. We can't hope to outrun them, but we have to be ready if they make a mistake."*

Trey kept the ship on course at the navigational column while Cyrith and Xander stared intently at the view screens. Aaron and Donovan waited for instructions from one of the two senior Developers. Since almost all of their time had been devoted to building the chronotrace, they had not been prepped for any specific role in case of attack.

"What should the two of us do?" Aaron asked.

Cyrith kept his eyes on the navigation charts and gave no reply. Dozens of smaller ships issued forth from the derringers.

One of the screens switched to a view of the half-built cargo bay where the assessors assigned to the fleet began pouring in, racing to their ships. The collection of vapors, lancers, and skiffs was frighteningly small compared to the Delegation fleet. And the praxis and the hovland cruisers were nothing compared to the massive derringers they would be going up against.

I've got to do something, Aaron thought to himself. *I'm of no use here.*

He looked to Donovan, but he was as wrapped up in the readouts as everyone else.

Aaron was about to repeat his question when Xander's thought cut him off.

"We have an incoming audio transmission. It's the leader of the Delegation fleet. Shall I accept?"

"Send it through," Cyrith answered, immediately shifting his focus to the audio channel.

A husky, indignant voice filled the bridge.

"Attention. This is Sentinel Orin of the assault ship *Torrent*. You are in possession of a Delegation space station, seized in the year 2152 Sovereign Domain. We demand that you hand over the ship at once or face immediate boarding."

Cyrith sent Xander an order over the Dev channel. *"Stall him."*

Xander cleared his throat. "You have no jurisdiction on this planet, Sentinel Orin. This ship belongs to the Collective. We declared our independence from the Delegation years ago."

"The Collective? Is that what you're calling yourselves now? Fine. You can declare your independence all you want, but I've got three hundred venators headed your way that say otherwise. You know full well who created that ship and I did not jaunt six thousand steorra across the galaxy to jaw with one of the Doctor's lackeys," answered the sentinel gruffly.

Aaron checked the navigation map. It seemed like half of it was flashing red. Crimson dots continued to stream forth from the larger ships, over a hundred now, and more coming by the microslice.

"Perhaps we can negotiate. We have valuable technology to offer—" Xander started to answer.

"There will be no negotiation. You tried to eradicate us and we're here to return the favor. Tell that to the Doctor, tell that to the defectors who betrayed us. We are coming and there is nothing you can do to stop us. Prepare for boarding." The commander's voice rang in Aaron's ears as the audio cut out.

A sea of red swarmed the navigation screen. The Developers stared blankly at the impending destruction it represented.

"Sentinel Orin has not changed," Cyrith commented. *"Brute force is the only language he understands. But he knows what this space station is capable of. He will do everything possible to see we do not clear the atmosphere."* For the first time

since Aaron had known Cyrith, his face looked noticeably troubled. He cast his brooding gaze towards Aaron. Perhaps it was only a coincidence, but the timing made it seem as if Cyrith blamed Aaron somehow for what was unfolding.

"What can we do to help?" Aaron repeated his earlier question.

But Cyrith's mind was paralyzed by indecision. He was a researcher. He had no way of knowing what to do in a situation like this. His expression darkened with each passing moment.

"Let's go," Aaron told Donovan. *"We need to get the chronotrace working. If we could map their ship we could back trace their communications and security protocols, jam their signals, and find out how to drain their ships' power."*

"You go on without me. I'll stay here. It would only be a waste of time."

"But there's nothing for us to do here. Do you want to just sit here and watch the Delegation tear the ship apart?"

Donovan's mind withdrew. His eyes locked on to the various view screens, consuming the incoming data with grim fascination. Aaron never felt more distant from his friend than at that moment.

Aaron understood Donovan's response. It was a hopeless plan after all, but the alternative was even more hopeless. The crash of the *Nebula*, the Delegation attack, their failure to construct the chronotrace in time, everything was falling apart. He had to do something.

Aaron turned and left, stepping onto the black lev disc waiting outside the door. At least some things were still in order aboard the ship. For now.

As the circle took off, he wondered whether or not he'd have time to do what he was planning and whether the Collective stood any chance at surviving this attack even if he succeeded.

Aaron floated through the lengthy metal corridors as fast as the disc would go, his silver robe plastered against his skin. Why did they have to put the lab on the outer rim of the ship? Even though the bridge was centrally located, it took a few microslices to get to where he was going. At least there was no other traffic to slow him down. The containment teams were on the opposite side of the ship, closer to the direction from which the Delegation approached.

He clung to the possibility of the chronotrace as the last hope of the Collective. If only the *Nebula* could hold out long enough for him to find a way to get it working, they might be able to find a way to disable the Delegation ships.

Aaron connected his mind to the tactical screens back on the bridge. The Delegation venators were over three quarters of the way to the *Nebula* by now. They may have been numerous, but they were only about half the length of a lancer and had short, broad wings. Their cockpits were covered by rectangular, tinted windows. Maybe they were only drones and the boarding threat was a bluff.

His stomach fluttered. At this point he wasn't sure what he was more anxious about, the impending attack, or the impossibility of fixing the chronotrace in time.

The moment he arrived at the lab, the hallway emergency lighting flashed on, the crimson hue signaling that the ship was under attack. The locus energy shields surrounding the ship would hold off the venators for a while, but they would not hold up forever.

He checked the view from the bridge again, expecting to see the *Nebula* under fire, but it wasn't. Roughly a third of the venators had met the Collective fleet in the air and chosen to engage it. They exchanged locus pulser and disruptor fire, lighting up the dust filled air with white and yellow energy beams. But that wasn't what had sounded the alarm. It was the more than one hundred venators who had simply flown around or past the Collective forces and landed on the *Nebula'* hull. They did not opened fire on the space station. Instead, they landed on the invisible shield surrounding the ship. Right before making contact with the shield, the ships morphed. Their panels and wings shifted in place, reconfiguring themselves into enormous, metallic exoskeletons, with large locus pulse cannons mounted on one arm and enormous blue energy blades springing forth from the other.

Aaron's skin bristled in fear.

"What are those?" he queried the *Nebula's* esolace.

Venators, came the answer. *A hybrid short range space craft combined with an oversized armatus battle suit. A one-man craft equally capable of securing land targets or harassing airborne enemies. Originally created by Factor Ten forces and then appropriated for use by the Delegation in the Terminus Conflict where they were used almost exclusively by elite, escalon attack forces.*

The facts blazed through Aaron's mind as the door whisked open. He stepped inside the lab. He set the chronotrace into its seating on top of the celerium column.

Various images from the bridge screens flashed before him. The venator battle suits were using their cross stream blades to cut through the *Nebula's* shields. Wherever they did, glowing gashes opened up, suspended in midair like floating green scars. The venators jumped through the openings, landing on the hull and repeating the procedure, this time opening a gash in the fuselage.

With that tactic, they were going to take control of the ship sooner than he thought.

Aaron hurriedly instructed the inert chronotrace to power

up. This time he did not debate within himself about the proper course to take to run his experiment. There was only one choice which made any sense at this point, the only one they had not tried.

He accessed the logs and referenced the sub-rational algorithm Gavin had detailed there, insetting this routine into the chronotrace's temporal sequencing module. It was not even that much of a change, just a small shift in the logic, a minuscule part of the overall design, really. It should not have made any difference by conventional wisdom and all known laws of science, but Aaron didn't care. What good were the laws of science when an army of attack ships was bearing down on you?

With the alternate algorithm in place, Aaron sent a mental command to the device to initiate the trace. The sound of dozens of booted feet running past the door filled the lab as the chronotrace began to glow. A check of the security logs showed that squads of somatarchs were being sent to deal with the venators who had breached the hull. They were not entering at a single point, as expected, but in every section of the ship.

The chronotrace scattered light all around Aaron as it completed the initial scan. Now came the real test. All he wanted to see was whether it would play back his presence in the room. The entire sequence would take only a fraction of a microslice, but, if successful, it might change everything in this battle.

The projection commenced, spinning time in reverse. He waited, and waited, holding his breath and then... his hands and legs started to blur. He spun around and stood face to face with a mirror image of himself. The inverted echoes of the somatarchs swept past the lab backwards. His copy backed out through the open door and stepped onto the black disc outside.

The trace had worked! The new algorithm had made zoetic

mapping possible and the answer had been right there in Gavin's notes the whole time. He cursed his foolishness, but this was no time to wallow in past failures. He did not know how much time he had left.

His skin tingling in anticipation, he sped up the trace and instructed the chronotrace to shift the scan location so he could find out what was happening on the Delegation ships. As the trace unfolded, a strange sensation washed over him. It wasn't just the newness of this technology, as unfamiliar as it was, but the nagging suspicion that the venators boarding the *Nebula* were not the biggest threat they would have to face.

THIRTY-THREE
STOW AWAY

Two Delegation soldiers stepped over the bodies of the fallen somatarchs. The shredded remains of a dozen more lay behind them, victims of a locus pulse grenade which had ripped through them like ten thousand tiny cutters shooting out from the point of detonation. The scrap metal from several contingency probes lay mixed in with the bodies.

The remains of the Delegation forces were less conspicuous. Four black and gray uniforms and an equal number of helmets lay in disarray on the floor at the edge of the mangled clump of dead somatarchs. A dozen silvery oscillathe pistols, their sheen now tarnished by spattered blood, told the story of how the soldiers had met their end.

"Sentinel Orin, we've secured the hallway leading to the bridge," said one of the soldiers. His face was hidden behind the dark visor covering the front of his helmet.

Orin's audio response came inside his headgear, as clear as if he'd been standing right next to the soldier. "Excellent. Hold that position. We'll all rush the bridge together on my command. They won't stand a chance."

"Affirmative," replied the soldier, disconnecting from his audio link with the commander.

"So we're just supposed to sit here and hope they don't send anything more at us? Just the two of us," said the other soldier in the hallway. He was a little shorter than the first, but in their uniforms they were otherwise identical.

"Sounds about right," his companion answered.

The two men separated and took a knee beside either wall.

The smaller soldier grunted inside his helmet. "Casper, you saw what those whispering weapons did to our team. Whatever they are, they can kill escalons. We never lose men in close combat and we've already lost half of the ones who breached the hull." Despite his concern, it didn't sound like he cared as much about the lost lives as he did about the success of the mission.

"The other four teams are still mostly intact," Casper said. "And we know how to fight them now, just don't engage them up close. The superior range of our pulsers should give us the other advantage. The others won't make the same mistake we did."

The other soldier snorted into his mask. "I just hope they don't empty out the body farm on us. Those things we fought, they looked human, but they weren't, you know? Never saw anything like that."

"These lab coats are all freaks if you ask me," Casper said.

"You think the Doctor is still in charge?" asked the other man.

"I hope so. His day has been a long time coming."

Another voice, not belonging to the sentinel, or to either of the two men in the hallway burst into their headsets.

"We're nearly finished mopping up the Deliverance fleet. All we really have left is the praxis," the new voice reported.

"Keep up the hurt," Sentinel Orin's voice came over the

audio. "We'll have the bridge secured soon before they even clear the atmosphere. Send word when you've zeroed out the Deliverance fleet."

"I look forward to joining you back on the *Nebula*," the new voice informed them.

"It's a glorious day for the Delegation!" Sentinel Orin declared.

At that point Aaron paused the trace. The two soldiers froze where they were, facing the door which led to the Command Center. The processing for the short sequence he had just observed had taken less than two microslices. There was no point in continuing further. He had what he sought. It was time to put it into action.

"Cyrith, I've discovered the encryption key the Delegation is using for their communication." Aaron sent the message over the Developer channel.

Xander's mind responded back instead. *"They weren't communicating over a secure audio channel?"*

"Of course they were, but I decoded it using the chronotrace —I've got it working! And another thing, Xander, what are we doing about the units converging on the bridge? You need to send a team to—"

Xander seemed almost angered by Aaron's report. *"What team? The assessors went with the fleet. And the venator soldiers have taken out most of the somatarchs we had on board. We're totally outmanned. I recalled a unit of ten to the bridge once we got boarded and I've ordered another three units to head to the bridge, but they will probably get slaughtered on their way. The escalons are too smart for them."*

"But what about the omniclast? We've almost broken the atmosphere, haven't we?"

"It doesn't matter. The weapon still has to charge once we get into space. The bridge will never hold out that long."

Xander's thoughts were harried, scattered, disordered. *"Jamming their communications now would be pointless. The* Nebula *is overrun."*

Aaron stood for a long time without moving, Xander's panic spreading through him like an infection. This paralysis of indecision might have gone on for even longer had it not been for the sound of soft footsteps at the door.

His muscles tensed. It wasn't a somatarch, they never moved with that level of subtlety. It had to be one of the soldiers. He looked around the lab for anything he could use to defend himself. He grabbed the first suitable thing he found, a metal canister stored on a nearby shelf and lifted it with shaking hands. It had a nice heft to it, but he doubted it would be enough to take out a soldier in body armor.

A yellow glow appeared on the surface of the door, as if it were being heated at a single point. A radiant sliver poked through the metal at that point. It quickly traced a large hole in the door, moving through the thick metal like it wasn't there. The circle complete, the inner part of the door toppled to the floor revealing a man wearing a dust-covered jacket and weathered pants. His face was nondescript, but the knowing glint in his eyes gave him away. It was the defector Gavin.

Gavin extinguished his cutter blade.

"Thank goodness. I finally found you," he said.

Aaron drew back from him, raising the canister above his head.

"Don't come any closer. I'll hit you with this, I promise I will." Though he looked like any other scientist, anyone who could escape the Collective was as deadly as the Delegation soldiers who had boarded the ship. But what was he doing on the *Nebula*? Had he joined the Delegation somehow? Maybe he had been working for them all along.

Aaron connected his mind to the security channel to warn the bridge, maybe even call for a contingent of somatarchs, but the channel was down. His mind scrambled to connect to any of the other channels. They were all down. The *Nebula's* esolace had vanished and that could mean only one thing: the Delegation must already be in control of the bridge. Aaron was on his own.

"I know you don't remember me." Gavin raised his hands non-threateningly and yet stepping across the threshold. Aaron thought he caught a white shimmer wash over him, but it may have simply been a trick of the light as Gavin passed from the corridor into the lab.

Aaron waved the canister in front of him. "I've called security. They'll be here in less than a microslice," he bluffed.

"I'm a memorant. You should know you can't get away with lying to someone like me," Gavin said. "Besides, even if I wasn't, I've got this." Here he pulled a chronotrace from a bag he wore slung across his shoulder. It was slightly smaller than the one Aaron had built, but otherwise very similar.

So that's how he found me.

He had to get out of here. But with Gavin standing right smack in the middle of the door there was no way around him. Aaron began to slide forward surreptitiously in the hope of getting close enough to knock his adversary down and then sprint away before he had a chance to get up.

"I know why you're here, I've seen the data on you." Aaron continue forward cautiously. "You're trying to destroy this ship and eliminate the Collective."

"Actually, I think the Delegation is doing just fine on that front. I'm here for you."

Aaron halted, caught off guard by the unexpectedness of Gavin's statement.

"Me? What do you want with me?" he asked.

"I've come to rescue you, the same way you rescued me. This is not where you belong. This is not who you are. They've remapped you. Aaron isn't your real name. It's—"

"You expect me to believe you—a traitor to the Collective?" Aaron cut him off, risking another step forward. Why hadn't Gavin reacted to his advances? Surely as a memorant he must have guessed Aaron's intentions.

Gavin shoved the chronotrace back in the bag and pulled out a vial of remin fluid instead. The green liquid glowed through the edges of his fingers as he stretched out his hand, offering the container to Aaron.

"I didn't expect you to believe me. Which is why I brought this." Now Gavin took a step forward.

"I'm sure it's laced with neural block to knock me unconscious. You can keep it," Aaron said.

"It wouldn't make any difference if it was. You can't be knocked out that way." Gavin shoved the vial back in his bag and took another step. Only three or four steps separated them now.

Aaron tensed, but he couldn't hurl the canister yet. He wanted to be sure he didn't miss. He would only get one shot.

Gavin picked up one of the metal trays off a lab table, grasping it with both hands. "The only thing that works is blunt force trauma. I came here to save you. Even if I have to hurt you to do it."

Aaron nodded grimly. He would have expected no less from someone like Gavin. The only surprise was that Gavin had gone through the pretense of wanting to help him first.

"We both have to do what we have to do," Aaron said.

"I'm sorry about this," Gavin responded with a look of

genuine regret. "I told myself I wouldn't ever beat you over the head again."

Aaron would have to knock the tray out of Gavin's hands before he could hit him with the canister. Gavin did not appear all that strong, so it would come down to a matter of timing and reflexes.

Aaron charged forward, swinging the canister like a club. While he connected with the tray, the canister ricocheted off like he'd hit a solid wall. He was so shocked, he nearly lost hold of it. He barely had the presence of mind to duck beneath Gavin's counter swing. Before Aaron could bring the canister back a round a line of soldiers in black and gray uniforms burst through the hole in the door.

At first Aaron expected them to join Gavin's attack, but the first one charged Gavin and the second came after him.

White neutralizer blasts leapt from their hands, striking Gavin in the back and Aaron in the chest. The blasts dissipated off Gavin's body in a shimmer of light, but Aaron felt a tingling weakness pulling him to the ground. He pitched forward onto a table. Everything went black momentarily.

When he opened his eyes, Gavin was wrestling with one of the Delegation soldiers. Gavin took several blows to the head and torso, but kept going, completely unfazed. Which is more, he was giving back better than he got. When it came to physical ability, Aaron had definitely misjudged him.

Gavin wailed on the soldier, sending him reeling. The helmet he wore was probably the only reason the soldier remained conscious and even that had a large crack in the visor. Still, he wouldn't back down. He kept struggling against the inexplicably powerful blows of the scientist as two of his companions rushed in to help. Both of them leapt on top of Gavin and he finally went down.

Aaron would have gladly left Gavin to his fate if another

three soldiers hadn't poured through the door. He realized that, for the moment, he and Gavin were on the same side, though it did not look promising for either of them. He scrambled back to his feet and dove at the incoming soldiers.

They blasted him with more neutralizing beams, but this time they affected Aaron even less. He staggered briefly, vertigo filling his brain, but the temporary blackout did not happen this time and a moment later he was fine. Still, his stumbling killed the momentum of his charge and when he didn't go down, the soldiers who had just come through the door barreled into him and brought him to the ground.

They pinned Aaron face first to the floor. One of the soldiers clamped his hands behind his back with a pair of metal casings. Something slammed against the wall, shaking the room. Trays and instruments went flying.

Gavin roared and the sound of more blows could be heard, followed by neutralizer blasts. Finally, Gavin's voice rose above the fracas. "I'm sorry. There are too many of them. I'll come back for you!" he cried out. This was followed by the sound of soft-soled feet fleeing the room.

"After him," shouted one of the soldiers and three of them rushed into the hall.

The two who remained pulled Aaron to his feet.

"What's your name?" asked one of them as he adjusted the fit of his helmet. His voice sounded artificial behind the tinted silver mask.

Aaron didn't answer. He was not about to cooperate with the enemy.

"How did you shake off our neutralizers?" he asked. "You don't have any visible equipment and you don't scan for any augmentations. Are you an escalon?"

"I don't know what you're talking about." Aaron stared confidently into the soldier's visor.

"There's no history of any escalons defecting, especially not to Deliverance," replied the other soldier.

"We can run a check on him when we get him back to the bridge," said his partner.

Then, shoving Aaron towards the ruined door, the two Delegation soldiers marched their prisoner to the center of the ship.

THIRTY-FOUR
CHANGE IN COMMAND

The bridge looked markedly different. Several dozen Delegation soldiers now occupied the area. Cyrith and the other Developers were nowhere to be seen. Traces of blood on the floor told him that at least some of those who had stayed to defend the bridge were most likely now dead. Hopefully all of them had been somatarchs.

The view screens no longer depicted the Delegation ships. Instead they showed various rooms inside the *Nebula*. Locations flashed by, snapshots from all parts of the ship. The various humming and machine noises from the places depicted added a low, chaotic white noise to the chatter of the soldiers analyzing the screens. The Delegation was using the ship's surveillance systems to search for something, but at first it was not apparent what that was. Corridors, rooms, vents, and even external shots of the ship appeared briefly before passing away. Most of the scenes were empty, though a few showed the remains of the Delegation's skirmishes with somatarchs. Others showed Delegation forces spreading out throughout the ship, perhaps engaged in the same search as those on the bridge. One screen, however, did not change. That was the screen following Gavin's progress through the ship's corridors.

The renegade raced through the hallways and corridors, unimpeded by the patrols of Delegation soldiers harrying his every step. Their red pulser fire sent low hissing noises over the audio. It should have scorched Gavin's body, but he ran through it like it was nothing more than a light show. The beams pelted him and disappeared. Little shimmers of white light spread across his clothing indicating where the beams had hit, but they otherwise had no effect. Since the Delegation soldiers' weapons appeared to be ineffective, they eventually gave up firing, but they did not give up the chase.

Besides the panels, the view from the windows had changed as well. The windows were now filled with stars. The *Nebula* had at last freed itself from the confines of the planet's turbulent atmosphere. The myriad stars wove an illuminated tapestry across the infinite dark more beautiful than anything ever crafted by the hand of men. One star in particular outshone the rest by far. It dominated the scene, ten times the size of any of the others and with a white hot center and a yellowish outer edge. This must have been this planetary system's central star, the one responsible for creating day and night on the planet below. Gazing upon the celestial mote woven into the stardust fabric, he felt a great longing to hold it in his hands, though he knew that was impossible. At that moment he forgot all about being captured and the boarding of the ship, swept up into the grandeur of the heavens before him.

The soldiers escorting him did not even give the windows so much as a look, but prodded him forward. He stumbled ahead, enwrapped in sidereal wonder.

*I came from somewhere out there...*he thought to himself. He could not say why that mattered and yet something pulled at him inside to know what that place was.

"Sentinel Orin, we've captured one of the members of Deliverance," said the soldier on Aaron's left.

A few of the troopers present were not wearing helmets. Those same men had solid black uniforms with silver trim at the collars and cuffs, and the outline of a nine-pointed star displayed on the chest.

The man the soldier addressed was short, but powerfully built. His hair grew full and thick on the top of his head, packed even more tightly than his muscled frame. This wooly profusion marched down the lower half of his face in the form of a dense beard, neatly trimmed.

Sentinel Orin gave Aaron a cursory look, more focused on watching Gavin's exploits on the screen in front of him.

Orin addressed the soldier. "Excellent. Maybe he can help us figure out how to gain control of this ship." He pointed towards the screen depicting Gavin who had just entered into the section of the *Nebula* containing the deep freeze storage vaults. Those vaults were hardly ever visited by the rest of the ship's population. They housed the members of the Collective who had yet to be awakened from cryo-sleep. "First, though, who is this friend of yours and what sort of shield is he wearing that our pulsers have no effect on him?"

"His name is Gavin, and he's not my friend," Aaron stated flatly. "He's a Collective defector."

"A defector? Well if so, it hardly looks like he's ready to join the Delegation."

"He may be a traitor, but he's no fool," Aaron said.

The sentinel took a step towards him and Aaron could tell by the flash in his eyes that he had his full attention. He thrust a thick finger in Aaron's face, opening his snarling mouth to speak, but a voice over the bridge's audio system cut him short.

"Sentinel Orin, this is commander Nestor. Is everything under control? Why are you still ascending?"

Orin kept his gaze fixed on Aaron, but the fire in his eyes cooled. "Not to worry, commander. We have taken possession of the bridge and are working to remedy the situation. The *Nebula's* safety measures sealed off the sections of the ship where the venators breached the Hull. We sustained some casualties in the effort, but nothing we can't handle. As we expected, these Deliverance dregs were no match for our escalons."

"If you've taken the bridge, what is keeping you from taking control of the ship?" Nestor asked.

Sentinel Orin turned from Aaron and began pacing in front of his men. He spoke into the air, as if rehearsing some grand speech. "It looks like they've installed some sort of fall-back navigation controls which are overriding the ones on the bridge. So far we have been unable to locate secondary Command Center."

"Understood. We'll hold off on boarding the *Nebula* in case they make a sortie or try to escape, but I'm worried about the omniclast. Now that you've cleared the atmosphere, they may attempt to charge it. If they decide to fire on us, we'd be husked in a microslice. If we get close enough to your position they'd have to hold off firing or risk getting consumed in the paroxysm."

"You're certain there are no reinforcements back in the planet's airspace or on the surface?" Orin asked.

"Nothing we can spot on our scanners."

"Good, proceed towards our position, but maintain a distance of a thousand clicks," Orin instructed.

"Affirmative. Nestor, out."

Orin's attention snapped back to the screen following Gavin's progress through the vaults. He waved in Aaron's direction without taking his eyes off the screen. "Scan this prisoner. Find out if he's an auger or a natural before we decide whether he's of any use to us or not."

One of the soldiers passed his gloved hand over the back of Aaron's own. A green light flashed from the glove, illuminating Aaron's skin before fading. Then the soldier studied the back of his glove. Glowing letters appeared in the air just above it. They scrolled by in a blur. Aaron couldn't read them, but the soldier cocked his head to the side, as if the information, whatever it was, was unexpected.

"Sir, you're not going to believe this," he said. "He's one of us."

"What?" the sentinel pulled himself away from the screen and came over to see the information projecting out of the soldier's glove. Orin's whiskers trembled, creating dissension among the ranks of his neatly kept beard.

"He's a sidereal scout. Sent to this sector of the galaxy seven years ago," the soldier said, reading the text aloud. "If everything went according to his flight plan, he would have arrived 185 days ago."

Orin gave Aaron a long, searching look. "You don't remember, do you, soldier? They blanked you."

Aaron glared back at the commander, wondering what sort of mind games the Delegation was playing with him. This was likely some type of interrogation tactic to get him to cooperate.

"I'm not part of the Delegation, if that's what you're getting at," he said.

"Standard, pull up his mnemonic," Orin said, addressing the soldier.

The standard pulled a metal square off his belt and flung it in front of him. The four corners split apart and hovered in the air, forming a rectangular shape. A semi-transparent, three dimensional image appeared inside the rectangle. It was a mirror image of

Aaron. The figure blinked when he blinked and its head moved when he moved. It took Aaron a moment to realize that this was little more than a high tech mirror. At the same time, he realized two more things. The first was that he had never seen what he looked like before. Except for the figure's mimicking of his movements it was like looking at a total stranger. The figure in the projection had shiny black hair and thick eyebrows. His cheeks were broad and flat and his mouth rather thin. His eyes were dark brown and slightly tapered at the edges. For a moment he suspected that the image might be a ruse, part of the Delegation's attempts at manipulating him. But after considering it further, he couldn't think what purpose Orin would have for showing his reflection.

The second thing he realized was that he looked nothing like any of the other members of the Collective. Not that he had ever really given much thought to their appearance before, but somehow seeing his reflection brought to mind the incredible homogeneity in the way they looked.

At a wave from the standard's hand, the image began to change. Aaron's likeness remained, but the clothes changed and the figure no longer mimicked his movements. He appeared dressed in a Delegation uniform and his hair was noticeably shorter.

"Kessen, our eternity, soldier," the image addressed him. It was definitely Aaron's voice. "If you're seeing this it means you've fallen into enemy hands. I'm here to remind you that you've got a mission to fulfill: bring the Deliverance renegades to justice. They may have wiped your mind, tampered with your system, done all sorts of things. That's what they do. But whatever you think now, you're not one of them. Your name is Matthew Yin. You're an escalon, serving as a sidereal scout in the Delegation forces. Every soldier that goes out on hyperspace missions is given a mnemonic. It's woven into the core of your generational map so that if its tampered with it'll kill you, kind of like the poison pills soldiers and spies once used. Only this code can also verify your identity if you get recovered by Delegation forces. As soon as you hear it from me—and only me, the corresponding code will trigger in your mind and you will be forced to respond with the counter code. That's how you—and the Delegation—will know it's been authenticated. Got that? Here it goes. 1-1-2-3-5-8-1-3-2-1-3-4-5-5."

The moment the image finished pronouncing the last "five," Aaron, completely apart from his own volition found himself speaking out loud in unison with the voice of his reflection, "8-9-1-4-4-2-3-3-3-7-7-6-1-0."

"Welcome home, soldier," said the reflection. Then the four corners of the mirror collapsed in on themselves and flew back onto the standard's belt. The image vanished and with it everything Aaron thought he knew about himself as well.

THIRTY-FIVE

ON ALL SIDES AND NONE

A wave of weakness washed over Aaron.

He wanted to believe that all of this was just some form of manipulation by the Delegation. The holographic mirror, the mnemonic, it had to be a clever contrivance on the part of his enemies, expert in the kind of psychological manipulation it took to bend the will of anyone they deemed useful. But the problem was, this theory did not explain his response. Where had those numbers he rattled off come from? And it wasn't just the numbers themselves, the recitation of the counter sign had unlocked a chain of realizations about his life in the Collective.

The first thing that hit him was just how vague and indistinct his memories were from the time before he had come out of cryo-sleep. This wasn't the first time he had experienced fuzziness regarding his past, but it was the first time he had really stopped to consider it. Before, whenever such impressions came over him, they vanished a moment later, replaced by the next task, the next activity, the next item on his constantly filled schedule.

He also realized that it was possible his scientific skills were not native to him. Through technologies such as the esolace and his bioseine, knowledge could be imparted in a very short time.

The last realization came in the form of his appearance. He could not get over how different he looked compared to the rest of the members of the Collective. And now that he thought about it, so did Donovan, the man he had been working with over the last few days and whom he considered his life long friend. He wondered if Donovan was part of the Delegation too.

A hollow cavity opened up inside him, threatening to swallow him whole. He had been robbed of his identity and swept up into the enemy's ranks in one fell swoop. How could he go on now? What was he supposed to do next?

"So...I'm one of you," Aaron admitted at length. Though it seemed all but certain the mnemonic was authentic and not some form of manipulation, he still didn't want to be part of the Delegation. His biases from the Collective were not something he could easily shake. It was hard enough just thinking of himself by his new, or rather, his old name—Matthew.

"That's right, soldier," Orin said. "You served under Commander Nestor's division so I'm sorry to say that we've never met before, but I'm glad we found you. You're a real diamond in the rough. You know this ship and that's what we need. We have to find out where the scum who are running this vessel are holed up."

Aaron—now Matthew—had a powerful desire to see the leaders of the Collective as well, to confront them with a thousand questions which had arisen in his mind. He made an attempt to connect to the *Nebula's* esolace again, but it remained down. "What are you going to do with this ship once you take control of it?" he asked.

Orin folded his arms. "Look, escalon, I don't have time to

get you up to speed on a battle plan that's been years in the making. Can you help us track down these traitors? If so, tell us what you know."

Matthew looked around the room. The screens continued to flip, roaming all over the *Nebula*, trying to find where Cyrith and Xander had fled to, but he knew they would never find them. The Developers were smart enough to have disabled surveillance wherever the override controls would have been located.

"They didn't tell me the location of the secondary piloting station and I no longer have access to the ship's information systems, what we call the esolace. You shut it down, didn't you?" Matthew replied.

Orin snorted. "No. I don't even know what you're talking about. This stuff is way too advanced for us. Deliverance must have shut it down themselves."

"Then I don't see how you'll ever find them, not in time at least."

"Great," Orin exclaimed, pressing his hand into his forehead. "So we're still as blind as—"

"Wait. There is one possibility," Matthew interrupted, an idea suddenly popping into his mind.

"Well? Out with it," Orin said.

"There is a device on board which can trace people's actions back through time. We could use it to find their location."

The sentinel responded with a blank look. "A device that what?"

"It plays back past events. It's called a chronotrace. We could use it to find out where the people on the bridge went," Matthew said.

"Okay. We've already hit every view we can access a dozen

times over so if you think it's worth a try, I'm game. Where's this device of yours?"

"In the lab where your men found me," Matthew said.

"All right, then. Get this soldier a weapon, officer." Orin gestured to the man on his right who had one of the silver stars on his chest. The man went over to a black case resting on the floor. Opening it up, Matthew saw that it had four extra pulsers. They had transparent, copper-tinted bodies with what looked like liquid inside them. The standard pulled one out and handed it to Matthew. Though he had no recollection of ever firing such a weapon, it felt surprisingly natural in his hand.

Orin swung his arm towards the direction of the exit. "All right, we'll divide up the strike teams. Officer Ferris, you keep the Tungsten unit here on the bridge. I'll head to the lab with Xenon. If this chrono gizmo of Yin's doesn't work, we'll need to keep looking. Let me know if you find anything."

"Yes, sir," replied the officer, who went back to the soldiers surveying the screens. "What do you want us to do with the target we chased into the storage vaults? It looks like he's started reviving the people in stasis and he's engaged the locus fields surrounding the entrance so we can't get in."

"He is no longer a priority," Orin said. "We've got escalon Yin to help us track down our targets. The vaults are detachable are they not?"

"Yes sir," Ferris responded.

"Then just eject them. Send him and the rest of that Deliverance brood to rot out in the nothing. We don't have time to waste on them."

Matthew stared at the screen trained on Gavin as Orin and Ferris discussed the man's fate. He had mixed feelings about Gavin now. Was the enemy of his enemy his friend, or just another enemy? He barely even knew which side he was on anymore. Whoever Gavin was, it didn't seem right letting his section of the ship float off into space.

Gavin leaned over a woman with short-cropped hair. Her eyes fluttered open. Her face had gone blue from the cold, but even so, something stirred in Matthew at the sight of her, making him wonder who she was.

"Gavin," she said, her lips moving stiffly. "Praise Numinae you're here."

"I'll get us out of here, don't worry. Every single one of you," he said, his breath puffing clouds of frozen air.

"And Adan? Have you found him too?" she asked. The look in her eyes showed that this Adan, whoever he was, was someone she cared deeply about.

Gavin's eyes dropped and his expression grew as frigid as the surrounding air. "It's complicated, Sierra...It's complicated."

The room jerked to the side at that moment. "What was that?" Sierra asked.

Matthew already knew the answer to her question and he didn't have the heart to stay and hear Gavin's reply. The vault had been released from the ship, cast adrift in space with only a limited time before the life support would exhaust itself, killing everyone inside.

Instruments and equipment from the lab littered the floor from the scuffle with the Delegation soldiers. The chronotrace remained intact, however, still resting on top of the ebony column of celerium.

"So this little thing is going to show us the past?" Orin asked, scratching his wooly beard.

"It should," Matthew said. "It's still relatively untested,

though, a prototype, really. I can't guarantee we'll find them before they charge up the omniclast or find some other way to stop you." It still felt like he was betraying Cyrith and the Collective. He wasn't sure who was in the right anymore.

Matthew used his mind to restart the chronotrace. Orin stared at the whirring half sphere and the white lights which filled the room as the device went through its initial scan. Once complete, Matthew sent the trace's point of origin in motion, heading towards the bridge to get the last recorded moment when the Collective was in control. From there, he could track them to see where they went.

Orin and the rest of the unit could see nothing but the flashing lights. The sentinel's face grew skeptical as more and more time went by and nothing happened.

"Sir, we've been monitoring the ship's sub matter intensifiers through the view screens," Ferris reported over Orin's in-suit audio. "Based on what we've seen, there are indications that the omniclast is charging."

"How long until it's ready to fire?" Orin asked.

"Less than thirty microslices by our estimation," Ferris answered.

Orin shook his head. "They won't fire," he said. "The Torrent is too close. They may be butchers, but they won't blow themselves up just to get us off the ship. That's insanity."

That reasoning made sense, but knowing the leaders of the Collective, Matthew didn't want to wait around and find out. They had little to no regard for human life. He wouldn't put anything past them.

Matthew sent for a snapshot from the chronotrace. It had gotten as far as events on the main bridge just before Cyrith and Xander left. Donovan was there with them, along with Trey, the chief engineer, and twenty somatarchs.

As Matthew engaged the playback and the lab transformed

into the scene from the chronotrace Sentinel Orin nodded in wonder and satisfaction.

"I have lost contact with the praxis," Cyrith informed those present.

"The escalons are closing in on us from all directions. I don't think we have enough somatarchs to survive if they come en masse, even with us directly controlling them." Xander's eyes flitted between half a dozen screens depicting the Delegation units advancing uncontested towards the bridge. Whenever groups of somatarchs did oppose them, their oscillathe guns lacked the range to take out the Delegation forces and they had little difficulty with the contingency probes. The conflicts inevitably ended as soon as the Delegation forces got close enough to fire their pulsers.

"We must retire to the auxiliary bridge," Cyrith declared. The somatarchs began filing out the door in response to Cyrith's mental order. The lead Developer continued, *"If they find and attempt to breach it as well, we will have no choice but to fire the omniclast. We will not let them take the* Nebula, *no matter the cost."*

Xander, Donovan, and Trey followed the somatarchs out, but Cyrith lingered, casting one last glance back at the bridge.

"I despise this planet. I should never have come back here." His silver coat shimmered with what would have appeared to be the beginnings of a terrible rage were it not for the look of complete impassivity which dominated his face. But the anger passed away as quickly as it came and Cyrith fled through the doorway, determined to maintain his fragile hold on the ship until the very end.

THIRTY-SIX

INSUBORDINATION

Matthew waited just long enough for the chronotrace to confirm that Cyrith and the others had arrived at the secondary bridge before he ended the trace. The device spun to a stop and its white lights faded. As it did so he reflected on the irony that it had been Cyrith and Xander who pushed him to finish the device in order to stop the Delegation and now that very same organization was using the device against them.

"That's an amazing piece of technology you've got there," Orin said. "Who invented it?"

"It was created by the man you chased into the storage vaults," Matthew replied, trying to push from his mind the recollection of what the Delegation had done to Gavin.

"Well, I'll give them this much, Deliverance had us beat when it came to non-military technology. We didn't realize just how advanced they were back on Kess until it was too late. But there is one force in the universe that no technology can overcome and that is man's thirst for vengeance."

Matthew wasn't sure he agreed with that last statement,

but the edge in the sentinel's voice told him that, whatever the Developers had done to Orin and his people, the emotions were still fresh.

"Have you seen enough?" Matthew asked.

"More than enough," Orin said. "The longer we tarry, the more time we give them to charge up the omniclast and blast our fleet into micro-dust."

"Let me take this with us, just in case." Matthew reached up and dislodged the chronotrace from its clamps on top of the celerium column. He shoved it inside a polymeric satchel he found in a drawer.

The sentinel cleared his throat and pointed at the door. "All right, escalons, let's move."

Everyone filed out of the lab, Orin and Matthew bringing up the rear. As they set out at a brisk pace through the corridors, Matthew addressed his new commander.

"Sir, if I may, you keep referring to me and the others as escalons. Is that some sort of rank?"

"Fair question. We're all escalons, actually," Orin said, speaking between breaths. "Towards the end of the Delegation's rule on our home world most of our army was converted into escalons. Without going into the details, they grafted anacite into our bones and juiced up our metabolism. That means we heal pretty fast if we get injured and we don't get affected by low frequency energy weapons like neutralizers and other stun based weapons. But don't go thinking you're invincible just because you got a body upgrade. As I always tell my men, the heart of a soldier is his greatest weapon, not his gear."

"Understood," Matthew said. As a member of the Collective, he was accustomed to the idea of being something more than human, but he was surprised to learn that the Delegation had their own forms of augmentation. He wondered if there were any natural humans left on this world or any other.

The escalons soon ran into the first of many passages blocked by glowing blue walls of locus energy. This was the *Nebula's* means of dealing with the breaches the venators had made in the hull, sealing off certain sections of the ship. The barriers meant that they were not able to take a direct route to the control center. Orin and his team seemed unfazed by this. They left the passage, finding an entrance to the maintenance shafts which ran beneath the ship. They were narrow enough that in most places the soldiers had to go single file, but they were relatively free of clutter so the soldiers kept up a brisk pace.

After running through the underbelly of the ship for several microslices they reached an access hatch, but it refused to budge. Their pulser weapons only damaged living things so they couldn't shoot their way through.

One of the soldiers pulled a small tube off his belt and twisted it. A thin blade of yellow light sprang from the end. The soldier used the utility cutter to open up a hole in the doorway similar to the way Gavin had broken into the lab.

Sentinel Orin spit on the floor in an odd display of excitement. "Soon, boys, soon. These Deliverance scabs will be ours."

Several of the soldiers nodded in response, but Matthew couldn't read their expressions behind their visored masks. It was odd not being able to read their thoughts. Everything felt so unfamiliar, so unnatural, like a puzzle with all the pieces put together, but in the wrong place.

"You keep talking about 'Deliverance,'" Matthew said while the soldier made the incision. "You're referring to the Collective, right?"

"Deliverance is the name they called themselves back on Kess," Orin answered. "They were a revolutionary group back then, new and influential, but the Delegation had so many enemies we barely noticed them. We had no idea what they were up to until it was too late."

"Cyrith told us that it was the Delegation that started the war."

"Humph. That's a load of tripe and he knows it."

"You looked like you recognized him when you saw him in the chronotrace. Is that right?"

"Oh yeah. Cyrith Crane. He was a brilliant generational scientist—one of the Delegation's brightest minds before Deliverance got a hold of him. I never thought he'd be the one leading this mess."

"So Cyrith wasn't the original leader of Deliverance? Do you know who was?"

"Unfortunately, no," Orin said. "Our intelligence says that he was known primarily as 'The Doctor,' but our knowledge is extremely dated. I assume a lot has changed since the Purge."

The escalon soldier finished cutting the hole through the hatch. Two more men carried away the slab he cut out, but a second hatch lay beyond the first. It was also sealed shut so the escalon set about carving another opening.

"Well, I certainly haven't met or heard about anyone who goes by that title," Matthew stated.

"Let's hope for his sake that he suffered a slow and miserable death out in the deep dark of space." A threatening look burned in Orin's eyes.

"You really hate him, don't you? Though you don't even know who he is," Matthew observed.

"I'll know him if I find him. And if he's still alive, I *will* find him," the sentinel said. "Deliverance, led by this man, fired the omniclast into our planet and set off a paroxysm that destroyed ninety-eight percent of life on Kess. The Purge left our planet a lifeless husk. The only deliverance they ever achieved was for themselves."

Not for the first time since hearing the mnemonic, Matthew found Sentinel Orin's words difficult to comprehend. The destruction of an entire planet? That did not seem possible to him. The Developers were cold and efficient but this...he couldn't fathom anyone committing such an atrocity.

"How did you find us—I mean, them? Kess must be half way across the galaxy," Matthew asked.

Orin's eyes sparkled in the dark, as if he had been waiting for Matthew to ask him the question.

"No one believed we would find them, but I refused to let them escape the consequences of their actions. So we sent out scouts. Space travel without using sidereal portals is extremely slow so we couldn't send off our ships until we knew where they were. We sent multiple scouts out to different systems, staggering the missions to give them time to track our enemy down. You were one of several we sent to this planet. We got word only yesterday from one of our scouts that this was where Deliverance fled to."

The escalon finished cutting the hole in the second hatch. His fellow soldiers silently removed the slab, pulling it through the first hole. Then the men of Xenon unit poured through.

"This is it." Orin's eyes lit up with a vengeful glimmer. "This is what we came for." He reached into a pouch on his belt and pulled out an orange pellet and popped it in his mouth. "Want some solec?" he asked, offering Matthew a second pellet.

"No thanks," Matthew said. A powerful drug like that would have certainly calmed his nerves, but it seemed like overkill. It would have been better to save it in case someone got injured.

Everyone kept quiet after that. As they pressed forward, Matthew grew anxious, wondering what he would feel when he saw Cyrith and the others. He didn't despise them the way

Orin seemed to, but if they really had killed billions of people, perhaps he should. It still all seemed so unreal.

A quarter of a slice later the soldiers of Xenon unit arrived at the final hatch, the one leading into the auxiliary control room. They had expected to find it guarded, or at least sealed, but it was neither. Instead the door to the opening sat off to the side, blackened on the edge so that it looked like it had been blown off its hinges. The charred body of a somatarch lay sprawled across the threshold, killed by pulser fire. Though it was no longer a threat, everyone instinctively pulled out their weapons.

Beyond the body, a ramp led down into the control room. More signs of battle littered the passage there. The burned bodies of at least a dozen somatarchs lay strewn about. The lead soldiers filed through, two abreast, picking their way through the scorched remains. In many cases, only snatches of the somatarchs' white uniforms gave any indication of their identity.

Even more surprising than the presence of the somatarchs, several Delegation uniforms lay scattered amongst the bodies. They must have been hit by oscillathe blasts, but how did they get here in the first place? And why hadn't they contacted Orin when they found the auxiliary bridge? Whoever they were, the number of scorched somatarchs scattered around the room showed they had not gone down without a fight.

The sentinel's team quietly descended towards the control room. They left the ramp, the soldiers fanning out to either side. The room was circular like the main bridge and almost as large. A ring of instrumentation occupied the center. This inner ring was divided into three sections with wide gaps between each. The panels were lit up with navigation data and status screens for all the ship's systems. Above those, curved view screens hung from the ceiling, each of them depicting the sub matter intensifiers for the omniclast on top of the ship. A curved polymeric chair sat in front of each section.

Matthew's eyes scanned the room for any sign of Cyrith and the other Developers, but he spotted nothing until one of the soldiers pointed at the instrument panel to their left. There, the upper part of Cyrith's body peeked out from the base. His silvery lab coat as charred, as was most of his face, but enough was left to see that it was unmistakably the remains of the lead Developer. An odd mix of emotions rushed through him at the sight. On some level Matthew knew that justice had been served, but even though his connection to the Collective had been entirely fabricated, he could not shake a sense of guilt for having joined their enemies.

Orin thrust two fingers forward, ordering his men to advance towards the panels, but they had barely taken two steps when a man rose up from behind the nearest section of instruments.

"Kessen, our eternity," the stranger said in hoarse and ragged tones. The man had stringy gray hair down to his shoulders and a beard that was little more than thick stubble. His hollow eyes shone dully, as if he had seen far too much to care any more. The most unsettling thing about him, though, was the fact that he wore the silver and black uniform of a Delegation soldier. "If you approach the instruments, or make any hostile movements whatsoever, I will fire the omniclast."

The man moved over to a panel which they could see. On the edge of it, nestled in with power level indicators, glowed a large white circle. His hand hovered over it, trembling slightly.

The soldiers stopped in their tracks, looking back to Orin. "Sir?" one of them addressed him.

"Hold," ordered the commander. "Who are you?"

"Just a prop in your play," said the renegade soldier, "You wouldn't know me or care if you did."

The commander snorted in frustration. "Listen, I am Sentinel Orin, Overseer of the Delegation forces from the planet of Kess. Identify yourself immediately or—"

"Or what? You'll order your soldiers to shoot me down? What do I care? You've already taken everything I have. It would be a small thing for you to take my life as well."

Orin's fingers clamped around his pulser, but he held back, his eyes fixed on the man's hand poised above the glowing white circle. Was the stranger just keeping them talking so the omniclast could fully charge? Or was he really going to fire?

"I don't know who you are, but you have no authority on this ship," Orin shouted. "The *Nebula* belongs to the Delegation. Now step away from the omniclast initiator or you'll reap the whirlwind."

The man leveled his sunken gaze at the commander.

"No, Sentinel Orin, it is you who has no authority on this ship. It's been taken over it in the name of all the people you oppressed, slaughtered, tortured, and maimed to maintain your grip on our world. Our slavery to the Delegation ends today."

Orin's nostrils flared and his ears flushed crimson.

"Soldier, have you gone mad? You're talking nonsense. What unit are you with? I order you to stand down immediately."

Don't lose your cool, Matthew thought. Something told him that this stranger was more dangerous than he appeared.

"We know why Deliverance destroyed Kess, sentinel, to end the Delegation atrocities that were ravaging our world. They would never have triggered The Purge if you had not created the omniclast first!" The man's face grew even more grim, his resolve strengthening with every word he uttered.

"Nonsense! The *Nebula* was only built as a last resort—"

"I stand here today, the voice of all the people you murdered and crushed beneath your feet, the fathers and mothers, the children, the soldiers, the innocents. This is the day their cries for mercy shall be answered." His hand quivered with excitement and anticipation above the white disc. Matthew had no doubt that he would fire the omniclast at any moment. The only question was why he hadn't done it yet.

"You're bluffing. You wouldn't—" Orin began, but the soldier beside him tapped him on the shoulder.

"Sir, we have a positive ID," the man said, lowering his voice. "The soldier is Kelm Brennan, an escalon."

"The sidereal scout who signaled us to come here? That's impossible," Orin muttered in response.

A wild-eyed smile percolated across Kelm's face.

Why isn't he firing the weapon? The question bore down on Matthew, pressing into his thoughts. Kelm had to have a reason. If only Matthew were a memorant and could read his mind.

"Yes, I summoned you here half way across the galaxy," Kelm said. "Kess was dying long before *Deliverance* destroyed it. And you are responsible for that. You poisoned the atmosphere knowing that only your augmented form of humanity would survive. Then you created the omniclast to ensure that no one would ever oppose you. But some of us did not forget the ones you killed, we did not lose hope that one day you would pay for your sins. And I am ready to die to see that happen."

As Kelm spoke, spittle ejected from his mouth, a faint, bitter shower of hatred and bile. And yet, something in his eyes betrayed the fact that he did not really want to die, did not expect to die, but planned on coming out of this encounter alive. Matthew couldn't say how he knew it, but he had a strong impression he had seen the eyes of a man bent on his own death before and they did not look like this.

At that moment two things happened at once.

Orin fired his weapon, shouting, "Take him down. Open

fire!" With instincts honed and trained by years of military experience, the escalons around him lay down a swath of echoing pulses along with their commander.

At that exact same moment Matthew noticed something shimmering in the air. A faint sprinkling of light that lay suspended between Kelm and the soldiers. It was Kelm's spittle. It had not dissolved in the air or fallen normally as it should have to the ground. Instead, little dots of it froze in midair. An invisible shield surrounded the instrument panels. Kelm had wanted them to fire all along.

"Stop..." Matthew shouted, but the volley had already been let loose.

Red pulser fire filled the room. It burst like sparks on the unseen barrier surrounding the controls, reflecting back the blasts and coating the room in burning scarlet beams. Matthew dove back into the tunnel, landing in the pile of dead somatarchs while screams of pain and horror echoed all around him.

THIRTY-SEVEN

THE CHRONOTRACE SEQUENCE

ONE OF THE SOLDIERS FELL HARD ON TOP OF MATTHEW. His helmet slammed into Matthew's skull and for a moment the tunnel went dark.

When Matthew came to, he struggled to shove the soldier's body off him. Part of his lab coat got caught on the soldier's belt and ripped off a large section of fabric when Matthew pushed him away. Somehow the chronotrace came loose in the process, or maybe it had slipped out of his satchel when he dove to the ground. Either way, it landed just beyond his reach.

The rain of locus pulses inside the control room had died. All was quiet. Matthew strained to see what was going on, but his dimmed vision did not allow him to make out anything beyond the tunnel. He tried to shake off the stupor he had fallen into, but everything seemed to happen in slow motion.

A light shot out from the chronotrace, much brighter than any the machine had ever emitted before. It forced Matthew to shield his eyes.

He had not initiated a trace or a playback and the device could not have engaged on its own unless it was malfunctioning. He stretched out his mind to connect to it and shut it down, but he could not sense anything there.

A breeze swirled amidst the blazing light. Fear that there had been a malfunction in the ship's environmental generators gripped him, but pulser fire shouldn't have done any harm to the ship. Gusts swept past him in all directions, growing stronger by the moment. The tunnel seemed to open up and glimpses of purple smoke broke through high above him.

Without warning, two rays of light seared his vision, bright as pulser beams. He had no time to react. The glowing shafts burned into his skin as they swept across his body. He thought he should have been killed, but it turned out not to be pulser fire, just a constant stream of heat pouring over him.

It may not have been pulser fire, but the rays burned painfully. He had no idea what was happening in the bridge, but he could not escape that way. It was a dead end. Facing the source of the heat down the corridor was his only way out. He only hoped it didn't get hotter further up.

Still covering his eyes against the flood of light, he struggled to his feet, taking only a single step before tripping over something on the floor.

As he slammed into the ground, he fell out of the scorching beams. A shadow fell upon him. Down near the floor the winds were not nearly as strong. Looking up, he saw an immense creature towering over him, twice as tall as himself. Though it had the frame of a human, it only took one look to realize that this was nothing from the world of men.

The creature's silver skin sparkled like starlight shining on the water. Strips of luminous fabric wrapped its metallic flesh, but only loosely. They floated and fluttered as if caught up in their own slow and gentle wind despite the swirling tempest overtaking the corridor. But the most unnatural aspect of the creature was the eyes. Beams of light poured forth from them, burning him again and scattering the shadows which had momentarily allowed him to see.

Matthew shrank back in terror. If he had not already been prone, he would have collapsed to the ground. His limbs grew heavy, like he was treading water. The sense that his death was near overwhelmed him. The creature was the source of the heat, a living weapon from some other world sent to destroy him and anything else that stood in its way.

And then he remembered that he had seen one of these creatures before. This was the same sort of being which had caused Gavin's trace to malfunction. Perhaps it was just some projection from the chronotrace then, another mistake like the Developers had claimed. But it felt too real, too terrible to be anything which existed in a mere projection. The longer he looked at it, the more convinced he became that one of these creatures had somehow boarded the *Nebula* and stood before him now.

"*Matthew,*" a voice spoke to him. "*Do not be afraid.*"

Though the creature's lips didn't move, he knew instinctively that the message came from the otherworldly being. The voice had sound, but it echoed directly into his thoughts, somewhat like the communications he received through his bioseine. It carried a frightening sense of power.

"What...what do you want with me?" Matthew ventured at last, mustering up every last bit of courage just to speak.

"*I am an eidos, a messenger from Numinae.*" The words resonated inside his head.

"Numinae," Matthew mumbled reflexively. Something about the name made him feel like he ought to know it, but he could not recall who it belonged to. "Who is he?"

"*The giver of life and the sustainer of all being,*" came back the otherworldly voice. "*You do not remember him because you choose to forget.*"

"But—" Matthew started to reply, but words failed him. In the face of such raw power, what could he say that would not be the cause of his undoing? His life was forfeit and he dared not anger this being who stood before him.

"Others may hide the knowledge of your Creator from you, but he may always be found again by the smallest effort. You, however, have made no such effort." The creature's eyes glowed brighter and Matthew cringed, fearing the worst.

But then, unexpectedly, his mind was drawn back to recent events. He remembered asking Donovan about the sub-rational. The word was really just a euphemism for the supernatural. Donovan had dismissed it along with Matthew, based on nothing more than the authority of the scientists. He had not given a second thought as to why they rejected it. He accepted their claims on blind faith.

But hadn't these same people also wiped out his memory? They could have lied to him a thousand times over without him ever knowing. Why should he trust anything they said? He wanted to believe the mind remapping was the real reason he had not bothered to consider such things, but he knew in his heart that he had no interest in anything he couldn't measure, quantify, or explain in empirical terms. He had been all too willing to allow the Collective consensus to hold sway over him in this, as in all other things.

Somehow, this realization restored some of Matthew's strength, enough at least to be able to respond.

"I am sorry," he said. "You're right. I—I didn't really think things like you existed, or this—this Numinae you speak of. What does he want from me?"

"He sent me to show you the way home. You may have forgotten him, but he has not forgotten you." The lights in the eidos' eyes softened and it became less painful to be in his presence. Though they remained white and without pupils,

Matthew thought that for the first time they appeared vaguely human.

"Home?" Matthew asked. The word felt strange to say. He had no concept of what it meant beyond the fact that it was a place where someone lived. It didn't fit the Collective's pursuit of a new world to colonize and he had no idea whether it meant anything to the Delegation.

And then a terrible thought occurred to him. What if the eidos was speaking of *its* home, what if it was referring to the place where creatures like this one dwelled? Matthew did not think he could survive one moment in a place native to such beings. They were creatures of light and he, nothing more than dust and ashes.

"Where is that?" he asked, his limbs quivering in fear.

"Your true home is far from here. It is a place where you will pass beyond time and space, beyond pain and suffering." The words of the eidos evoked both peace and dread at the same time. *"But you will not see that place today, for your time has not yet come. I am only here to set your feet on the path, that you may enter into that final rest one day."* The creature pointed a long smooth finger towards whatever lay behind Matthew. Like everything else in this strange vision the area remained swathed in wind and light. *"Hear me now. There are people you must save, people whom you alone can save. Seek out the remnant destined to survive and do whatever is in your power to lead them to safety. Heed the words of Numinae and live."*

The light grew brighter once again and nigh unbearable. The winds raged so fierce it was a wonder Matthew's clothes were not ripped from his body.

"What people?" he shouted into the wind, hoping that the eidos would still be able to hear him. "Who are they? How will I find them?"

And then, just as quickly as they arose, the winds subsided.

Had they not, they would certainly have torn him apart. The light faded and the eidos was nowhere to be found.

"Wait—I don't know if I can do this. I don't know what I'm supposed to do!"

An enduring silence was his only answer. The eidos had left and Matthew found himself once again alone in the tunnel, surrounded by the bodies of the fallen somatarchs.

Part of him wished he could remain there with these lifeless bodies. He had no idea how he could go on after this awful vision. But then he heard a small, gentle voice, like the rustling of the wind. *"Your success lies only in the attempt. Trust Numinae and though the stars fall down around you, he will see you through."*

The lights were gone. The chronotrace lay dark and still amongst the carnage. Matthew's face was covered by the charred remains of the somatarchs. He tried to wipe off the soot, but his hands came back streaked in black and he only succeeded in rubbing it in further. Burn marks ran down one arm and the top of his shoulder, but they were not severe.

Matthew caught the sound of movement coming from the control room.

Still not knowing what to do, he wobbled to his feet, his head so dizzy that he nearly fell back down again. After taking a moment to find his balance, he got his legs under him and rushed back down the ramp. Maybe the people he was meant to save were the Delegation soldiers in the control room. He stumbled towards the auxiliary bridge, hoping someone up ahead was still alive.

The soldiers of Xenon unit lay dead around the instrument panels, many of them so covered in burns that they were little more than charred remains. Matthew's eyes passed over them quickly, his attention focused on the center of the control room, beyond the invisible shield. Orin, badly burned and wincing in pain, was wrestling Kelm to get at the panel controlling the omniclast.

Numbers flashed across the view screens. 0:24...0:23... Kelm had initiated the omniclast firing sequence.

Matthew stared at the scene in shock. Perhaps he had misjudged Kelm, perhaps he truly did want to die. Or maybe he had set the omniclast to fire far enough away so that the *Nebula* would not be consumed in the blast. Wherever it was aimed, he had to stop it from firing. To do that he would first have to take out Kelm.

Matthew ran straight at the shield. It was based on the re-calibration of space which scattered all forms of energy directed towards it. Such barriers were mostly used on the outside of ships, but it was not unheard of to use it to protect high security areas inside as well. More importantly to Matthew's purpose, a shield such as this was not impenetrable.

"I should have killed all of you when I had the chance," Orin shouted as the two men crashed to the floor. Matthew lost sight of them behind the instrument panels.

He hit the invisible wall at 0:20.

It was an odd sensation passing through the shield, a little like trudging through a wall of sludge. His forward movement slowed almost to nothing. His legs dragged like they were being pulled backwards by unseen hands.

Matthew led with his pulser in hand, knowing he could fire it before the rest of his body passed through if he got a clear shot. A moment later, he felt the knuckles of his pulser hand pop free of the barrier. The two brawlers rolled into view, Orin on top of Kelm, blocking the shot. Matthew had been so caught up in their struggle that he had not noticed the bodies of

Xander, Trey, and Donovan nearby. They lay next to each other under the far left instrument panel, multiple pulser burns crisscrossing their bodies. The sight sent a shiver down his spine. He wondered if anyone would get off of this ship alive.

The timer on the screens read 0:17.

The sentinel fought to wrest something from Kelm's grasp. Matthew couldn't see what it was. His hand slipped free up to the wrist while his foot and nose escaped the invisible pull of the shield.

"Curse you!" Orin screamed, pulling back a bleeding, charred hand to pummel his opponent. At the same time a pulser went tumbling across the room. Both men abandoned their grappling and went scrambling for it. Kelm grabbed hold of it first, but Orin clamped both hands around his adversary's wrist, keeping him from aiming it at him. Orin's mangled hand was slowly losing its grip. If Matthew didn't do something quickly, Kelm would be able to fire the pulser.

The timer continued on to 0:14.

Matthew's entire right arm, the one with his pulser, slipped free, as did most of his head and his left leg. Orin shifted, moving in the way of Matthew's shot.

At 0:11 Orin lost his grip and Matthew heard the buzzing squelch of a pulser discharging. Orin cried out in pain and collapsed on top of the Delegation traitor. The sentinel was dead.

Matthew's right leg below the knee and his left arm below the elbow were still caught in the shield, but he had his thumb on the pulser's trigger, waiting to press it the moment he had an open shot.

Can I do this? The thought leapt into his mind. *Can I kill this man?* Matthew may have been a soldier with the Delegation, but he had no memory of that life. As far as he knew, he had never killed anyone before.

Kelm rolled Orin off him. His back still faced Matthew. Matthew had a clear shot, but he wavered. He was still pushing through the shield and the effort made it hard to steady his wrist. Sweat coated his palms, loosening his grip on his weapon. If he missed, he would give himself away to Kelm. Kelm might fire back before Matthew could get a second shot off. Matthew would be an easy target while trapped by the invisible shield.

In that moment of hesitation Kelm rose to his feet and turned. Their eyes locked.

The timer flashed 0:09 as Matthew broke free of the shield.

He fired, but the shot went well wide of Kelm, burying itself into one of the panels where it dissipated harmlessly into the glassy material.

Kelm whipped his gun up and instinctively Matthew dove to the side and hit the floor just as Kelm's pulser went off. A streak of heat whizzed over him, the shot just missing. It sailed past Matthew and ricocheted off the shield behind him. The beam launched straight back at Kelm, plunging into his chest.

"You?" The word shot from Kelm's mouth like a second volley. His eyes bulged in horrified recognition as if he realized who Matthew was just before the end. He clutched his chest, a bright red glow seeping out around his fingers. Then he fell to the floor, killed by his own weapon.

Matthew dashed over to the instrument panel and slammed his hand onto the omniclast override control, a bright red circle in the middle of the panel, just as the timer ticked to 0:06.

A silver smooth voice spoke into the air. "Generational signature not recognized. Override failed," it said.

A signature? Did it need Kelm to override it? Matthew's mind scrambled.

The time flipped to 0:04. He grabbed hold of Kelm's dead hand and dragged it up to hit the button again.

"Invalid input. Override failed," the voice said.

The screen turned to 0:02.

Panicking, Matthew did the only thing he could think of, he slammed his pulser into the panels. He brought it down over and over again. The panel shattered and cracked where his blows landed, but it would not go dark. Looking up, he saw the screens go to 0:00.

"Omniclast fully charged," said the toneless voice. "Awaiting command to fire on target."

The weapon was only charging?

Matthew ran to one of the other panels, searching for the visual controls. A carousel of various views caught his eye and he ran his finger along them and flicked to the ones which showed the omniclast accumulators. As far as he could tell, none of them had fired. With a few more gestures he switched the screens to show the derringer assault ships of the Delegation still floating out in space, unharmed and intact.

"Yes!" he shouted into the empty room. He let his head fall forward against the panels and whispered into the glass the two most appropriate words he could think of. "Thank you."

THIRTY-EIGHT
AND SO THE WORLD ENDS

Matthew's relief at avoiding the paroxysm distracted him to the point that he never heard the shuffling charge coming.

At the last moment, his attacker's guttural cry alerted him, but he could not turn in time to avoid the two quick stabs into his lower back. Though his bioseine instantly squelched the raging hot flash of pain, his pulser fell clattering from his hands and he lost all strength in his legs. He slid down the instrument panel, crumpling to the floor.

Looking up, he saw a man with ragged silver hair drawn into matted tendrils and a shriveled, malevolent face. His robes were as tattered and shredded as the patchwork patterns of missing hair on his head. Two jagged knives made from pieces of scrap metal were strapped to his hands. Both of them dripped with blood. But it wasn't the makeshift blades that seized Matthew's heart with dread, it was the wild, primal intelligence in those bloodshot eyes. Matthew wondered if this might be some failed experiment of the Developers, some mish-mash of humanity with something older, something much more brutish. Yet for all the man's savagery and inhuman appearance, a cold, cunning light burned white hot out of the depths of his shadowy glare.

"Leave my ship alone," the man said, saliva pooling at the edges of his grimy mouth. He kicked Matthew's pulser into the base of one of the panels. The weapon ricocheted off the metal and landed near the bodies of the three dead Developers.

Matthew's lower body refused to move, but he grabbed at his attacker's legs in a feeble attempt to trip him.

The wild man kicked Matthew in the chin. Bursts of light danced over his eyes and several moments passed before the room stopped spinning. When Matthew recovered his senses, he spotted the stranger hovering over one of the undamaged instrument panels, well out of his reach. He sniffed them first and then pawed at them cautiously.

"What are you doing?" Matthew asked.

"Erasing the past," the man mumbled. "Have to clean up old mistakes." He gave the panel a long, distrustful look and then spit on it. When the surface lit up, he jumped back in shock. "Ah, I remember now. Pieces of the puzzle are still floating up there somewhere." He tapped his forehead, entangling one of his blades in his free ranging hair. Rather than take the time to unravel the mess he yanked the strands out with a loud grunt.

"Who are you? Why did you attack me?" Matthew demanded. His legs twitched, signaling the return of some strength, though not enough to stand.

"I am...I am...a doctor. I am here to cure a terrible disease," the man declared with a great sense of self-importance. "They are the disease." He waved at the dead bodies around the room. "Them and everyone like them. So much deviation. Humanity is a taint, an infection which I fear has stricken me as well. Yes, even me. We're all infected. It's time to purge the sickness. There's no turning back now." His head bowed and the shadows on his bony face deepened ominously.

The man's words confirmed what Matthew already suspected: he was insane. If he could not be reasoned with, Matthew had to keep him distracted long enough to figure out a way to stop him.

He started clawing his way towards the body of Orin. He had his eye on one thing: the commander's utility pouch.

"What are you doing with that panel? Why did you turn it on?" he asked.

The madman paused to study the panels before him.

"Now, where are those targeting controls?" the man mumbled. He tried pressing on the various shapes and symbols, but his weapons got in the way, clanging and scraping on the glass. "Cursed claws! When will I be rid of you?"

"You didn't answer my question. What are you planning on doing with that panel?" Matthew had arrived at Orin's side and was just about to reach for the utility pouch on his belt when the wild-eyed man shot him a murderous scowl.

"Stop barking you useless squawker! Can't you see I'm trying to think?" he shouted.

Matthew paused in his search, but the man swung his head back towards the glowing panels, his eyes eagerly pouring over the various controls.

The panel Matthew had cracked with his pistol caught the madman's eye. "You bruised my beastie, meddler. All your thrashing and smashing disabled the world breaker!" He jumped to his feet, frothing with white foamed vengeance.

Matthew froze where he was, afraid to say anything. He was certain the man meant to strike again and finish him off for good.

But his whirlwind expressions shifted again, as if another

mood had hit him over the head. An air of pride swelled across his gaunt face.

"No matter. I am a doctor! I am a genius. I must have installed a back door somewhere. Clever men always see things from two sides."

He moved to another panel and began flipping through several new sets of controls, waving his arms about in a frantic, but oddly purposeful fashion.

Matthew took advantage of the man's preoccupation and grabbed Orin's pouch and stick his hand inside.

"Ah, there it is," squealed the madman, his eyes landing on a series of red dots on the panel. He ran his fingers across the dots, punching them wildly. Images flashed by on the screens above, shifting between every possible part of the ship, intermixed with views outside of it. In the end they settled upon the two Delegation interstellars. The sight made Matthew's heart skip in his chest.

"Why are you looking at those ships?" Matthew asked. Was this deranged person even capable of operating the omniclast? Was he working with Kelm? Kelm had mentioned that there were others on his side, but Matthew doubted Kelm would have chosen someone like this as an ally.

"Ah, my old enemies," the man cried out. He stood erect, clasping his ragged robe in a grotesque caricature of elegance. "He led them back to me, no doubt to destroy me. But no one takes my life from me. Only I say whether I live or die." He glanced sideways at Matthew. Though his expression was vindictive and sinister, Matthew did not think it was directed at him this time. Hatred for the his enemies burned above all else in those eyes.

"Doctor—if you really are a doctor—aren't you supposed to help people? Can't you see there are people injured all around you?" Matthew kept talking, rifling through Orin's med pack until he found the packet of solec. He popped two of the pills into his mouth and waited for them to take effect. If they were of typical potency, it would not be long.

"What?" the man screamed at the panel, pulling at what little hair he had left. "The level was set to fifty percent? That won't do."

He began pounding the panel with his fists over and over. At first Matthew thought it was out of frustration, but the status screens on the omniclast targeting range increased each time he did. Kelm had set the range to roughly fifty percent, enough to hit the Delegation ships, but not much beyond. By increasing the levels to full, the omniclast's attack would pass right through the fleet and straight down onto the surface of the planet, triggering a paroxysm there as well.

"You can't do that," Matthew yelled at him. "You'll kill everyone—you'll destroy this ship, you'll destroy the entire planet."

The man flashed his reddened eyes at Matthew. They had never looked more lucid.

"That is the point."

Whatever dark purpose drove his heart, the tone of his voice made it clear there would be no turning him aside from it. He was bent on the destruction not only of the Delegation and the *Nebula*, but of the planet Nai as well. This wasn't Kelm. He was infinitely more dangerous. This 'doctor' meant to snuff out the lives of as many of his patients as possible. And if he died in the process, so be it. Or perhaps that was his main objective and the rest was simply an unfortunate, but necessary consequence.

Matthew had to find some way to stop him, but the solec wasn't working fast enough. He could barely move his feet, much less stand on his own power.

The doctor's hand shot out over the large white circle

which reappeared on the instrument panel beneath the cracked glass.

"If only they had listened to me, it never would have come to this," railed the doctor. "We were supposed to have a new beginning here, to start humanity over from scratch and remove all of the deviations, but he would not have it. The Everlord suffers no challengers to his throne." His hand quivered over the circle excitedly.

"Please, don't do this," Matthew begged.

"I offered them life. I offered them peace, but they chose rebellion. But there is more than one force in this universe with the power to create and destroy," he rattled on. "And now they will all pay for their crimes. Now death comes swiftly!"

His palm slammed down onto the white circle.

"Input ignored," came a silvery smooth voice into the chamber. "Omniclast is already at full power. Awaiting command to fire."

Matthew had to stop this man before he could issue the command. He pounded his legs, but all he managed to do was bend his knees a little.

"Work, you useless stumps," he muttered.

"Ah, fully charged already? How fortuitous," the doctor chirped gleefully.

"You can't do this," Matthew said. "Please, please, you can't possibly have any reason for wanting to kill all of these people."

"There must be peace, whatever the cost. I promised them peace, and it is peace which I shall give. My peace." For the first time the edge in his voice faded. An almost human smile etched itself across his face.

"Doctor—whoever you are, you have to stop this," Matthew pleaded. His legs trembled encouragingly, but they were still coming back to life, he did not yet have the strength to stand. No matter. He could wait no longer. He scraped along the floor in the direction of his cast off pulser, a few strides beyond the bodies of the three dead Developers. He had to risk the doctor seeing what he was trying to do. There was no time left for subtlety.

The doctor leaned forward, grinning contentedly and surveying the panel. "This is where it all began and this is where it will end. The one freedom a man has in life is to choose the time and manner of his own death. I will be free from pain and suffering. We will all be," he cooed into the glowing instruments.

"Are you sure this world is all there is? Are you sure you'll find peace on the other side of death?" Matthew clawed his way across the room trying to keep the man babbling. He was halfway to the Developers' bodies now.

"You think you know the Everlord, do you?" The doctor snarled, but he kept his eyes fixed on the panels and had yet to turn towards Matthew. "Ah, but you do not know him like I do. You haven't seen his *other* side. He refuses to allow his creatures one moment of unfettered freedom. He lays claim to everything. But if he has given me the power of death, why should it be a sin to use it? And if it is a sin, when no one is left to remember it, how can it be charged against me? If this is what it takes to blot out my transgressions, so be it."

Matthew's strength continued to trickle back. He worked himself up into a crawling position. All it would take was a word from the doctor and everything would be lost—the Delegation fleet, the *Nebula*, perhaps humanity itself.

The doctor turned and regarded Matthew as he reached the bodies of the three Developers, but then he looked past him to the charred remains of a forth corpse nearby. A look of mild surprise registered upon his face.

"Cyrith? Is that you?" Something approaching pity arose in

his voice. "I see that you chose death as well. A wise decision. You could never hope to replace me."

He doesn't see the gun, Matthew realized.

The doctor turned back to the panel, losing himself again in silent rapture as he surveyed the fully charged accumulators.

Matthew had to destroy this man. He scrambled on his knees and elbows over the last few paces, grabbing the pulser at last. He slammed his thumb onto the firing trigger, aiming for the doctor's head.

The gun failed to fire.

It was then that Matthew noticed that the power chamber of the weapon had cracked. It must have happened when he was slamming it into the panels.

He had no time to panic. In the wake of his failure, he tried to stand and rush the doctor, but though he managed to totter onto his feet his legs locked up like stone.

He got two steps before an oblivious smile quivered onto the doctor's lips. He let out a long, shuddering sigh.

"Fire the omniclast."

The screens flipped to show the outside of the ship. An effulgent emerald blast erupted from the intensifiers on top and streaked across the screen. In moments, they reached the Delegation ships, consuming them in a verdant flash. From there they shot on through space, heading straight for the foggy green ball below—the planet of Nai.

Matthew could not watch. He struggled to his feet, sheer terror lending him the last bit of strength his legs needed to begin functioning once again.

A serene expression settled upon the madman's face. "And so the world ends. This time for good."

Then the doctor closed his eyes and waited for oblivion to come.

THIRTY-NINE

THE PAROXYSM

The doctor's head rested against the instrument panel. His eyes remained closed, caught up in whatever twisted bliss he was wandering in. The depraved man's words echoed in Matthew's mind.

"And so the world ends..."

And yet, in all of his desperation to stop the omniclast, he had forgotten his encounter with the eidos. Those words came back to him now.

There are people you must save, people whom you alone can save...

Yes, he had to find them. If only he knew who those people were.

But before that he had to get off this ship—if there was even time.

Ignoring the motionless madman, he scanned the screen showing the Delegation ships. They were all gone now, consumed in that terrible, agitated cloud of green brilliance. The intensity reminded him of the burning gaze of the eidos from the corridor. The glowing sphere bubbled and frothed as it grew. All matter it came into contact with would be annihilated in the insatiable paroxysm. It would not take long before that expanding destruction reached the *Nebula* and devoured it as well.

Matthew ran towards the exit, expecting to hit the shield again, but he passed through the area unhindered. The doctor must have disabled it in all his mad pounding against the panels. Stepping into the carnage outside the instrument panels, Matthew scooped up one of the cast off helmets from the vaporized Delegation soldiers and shoved it on his head.

"Hello? Is anyone there? Anyone? This is escalon Matthew Yin," he said, unsure how to trigger the audio system in the helmet. When he got no answer he tried again. "Is there anyone who can hear me? Sentinel Orin is dead. The omniclast has been fired. Is anyone getting this?"

He started running towards the tunnel, still hailing the Delegation via the helmet as he went, but no one answered.

"Technology," Matthew muttered under his breath, realizing he had no idea how to operate the helmet. He cast it off in frustration and ran from the room.

He reached an access shaft in the ceiling half a microslice later. Racing up to the wall so fast he barely touched the rungs, he shot out of the floor on the main level of the *Nebula*. It was near one of the sectors the Delegation soldiers had invaded. The translucent barrier of locus energy sealed off this section of the ship where the breach had occurred. Beyond the sheet of energy waited the empty vacuum of space and, hopefully, one of the abandoned Delegation venators the escalons had used to board the ship. There were no ships left in the Collective fleet and the *Nebula's* escape pods would only get him to the surface of the planet. With the omniclast eating through Nai's crust, that would only relocate the place of his death. He had to get

out into open space, far from the *Nebula,* and then figure out
what to do from there.

To get to the venator, he had to get through the vacuum
first. Unlike the Delegation soldiers, he had no suit to protect
him. It would have taken precious time to go back and grab one
from the dead soldiers, and they were probably damaged
beyond repair anyway. But the *Nebula* was equipped with
exactly what he needed.

He moved over to one of the safety panels on the side of the
passage. He pressed a section of the floor with his foot and it
slid away, revealing a compartment with a stack of small triangular plates embedded into a piece of foam. Above the foam in
another compartment hung a silver helmet with a green tinted
visor, very similar to the kind the Delegation soldiers wore.

Matthew pulled out one of the plates and slapped it onto
his chest. The other plates, bound together via a low power
axom field, floated after the first, wrapping themselves around
him and forming a tessellated metallic suit that covered his
entire frame. After the plates locked into place, he grabbed the
helmet and shoved it onto his head where it formed a seal with
the plates around his neck.

Protected inside the suit, he headed towards the locus
barrier in the middle of the hallway. Though the shimmering
wall kept out almost everything else, the material in Matthew's
suit allowed him to pass through. He stepped safely into the
vacuum, his suit providing him with oxygen through the two
circular converter panels on the back.

This section of hallway lacked any gravity. Matthew pushed
off the floor and drifted towards the ceiling. A few moments
later he spotted the breach in the hull. Using his hands to thrust
himself back to the floor, he rebounded back up to the opening.

He breathed a sigh of relief at the sight of one of the venators standing motionless, its feet latched onto the *Nebula's* outer surface by some invisible bond. It towered above him, four times his height. It had a human shape, though the head was more like an elongated cone left over from the vehicle's ship form with the tip pointed downwards, like a giant beak.

Matthew slipped through the breach and out into open space. The brilliant green light of the paroxysm expanded off in the distance. It had swelled to five times its previous diameter, blocking out his view of the planet Nai. At that rate, he did not have long before it reached the *Nebula*.

Matthew shot upwards toward the exoskeleton's body, gripping the many protrusions which ran along the machine's channeled surface. He flipped around to the back of the ship and spotted a rectangular opening.

He ducked inside and the hatch sealed shut behind him. As he nestled into the venator's cramped cockpit he took stock of the ship's interior. The cockpit was little more than a human-shaped cavity with a separate space for his arms, head, and legs. He settled in and then realized another terrible truth: he had no idea how to operate this ship.

His hopes plummeted.

A blue light flashed across his eyes and he squinted instinctively, afraid it might be some sort of alarm system.

"Identification scan failed," came a hollow sounding voice inside the cockpit.

"Oh, so this thing talks. Great. How do we transform the ship and launch?" Matthew asked.

"Maintain your eyes open for the scan," said the ship.

Matthew kept his eyes open as wide as possible while the blue light flashed over them again.

"Pilot identified. Escalon Matthew Yin. You are authorized to pilot this vehicle. Welcome aboard."

Soon the cockpit instruments lit up around him and the

scanner screen appeared, translucent and superimposed over his vision.

Large green sensors flashed in front of him in the shape of hands. He pressed his palms against them. Small suction cups connected with his body all along his limbs and torso.

"Okay, please launch the ship," Matthew said.

"The ship will mimic your movement while in exoskeleton form. Or would you prefer to transition to full flight mode?"

"Flight mode, yes—full flight mode—now!"

The venator's metallic knees flexed and the giant machine leapt into space, leaving the *Nebula* behind. Once they cleared the hull, the armatus' outer panels began to shift and swivel in all directions, re-forming the venator into a small, triangular space ship with two thrusters at the rear. As he pulled away from the massive space station, Matthew kept his eyes trained on the spatial map superimposed over his vision. The paroxysm dominated the read out, but off to his left, a tiny spec moved parallel to the blast and away from the *Nebula*.

"Can you zoom in on that object?" Matthew asked.

The object grew larger until it filled about half the screen. It was the jettisoned storage module from the *Nebula*. He had completely forgotten about it in the fight with Kelm and the doctor. Gavin and the other Collectives still in cryo had been cast adrift and left to die. Based on their trajectory the little compartment would be consumed by the blast around the same time as the *Nebula*.

*There are people you must save...*the words of the eidos echoed again through his memory. He wasn't certain whether these were the people the eidos was referring to or whether anyone on that module was even still alive, but the *Nebula* was lost, along with the Delegation ships and everyone on the planet below. These were the only people he *could* save.

A distance indicator appeared below the module on the scanner. It read two hundred fifteen clicks.

"How do I make this ship go faster?" Matthew asked.

"The thruster controls are near your thumbs. Your right hand controls forward thrust and your left the drift."

Matthew touched the tiny balls near his thumbs. After a few moments of experimentation he found that by pressing on them or pushing them in different directions and with different levels of pressure he could make the ship go more or less wherever he wanted it to go. He engaged the thrusters at full and the venator shot off towards the wayward module.

His newly acquired ship streaked across the empty void, covering the distance between the module and the *Nebula* in little more than a microslice. In that time the paroxysm continued to grow at an ever increasing rate. Would he be able to reach Gavin's module in time? And would he be able to outdistance the blast if he did?

"How far is the paroxysm?" Matthew asked.

"Two hundred and six clicks," came the dry response.

He decreased the velocity as he prepared for the approach. The light from the paroxysm reflected off the metal hull of the module like a polished jewel. The storage compartment was rotating slightly and he soon spotted some maintenance rungs on its underside. He cut the velocity more and more the closer he got. He wanted to ensure he could land on the module without bouncing off.

"Open up an audio transmission to that module," he told the ship.

"External audio engaged," the venator replied. *"While active, you will need to preface any verbal commands to your ship with my call sign."*

"And what's that?" Matthew asked impatiently.

"Venator EC-2."

"Got it," Matthew said. "Attention, Gavin, this is Aaron from the interstellar *Nebula*, are you there?" The module's guide lights were off. It might be that the power was already gone. Without power, there was little chance anyone inside was still alive.

Matthew hoped the audio had simply malfunctioned or that they had disengaged it to conserve power. He repeated his call, "Gavin, this is Aaron, can you hear me?" Silence once again.

He studied the approaching blossom of destruction depicted on his scanners.

"Venator EC-2, how much time before the paroxysm overtakes this ship?"

"*1.2 microslices*," answered the disembodied voice.

The thought crossed his mind again that everyone on the module might already be dead. Perhaps he was risking his life for nothing.

No. He couldn't know that until he got inside the ship. He had to see this through.

It took almost half a microslice to close the remaining distance.

"Transform the ship into exoskeleton mode," Matthew said.

The venator responded by shifting around him, morphing itself back into its bipedal form. The feet clamped onto the surface of the module through the same axom attractors that kept them on the *Nebula*. His momentum halted, he used his own body movements to control the ship. He pulled the venator's feet up and rolled the exoskeleton around until he was crawling on the bottom of the storage unit, gripping a pair of maintenance rungs which were still intact.

The intensity of the paroxysm made it look like a massive star forming in space. The expanding wave of oblivion threatened to wash over him at any moment. Matthew shoved the head of the venator into two of the rungs.

"Venator EC-2, Shift back into full flight mode," he commanded.

Several sections of the venator scraped against the bottom of the storage module during transition, but the rungs held. Matthew hit the thrusters the moment the ship reassembled. Emerald light streamed everywhere. Based on the scanner read out, they were on the very edge of the paroxysm, but somehow they still had a fraction of a click between themselves and oblivion. Matthew half shut his eyes, wondering if this would be the end. But just like that, the next moment the venator pulled away, surging out into the empty black.

"Is someone out there?" came a feeble voice over the venator's audio as the ship pulled away from the entropic blast.

Matthew flinched at the unexpected transmission. Someone must have heard his ship scraping against the module and reengaged the audio.

"This is Aaron from the *Nebula*. Is that you, Gavin?" Matthew asked. Elation and terror warred inside of him. He was thrilled that there were survivors, but his eyes stayed glued to the scanner, watching as the paroxysm overwhelmed the nearby space station.

"Aaron? What are you doing out there?" Gavin's voice brightened, though he still sounded incredibly weak.

"Just giving you a little push, that's all," Matthew said. The venator and the space module pulled further and further out into the deep nothingness of space. The *Nebula* was gone, consumed in a matter of moments, but the deadly light which had claimed it was no longer as close.

Matthew let out a deep sigh. They were safe.

Thank you, Numinae...wherever you are. He was convinced that this was what the eidos had sent him to do.

"Why? Why did you come for us?" Gavin asked.

Matthew thought for a while on how best to answer. A short time ago he could have cared less about the person asking the question. He had considered him a traitor. Now he was overjoyed to have just saved his life. How quickly things had changed.

"Someone told me I should," was all he said. He didn't think it was the right time to mention the eidos. It still felt a little unreal to him even now.

"You are an answer to my prayers," Gavin said, breathing heavily.

"I believe you," Matthew said. "I only wish I had listened to you before. Maybe somehow we could have saved the *Nebula*."

"I doubt it," Gavin said. "But you're here now. That is what matters."

They continued to pull away from the paroxysm. Eventually it would stop expanding, but not until it had run its course. Until then, they had to keep as far away from it as possible.

"I have to confess I was beginning to doubt whether you would come for me this time," Gavin said. "But I should have learned by now never to count you out, or our mutual friend."

"Our mutual friend?"

"The one who sent you to save me. The same one who sent me to bring you home."

So had he guessed about the eidos after all? Perhaps memorants could read thoughts even when they couldn't see you.

"Home..." Matthew repeated that word, wondering once again where exactly that might be.

"We'll go back there—together."

"Gavin, are there any other survivors besides you?"

"Approximately thirty. I put them back into cryo-sleep to conserve energy and resources. But even so...I think we're down to less than thirty microslices of artificial atmosphere.

"You need to get us out of this module. How big is your ship?"

Now the weakness in Matthew's hastily conceived plan became clear. His ship would hold only a single occupant and they had nowhere else to go. He had saved them from oblivion only to lead them to die out in the void. If the omniclast hadn't hit the planet, he could have guided them back to the surface, but out in the midst of space there was nothing but death and emptiness. Even the distant star, as bright as it shined, appeared cold and uncaring to him now.

Matthew's voice caught in his throat as he struggled to find the right words to inform Gavin about the reality of the situation.

"You don't have enough room for us, do you?" Gavin said, breaking the silence.

"I don't," Matthew admitted. "They fired the omniclast. I was in such a panic to get you out of the way of the paroxysm I didn't think about what would happen if I actually managed to save you. The *Nebula* is gone. The Delegation ships are gone too. They hit the planet as well. There's nowhere left for us to go."

"Nai? They fired on the planet? But—but the Welkin, the Sentients...Senya..." His voice sounded more faint than ever.

"You had friends down there?" Matthew asked. Though Gavin gave no reply, his muffled sobs told Matthew all he needed to know.

The venator and the storage module drifted along in the desolation of space. Matthew had no words to comfort this grieving man. There was nothing he could say.

The thrusters flickered feebly behind them. It seemed like a useless expenditure of power now. Nai would be destroyed, like the planet Kess before it. The last remnants of humanity had fought each other into extinction. For all Matthew knew, he, Gavin, and the thirty prisoners clinging to life inside the frigid storage vault were all that was left of the human race.

"Seek out the remnant destined to survive," the eidos had told him. Was this it? Were these the only people meant to survive? If so, for how long? The few microslices until the oxygen ran out? Why hadn't he been able to stop the doctor from firing the weapon? Or why had Numinae even left it up to him in the first place? Couldn't the eidos have stopped all of this if he had wanted to? Matthew couldn't help but think that maybe Numinae had chosen the wrong person.

"Fly us to the planet's surface," Gavin said.

"But the omniclast—"

"The paroxysm will take some time to destroy something as large as a planet. At least there we can breathe the open air and die as men. I don't want to freeze to death out here, buried in all of this cold emptiness."

Gavin's words only deepened Matthew's sense of hopelessness. Perhaps he was right. Perhaps it would be best to die with their feet on the ground instead of out here in the midst of space. There might yet be some island of rock down there amidst the destruction where they could wait until the end came upon them.

Though he didn't even know him, Gavin had still tried to save him. If nothing else, at least Matthew owed it to him to honor his dying wish.

"Very well," he agreed, engaging the lateral thrusters to begin changing course.

"Besides," Gavin said. "Paroxysms are unpredictable. It may be that this one will expend itself before it destroys everything. Numinae may yet spare us in the end."

Matthew wanted to believe that. But Gavin hadn't seen the power levels on the omniclast when it fired. There was no doubt in Matthew's mind the paroxysm would erase every last vestige of life on the planet's surface. It would burn hundreds of micro-clicks down into the crust, leaving a world devoid of topography, divested of its atmosphere, and no longer able to support life. He did not mention these things to Gavin. It was enough that his body was going to die, Matthew refused to kill his spirit as well.

The venator and the storage module circled around and set themselves on a course for the planet. They could not head directly for it because of the massive paroxysm, but the venator was fast enough to skirt around the edge of the blast and make for the far side of the planet. Because of the longer route they would be forced to take, Matthew risked accelerating to maximum speed to ensure that Gavin and the others reached the surface before the module's air supply ran out.

As they passed beyond the malevolent, verdant glare of the paroxysm, it continued to convulse and grow like some interstellar disease, but now Matthew got his first view of planet Nai. A third of the world was lit up by a nightmarish green glow. No clouds were visible through that awful brightness, but the ones beyond the blast seemed to writhe in fear, anticipating their imminent demise.

A distance indicator on the scanners told him that they had about five thousand clicks before they hit Nai's atmosphere. A short time later, Matthew noticed a blip on his navigational screen which appeared around the edge of the planet. He stared at it for some time, waiting for the venator's scanners to tell him what it was. The way it was moving made him cautiously optimistic. It didn't seem to be in any fixed orbit, it seemed to be moving on its own.

And then the most wonderful words he could have imagined sounded over the venator's audio system.

"Ship identified. Derringer class attack ship with interstellar capabilities."

Matthew took in a sharp breath. "What? But that's impossible," he muttered.

"What is it?" came Gavin's startled voice.

"It's a—" Matthew began, but the in-ship audio cut him off.

"Incoming transmission from the derringer. Do you wish to accept?"

"Yes, yes!" he shouted. "Venator EC-2, open up the channel and broadcast it to the module," he instructed. "Gavin, we've made contact with one of the Delegation ships. One of them must have survived!" he exclaimed. "We're not going to die. We're going to make it after all."

Emotion overcame him. All he could do was sit and listen to the incoming message as tears streaked down his quivering cheeks.

FORTY

THE RADIX

The incoming message was breathtakingly clear, the voice on the other end pointed and direct.

"Venator EC-2 this is the derringer *Radix*, please respond with your status and identify yourself."

Matthew blanked for a moment, unsure of how to respond. Then he remembered that this was a Delegation ship and that he was actually still a part of their army. Giving a straightforward answer seemed the best option.

"This is escalon Matthew Yin, sidereal scout class. I have a jettisoned module from the *Nebula* in tow with approximately thirty survivors and life support is running extremely low. Request permission to approach the *Radix* and board."

A long pause followed. Matthew wondered if they were double checking his identity or simply debating whether or not to agree to his request.

"Sentinel Yin, this is Commander Farin of the *Radix*," came back a different voice. It sounded much more pleasant than the first. "Forgive the delay in our reply, but we thought you were dead, sir. No one has heard from you in over seven years."

Sentinel Yin? Matthew wondered if he had heard that right, but he thought it best not to question it for now. Perhaps Farin had simply misspoken.

"Yes, well, it's been a bit of a rough ride. But right now, I need to get back to the fleet. These people I've got out here don't have much time left."

More hesitation followed. "...Understood. You're cleared to approach, Sentinel."

There it was again: sentinel.

"Excellent." Matthew said calmly, though inside his mind was spinning. He adjusted the course of the venator to head for the derringer. "We owe you one."

"You should expect nothing less," Farin replied. "Remnant takes care of its own."

Remnant? Now Matthew was doubly confused. The scanner identified the *Radix* as a Delegation ship. Who was Remnant? And now that he thought about it, how had this ship even survived the paroxysm? A hundred questions crowded his mind, but he didn't want to act too confused and give Farin cause for alarm.

"Commander, about the Delegation, what is the status on the rest of the fleet?" Matthew asked.

"We are free, Sentinel Yin. Our Delegation oppressors have been eliminated." Farin's voice swelled with pride.

Matthew sat there staring at his scanner as the full significance of that sentence set in. Whoever Remnant was, apparently they were not part of the Delegation, but had somehow come into possession of one of their ships.

The words of the eidos came back to him again. *"Seek out the remnant destined to survive and do whatever is in your power to lead them to safety."* The remnant. Could these words have been referring to the people on this ship? If so, it didn't seem like they were the ones who needed to be led to safety, but Matthew himself.

"I understand you have not been apprised of the changes in our strategy, Sentinel, due to your long absence," Farin continued. "But it became clear that forcing Orin into an agreement was no longer a viable option."

"I see," Matthew said, still trying to puzzle things together in his mind. "That explains what happened with the omniclast."

"Well, it does and it doesn't," Farin replied. "Kelm's team was not supposed to fire it at full power. We never intended to leave this world uninhabitable as well. Were you onboard the *Nebula*? Do you know what happened?"

With each new bit of information, the mystery began to unravel for Matthew. Kelm had not boarded the *Nebula* alone. He had said others were working with him, but until now Matthew had no idea who those others might be. The rest of Kelm's team must have died in the fight for the secondary bridge. If Kelm and Farin were both a part of this Remnant faction, it seemed probable that the same sort of betrayal might have happened aboard the *Radix* as well. If Farin's men had successfully taken over one of the Delegation's ship that would explain why they had been able to escape the omniclast attack. Knowing what was coming, they would have sent the ship out of range before the omniclast fired.

But all of these suppositions left Matthew with a much larger question: what role had he played in all of this? If he had really been a part of this Remnant faction as Farin seemed to think, was he responsible in some way for the ever growing blight consuming the planet below?

"Sentinel?" Farin spoke up after a long silence.

"Yes, sorry," Matthew said. "It's just...it's a lot to take in."

"I completely understand." The audio went silent yet again and when Farin came back his voice sounded a bit more anxious. "Sentinel Yin, much has changed since you left on your mission. I've talked things over with some of the other officers and we think it might be best if we gave you some time before resuming your duties, at least for now."

Matthew had no interest in leading anyone so this development meant little to him, but he wondered what effect it might have on his situation going forward. For now, though, he thought it best to simply go along with whatever the commander said.

"Of course, Commander Farin," Matthew said. "I'm in no condition to resume my duties anyhow."

"We can discuss your situation further once you get onboard. For now, I am going to turn you over to Crew Chief Tulloc. He'll direct your ship to the cargo bay while I organize a team to meet you."

"Sounds good. Thank you again, Commander. We owe you our lives," Matthew said.

"This is a great day, Sentinel Yin," Farin said, his voice swelling with confidence. "Not only have we avenged ourselves on Deliverance and liberated the Remnant out from under the oppressive Delegation, but you are alive beyond what anyone ever hoped or dreamed."

Matthew raised himself up out of the venator's cockpit and threw his legs over the side of the ship. Dozens of other ships crowded the long cargo bay, all of unfamiliar designs, but Matthew had no time to take them in. Farin, the commander of the derringer *Radix*, stood a few paces away, waiting to greet him. A dozen Delegation soldiers flanked him on either side, though none of them wore helmets as they had onboard the *Nebula,* and the silver stars on their chests had been removed. They were a mixture of hair colors and skin tones in marked contrast to the people who formed the Collective. The commander was a short man who had reddish hair and a light complexion.

Matthew slid off the fuselage and stood before him.

"Commander Farin," Matthew saluted the smaller man.

"Sentinel Yin," Farin said, returning the salute.

"It's good to see you." Matthew felt awkward in front of these soldiers. They regarded him with expectant looks, but he had no idea who they were.

Near the outer hatch of the storage compartment, a team of medical personnel were positioning a mobile ramp.

"Welcome aboard the *Radix*," Farin continued. "You need not worry about the survivors. Our men will see that they are properly taken care of."

Farin's words were friendly enough, but Matthew sensed a tension between them. He wondered what his relationship with this man had been, and if Matthew's reappearance now, after all this time, might not pose some sort of complication for Farin or the faction he represented.

"I'm sure you will do everything you can for them," Matthew said.

"Of course. While they're being taken care of, I'd like you to come with me and fill us in on what happened to you during the years you were on your mission—if you're feeling up to it." Farin gestured towards the exit located in the large alcove at the other end of the bay.

"I'd be happy to, but before I do, I'd like to talk with one of the survivors in particular if that's all right." Matthew not only wanted to see Gavin to make sure he was all right, but he was anxious to find out just what was in that vial of remin fluid he had.

Farin's gaze shifted from side to side. Perhaps his suggestion had been more important to him than the he had let on.

"Crew Chief Tulloc said they were all in cryo-sleep. Are you sure this person will be in any condition to talk to you?" Farin asked.

"One of them stayed awake during the module's ejection. He was trying to give me some important information back on the *Nebula*. If we wait for him, it might help answer some of your questions."

Farin pulled on the edges of his sleeves as if straightening them were a part of his cognitive process. Once the wrinkles had been smoothed, he gave Matthew a curt nod.

"Very well. If you think this man has valuable information, of course we will wait for him. What is a slight delay after all these years?"

Farin and Matthew made their way to the storage module on the other side of the venator. The soldiers followed.

The medical team had already released the outer hatch and a frigid mist billowed around the opening. They watched as the first of the *Radix* personnel, men and women in dark blue plastic suits, entered the craft via a portable metal ramp.

"So was this...information the reason you went out in the venator to rescue these people? Or were you just fleeing the *Nebula* and happened upon them?" Farin asked as they waited for the survivors to emerge.

Matthew stared off into space, trying to decide how to explain what had led him to go after Gavin and the others. He doubted Farin would understand or believe him if he told him about the eidos.

"Sentinel Orin cast them adrift. They would have been caught in the paroxysm if I didn't go after them."

"But they were part of Deliverance weren't they? Why go to all the trouble to save them?"

"Actually, I don't think they were." Something told Matthew that this was more than just a hunch, but he couldn't say how he knew this.

At that moment the first of the survivors emerged from the vault. A man with blue skin and frost covered hair tottered forward, his eyes taking in and searching the crowd of ships. But his near brush with death had not diminished the brightness in his eyes and Matthew recognized Gavin despite his bizarre appearance.

The medical team attempted to load him onto a floating black gurney, but when Gavin saw Matthew, he shoved them aside and hobbled down the ramp. The medics easily pulled him back, weak as he was, but Gavin continued to resist.

"It's all right. Let him through, let him through," Farin ordered. The medics acquiesced, letting Gavin stumble half-frozen down the ramp towards his rescuer.

Gavin embraced Matthew. "Thank you, my friend," he whispered. His skin was ice cold, but Matthew grew warm inside at those words. Up until now he had known that saving them was the right thing, but it had been an abstract understanding. The frigid chattering of Gavin's teeth on his shoulder sent the full weight of what Matthew had done pressing down on him. He had saved this man's life. Whatever else he did from here on out, he would always have that.

"I'm just glad you're alive," Matthew said.

"I know you do not remember it, but this is not the first time you have saved my life."

"I would gladly do it again if I had to."

Commander Farin coughed and adjusted his collar, reminding Matthew of his presence and his desire to speak with him privately.

"I have something for you," Gavin said. He tried inserting his hand into his tunic, but the cloth was too stiff and stuck to his skin. It quickly became apparent that he would not be able to retrieve what he was looking for until he had warmed up. "Well, it's probably frozen anyway."

Farin gave Matthew an impatient, questioning look.

"Would it be okay if Gavin came with us to our meeting?" Matthew asked. Farin's face stiffened so that it looked almost as frozen as Gavin's. "He was an important member of Deliverance, but he defected from them once he realized what they were doing. I think you will find the information he has to offer just as vital, if not more so, than what I have to say."

Farin raised a skeptical eyebrow. "I'm sure what Sentinel Yin says is accurate," he said, addressing Gavin, "but you're half-frozen. I don't think sitting through a long interview would be the most helpful thing for you at this moment. I'm eager to learn what you know, but for now it would be best if—"

A voice sounded right next to the commander, interrupting him. It took Matthew a moment to realize that it came from an audio piece embedded in Farin's collar.

"Sir, we've spotted another ship coming out of the planet's atmosphere. It looks like they are fleeing the paroxysm. They are attempting to make contact with us." said the voice.

"What type of ship?" Farin asked.

"A praxis cruiser, sir, a part of the Deliverance fleet."

Farin's brow knit together. "But the Delegation destroyed them all, how is that possible?"

"It must have escaped somehow," the man on the other end conjectured.

Gavin lurched forward and placed his hand on Farin's shoulder. "Commander, if I may—" he started to say before the soldiers yanked him violently back.

Farin huffed and swatted away the soldiers swarming in to protect him.

"Let the man speak. Can't you see he isn't any threat?"

Gavin was allowed to stand on his own again as he addressed the commander.

"Forgive me for speaking out of turn, but I believe I know who is on that ship. It is being piloted by the rest of the defectors from the Collective," Gavin declared. "They call themselves the Sentients."

"And you know this how?" Farin asked.

"Because I was the commander of that ship."

Farin cast a sharp glance towards Matthew. "Is this true, Sentinel?" he asked.

"I don't have any reason to doubt what Gavin says," Matthew said.

Farin drew himself up until he had nearly risen to the level of Gavin's shoulders, as if he would be able to size Gavin up better if the two of them were closer in height. Everyone around Farin, Gavin especially, stared at him, waiting to hear how the commander would respond.

Farin took an unusually long amount of time to consider his reply. With each passing moment the suspicion that he might order an attack on the ship grew stronger in Matthew's mind.

At last the commander ventured a reply. "Are we within firing range yet?" he asked.

The question sent a chill as cold as Gavin's skin down Matthew's back.

"No, sir, but they will be soon," answered the voice over the audio.

The little color Gavin's face had begun to gain quickly vanished.

"They would be foolish to attack a ship of this size," Farin said. "Although they have a fair amount of firepower, we far outclass them in size and range. They would never penetrate our shields. Send their audio through straight to me, but give word to prepare the fleet for launch."

"Commander Farin, what are you doing?" Matthew asked, unable to restrain himself any longer.

Farin's expression was enigmatic. "Assessing the situation," he said. The response wasn't exactly cold, but neither was it friendly. Matthew sensed that pressing him on the issue would only make matters worse so he forced himself to hold his tongue.

A nervous voice came over the audio channel. "Greetings. My name is Nance and I am in command of the praxis *Maven*,"

"This is Commander Farin of the derringer *Radix*. You realize that you are flying directly into our sovereign zone. What are your intentions?" he asked. "I assure you that we are a fully functioning assault ship."

"Yes, we came across the remains of the Collective fleet you destroyed. Our intentions are entirely peaceful, I can assure you. But the paroxysm..." Nance's voice strained to hold back the emotion. "The planet is no longer safe and our vessel is not equipped for long term survival in space."

"Clearly." Farin was unmoved by Nance's plea. "So what is it that you seek?"

"We seek refuge on your ship. We cast ourselves on your mercy and place our ship at your disposal, if only you will grant us safe harbor. Please, we have nowhere else to turn."

Again Farin paused, considering. Each hesitation on the commander's part strained Matthew's nerves closer to the breaking point. Surely Farin wouldn't just abandon them to their deaths!

"How many passengers and crew are aboard your ship?"

"Over six hundred, including many women and children," Nance said.

"I see," Farin said, still pondering. "You realize that you are asking me to take on a significant burden, Commander Nance. The *Radix's* resources are not unlimited."

"I understand." Nance's voice shaky. "but there is a great deal of advanced technology on this ship. You are welcome to plumb its depths and use it as you see fit. Just take us in; that is all we ask."

Matthew's eyes flitted between Farin's complacent face and Gavin's tormented one. Seeing the pained look on the face of the man who had risked his life to come save him, Matthew decided to speak up where Gavin could not. He knew he had some sort of leverage with Farin and he decided now was the time to find out just how much.

"Commander Farin, I know the kind of technology Deliverance possesses. If we are being presented with a peaceful means of acquiring some of it, I think we would do well to take advantage of the opportunity."

Farin pulled him aside and addressed him in low tones, though Matthew suspected that most of the people around them could still hear what he was saying.

"An interesting suggestion, Sentinel, but I thought we agreed you would wait to resume your authority until after you had been brought up to speed? Perhaps you think I am being callous by not simply granting their request, but I do not want to do anything that will jeopardize the freedom we have worked so hard to achieve."

"I understand, but—" Matthew checked his response. As much as he feared for the lives of those onboard the *Maven,* starting off his relationship with the commander in an argument hardly seemed the best way to ensure their safety. "I leave it to your discretion, then."

Farin smoothed the front of his uniform in contented fashion. Returning to the gathered group, he raised his voice and addressed the *Maven* once again.

"You have permission to approach," he informed Nance. "Our chief navigator will direct you from here on out, but Commander Nance—we reserve the right to remove you from this ship if you show the slightest signs of hostility or if your people prove to be too much of a burden."

"Of course, Commander. Thank you. I promise you will not regret this," Nance effused.

Farin gave quick instructions to the bridge, directing them to receive the praxis in the cargo bay with a large contingent from the security force. This made Matthew nervous, but Farin assured him it was merely a precaution.

Matthew watched as the tension drained from Gavin's face. He even imagined he saw a touch of color return to his cheeks.

"It is time for us to retire to the council room," Farin said.

"And Gavin? Will he be allowed to come with us?" Matthew asked.

"Commander Farin," Gavin spoke up before he could respond. "I would actually prefer to stay while the others disembark. That way I can be here when the praxis lands as well. I am sure my friends will be disoriented waking from cryo-sleep and I think a familiar face would be helpful."

"I agree." The commander nodded satisfactorily. "That will make the situation much easier. We can meet with you once you've made a full recovery."

Farin made to go, but Matthew hesitated, still unsure whether it was wise to leave Gavin here alone.

"I'll be fine," Gavin said. The look in his eyes told Matthew that he could take care of himself. Matthew only wondered if he could say the same thing.

"I'll see you again soon, then," Matthew said.

Farin set out for the exit at a brisk pace with Matthew at his side. The last thing they saw as they headed out the door was the next survivor being helped off the module, a woman with short blonde hair and a beautiful face, pale and blue though it was. Gavin embraced her warmly and then he and the medical staff helped her onto a floating gurney. Matthew recognized her as the one Gavin had been reviving back on the *Nebula*. The one called Sierra.

FORTY-ONE
REMNANT

The council room Farin brought Matthew to was much larger than he had anticipated. It was filled with black chairs arranged in concentric circles, close to a hundred seats in all. Farin and Matthew were the only occupants of the room. The soldiers were ordered to guard the doorway outside.

In the center of the chamber floated a transparent image of the planet Nai. The paroxysm had consumed nearly seventy-five percent of the planet by now. In the projection, the paroxysm appeared as a molten glow seeping over the surface. In the parts that still remained untouched, blue flares pulsed beneath the clouds. These, Farin informed him, represented elevated levels of seismic activity. There were at least a hundred such areas that Matthew could see.

"This is very different from what happened when Kess was destroyed," Commander Farin said. "It's almost as if the planet were reacting to the paroxysm somehow, like an immune system struggling to fight off a deadly disease."

Matthew pulled away his eyes from the devastation. He wished Farin would turn the projection off. "Even though this is just a single planet in a vast universe, I can't help but think that everything has changed. Planets are not supposed to just die like this."

The two men sat down and regarded each other. It was time to be honest; Matthew had put this off long enough. Though he was not sure to what extent he could truly trust the commander, the only way forward, and probably the only way he would ever find his place among these people was to tell the truth.

"There's something you need to know before we start," Matthew said.

"Very well, say what you have to say," Farin said. The doubt in his eyes gave Matthew pause, but he had made his decision.

"I have no memory of this ship. I have no memory of Kess, of you, of anything. I only found out that I was a Delegation soldier just before the *Nebula* was destroyed. I'm sorry I didn't tell you sooner, but I was afraid you might not help us if you knew what had happened to me."

To Matthew's surprise, the reservations in Farin's eyes faded.

"I'm actually glad you didn't. If representatives from the other factions had found out about it, it might have given them occasion to doubt your ability to lead us again."

"Other factions? But I thought Remnant was in control of the ship." Matthew's worries shifted away from his own situation back to Gavin and the prisoners. Perhaps the *Radix* was not as safe a place as he had assumed.

"Yes, but Remnant is not a monolith. It is made up of around fifteen hundred people, but within that larger group there are three major divisions. My faction, the Consortium, has the fewest members, but we are the most technically trained and have the most military experience, so most of the command of the ship falls under us. The prominent role we play, however, does not sit well with the other two groups, the Thurim and the Chanters."

"What are you saying?" Matthew looked Farin in the eye. The commander returned his stare with a look that was both calculating and desperate.

"What I am saying, Sentinel Yin, is that the future of Remnant hangs by a thread. I'm sure the other commanders would have headed down to the cargo bay to attempt to sway you to their side if they had known of your arrival, which is why I wanted to get you out of there as soon as possible."

"But how can you be divided? Remnant just managed to take down both the Delegation and Deliverance. That must have taken tremendous planning. I don't see how a fractured group of people could have pulled something like that off."

"That's just it," Farin said. "It was the attack on Deliverance and the Delegation which held us together. At this moment, it is too early to tell where things will end up, but let's just say that the three factions have a less than amicable history and I do not foresee things remaining in their present state. Without a common enemy, there is great danger that our differences will cause our alliance to splinter apart."

Matthew leaned back in his chair, unsettled by Farin's words. Would there be another conflict on this ship the way there had been on the *Nebula*? Could peace ever exist in a world were men seemed bent on each others' destruction?

Farin continued. "Listen, those of us in the Consortium knew about the Doctor's ability to do memory wipes. We knew when you volunteered for the mission there was a high chance that if you got captured they would erase your mind. And based on your answers from the venator, I suspected as much. That's another reason why I didn't want you stepping back into your old position right away."

"And what exactly was my old position, Commander?"

"You were to replace Sentinel Orin once we defeated the Delegation. Everyone wanted you to lead us. You are the one that brought us together in the beginning and made us believe we could come out from under the Delegation's tyranny. I was never in favor of you taking the mission, but the Delegation hand picked you and it would have raised suspicion if you had tried to avoid it."

"And what do you think your people want now? That was a long time ago. Do they still expect me to lead them?" Matthew ventured, uncomfortable with the idea, but wanting to know what these people expected of him.

"I cannot say for sure. I think first you might have to remember who you were. The old Matthew Yin, that is who they would follow, that is who might be able to keep us together. But apart from that..." Farin shook his head, doubt returning to his face.

"Yes, that is a problem," Matthew said. He didn't want to lead anyone, but he did want to help these people and he definitely wanted to know who he was. Not for the last time, he wondered just exactly what Gavin's vial of remin fluid contained.

Matthew welcomed Gavin inside his new quarters. Though Farin had called it a "capital room," it was rather sparsely furnished. It was a cabin with a bed, a table, two storage vaults in the walls, two chairs and a small lev vent where supplies could be sent and received.

Nearly six slices had passed since they arrived on the *Radix*. Gavin had his color back, what there was of it at least, since he was naturally rather pale.

"How are the other prisoners?" Matthew asked.

"Warmer," Gavin said, smiling. "And anxious to see you again. One in particular."

Matthew nodded politely. He was looking forward to meeting them, but he was not all that excited about the prospect of staring at them blankly while they asked him questions he had no answer to.

"And the passengers and crew from the *Maven*? Farin told me he was trying to find places for them, but that it might be a few days before everyone had permanent quarters."

"Yes, I think it will work out. Most of them are still struggling with the loss of their home world, but some of them will be coming to the mess hall tonight if you'd like to see them. You have friends there as well."

"What did you tell them about me?" Matthew asked. "Do they know that I've lost my memory?"

"I told some of the Sentients, but with the Werin, the natives, I simply told them that you're not well, that you're recovering from your mission."

Matthew rapped his fingers on the table. He didn't think he could wait a moment longer.

"So you brought the vial?" he asked.

Gavin gave him a blank look. "You know, I completely forgot," he said, his mouth going slack.

"But I thought memorants never forgot?" Matthew shot back, shaking his head in disbelief.

A knowing grin spread across Gavin's face. "You thought right," he said, reaching into his tunic and pulling out a vial of glowing green liquid.

"Gavin, you're horrible," Matthew chided him.

He wanted so much to grab hold of the vial, but his hands were so covered in sweat he was afraid he might drop it.

"I feel as though I've waited my whole life for this,"

Matthew said. Gavin placed the vial on the table in front of him.

"I believe you're not too far off with that remark," Gavin said.

Matthew cautiously took it and pulled it across the table.

"How much is in here? Is it just my time on Nai? Everything from the last time we met? Further back?"

"Just the last six months," Gavin said. "Everything up to right before you were captured by the Collective, but I can get much more with the chronotrace now that we have more time."

"That's more than enough for now," Matthew said, staring at the precious liquid. "I don't think I could take it all at once."

"That day will come—for both of us," Gavin assured him.

"So is Matthew my real name? Matthew Yin?"

Gavin nodded.

"And you knew that when you found me on the *Nebula*?"

Gavin nodded again. "Yes. I knew about Kelm's plan to destroy the *Nebula*, too. I didn't think I would be able to convince you to get off in time, but I had to try. Unfortunately, it turns out I was right; I'm not very persuasive. I was going to use the miasma channel, but then the Delegation showed up."

"You knew the *Nebula* was going to be destroyed and you came anyway," Matthew said.

"You would have done the same for me."

Matthew hoped Gavin was right. But he wouldn't know for sure until he drank that vial of remin fluid.

"What are you waiting for?" Gavin asked.

"This may sound strange, but I'm scared," Matthew confessed. "What if I don't like the person I was, what if I end up regretting the choices I've made, the things I've done?"

"I understand your reservations, but facing the past is the only way we can move beyond it. Would you like me to leave you alone?"

"No, no," Matthew said. "You're the one who made this possible. I want you to be here when I open my eyes again and remember who I am."

"All right," Gavin said gently.

Matthew pulled the top off the vial. A bitter, pungent smell crept up his nose and made him want to pull back, but he resisted the urge and brought the liquid up to his lips.

Finally. He sighed, still finding it hard to believe this moment had arrived.

With a flick of his wrist he drained the liquid into his mouth, absorbing it into his body in eager, ravenous gulps. The metallic taste overpowered his senses, making it hard to swallow, but he did not care. He drained the vial as quickly as his body would allow.

With each gulp, the memories came flooding back, washing over him like waves of cleansing, purifying waters. He saw the crash of his ship as a Delegation scout. He watched as somatarchs dragged him onto a lev from the remains of his shattered jaunter and presented him before Darius. The same cold light of cruelty and genius that had been there when he fired the omniclast gleamed in his eyes. Matthew's time in the vault and the Institute flashed before him as well. Then came his rescue by Will, the failed attempt to distribute the virus and kill the Developers, the storms and quakes which destroyed Oasis and Manx Core. It all came back to him, each memory rolling past like drifts of sand, wafting over the desert floor. He ran to every memory with open arms, each one more precious than the last.

This is my life, he thought. *How precious is the gift of memory, the inhale and exhale of the mind itself. We may be more than our memories, but we are certainly not less.*

For the first time in many years, Matthew Yin, sidereal scout from the planet Kess, was whole again, or nearly so. He gazed back across the table at his friend and wept freely. He smiled and cried for all he had been given and all that he had lost. And all the while inside, praise welled up spontaneously within him, praise to the one who had never forgotten him, never wavered, even when life and the vagaries of time had ripped from him everything he held dear.

The day after the battle which was being called the Second Great Purge, a banquet was planned. Ostensibly, it was to celebrate Remnant's victory and welcome the people of the *Maven*, but there would be more to it than that. Speeches from the leaders of each of the three groups which formed Remnant would be given. One from Matthew would be delivered as well. It was certainly the most important moment of his life thus far. The future of their little orbital vestige of the human race might depend on the words that were spoken this day, but he tried not to think about it too much. It was still morning and the banquet seemed far away. Matthew's thoughts were on other things at the moment, namely, Sierra.

He had wanted to see her yesterday, immediately after drinking the remin fluid, but Gavin had informed him that she would likely not be cleared from medical until the following day.

Before Gavin left, Matthew asked him to arrange a meeting with her first thing in the morning. The rest of his day had already been filled with meetings and preparations for the banquet and he had his speech to write.

Any moment she would walk through the door of his quarters. Whatever else happened on this day, for him it would be remembered as much for what was said between himself and Sierra as for anything that happened in the banquet hall. He pulled against the collar of his black uniform which chafed against his neck. He didn't like wearing it. It felt too stiff and formal, but he had another meeting directly after he finished with Sierra and he needed to look the part of the enterprising and aspiring leader of Remnant.

How differently things would have turned out if I knew what I know now, he thought as he waited. Having the memories again was not the same as if he had never lost them. His time on Nai had changed him. He could never fully go back to the person he had been before.

Much of his memory still remained a mystery even after drinking the remin. All he remembered from before he arrived at Nai were a few snatches about his double mission: to find the Deliverance base and to get word back to Remnant and then leverage that knowledge in Remnant's plot to overthrow the Delegation.

But he did remember two details that had nothing to do with his mission. As his jaunter was going down, its engines stalling in the unexpected turbulence of a high altitude storm, his thoughts had gone to his family. Though all of them had perished in The Great Purge back on Kess, he thought of them every single day.

And his last thought, just before his jaunter hit the sand, was of Numinae and the vision from the eidos. Matthew now realized that what he had seen in the chronotrace aboard the *Nebula* had actually occurred back on Kess, though how the device had recorded it he did not know, for that vision had taken place over seven years before. Maybe that vision hadn't been from the chronotrace at all, but a memory that had somehow been triggered when he hit his head in the tunnel.

Whatever the reason, this revelation made him even more certain that Remnant was in fact the reason he had been spared from the Second Purge. They needed him, they needed leadership. They had the opportunity to start over, to put the wars and conflicts behind them and this might be humanity's last chance at doing so. He only prayed that Numinae would give him wisdom, for in and of himself he had little confidence in his ability to guide these people.

At last the door slid open and all thoughts of his military life and the wars of the past vanished as Sierra's slender figure appeared before him. She wore a plain, unadorned white gown made from loose fitting fabric. It was the perfect contrast to his stifling black attire. Her face was pale and her eyes were tired and apprehensive, but to Matthew she had never looked more beautiful.

"Sierra," he said, his heart quickening as he spoke her name.

She stood with her hand against the door frame as though a great gulf and not a single step spanned the distance between them.

"Hello...Matthew," she said. "Or should I call you Adan?"

"Matthew is fine," he said. "Though it really doesn't matter. All that matters is that you're here."

Neither one of them seemed willing to move or say anything more for several nervous moments until at last Matthew worked up the courage to speak again.

"I know it's only been a few days since we last saw each other, but it feels like I've lived another life since then. I guess Gavin told you that I know who I am now. And I wanted you to know that a lot has changed, including my feelings for you."

Sierra gripped the frame of the doorway. "I understand—" she began.

"Wait, let me finish," he interrupted. "I didn't know before what to call what I felt for you, but I do now. Your compassion, the way you listen, your tenderness. I felt close to you from the very first moment, I just didn't have a name for it."

She ventured a timid smile, but doubt lingered in her eyes. "So what exactly are you saying? You know I can't read minds like you."

"I'm saying that...I love you, Sierra."

Sierra released her hold on the doorway and fell into his arms. As tightly as she clung to him, Matthew could not imagine a gentler embrace. The warmth of her arms flowed through the rigid fabric of his suit as the ship, his quarters, the world entire, floated away until only the two of them were left.

"I love you too," she murmured in his ear.

Matthew might have stayed in her arms forever if Sierra had not pulled back and looked up into his eyes.

"There is one thing I need to know, though," she said. "I was just wondering if—if there wasn't someone else in your life before...before you came here. Did you...have a family?"

Matthew searched her face, wondering what had caused her to ask such a question at that moment. After a bit of reflection, he thought he knew. "Yes. But they're all dead now," he said. "If you're asking if I was ever married, though, the answer is no. No, there was never anyone like that in my life."

The last of her doubts fled from her face. "I'm sorry," she said, tenderly. "Were they killed in the—in what happened on your home world?"

"I still don't have all the details, but my father and mother died sometime before the Purge. I was adopted and taken in by the Yin family."

"And what about your adopted family? What happened to them?"

"My adopted father actually died before I was old enough to remember him. I was raised, more or less, by my sister, Sun li. I don't remember much about her, though I do remember her husband. His name was Bunyan. My memories are sketchy that far back though. The remin fluid Gavin gave me only went back about six months."

"It must be hard, remembering people and knowing that they are all gone."

"Yes and no. I do feel the loss. It's fresh now, almost like it just happened even though it was a long time ago. And yet I am grateful for having known them at all. When I sit back and think of all the people Numinae sent into my life, it fills my heart with gratitude. He could have left me to die with my parents; he could have let me die in the Great Purge; he could have let me die when my ship crashed on the planet Nai; he could have let me be killed in Manx Core, or on the *Nebula*, but he didn't. He preserved me through all of this for no reason other than his goodness."

A shadow passed over Sierra's face at these words. With his abilities as a memorant now restored, Matthew saw her thoughts turn to those who had been killed since the destruction of Oasis.

"I know we should be thankful for the people we do have, but it's hard sometimes," she confessed.

"Yes. Yes it is." He could feel the weight of her internal struggles and sorrow pulling her down.

"Did they tell you about Tarn?" she asked. From the look on her face he could already tell what she was going to say.

"He didn't make it, then. They—the Collective would have had no use for taking a Wayman prisoner..."

Sierra hurriedly brushed away the tears which fell from her eyes. Matthew let out a long sigh and his joy began to dim.

"Did you know of Numinae back on Kess?" Sierra asked after a long painful silence.

"Yes, though again, I don't remember much."

"And did you ever have a hard time believing in him or trusting him back then? Or even now, after all that's happened?" Sierra's troubled expression reminded him of how he felt when he had asked a similar question of Zain.

"Faith is certainly not an easy path. And the hardest thing, I think, is that Numinae often turns out to be different than what we imagine. But we are not to think of him as how we would like him to be, but as he really is. It's hard, but it gives us strength, because it forces us to go beyond our simple conceptions and understandings. The essence of knowledge is not the accumulation of information, but surrendering to the truth."

"Hmm," she mused. "If that's so, then maybe my doubts come not so much from my not knowing who he is, but from my unwillingness to accept who he reveals himself to be."

He placed his hand on the side of her face, his hope renewed by the light of her eyes. "There is so much we do not know, but we have a lifetime to discover it," he said. "As many years as Numinae sees fit to grant us."

FORTY-TWO

ALL THINGS ARE PASSING

Raif gave Matthew a playful punch in the arm as they walked into the hallway outside the council room.

"Ow!" Matthew clutched his arm and grimaced, though it really didn't hurt that much. "What was that for?"

"For knocking them dead in the meeting. You and Gavin really had them under your spell. You weren't using mind tricks on us, were you?" Raif joked.

Gavin walked up behind them. "Uh oh. If you're saying I did well, does that mean you're going to punch me too?"

"Nah," Raif replied with a full-toothed grin. "I was going to punch you either way." He made as if he meant to give Gavin a shot to the arm, but then pulled his fist back with a laugh.

Whatever the circumstances, Raif's playfulness was the one constant Matthew could count on. Even though the meeting they had just left had been filled with posturing and tense debate between the various factions represented on the *Radix,* he was in high spirits as always.

As Farin had warned, there were indeed deep differences amongst the groups about how to move forward. The one positive thing Matthew took away from the meeting was the sense that most of the people gathered were weary of war and ready for a new beginning. Perhaps the speeches and ceremonies scheduled to take place during the banquet would do a better job at fostering a stronger bond between the various groups involved.

Matthew thought Gavin's presence had been an important factor in keeping the meeting from veering off course. As such an advanced memorant, he could sense the mood not just of individuals, but of the group as a whole. He always seemed to know the right thing to say. But it wasn't just his ability to read the crowd that allowed him to be such a calming influence. The more he spoke, the more obvious it became how valuable his insights and experiences would be when it came to the daunting task of reestablishing the human race on a new world. Everyone knew they could not survive on the *Radix* forever.

"So, are you heading with us to the ceremony?" Matthew asked.

"Well, I need to go back to my quarters first. I think I'm going to try a new hair color for the big shindig." Raif pretended to strike a solemn air. "Maybe I'll go for green this time to commemorate the occasion—new beginning and all that."

"You're serious?" Gavin asked.

Raif gave him one of his trademark deadpan looks. His orange hair did look a bit faded. "When am I ever serious?"

"When you're talking about ships and vintage tech," Matthew said.

"Okay, whatever." Raif rolled his eyes. "Actually, I do need to swing by and pick up Cade. You two go on ahead without me, eh?"

"All right, Raif," Gavin said. "Just don't take so long on your hair that you miss the ceremony."

"Got it, genius." Raif formed his hands into the shape of two pistols. Giving them both a parting shot, he winked and took his leave.

Gavin and Matthew turned and headed down the corridor toward the banquet hall. After they got past the congested area outside the council room, Matthew caught sight of the endless expanse of space through one of the windows in the hallway. The smoldering husk of Nai loomed large in the distance. It was no longer green, the cloudy atmosphere having been consumed by the paroxysm. What remained was a smooth, featureless black sphere with little flecks of blue. It looked in some ways like a giant ball of celerium. Matthew had seen the pictures of Kess after the first Great Purge and it had looked very similar, except the flecks there had been more red. No human life could exist on Nai now. Even if some of the Welkin had fled deep enough into the Viscera to avoid the excoriation, they would soon suffocate and die from the lack of an atmosphere. The only reason the people of Kess had managed to avoid extermination during the First Great Purge was because they were able to retreat into specially outfitted bunkers buried deep enough underground to withstand the attack and sustain them afterwards. After that they had begun building ships and moving the survivors into space, much the way Remnant was being forced to do now.

As Matthew stared at the lifeless husk, a great sadness arose within him, threatening to cloud all the hopefulness he had taken from the meeting.

"Why? Why do you think Darius destroyed the planet?" he asked Gavin, "Wouldn't destroying the Delegation have been enough?"

Gavin sighed as he often did when speaking about his former mentor. "I don't know," he said. "From your description of him, it sounds like he lost all sense of reason. Perhaps some day we could use the chronotrace to go back and find out what he was thinking, but I doubt even then it would make much sense."

"His brain might have been injured in the storm that destroyed Oasis," Matthew said. "Still, he knew enough to operate the instrument panel. I have no doubt that at some level he knew exactly what he was doing."

Gavin walked more slowly, as if the subject drained him. "Did you know that before he became the leader of Deliverance and the Collective, before he became 'The Doctor,' he was studying to become a priest?"

"Darius? Are you sure?"

"I found an entry about it in the Delegation records. They have few details about him, but that was one. I found it odd, too. But I think his defiance of his Creator makes more sense knowing that he had consciously chosen a different path."

"Still, that's a disturbing thought," Matthew said. "I can't imagine anyone who knew Numinae would turn from him so completely."

"It is a danger we all face," Gavin said. "Some follow him at first because they think he is a certain way, and when they find out he is not what they wanted, they turn and follow their own desires instead."

Matthew shook his head, wondering if the Delegation records were accurate. The man he saw in the control room on the *Nebula* hated Numinae, that much was certain. How he had come to that point only Darius would ever know.

They moved past the window and arrived at the access shaft. When the doorway opened they stepped onto the black disc waiting for them and descended to the Gathering Hall level.

"Your meeting with Sierra," Gavin said, changing the subject, "I take it that it went well?"

Matthew knew Gavin was just trying to cheer him up, but he was more than willing to shift the conversation to happier things. "Yes," he said. "Speaking of things which are hard to believe, she is rather incredible, isn't she?"

"Your relationship with her is a blessing," Gavin said.

The black disc stopped and the door opened into a wide hallway. Several people were moving down the new passage. Their chatter filled the space with a buoyant, bubbling energy.

"Yes, I know," Matthew said. "But I am a little nervous about what to do next."

"Then I guess I'll just have to keep training you," Gavin said in a spirited tone.

"I thought all you knew about was being a memorant and a scientist."

Gavin regarded him warmly. "I didn't tell you that I used the chronotrace to recover my own memories as well, did I?"

Matthew shook his head, surprised Gavin had failed to mention something so significant.

"I'm sorry, I should have told you before. But I knew how busy you were and I was waiting for the right time," Gavin apologized. "One of the things I apparently learned during my time with the Welkin, though, may be of use to you in your present situation."

"Yes, and what is that?"

A spontaneous grin danced across Gavin's face. "Let's just say you're not the only one who has won the heart of a woman," he teased.

Matthew searched his friend's eyes and instantly read what Gavin meant. "Senya," he exclaimed. "You and Senya...Oh, that's—that's wonderful!" He wrapped his arm around his friend's shoulder, overjoyed that Gavin had given his heart to such a noble, caring woman.

And, so, stride for stride, they bounded down the hall. If

they had been floating through the air on an axom field, Matthew could hardly have felt much lighter.

———

Gavin and Matthew arrived intentionally early for the awards banquet that was to take place that evening. In addition to the food and the speeches, soldiers who had served with distinction in the recent conflict were to be honored, as was Matthew for his role in the destruction of Deliverance and the Delegation. He had tried to argue against receiving any accolades on his part since it was Kelm and others who had coordinated the attack, but he was being given credit for freeing Kelm from prison and for making an ally out of Gavin. More importantly, following Farin's line of thinking, the bestowing of honors upon him would serve to introduce, or rather re-introduce, him to the larger Remnant population. Commander Farin insisted that this would be an important first step in him taking a more prominent role within the fledgling community of survivors.

Matthew felt ill at ease about so much being thrust upon him so quickly, but he was determined to bear this burden as well as possible and hopefully learn as he went along.

The Gathering Hall where everything was to take place was easily the largest room on the ship next to the cargo bay. The ceilings rose to three times his height and the long, rectangular space could hold over five hundred people. Row upon row of floating benches lined either side of the room. A gap ran down the middle with space for five or six people to walk abreast.

Gavin and Matthew were not the only ones who had decided to arrive early. Close to fifty people were already gathered in the great hall, milling about amidst the rows of benches. Scattered laughter erupted here and there while some whispered solemnly amongst themselves and wore sad expressions. Only about a third of those gathered belonged to the Remnant faction. Amongst the Remnants the fashions varied depending on which branch a person belonged to. Those belonging to the Consortium wore mostly outfits consisting of long robes with exaggerated, three tiered shoulders. They wore flat, triangular hats as well. Their clothing came mostly in umber, burgundy, or light gray hues, though a few of the women wore purple or deep blue dresses. The Chanters wore austere robes, both the men and the women. The color range exhibited about as much variety as the plain clothing, running in whites, beiges, and the occasional tan. Members of the Thurim were the most elaborately dressed of all. The men wore multi-plated shirts with matching headgear and short skirts while the women wore mosaic-like dresses that shimmered and sparkled in the light.

A handful of Sentients were present as well. Though they wore no hats, and had rather drab blue and gray robes, their outfits were accented by multi-colored scarves worn about the neck reminiscent of the kaffs of the Waymen.

The rest of those present, close to half, were Werin. None of them wore the traditional clothing of the Welkin or Waymen. Instead they were clothed in one-piece jumpers of green fabric with stylized patterns suggesting swirling winds or fields of stars. They were simple designs, but caught the eye. Matthew found it encouraging that he could not tell based on their attire which were Welkin and which were Waymen.

Gavin and Matthew had been instructed to sit in the front and were politely making their way through the small crowd when they heard a loud, shrill voice pipe up from off to the side.

"Hayden! Hey, Hayden! Wait up!"

Matthew turned to see, coming in through one of the side

entrances, a little Welkin girl with big eyes, padding across the floor between two older boys. It was Lila, along with her brothers Jarem and Halel. They were dressed in the same green outfits the other Werin were wearing. The boys had their trimmed down to their shoulders and the little girl's hair was neatly braided down one side.

"Lila," Matthew answered her mispronunciation of his old name, bending down and opening his arms wide as she ran headlong into them. He swept her up off the floor, her legs dangling so that her feet brushed against his knees.

"You know you don't deserve a hug," Lila said, teasing.

"Oh, don't I?" Matthew said.

"No. You've been gone for forty-leven days and when you finally did come back, you went a whole other day without seeing me."

"Is that so?" Matthew said, unable to defend himself.

"And the only reason you're seeing me now is because of this big fancy feast," she continued on with her half-serious complaint.

"Jarem and Halel," Gavin addressed the two boys arriving behind her, both suppressing grins at their sister's behavior despite themselves. They placed their hands on Gavin's shoulder and nodded respectfully, giving him the traditional Welkin greeting.

Matthew set Lila down. "Well, I just didn't want to see you until you were all dressed up," he said, getting a comical frown in response.

"Where is your mother?" Gavin asked the children.

"She's been working in the infirmary," Jarem said. "She told us to come ahead on our own and she would meet us here."

"So why didn't you tell me you lived in a big metal ship, Hayden? Huh? Huh?" Lila continued pestering him, poking him in the stomach.

Matthew's hands shot underneath one of her arm pits to tickle her. "Because I didn't know, silly. I lost my memory, remember?" he said over her squealing laughter. The tickling didn't last long, though, as her cackling drew the attention of nearly everyone around them and Matthew promptly tucked his hands behind his back. "So what do you think of this place? Is there enough room for you to run around in here without causing too much trouble?"

Lila put her hands on her hips. "That's the problem. They won't let me go *anywhere* around here."

"You would get lost if they did," Halel said.

"Well, I can find my way around better than you," she quipped, grinning.

Halel huffed, but didn't take the bait. Both he and Jarem appeared markedly older since he'd seen them last in the battle at the Basin. Lila clung to Matthew's side to shield herself from their disapproving scowls.

"Hey, Mendigo, do you think Hayden is going to join our knit now?"

"That would be up to him," Gavin said.

Lila looked up at Matthew expectantly, "Oh, please, Hayden, please?"

"I would love nothing more," he said.

Lila let out a squeal of delight. "Ooo! Do I get to name you, still? Oh, please, please, please."

"Well, I don't know. I think I may have already had one too many names," Matthew said.

Lila's lower lip dropped into a pout. "But Hayden is such an awful name and that new name they said you had, I can't even pronounce it. It sounds like a sneeze. What was it? Atchoo?"

Gavin smiled at the precocious little girl. "What name did you have in mind?"

"Um, oh, I don't know. How about Teo?" Lila scrunched up her nose, not all that convinced about her suggestion.

Matthew chuckled. "Well, maybe," he said. "I'll have to think about it."

"Come on, you owe me one!" Lila insisted, poking him again.

"Lila, are you behaving yourself?" came Senya's voice from behind Matthew.

Matthew turned to see Senya and Sierra walking in side by side through one of the entryways, their faces aglow. Senya wore a long green dress with a dark blue kaff around her neck. Sierra was adorned in a light blue dress with a white kaff as well, though she wore hers around her waist. She had her hair pulled back in a way that Matthew had never seen before. It showed more of her kind, soft face, and accented the beauty of her high, round cheeks.

"Mama," Lila waved at her mother. "It's not my fault. What else am I supposed to do around all these boys? A girl's gotta stick up for herself, you know."

Senya gave her a cautionary look, but it was more of a gentle reproach. The two women swept across the room in their flowing dresses, each locking eyes with the man they loved.

"It's so good to see you," Matthew said as he embraced Sierra. Beside him, Senya and Gavin did the same.

"I wouldn't want to miss your big moment," Sierra said, her eyes sparkling with pride.

"Hello, Sierra." Gavin shifted to greet her with a friendly embrace. At the same time Senya hugged Matthew tightly. It brought back memories of his time in her home in the Viscera. She had washed his face with a cool, damp cloth then, and fed him the most delicious meal he had ever tasted.

"Senya, I've missed you," Matthew said. "I'm sorry I couldn't come sooner, but I have not forgotten you."

"You have been in my prayers," Senya said, her eyes glistening with held back tears. "Every day."

"Thank you," Matthew said quietly, feeling a pull of emotion at the back of his throat and unable to say more for fear that it might break through.

"No. Thank *you*," she said. "You risked your life to save us from the Wayman city and, beyond that, you saved Gavin. I will forever be grateful to you for that." The tears began to trickle down her cheeks.

"Mama," Lila said, tugging at her mother's arm. "Are you going to cry this whole time?"

"Perhaps, Lila," she said, pulling her daughter close. "Perhaps."

Gavin wrapped his arms around both of them. "Numinae gives us strength in our weakness. Crying draws us closer to him."

Sierra snuck her arm in behind Matthew and drew in close. "I want to thank you, too," she said. "For protecting me. For keeping your promise even when you did not remember it."

Matthew let out a heavy sigh. He did not deserve the love and friendship of these people, but was thankful for it all the same.

"You did just as much, if not more, for me," he said.

"I would die for you," she whispered in his ear.

Matthew closed his eyes and allowed himself to cherish the moment. From the far end of the room where the raised platform stood, he could sense the lights coming up to full. Around the edges of the room, more and more people were piling in. Some began looking for a seat. Soon Matthew would have to make his way up front and give his speech. It was the last thing he wanted to do. He longed to stay beside Sierra, Gavin, Senya, and the children, to keep them close for as long as he could.

He opened his eyes and gazed out over the large, semicircular stage. He did not have all the answers. Their future was far from certain and he could not protect and love them all perfectly. Only Numinae could do that. But the mercy of his Creator was far greater than he could comprehend. He drew strength from that knowledge and from the fact that, as Gavin had said, his strength shines through in our weakness. And that was a good thing to remember in a frail and fallen world.

EPILOGUE

Matthew got up from the polymeric chair, the last events of the chronotrace sequence playing out around him.

"It's hard to believe that it all happened that way," Sierra said as she sauntered into the room. She wore a plain dress, after the fashion of the Welkin women, only hers was pearl blue and not the typical green or brown. She had just changed after coming back from the medical ward, but judging from her swollen belly, she would not be serving the sick and injured for very much longer. Matthew knew she would miss it, but he also knew she would make an even more wonderful mother than nurse, and that was saying something.

"In my mind, it's still as if it just happened," Matthew replied. For a memorant, everything was always fresh. It was both a blessing and a curse. "Even the parts I had forgotten and the parts where I wasn't even conscious."

"Why do you always start back at the Institute?" Sierra asked, coming up to him and giving him a light kiss on the cheek.

"You're so kind to me," he told her.

"Then maybe you can return the favor and answer my question." The corners of her mouth crept up playfully.

Matthew laughed, but Sierra's face turned serious. There was no hiding anything from her.

"I'm afraid," he said.

"Afraid of what?"

"Afraid of going back farther," he admitted. "I don't like going too far back. I'm afraid I might start thinking like the old Matthew again. I like the way I am now."

She took his hand in hers. "I found out about my past and I'm still the same person, aren't I?"

Matthew shifted awkwardly and stared out the chamber's window into the sea of stars. The blackened husk of Nai floated like a baleful, exposed eye beneath them, a visual scar amongst the otherwise beautiful vista. The *Radix* had yet to initiate its interstellar voyage. They still had not found a planet they were sure would be able to support them, but the *Radix* would hold them for some time yet. The stars always made him think of Will, and Zain, and all the others he had lost. He imagined that there might be a light somewhere out there in the universe for every person who had passed on to the Eversky, waiting vigilantly to transform back into a body of flesh at the end of days. In the meantime they gave light to a cold, dark universe, warming it by their memory. It was foolish fancy, he knew, but memory was a bit like that, sparks of light in a wasteland of forgetfulness, ever present and yet impossibly far away.

"Well, aren't I the same?" Sierra repeated her question. "Matthew, don't go wandering across the whole universe with that mind of yours again, not while your beloved wife stands before you, holding your hand."

"Yes, you are most definitely the same person," he said, giving up his musings. "But you did not serve with the escalons, you did not plot to start a rebellion. I've spoken with Farin at length about my involvement with the formation of Remnant so I already know many of the details. I'm just reluctant to go further back and find out what role I played in the Delegation's wars. Besides, I've been so busy."

Sierra gazed thoughtfully at her protruding belly. She took Matthew's hand, guiding it to her burgeoning midsection. *"But what about him? Don't you think he will want to know who his father was? And there might be wonderful things there, too, have you ever thought of that? Maybe there are people you need to remember, more stars to sprinkle in your sky."*

A gentle warmth spread through him. He always appreciated it when she paid attention to his background thoughts. It did not come natural to her so it meant she was making an effort to understand him better.

"I suppose you're right," he said.

"I am always right, you know that," she said, giggling.

"I'll tell you what, Mrs. Right," he placed his hands upon her shoulders and regarded her tenderly. "I'll set the trace to go back, say, to my birth. Would that satisfy you?"

"Oh no, I want to know about your parents, too." She laughed as he threw his hands up in response. "And your grandparents, and their parents, and their parents, and on and on and on—the whole history of your family, as far back as we've got power to make the chronotrace go."

Matthew gave her nose a lighthearted tug. "You are incorrigible," he told her. "Hopeless. I don't know what I am going to do with you."

"All right, I'll compromise," she shot back, feigning attrition. "You only have to go back to your birth...today. After that you can do one generation each day so you don't get overwhelmed. You do have work to do after all."

"As if I could experience my entire life in one day...well, you know what? Fine, I'll start the trace going and we'll see where it ends up, how about that? Do you want to stay and watch it with me? It's only my entire life after all, but it might take a little while to get to the start and I know how you dislike waiting."

"I've got the perfect idea," she said, taking him by the hand and strolling up to the window of stars. As the two of them walked, a pair of polymeric chairs floated along behind them, obeying her mental command. When they arrived at the wide opening, the chairs settled in neatly behind them. They sat down in front of the intergalactic canvas, a vast spray of stars whose light reflected in the twinkling of her eyes. "My feet are killing me. Why don't we sit here and wait while the trace runs its course and take in the view? It is almost as beautiful as you."

Matthew nodded. He could think of no better way to spend the rest of the evening than gazing at the stars beside the woman he loved. The past, as far as he was concerned, could wait. Today had more than enough life of its own.

GLOSSARY

Acretian \ah-CREE-shun\ Stone: A stone which is poured out in liquid form. It sets quickly but can easily be formed and smoothed for some time even after it sets. It is similar in function to synth metal and char.

Almamenth \AHL-muh-menth\: Compound in the form of a paste which provides nutrients and strength to the user. Meant to be applied on the skin and absorbed over time into the body.

Anacite \AN-uh-sight\: An organic metal hybrid which is harder than iron, but light and self repairing. Grafted into the bones of escalon soldiers.

Ancillary Rim: Outermost district of Oasis.

Andros \AN-drohz\: Derogatory term used by members of the Collective to refer to people lacking a bioseine.

Annex: A building connected to the Institute in the central district of Oasis from which the Developers administer the esolace.

Articulator: A large, bulbous piece of equipment with

dozens of retractable cables. Used for remapping operations in order to wipe people's thoughts and manipulate their memories.

Assessors: The security force of Oasis. They have more access to control of the esolace than typical members of the Collective, but are themselves controlled by the Developers.

Atmos \AT-mohs\ Array: This powerful battery of machines keeps the environment of Oasis at a constant level and protects it from the storms that afflict the rest of the planet.

Atol \ah-TOHL\: Hot, grainy drink consumed by the Werin.

Axis Prime: The central district of Oasis. This is where the Institute and the Annex are located.

Axom Field: Localized field used to attract objects from a distance.

Azanya \ah-ZAHN-yuh\: Large tent used for Waymen dwellings, typically housing an eclectic group of Waymen who are not necessarily related.

Bioseine \BAHY-oh-sahyn\: An organic augmentation grafted into the people of the Collective which regulates their health and allows them to access the esolace. It can also allow people to communicate mentally with each other even when the esolace is not present.

Bismine \BIZ-mahyn\: Yellowish crystals which absorb light and produce inordinate amounts of energy for their size. This is the main power source for all Oasis technology.

Blank: Term referring to someone or something without a bioseine or the ability to connect to the esolace.

Canter: Religious leader amongst the Waymen.

Celerium \suh-LEER-ee-um\: Mineral that is capable of increasing the power efficiency of any machine to incredible levels. It is black with blue flecks and is nearly indestructible.

Citus Axomvac: Long, narrow, two passenger ship with no offensive capabilities, but extremely fast. Used primarily for picking up and dropping off supplies or recovering downed ships with their axom field generators.

Click: Measurement of distance, roughly equivalent to about 2 km or 1.25 miles. A click is composed of a thousand spans (see 'span').

The Collective: Name for the general population of Oasis.

Compa \COM-pah\: General word of familiarity used by Welkin to refer to someone with whom they are on friendly terms.

Developers/Devs: Also called Administrators, they run and maintain the esolace and the entire Oasis infrastructure. They have control over the lives of everyone connected to the esolace.

Deton: Compound of various rocks dried together. When struck with sudden force it explodes producing a concussive effect.

Dispersion Band: A black band worn about the wrist. It blocks all bioseine connections as well as all forms of energy or kinetic attacks. It also creates a distracting, shimmering screen around the wearer which prohibits memorants from reading the wearer's thoughts, however a skilled memorant using the miasma channel can circumvent it. It can only absorb a certain amount of energy at a time, however. Concentrated streams of energy focused on it will knock it out temporarily. This device was worn by Malthus during the events of *Awakening the Sentients* and given to Gavin just before he died.

Disruptor: Energy weapon capable of temporarily knocking out power in ships and other devices.

Escalon \EHS-kuh-lahn\: Organically augmented soldiers that have accelerated metabolisms and anacite infused bones. They heal very quickly and are hard to stun except through blunt force.

Esolace \E-soh-luhs\: The molecular, city-wide network which connects everyone inside Oasis, allowing them access to all of the communication and informational resources of the Collective, including the ability to interface with all esolace enabled devices.

Etram: Type of stone which found in the vadis where water collects on the surface. Has a sponge-like consistency when wet, but when dry is a hard, porous rock. It draws water from underground reservoirs and dries on its own, going through cycles of moisture and desiccation.

Extractor: A small device that mimics some of the functionality of the esolace such as information storage and retrieval. Usually worn by assessors in the form of a torc about the neck.

Falon \FAH-luhn\: A member of the special guard assigned to protect a Reeve.

Fero \FAIR-oh\: A hollow metal tube, used as a club and also a horn of warning by the Welkin.

Garrick \GAIR-ik\: Coat with many hidden compartments typically worn by Waymen for desert travel.

Hard Link: The act of connecting to someone's bioseine when they are unconscious.

Hogar \ho-GAHR\: Multi-chamber tent-like structure, used by the Welkin for living quarters.

Ishto \EESH-toh\: Welkin word for children. Could also be translated "rascal". Feminine form is 'ishta'.

Kaff \KAF\: Turban wrapped around the head and worn by Waymen for desert travel.

Kindred: Name of the language spoken by both Welkin and Waymen, though they use different dialects.

Knit: Societal organization amongst the Welkin consisting of groups of families; a tribe.

Lentes \LEN-teyz\: Small circular lenses with polymeric padding around the edges which forms a seal around the eye so they can stay in place. They allow a person to see in the dark and to magnify what is seen.

Locus energy: Energy source which holds together non-living matter. It can be focused into various strains to be used in weapons, as energy sources, or to create barriers of various sorts.

Lucine \LOO-sahyn\: A gel used to augment the range at which a bioseine can connect to other minds or esolace enabled devices. Its development was abandoned due to potentially deadly side effects.

Lumin \LOO-min\: A small device, usually round, which functions as a light source.

Maneusis \muh-NOO-sis\: Religious leader amongst the Welkin who passes on the traditions and beliefs about Numinae.

Memorant: Someone with the ability to probe the thoughts of another person. Memorants also have the ability to absorb and process vast amounts of information when connected to the esolace, far more than ordinary people.

Mendax Generator: A small sphere which projects realistic images of people, machines, or other discreet simulated entities. A highly advanced form of projection, it is capable of reacting to the environment surrounding it, including the behavior of intelligent beings. It is only effective against people with a bioseine, however, as it projects the illusion directly into their mind.

Microslice: Unit of time roughly equivalent to 54 seconds. There are 100 microslices in a slice. (See also slice, nanoslice)

Mosh: A lumpy paste eaten by Werin, made from sere

powder mixed with water. Tastes like a mixture of peas and rice.

Nanoslice: Unit of time roughly equivalent to 0.54 seconds. There are 100 nanoslices in a microslice. (See also slice, microslice)

Oscillathe \AH-sil-ley*th***:** A class of weapon which comes in various sizes and forms, but which shoots forth an evanescence wave which dissolves or disintegrates living, organic matter by disrupting the zoetic forces which hold it together. The wave frequency can be diminished so that it merely stuns its victim.

Pallium \PAL-ee-um\ Generator: Small, bismine powered device which confuses anyone nearby with a bioseine into not being able to detect their presence. Not effective against large systems like the esolace or the quorum, but very useful against people who are not otherwise aware of the wearer's presence.

Pinion: Short javelin; principle weapon of the Waymen.

Praxis cruiser: Largest class of ship in the Collective fleet, armed with oscillathe cannons, locus pulsers, and dozens of antipersonnel guns. The praxis cruisers are the largest in the fleet, but not capable of interstellar travel.

Raker: Large, floating cargo ships which have locus energy barriers on top of them to protect their contents.

Reeve: Title for the leader of a Wayman thral (tribe).

Remin fluid: Liquid capable of storing memories. The memories can be recovered by drinking the fluid.

Sar \SAHR\: A Wayman camp.

Sere \SAIR-ey\: A soft, chalky rock that grows slowly over time in certain environments. It can be turned into a powder and if prepared properly, later reconstituted in water to use as food. The principal ingredient in mosh.

Service Ring: The district in Oasis between the Ancillary Rim and Axis Prime.

Sentients: Name of the survivors of the storm that destroyed Oasis who chose to try and break free from the Collective.

Shiv: Term used by Waymen meaning roughly "warrior" or "soldier". Also refers to the knife-like weapons these warriors use in battle.

Shim: A derogatory term for another person used by the Waymen. Roughly translated it means someone of little worth or importance.

Sidereal Portal: An interstellar gateway, allowing for instantaneous traversal of near infinite distances. Each portal requires a matching one at the point of origin.

Sidereal Jaunter: A small, one man interstellar space ship. The pilots of these ships utilize cryo-sleep to avoid aging over the long journeys these ships are capable of.

Slice: Unit of time roughly equivalent to 1.5 hours. There are 20 slices in a day. (See also microslice, nanoslice)

Solec: Drug with restorative and metabolism increasing properties. Very powerful but with negative side effects including extreme weakness and tiredness once it wears off.

Somatarch \SOH-muh-tahrk\: Mindless, soulless being which looks like an ordinary human but is controlled by the Developers and has no will or personality of its own. Used primarily for military and intelligence gathering purposes. Also referred to as "ghosts" or "the soulless" by Waymen and "hollow men" by the Sentients.

Sopor \SOH-pohr\: Also referred to as 'naptrap'. A powder made from combining the powders of griff and pheus rocks which will make a person unconscious nearly instantly if enough of it is inhaled. A handful of the powder can put an average size person to sleep for several.

Sovos \SOH-vohs\: Also known as a 'sand duster'. A small, open-topped ship which is faster than a lev and may also be outfitted with weapons. Seats around eight to ten people.

Span: Unit of measurement roughly equivalent to about 2 meters or 6.5 feet. A thousand spans is equal to a click (see 'click'). Also used in the expression 'a ten span' which is the way weeks are denoted (though obviously weeks are ten days instead of seven. Months are also only twenty days, so two ten spans, and there are only 200 days in a year).

Standard: Lowest ranking soldier in the Delegation army.

Steorra: Distance for measuring space travel. Equivalent to about 1000 light years.

Sunder: A Wayman with authority over a group of shivs. They are chosen by the Reeves from amongst the most brutal and ruthless members of the thral. It is not unusual for the next Reeve of a thral to come from amongst the ranks of the Sunders.

Taline \TEY-leen\: A rock that can easily be turned into powder and mixed with water to form an acid that eats through most forms of metal.

Tasada \tuh-SAH-duh\: Name for the eternal city in Waymen lore.

Thral: Societal organization of Waymen with fairly fluid membership held together by a powerful leader (the Reeve).

Throng: A Wayman raiding party.

Vacants: Fully grown adult bodies with no memory or personality. They are used by the Developers for creating somatarchs.

Vadi \VAH-dee\: A geographical formation of living rock which accumulates water over time. Waymen usually make their camps close to vadis.

Vapors: Round, fast assault vehicles which have blink

thrusters which allow them to seem to teleport over short distances. They use oscillathe pulses as their primary weapons.

Vast: Term used by the Werin to refer to the planet's surface.

Viand \VAHY-and\ Stream: A molecular distribution system responsible for the sustenance and health of everyone connected to the esolace. When connected to this, a person has no need to sleep or eat and is protected from all forms of disease.

Virid \VEER-id\ Ridge: Elevated area on the perimeter of Oasis where the atmos generators are located.

Viscera: Name the Welkin use for the underground cavities of the planet in which they live.

Waymen: General term for the people who live on the planet's surface. They are nomadic and often raid others for supplies and goods. Though they claim to be distinct from the Welkin, they often absorb members of the Welkin into their numbers.

Welkin: Name of the people who live beneath the surface of the Vast.

Werin \WAIR-in\: Name used by the Welkin to refer to all people, whether Welkin or Waymen. The Welkin believe that the Waymen and Welkin are simply two groups of the same people, but most Waymen do not share this view.

Yeso \YEHS-oh\: Made from cretan powder and umor oil, it is used by the Werin to set broken bones until they heal.

Zoelith \ZOH-uh-lith\: A small tool used to 'turn on/off' someone with a bioseine and also to perform 'maintenance' on their bioseine.

Zoetic \ZOH-eh-tik\ pulse/source: Detectable energy signature given off by living creatures.

ABOUT THE AUTHOR

DJ Edwardson always wanted to invent the hovercraft. Not some floaty balloon contraption, but the real McCoy, with levitation and jump jets and cool track lights down the side just because. But he found that not being a scientist or an inventor or a multi-billion dollar venture capitalist put a bit of a damper on that career path so he settled for the next best thing, writing fiction.

But he doesn't just write about exotic gadgets. He's invented all sorts of things that will probably never make it out of that "what if" stage, at least not in his lifetime. He also writes about things that aren't "things" at all, like friendship, courage, love, and faith. And those are even more exciting than hovercraft.

To find out more about his writing visit:
www.djedwardson.com

READ HOW IT ALL BEGAN

Discover the secrets of Matthew's past
in the prequel to *The Chronotrace Sequence*.

Truth, honor, faith: these are the true strengths of a warrior.

For Sun li the Code is more than a way of fighting; it's a way of
life. But her beliefs are not enough to save her father from the
wasting disease ravaging their planet.

The only hope for a cure lies in the hands of an underworld
insider, whose price requires Sun li to follow him into a war
between drone armies and cybernetically enhanced humans.
But as the code teaches, sometimes the most difficult battles are
the ones we fight within.

Available in e-book only

ALSO BY DJ EDWARDSON

A hero is measured by the size of his heart.

Every century a motley is born. Though only children, their patchwork skin marks them as dangerous, especially to those who know about the first motley. That one nearly destroyed the world.

But a chance meeting with Roderick the tailor may hold the key to breaking the curse. Roderick has no sword or armor or power of his own. He's not even rich. But what he does have is a heart moved by compassion for a hunted boy.

Will this be the last motley?

Available in print and e-book formats